A JUNE OF ORDINARY MURDERS

A JUNE OF ORDINARY MURDERS

Conor Brady

Minotaur Books

A Thomas Dunne Book
New York

This is a work of fiction. All of the characters, organizations, and events portrayed in this novel are either products of the author's imagination or are used fictitiously.

A THOMAS DUNNE BOOK FOR MINOTAUR BOOKS.
An imprint of St. Martin's Publishing Group.

www.thomasdunnebooks.com
www.minotaurbooks.com

Library of Congress Cataloging-in-Publication Data

Brady, Conor.
    A June of ordinary murders / Conor Brady. — First U.S. edition.
        p. cm.
    ISBN 978-1-250-05756-3 (hardcover)
    ISBN 978-1-4668-6126-8 (e-book)
    1. Police—Ireland—Dublin—Fiction. 2. Murder—Investigation—Fiction. 3. Ireland—Politics and government—1837–1901—Fiction. 4. Ireland—Social life and customs—19th century—Fiction. I. Title.
    PR6102.R3343J86 2015
    823'.92—dc23

                                                                    2014042137

Minotaur books may be purchased for educational, business, or promotional use. For information on bulk purchases, please contact the Macmillan Corporate and Premium Sales Department at 1-800-221-7945, extension 5442, or write to specialmarkets@macmillan.com.

First published in Great Britain by New Island Books

First U.S. Edition: April 2015

10 9 8 7 6 5 4 3 2 1

For Ann, Neil and Conor,
with great thanks for their love and patience

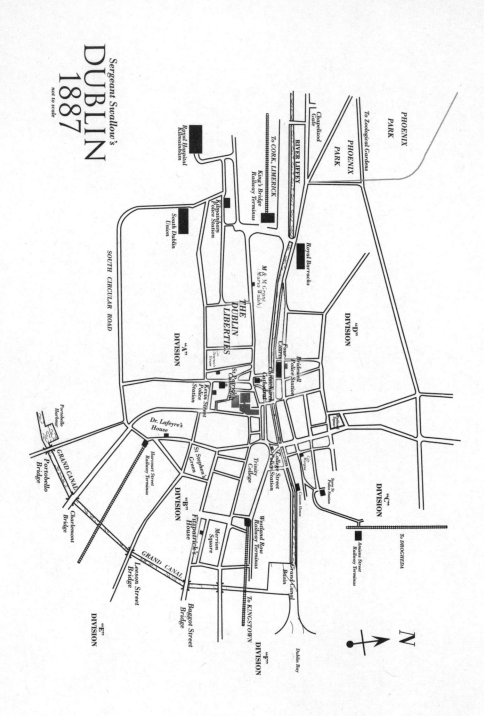

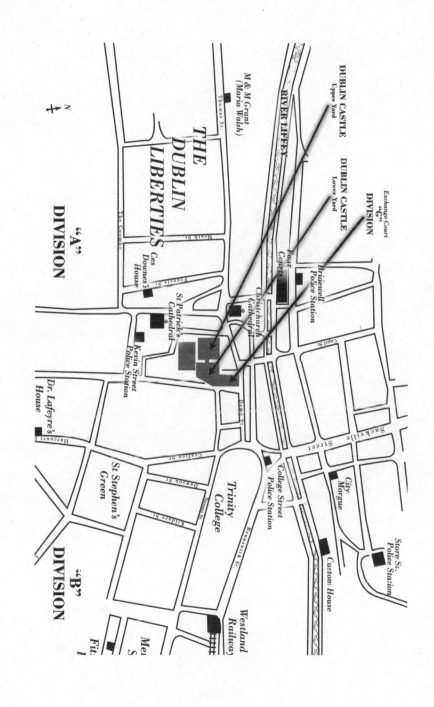

ACKNOWLEDGMENTS

Many people, albeit unwittingly, have had a hand in forming the career of Detective Sergeant Joe Swallow. They include two good friends, now sadly departed: Gregory Allen, founder and first curator of the Garda Museum, and Tom O'Reilly, former Deputy Commissioner of the Garda Siochána. Much of their lore of Dublin policing is woven into the story.

The creation of Swallow also owes an amount to historian Jim O'Herlihy whose meticulous research provides an essential backdrop to any description of Irish policing prior to independence. Similarly, Professor Donal McCracken, in his biography of John Mallon, the head of G Division of the Dublin Metropolitan Police, has put flesh and blood on key personalities in the Dublin Castle administration of the period.

Thus, even if Joe Swallow is an invention he is not unreal. I imagine that his ghost, along with the rest of the G-men, perhaps lingers in the courts and the narrow lanes around Dublin Castle. There may be something of their presence in the surviving brickwork of the old Police Office in the Lower Yard or in the granite of the Palace Street or Ship Street Gates.

My late friend and former colleague, Caroline Walsh, Literary Editor of *The Irish Times*, told me instantly, when she learned that the tale of Joe Swallow was in gestation, 'send it to Dermot Bolger for New Island.'

And so I did. I would like to thank Dermot for his immediate support and encouragement and likewise I wish to thank Edwin Higel and his team at New Island. They have been constant in their enthusiasm and professionalism.

All errors, inconsistencies and heresies in the story are, of course, of my own making.

Conor Brady
January 2012

Friday June 17th, 1887

ONE

The place where the bodies of the adult and the child were found was cool and shadowed before the sun burned off the morning mist.

It was on wooded ground that sloped down towards the river with a view across the city towards the mountains. Swallow knew it well. When the muttering constable with sleep in his eyes and clutching the crime report dragged himself up to the detective office from the Lower Yard of Dublin Castle, he could see it in his mind's eye.

This was where the boundary wall of the Phoenix Park met the granite pillars of the Chapelizod Gate, and where beech and pine trees formed a small, dense copse close by.

At this point, the trees are trained by the wind that funnels along the valley of the River Liffey towards Dublin Bay, inclining them eastward as if permanently pointing the way to the city. Outside the wall the ground falls away towards the river with the open fields and the village of Chapelizod beyond.

It was here, just inside the boundary wall of the park, that a keeper found the two bodies on the third morning of the extraordinary heatwave that settled on the island of Ireland in the third week of June, 1887.

In a few days' time the country, along with Great Britain's other territories and possessions across the globe, would mark the Golden Jubilee of Queen Victoria's ascent to the throne. It was as if the blue skies and sunlit days had been specially arranged to honour the Queen and Empress of half a century.

Though it was scarcely 7 o'clock, Swallow could feel the warmth of the coming day on the nape of his neck as the police side-car bucked and swayed along Chesterfield Avenue across the park to where the bodies had been found. The city temperature had touched 86 degrees yesterday. Now the strengthening morning sun presaged more of the same.

Dublin always took a more leisurely start to its morning, later than other cities in the industrious reign of Queen Victoria. At this early hour, the police vehicle was the only traffic on the broad, two-mile carriageway that bisects the Phoenix Park.

Swallow had put in a fetid night as duty sergeant at the G-Division detective office at Exchange Court. There were few places more cheerless in which to spend any night. Huddled in against the northern flank of Dublin Castle, chilled in winter and airless in summer, Exchange Court had the reputation of being the unhealthiest building in the maze of blocks and alleyways that had spread out around King John's original castle to house the administration of Ireland.

Dublin's police districts were denominated alphabetically. They went from the A, covering the crowded Liberties with its hungry alleys and courts and its primitive sanitation, to the F, serving the genteel coast from Blackrock to Dalkey with its spacious villas and elegant terraces.

The plain-clothes G Division based at Exchange Court was supposedly the elite of the Dublin Metropolitan Police. Its members often grumbled over the paradox of its having probably the least salubrious accommodation of all the force.

The report of the discovery of the bodies – a man and a boy, it was said – had come in a few minutes before Swallow was due to finish his shift at 6 a.m. Now the sun's faint warmth hinted of the denied pleasure of sleep. Behind the police vehicle, the day was forming over Dublin.

Here the city seemed far behind. The spreading acres of the great municipal park – the largest in the Empire, it was said – were a pattern of greens. Beech, oak, chestnut and maple rose over a mantle of meadow-grass.

At the base of the soaring Wellington Monument, erected through public subscription to commemorate the Dublin-born victor of Waterloo, a herd of the park deer grazed the soft morning grass. Picking up the sound of the police carriage, the timid animals started to move away from the open space to the cover of the nearby trees.

Swallow turned to gaze back across the park towards the bay and the mountains. Harriet would be going to her examination desk at the teacher training college soon. The first of her summer tests would start at 9 o'clock. It would be a trying day for his young sister, cooped up in a stuffy hall with the sun beating down outside. He smiled inwardly imagining her impatience as she would fill foolscap pages through the morning with commentaries on Shakespeare and the English Romantic Poets.

As they came abreast of the Viceregal Lodge, the residence of the Queen's deputy in Ireland, the police driver hauled the car sharply to the left, veering away from the avenue onto a narrow lane known as Acres Road. The centrifugal force of the turn obliged Swallow to clutch the brass centre-rail of the vehicle, just above the embossed harp-and-crown emblem of the Dublin Metropolitan Police.

The two Bridewell constables he had collected from their beats planted booted feet against the car's duckboard to hold their balance. The younger nudged his companion and grinned.

'Jesus, it's as well we didn't get any breakfast, what?'

By rights, Swallow reckoned, he should be at Maria Walsh's going through a plate of something substantial himself by now, and maybe addressing himself to a pint of Guinness's porter or a mellow Tullamore whiskey. For a moment he visualised himself in her parlour above the public house on Thomas Street, his current 'domicile', as police terminology referred to such arrangements.

Now the side-car was on a narrow, grassy track, leading across the open parkland.

There was a cluster of uniforms by the copse within sight of the Chapelizod Gate. A full-bearded sergeant and two constables from the A-Division station at Kilmainham stood beside a white-haired friar. In spite of the sunshine and the incipient heat of the morning, the priest looked pale and cold.

A few yards away, a park-keeper with a shotgun broken open across his arm was in conversation with some civilians. His gun dog sat obediently on the grass beside him, its nose twitching at the interesting scents of the morning air. From somewhere beyond the boundary wall, Swallow heard the morning squawks and clucks of barnyard fowl.

He had been to this place before. Five years earlier the copse was one of dozens of locations in the park he had searched with colleagues investigating the murders of Ireland's two most senior government officials, Chief Secretary Lord Cavendish and Under-Secretary Burke, by members of the extremist group, the 'Invincibles.'

The driver dragged on the reins and slowed the vehicle to a halt 20 yards from the group. Swallow and the two constables dismounted and strode across the grass. He recognised the bearded sergeant as Stephen Doolan, with whom he had worked before. He introduced himself for the benefit of the others.

'Detective Sergeant Swallow, G Division. Where are they?'

'In the trees,' Doolan nodded towards the copse. 'The park-keeper found them around an hour and a half ago, a man and a child – a boy.'

The copse had been planted a century previously by the park architects so that it formed a bower or primitive pergola. From where he stood, Swallow could see a contoured shape under a grey blanket between the trunks of two giant beeches.

'I've kept everyone a way back from the scene since we got here, including the priest,' Doolan said, gesturing towards the civilians. 'What might have happened before that, I don't know.'

Swallow grunted in approval. Not every uniformed DMP sergeant knew or cared enough about crime investigation to preserve a scene properly, but the veteran Doolan knew his business. Swallow and he went back a long way.

They walked the few yards to the copse. The sun had started to filter through the branches of the high beech, dappling the ground underfoot. Swallow saw that there was not just one, but two blankets.

He dropped to his haunches by the trunk of one of the trees. Doolan brought his bulk down on one knee and grasped the nearer blanket.

'D'you want to see the man or the child first?'

'Let's see the man.'

Swallow was unsure why he felt it might be easier that way. Perhaps he wanted to put off what he knew would be the more unpalatable sight. He indicated the covered shape on the ground, and Doolan lifted the grey blanket.

The body appeared to be that of a slightly built man, clothed in a dark jacket and trousers with an off-white shirt. It lay on its back, what remained of the face turned to the morning sky.

Swallow instinctively removed his hat as a gesture of respect.

The features had been terribly mutilated. The eyes were sockets of red turning to black. The skin, from the jawline to the forehead and from one ear to the other, was marked with a series of gashes. Only bloodied gristle remained of the nose. There was a full head of dark brown hair, cut short. Swallow reckoned him to be young, maybe in his twenties.

Doolan folded the blanket and dropped to one knee. 'You wouldn't see many as bad as that,' he said softly.

Swallow concurred silently. More than 20 years as a city policeman had inured him to sights of death and injury. Momentarily, he was reminded of a scene from his days in uniform where a young inmate had put her face in a mincing machine at the kitchens of the Richmond Asylum.

He had taught himself to isolate his emotions at times like this. His technique involved not thinking of what lay before him as an individual human being who had been breathing, eating, drinking or perhaps making love just a few hours previously. That would come later when they would have a name and an identity, humanising this broken thing on the ground.

What was important for now was detail. He drew out his notebook and pencil and started to record what he saw.

The left arm was flung out to the side at an angle of 45 degrees, the right arm folded across the chest.

The clothing was not noticeably disturbed. The jacket and trousers were clean and seemed in good repair. An off-white cotton shirt, buttoned to the neck but collarless, was spattered with blood. Seven or eight feet from the head a black, soft-brimmed hat lay upturned on the ground.

On the left side of the forehead, just below the hairline, there was a clear, circular hole, the size of a small coin. It formed the apex of an acute triangle with its base at the two craters where the eyes had once been. Swallow drew an oval to represent the face on the open page of the notebook and marked the location of the wound in relation to the eye cavities.

He moved close to the corpse and squatted so that he could examine the clothing by touch. He felt the fabric of the jacket between his thumb and forefinger. It was relatively new, but of indifferent quality.

When he touched his fingers against the corpse's right hand it was cold and solid.

He moved to the feet of the corpse and squatted again. The boots showed wear, but they had been neatly patched in two places on the uppers. He drew two outlines in the notebook and marked the location of the patches on each one.

Doolan rose to his full height and moved to where the other blanket was draped across a smaller form a couple of feet away.

'This won't be easy either,' Doolan said. He lifted the second blanket to reveal a small, huddled form, lying in the foetal position on its right side with bare legs drawn up towards the stomach. The boy was perhaps 8 or 9 years old. His hands were clasped together in front of him with the fingers interlocked. The head was turned upward across the left shoulder, so Swallow could see the same destruction of the face, just as with the adult lying nearby.

The eyes were all but gone under the open lids. In their place were two small caverns of bloodied space. On the pale forehead, above where the left eye should have been, the same circular wound penetrated through flesh and bone to reveal brain matter within the skull. The dark hair, cut short, looked healthy and glossy. The child's mouth was open with the gums visible as if he were still screaming in the shock tremor that marked the end of his life.

A scene from his childhood years in the County Kildare countryside swam into his mind.

A man ploughing the land near Swallow's home at Newcroft had uncovered what appeared to be human bones. At first, he thought they were the remains of famine victims, perhaps a family that had starved or died of exposure or disease. When the priest was called he told the farmer that he had stumbled on a prehistoric burial chamber. People travelled long distances to see it as the news spread.

Swallow's father had taken him by the hand across the fields to gaze down at the yellow-grey bones in the pit. One of the smaller skeletons was crouched in the same foetal position as the dead child he was now looking at.

A few days later, men came from the new museum in Dublin and took the bones away in a wooden box. They stopped at the Swallow family pub, Newcroft House, before taking the open car that brought them to the train at the town of Kildare. While they were drinking, one of the men from the museum told his father that the skeletons were 4,000 years old.

He got to his feet. 'Have we any identification at all, Stephen?'

'Nothing. I went through the pockets. There's no wallet, no watch, no rings on any of the fingers, no letters. Not even a tram ticket. Nothing in the lad's pockets either.'

Swallow pointed to the circular wound on the forehead. 'What do you make of that? And the same mark on the child?'

Doolan scratched his chin through his dark beard as if seeking inspiration. 'They're surely bullet wounds. But there should be exit wounds too. And I can't see any.'

Swallow moved back to squat beside the body again. He went through the pockets of the trousers and jacket. Doolan was right. There was nothing.

'Do you think the park-keeper might have lifted a wallet or a watch? Or anyone else?'

Doolan shook his head. 'I can't say it didn't happen. The park-keeper's fairly shaken himself, though. He lives down in the village in Chapelizod. He says it was the dog that brought him over here, barking and yelping.'

Swallow reached to the adult corpse's left arm from where it lay across the grass. The hand was surprisingly small. There were no signs of physical labour.

Swallow concentrated on the two bodies, trying to study the features. Father and son, perhaps? The destruction of the faces made it difficult to measure likeness.

'What time were they found?'

'The park-keeper turned up at the police station in Chapelizod about 5.30 or so. They sent for the priest and they telegraphed to the Commissioner's office at Dublin Castle. The message was relayed on to me at Kilmainham. I sent one of my lads to notify the G Division.'

The police chain of communication was slow and cumbersome. The Dublin Metropolitan Police area stretched well beyond the city proper, encompassing the great space of the Phoenix Park and many of the villages and hamlets on its periphery. Nearly all of the big DMP stations were linked by a communications system known as the ABC Telegraph. Only a few of the larger stations were connected to the new telephone system that was in the early stages of installation across the city.

Outside of the Metropolitan District, policing was the responsibility of the Royal Irish Constabulary. Arguably the most effective communications link between the two forces was the fact that their respective headquarters' offices were located in proximity to each other in the Lower Yard at Dublin Castle.

'Do we know any reason why the park-keeper was out so early?'

Doolan shrugged. 'He says he was watching for a couple of stray dogs that've been giving trouble. We haven't any report of that but we can check it. He might have been planning on bringing home a few rabbits or even a deer. He wouldn't usually start work until 8 o'clock.'

Swallow cursed silently. Close on two hours had been lost, part of which he had spent in the detective office at Exchange Court, shuffling useless paperwork to bring him to the end of his night shift. It was time that might have seen the disappearance of valuable clues, or enabled a perpetrator to get far away from the scene of the crime.

With more than 20 years in plain clothes, Swallow was one of the G Division's most experienced serious crime investigators. There had scarcely been a murder or suspicious death in the city during the past decade to which he had not been assigned. That the Dublin Metropolitan Police had been able to claim the highest rate of crime detection of any urban area in Britain and Ireland was in some considerable part attributable to the skills of Detective Sergeant Joe Swallow.

When three of the 'Invincibles' went to the gallows for the murders of Lord Cavendish and Mr Burke, Swallow got a commendation. His boss, the legendary Detective Superintendent John Mallon, had been promoted. Some of Swallow's colleagues told him that he should have done better out of the case himself, maybe with promotion to inspector. Swallow thought so too. In fact he was bloody sure of it. He had seen others promoted having achieved much less. It was not easy to avoid feeling bitter.

And he could have done without this situation, he told himself. He had got through his week of night duty without a major crime being reported. A couple of years ago that would have been a disappointment. He would have relished the thrill of a new case, the challenge of the unknown, the satisfaction of putting the pieces of a puzzle together to see it emerge finally as a coherent picture.

This time he had been looking forward to his two leave-days. He would have slept late in the mornings and then maybe spent the warm June afternoons with his board and colours, painting at Sandycove Harbour or by the rocks at Scotsman's Bay, behind Kingstown. He liked seascapes for the way they constantly changed, even as he worked. It meant that nobody could say he had got the wrong colour in the sky or that he had exaggerated the height of the waves.

For as long as he could remember he had been a sketcher, scratching away with a pencil stump as a boy, drawing dogs or birds or the outline of a hill or the detail of a building. In the budding stages of his romantic involvement with Maria Walsh, she had introduced him to her younger sister, Lily Grant, who was a teacher of art at Alexandra College. She encouraged him to experiment with watercolours and offered to guide him in his early efforts. He still liked to sketch, but there was something especially pleasurable in working the colour washes in and around the pencil outlines.

Even his immediate plan for the day was forfeit now. He had arranged to collect his sister at the college in Blackrock in the afternoon, when her examination would be finished. They would walk the length of the sea road to Kingstown and she would tell him about the examination paper in the morning and how she had got on.

Then he would take her to afternoon tea at Mr Gresham's Marine Hotel, looking down over the harbour, busy with yachts and ships and with passengers getting on and off the mail packets.

Swallow took his role as an older brother seriously. Harriet had hardly known her father. After he died, her brother had filled much of the void in her childhood world. He was her security, her counsellor and her confidant.

When she had been offered a place at teacher training college a year ago it had signalled a problem. It meant she would leave her mother to operate the public house and grocery store at Newcroft. Running the business was a hard task for a widow, dependent on hired help.

An obvious solution might be for Swallow to go home to run the place. After more than 20 years' service with the police he was eligible for a decent pension. A detective sergeant's pay was more than adequate for a single man. He had made some modest investments and savings too: a few shares in the tram companies and the new Dublin gas company, and a small accumulation of cash in a savings account in a Dame Street bank.

There was the complication of his relationship with Maria Walsh. He was a single man. She was an attractive widow with her well-established public house that she had inherited from her family in Thomas Street, just 15 minutes' walk from the Castle. There was the age gap between them. He was fit and strong for his 42 years. She was looking at 30. Without planning it, their lives had become enmeshed.

But Swallow was not of a mind to abandon the life to which he had become accustomed in order to return to rural Kildare or even to become Maria Walsh's partner in running her business. At least it was not what he wanted to do just yet.

It was important to be in Dublin while Harriet was in training college. She needed his guidance as she came to know the world. Increasingly, he worried about what was in her head concerning politics. She had begun to mention too often, he thought, what she referred to as 'Ireland's distress.'

When he encountered his sister recently in a café in Westmoreland Street with a young man, Harriet introduced her brother using an Irish language form of his name – *Seosamh*.

Swallow did not conceal his irritation. 'You're going to confuse people,' he told her sharply. 'If I change the name I was given at birth I'll let you know.'

Harriet introduced the young man as Mr O'Donnell. He was '*Seamus*' but if Swallow preferred he could call him 'James,' she added.

Within a few minutes of opening the conversation, O'Donnell had used the same phrase that she had used about Ireland's distress, but it was with an undertone of aggression that rang a warning bell in Swallow's policeman's head. When they parted, he scribbled the name 'James O'Donnell' in his notebook.

In Swallow's experience, Ireland's distress was too often invoked as a cover for what was simply crime. Violence, misappropriation of funds, even murder could be presented under the guise of patriotism. It was not that he doubted the sincerity of some of the politicals, as they were referred to in police parlance. Many of them were honourable people, he acknowledged. But good causes could also be exploited.

His boss, John Mallon, had a saying: 'you can buy a lot of patriotism in Dublin for a fiver.' The veteran detective had made quite a few such purchases in building up his intelligence network over the years.

Lately, Swallow noticed, Harriet had begun to disparage the various celebrations that were being planned to take place around the city to mark the Golden Jubilee of Victoria's ascent to the throne.

1887 was to be a year of self-congratulation for the Empire upon which it was proclaimed the sun would never set. But conditions in Ireland were not conducive to celebration.

The 'land war' continued to rage across the country as smallholders fought to free themselves from crippling rents. The Dublin Castle authorities, under the direction of a new and tough Chief Secretary, Arthur Balfour, responded with draconian crime legislation, additional powers for the police and additional prison spaces for those who demanded reform. Irish nationalists argued that there was nothing for their country to celebrate. There were urgings to boycott or disrupt public events.

But there would be no visit to Kingstown and no afternoon tea with his sister at Mr Gresham's Marine Hotel today. The bodies of the man and child on the ground between the beech trees had put paid to that.

Doolan removed his helmet and wiped his forehead with his uniform sleeve.

'How long do you think they're dead?'

'Just a few hours, I'd say. The man's still in rigor mortis. That usually begins after about three hours. He died sometime last night, maybe in the early hours of this morning.'

'Christ, I've seen a lot over the years – as you have. But a father and child butchered like that...' Doolan said.

'You'd say they're father and son?' Swallow asked.

'Well, it's a guess. But they could be. I don't see anything indicating a struggle,' Doolan said hurriedly, moving from speculation to more certain ground. 'But nobody here would have seen anything in the night or even heard shots. The lodge at the gate isn't occupied any longer. Maybe they were killed somewhere else?'

Swallow shook his head.

'I think they died here. You can see the lividity there in the hands and the arms where the blood gathers. The bodies weren't moved after death.'

He pointed to the ground. 'If you look on the moss and grass around the two of them there, you'll see that there are small blood-stains. They're in a pattern around the head and shoulders on the ground as well as on his clothes. They bled here. They died here.'

Doolan shrugged. 'I suppose you're paid more than I am to know about these things. What do you want done now?'

'We need to get a message down to Doctor Lafeyre at Harcourt Street. Tell him he's needed up here. We need to get the photographic technician too. You'll have to clear that with the Commissioner's office. I want photographs here before the bodies are moved.'

Swallow stepped back from the bodies to the edge of the copse. It was still cool and dark in the trees, and he winced slightly as the strengthening morning sun hit his eyes.

Everything he had seen so far boded badly.

This was not going to be a routine inquiry. It was not the result of a drunken brawl or a random criminal encounter. The remote location meant it was unlikely there were any witnesses. The extent of the damage inflicted on the corpses confirmed the application of singular brutality in the execution of the crime. The absence of any identifying clues especially worried him. Not knowing the identity of a crime victim multiplied the police task of investigation many times over.

The only positive he could see was that there was nothing to suggest any political dimension to this case.

G Division divided all crime into two categories: 'special' or 'ordinary.' The absolute priority was 'special crime' – anything with an element of politics or subversion. 'Ordinary crime' might be serious, but it took second place to security or politically related issues. Swallow's instinct told him that these were 'ordinary murders.'

He stepped back out of the copse and into the full light, allowing his gaze to travel across the scene through a full 360 degrees.

He tried to imagine the final moments of what had been acted out here. Was the boy shot first? Did the man witness the terrible sight of his young son – assuming that they were parent and child – being killed before his eyes? Or was the parent shot first? Did he see the child's terror in the last fraction of time that he was given, knowing too with certainty that the boy would follow into the darkness?

It was incongruous, he thought, that such brutalities were often uncovered in beautiful places.

So it was here. The green park rippled away towards the city, punctuated with breaks of trees. Although he could not see the river from where he stood, a faint morning mist rising from beyond the Chapelizod Gate marked its route down the valley to the city and the bay. In the distance, over the city, he could see the rising plume of steam from Guinness's brewery at St James's Gate. He got the faint, sweet aroma of roasting barley and hops on the air.

There was no way of knowing how the man and the boy had come to this place. Had they walked or ridden? Had they been driven? Had they come from the city during the night, along the wide expanse of Chesterfield Avenue, or had they entered the park through the gate nearby? If they had come through the village of Chapelizod there was a better probability of witnesses. Perhaps even of identification.

Swallow glumly told himself the chances were slim. The dead man and child were no villagers. The light clothing and the soft hands suggested a city type. Other questions followed. What time had they come? Were they alone? Why had they come to this remote, out-of-the-way corner of the great park? And what motive could there be for such brutal killings? Robbery might be a possibility, given the absence of any money, a watch or a wallet. Could there be some motive of revenge? Or some set of relationships gone violently wrong? Until he had identification the lives of the man and boy would be unknowable.

He gave instructions to Doolan.

'Get every man you can collect, Stephen. Have them search the ground thoroughly from here to the road beyond. Collect anything they find, buttons, coins, clay pipes, cigarette ends. I want anything that looks like a good footprint or a wheel-track to be marked out for plaster-casting. How many men can you raise?'

'We'll pull them off the regular beats on the A Division. I can get a dozen.'

Swallow nodded. 'You'll need more. You'll have to preserve the scene until Dr Lafeyre is done and the photographer too. Contact D Division too. Get them to send everyone they have as well.'

He pointed towards the end of the track where it exited the park at the Chapelizod Gate.

'Get a party to follow the road right down to the gate. You'll need a line of men across the grass, three feet apart, six men each side. Then go the other direction and follow the road up to Chesterfield Avenue. If there's a gun or cartridges or anything discarded they'll probably be somewhere along the track.'

Doolan hurriedly noted the instructions in his pocketbook.

'That's all understood. I'll send down to the city for more men, but it'll take a while to cover all the ground. I'll have both ends of the road closed and we'll the seal off the extended scene.'

He gestured to where the white-haired friar was standing patiently beside the road, clutching his box of holy oils.

'We asked Father Laurence from the Merchants' Quay friary to come out with us earlier. God bless him, he's been standing there for more than an hour. Are you happy to let him up there to give them their last rites?'

Swallow glanced over at the priest in his brown habit. He had forgotten about him and felt momentarily guilty. 'That's fine as long as he doesn't interfere with anything. Send a constable up with him to make sure.'

Doolan went to deploy his men and Swallow walked over to where the park-keeper stood with his gun and dog.

The man was perhaps 40 years of age, thin and wiry. He was agitated, his eyes darting around as if expecting some new catastrophe to descend, but he offered a consistent account of what he had seen and found.

Swallow thought he might have been mildly hysterical. That would not rule him out as a suspect. He had experienced cases of violence where the criminal, confronted with a full realisation of what he had done, had gone into shock.

'I want to see your hands and to examine your clothes,' Swallow told him. 'Have you any objection?'

The man seemed startled. He shrugged and stammered, 'No... no.'

'Take off your jacket,' Swallow commanded, 'and put your hands out in front of you with the palms up.'

He gave Swallow the blue official jacket. It was worn and it smelled of woodsmoke and sweat. Inside, the lining was holed and torn. But there were no stains or damp spots that might indicate hurried washing. The pockets contained a few pennies, a pipe and a tobacco pouch, a dirty handkerchief and rosary beads.

He scrutinised the man's extended hands and turned them over. They were calloused and ingrained. Rims of black dirt lay under the fingernails, but there was no blood. These were not the hands or the clothing of a man who had committed the butchery in the copse of pine and beech.

'All right,' Swallow conceded. 'Go along with the constables. Make your statement and then go home. You've had a bad morning.'

Swallow estimated that even if the man was a poacher on the side, he was in this instance at least an honest witness.

Doolan came across the grass, having briefed his men. He drew his half-hunter watch from his pocket and read the hour. It was coming up to 9 o'clock.

'Do you want some breakfast? They'll still be serving in the canteen at Kilmainham. You'll want to make a report to the Castle – to get some of your own fellows up here from Exchange Court.'

Swallow had eaten nothing since midnight in Exchange Court when he had taken his sandwiches, prepared for him earlier by Maria's house-keeper. He was thirsty too. In earlier years, he might have finished his night-duty tour with a couple of pints of stout and perhaps a Tullam-ore or two in one of the early-morning houses licensed to serve drink to drovers, dealers and others whose livelihood would have them on the streets before the city was properly awake.

The normal arrangements for refreshment and sustenance would not apply for the foreseeable future. He had a full agenda. He had to advise his superiors at Exchange Court of the details of the crime. He needed experienced detectives on the ground.

Standard procedure would oblige him to open a 'murder book.' An investigation into a crime like this could take weeks or months. Police practice required that every jot of information, every witness interviewed and every statement taken be meticulously recorded in the murder book, checked and then cross-checked.

Swallow reckoned that he had an hour before Dr Harry Lafeyre, the city medical examiner, would get to the scene along with the police photographic technician.

He would have to eat at some point, and it was going to be a long day ahead. He knew too that at this stage of his investigation even the sight of mutilated bodies would not interfere with his appetite. That would come later, perhaps, when names had been put on them, when the lifeless corpses were no longer just nameless flesh and bone.

He climbed aboard the Kilmainham side-car. 'Breakfast it will be then, Stephen,' he answered Doolan. 'They say an army marches on its stomach, but I can tell you that in my experience so does a murder investigation.'

The driver snapped the reins, drawing the horse from its feast of meadow-grass, and turned the car back towards the city.

TWO

'Pisspot' Ces Downes died in the front bedroom of her house overlooking Francis Street, in Dublin's Liberties, four days before the Queen's Jubilee, on the third day of the heatwave. She breathed her last just after 8 o'clock in the evening, about the same time that Joe Swallow completed his initial report on the Chapelizod Gate murders and signed himself out of the detective office at Exchange Court.

The news had spread during the week that the woman with a killer's reputation who had spun a spider's web of crime across the city for more than 20 years was on her deathbed. As quickly as the news percolated through the streets and the public houses and even the police stations, the question was being asked: What would happen when she was gone?

There were differing versions of how 'Pisspot' Ces – Cecilia Downes – had got her nickname. One was that she kept a porcelain pot brimming with sovereigns hidden in a secret room at the top of the three-storey house in Francis Street. Another was that when she drank porter she did so from a circular, two-handled vessel that looked as if it had been designed for sanitary purposes.

Many years before, Joe Swallow had heard what he believed to be the more accurate account of it. His source was Stephen Doolan who was then working in plain clothes from the DMP station at College Street.

Swallow and Doolan had spent a fruitless week trying to recover a haul of silver plate taken in broad daylight from a judge's house on St Stephen's Green. The word around the city was that 'Pisspot' Ces had already found a buyer for it in Manchester. Now they had taken two high stools in front of a pair of pints in Mulligan's public house, behind the DMP station.

The two policemen were in gloomy mood, anticipating the censure that would descend upon them from on high for their failure to restore His Lordship's plate.

'She's as hardened and vicious a criminal as you'll meet, that one,' Doolan said, as he squared up to his pint of Guinness's porter. 'And she has an eye for good silver.'

He raised the tumbler to his lips and downed a third of his pint.

'That's what she started with – silver. Did you know that?'

He ran the back of his hand across his mouth, drawing the frothy trace of the porter off the bristles of his moustache. 'As I heard it from one of the old-timers in College Street, she was only a young one at the time. She went to service in a big house in Merrion Square, I think it was. The housekeeper found a clutch of silver spoons hidden away under a petticoat. When she saw the set of spoons neatly wrapped away she told her she was calling the police.'

He shook his head gravely.

'That was where she made the mistake – the housekeeper, that is. Ces Downes drew up a cast-iron chamber-pot from under the bed and battered her with it across the skull a dozen times. That woman never walked or talked properly afterwards.'

Doolan raised his glass again.

'I heard that from one of the men that took Ces Downes to the Bridwell, still shouting that if she had a chance, she'd finish the ould bitch off. But you know, the extraordinary thing is that she was never charged for it. She could have been done at the very least for assault and battery, maybe even attempted murder. You won't find any of it in the records at the Dublin Criminal Registry.'

Whether the tale was true or not, it had gained acceptance in the world of Dublin crime. It became another thread in the mystery that was 'Pisspot' Ces Downes.

Even in the closing days of her life, nobody in authority could have put their hands on any documentation to confirm where Ces was born or what her name had been before she married her late husband, Tommy 'The Cutter' Byrne.

Searches by successive investigators over the years in the Registry of Births, Deaths and Marriages had yielded nothing. Trawls through the post office and the savings banks, facilitated by co-operative officials, found no trace of her supposed crime-funded fortune. There was nothing of use in her file in the Dublin Criminal Registry, the DMP's vast repository of information held at Dublin Castle on those who came to their notice during the investigation of crime.

A decade previously, after her husband had died of consumption, she paid cash down for what had once been the home of a prosperous wool-merchant on Francis Street.

The once-elegant town house was within the hearing of the bells of the city's two cathedrals: Christ Church and St Patrick's. It became the headquarters of Ces Downes's criminal operations. The fine reception rooms became dormitories for travelling criminals. The spacious kitchens and pantries became storehouses for junk and stolen property. The Italianate plasterwork on the ceilings crumbled. What had once been a showpiece of Georgian architecture and workmanship degenerated into a squalid doss-house.

A wisecracking G-man remarked perceptively that Pisspot Ces and her house on Francis Street deteriorated together. Never abstemious, she drank heavily and steadily after Tommy's death. The sharp, strong features turned to sagging flesh. The once-glossy hair that she wore curling to her shoulders gradually turned from black to a yellow-grey.

Ces Downes kept the top floor of the mansion as her citadel, sharing it with two Staffordshire fighting dogs that reputedly slept one at each side of her bed at night. Few of her criminal foot-soldiers had access to the top floor. Only her most trusted lieutenants ever got beyond the landing. When she saw visitors on business it was in a dilapidated, dirty room at street level that had once been the wool-merchant's counting office.

As Ces Downes's criminal enterprises consolidated, upwards of half a dozen young men – her 'lads,' as she referred to them – operated as her muscle.

Two of them in particular, Vinny Cussen and Charlie Vanucchi, were toughened criminals. Cussen was squat and red-haired with a physique like a small horse. Vanucchi's tall frame and sallow, dark looks betokened his Neapolitan forebears, who had come to Dublin as street pedlars three generations previously.

There were rumours that Ces had children. Some of the G-Division detectives had picked up a whisper that she had a son who was one of the top criminals in Liverpool. A young woman who came to visit her once at Francis Street was spoken of as being her daughter.

Somebody else said she was Ces's fence – a receiver of stolen goods – in London. But she would neither deny nor confirm any of it on the many occasions when she was interviewed in connection with one crime or another.

Nor was it easy to say how or why Pisspot Ces Downes had emerged as one of the acknowledged principals of Dublin's criminal underworld during the 1870s and 1880s. Some policemen believed there was a clue in the bail records of the Dublin Magistrates Courts. While it was impossible to find any trace of her in any other official register, the books there showed that she had begun to offer herself as a bail-bondsman at some time at the beginning of that period.

Bail was difficult in the Dublin courts for a suspected criminal accused of housebreaking or robbery or picking pockets. Victorian Dublin, in common with every other major city of the United Kingdom, placed a premium on the protection of property. The city's policing and courts system reflected that. But bail in some circumstances might be a possibility if someone was willing to put up a heavy bond. Ces Downes seemed to have the funds to do so.

She had no convictions for violence, but it was generally believed that a Belfast criminal who was found with his throat cut on Usher's Island had died at Ces Downes's own hand. His error, it seems, was thinking that he could undercut Downes and supply cheap, bootleg whiskey to certain public houses on the Dublin quays.

And it was known that when a small-time fence across the river in Mary Street refused to pay Vinny Cussen the agreed value of a collection of stolen watches, Ces Downes ordered that he be brought over to Francis Street for some persuasion. He was never seen alive again. Tentative identification of a battered corpse taken from the river at Islandbridge a month later indicated his likely violent end.

She seemed to have influence in unlikely places. It was known that when a drunken doctor had refused treatment to a sick woman at the Long Lane Dispensary, Ces Downes somehow arranged it so that she was admitted as a patient at Dr Steevens' Hospital. The woman even got a sulky apology from the dispensary.

She had the reputation of being able to persuade certain landlords to hold off from raising rents or evicting certain tenants who were in her favour and who were having difficulty meeting their bills. It was said, although never proven, that she had influence with lawyers and even with some judges.

Over the years she built a network of operators from the poverty-stricken classes that inhabited the courts and alleyways and tenements of Dublin city. Ces Downes was a protector, a fixer, a money lender and a counsellor as well as being a woman who was personally capable of extreme violence.

G Division knew that her criminal interests ran virtually the entire gamut of the underside of Dublin life. She received stolen property. She operated rings of 'dippers' – young girls who picked pockets in the streets or at race meetings. She funded pitch and toss schools. She staked cash for the illicit distilling of alcohol. Although it could never be established that she was directly involved in prostitution, she readily went bail for girls from the red-light districts around Montgomery Street or in the courts and alleys off Grafton Street whenever the DMP felt it was necessary, for appearances' sake, to make some arrests.

If Ces Downes had connections to any of the 'politicals,' the Land Leaguers, the Fenians, the Invincibles or any of the splinter groups, G Division rarely found any traces of them. She stayed clear of the well-known figures who claimed to be pursuing the interests of the worker or the small farmer or advancing the cause of patriotic nationalism.

But the G-men often found that there was cross-membership down the ranks between the ordinary criminal and the politicals. Housebreakers, robbers, prostitutes, receivers, pickpockets and miscreants of various types would frequently invoke political motivation when arrested or charged. Sometimes, in Swallow's experience, the claims were genuine. Often they were expedient, or a desperate attempt when caught red-handed to do a deal as an informant with a G-man.

Estimates of Ces's age put her somewhere in her forties. But the heart disease that slowly drained the strength from her body had turned her yellow and gaunt and seemed to shrink her frame. Since the early springtime she had grown visibly more frail each week, and from the early summer she had not been able to spend more than an hour or two of any day on her feet.

In more recent years, as she had gradually succumbed to the illness that finally ended her life, she had devolved much of the running of her organisation to her two lieutenants – Vinny Cussen and Charlie Vanucchi.

The question now was which of these two potential heirs would take her place. Both were brutal men. Their victims included people who could not pay their debts to Ces Downes's criminal empire, troublesome publicans and potential witnesses in court cases. Some of those who crossed Cussen and Vanucchi disappeared, like the fence from Mary Street who refused to pay for the stolen watches, and were never seen again. Others ended up in hospital or badly mutilated.

Charlie Vanucchi ran as many as a dozen burglary and housebreaking teams simultaneously. It was said that Charlie could accurately describe the interior and layout of every fine house and business premises between the two canals that circle Dublin city centre.

Vinny Cussen's reputation was largely built on poteen. He bought, transported, and when necessary manufactured the cheap, potent whiskey that his gangs supplied to public houses at a fraction of the cost of regular, bonded alcohol that was subject to excise tax.

Each of them regarded the other with the deepest hatred and suspicion.

As long as Ces Downes was in charge, they suffered each other in the confined world of Dublin criminality. But with her dead, would that uneasy co-existence be sustained? Most observers felt not. One man or the other would surely emerge as top dog, and it was unlikely that it would happen without a struggle.

Other questions followed. Would her successor operate according to the rules that she had dictated during her lifetime, or would the criminal network which she led try to extend beyond its traditional businesses and into new districts? Would the transition to a new leadership be peaceful, or would there be a bloodletting as a new order was established?

Pisspot Ces Downes had entered the last days of her life as the calendar turned to June. May had been seasonally warm, but June was to prove memorable for the extraordinarily high temperatures of its days and for the cloying humidity of its nights. Over the days and nights that she lay in her sick-room, at the front of her house in Francis Street, the more the conversations in the streets and courts and alleyways seemed to bespeak the uncertainties in what lay ahead.

Unidentified visitors sometimes came at night to Francis Street and were admitted on her instruction to her third-floor citadel. Invariably the visitors' features were hidden by unseasonal scarves and headgear. None took more than a few minutes with her. The exceptions were a friar from the Franciscan Church at Merchants' Quay and two black-robed nuns who spent an hour by her bedside one afternoon and then slipped out into the street.

The gathering heat and the bad air of the June days hurried her end. She would have no doctors. She dulled the pain with laudanum in brandy until she was no longer able to swallow. The 'lads' were by her bedside as she breathed her last.

On the evening that Ces Downes died, Charlie Vanucchi and Vinny Cussen came together to the front door of the house in Francis Street. Together, in a rare show of unity, they pinned the black crepe and the notice on the door, announcing her passing, shortly after 8 o'clock.

THREE

By 11 o'clock, when Dr Henry Lafeyre, the Dublin medical examiner, reached the copse of trees inside the Chapelizod Gate, the morning sun was climbing over the city. Untrammelled even by a single cloud, it had cleared the small hills that flank the bay to the south – Dalkey and Killiney. Then it set its course behind the dead volcanic peak of the Sugarloaf, past Two Rock and Three Rock. At midday it would burn steadily in a diamond sky above Djouce Mountain.

Joe Swallow worked productively and easily with Harry Lafeyre. Sometimes Swallow thought that, although he was ten years the senior of the medical examiner, the two men saw something of themselves in each other's life story.

Lafeyre, the forensic examiner and physician, had served for three years as Medical Officer with the Cape Colony Mounted Police in southern Africa. He was 'a copper with a stethoscope,' as he humorously recalled it.

Swallow would have been a doctor rather than a detective sergeant in the Dublin Metropolitan Police had he not drunk his way through two years of medical school, 'pissing away hard-earned savings from the family business,' as his father, in his final illness, had put it bitterly.

Brought together in the common purpose of solving crime in Dublin city over the past three years, a working relationship had developed into a mutually respectful sense of ease and even friendship.

There was another connection too. Harry Lafeyre had recently become engaged to Lily Grant, who was a teacher of art at Alexandra College, a city school for the education of young Protestant ladies. Lily was the younger sister of Maria Walsh, Swallow's landlady at Thomas Street.

'I suppose that makes us potential in-laws, except there isn't any law in it,' Lafeyre had quipped to Swallow when it transpired that the two Grant sisters had come to occupy places of significance in their respective lives.

Lafeyre's brougham carriage, driven by his general assistant, a dour young man named Scollan, trundled across the track and rolled to a stop beside the DMP car that had brought Swallow and Doolan back from their breakfast at the Kilmainham Station mess hall.

It had been a good breakfast. Once he got the aroma of frying bacon in his nostrils, Swallow had set aside his Catholic reservations about eating meat on Fridays. He recalled a comforting formula from his school catechism offering a dispensation in circumstances where meat might already have been prepared, perhaps by ill-informed or well-meaning Protestants. He allowed himself to imagine that the description might fit the mess cook.

He had telegraphed a preliminary report from Kilmainham to the Castle. By the time he and Doolan returned to the crime scene, three G-Division detectives had arrived from the day-shift at Exchange Court. Two of these, Tom Swift and Mick Feore, were now leading door-to-door inquiries in the houses on the park side of Chapelizod village.

The third, Pat Mossop, was seated in his shirtsleeves on the step of the side-car. Mossop was a 'Book Man.' Now he sat, filling in details in the big foolscap pages of the murder book, his slight frame perspiring through his white shirt.

When he could get him, Pat Mossop was Swallow's first choice in the role of Book Man. Appointing the Book Man was a key task for an investigator leading a serious criminal inquiry. He was the meticulous recorder of every detail and each scrap of information that came in. He was the one who would be expected to see connections or patterns in the material collected by the men on the ground. He had to have the ability to remember everything and forget nothing.

Swallow reckoned that Pat Mossop was probably the best Book Man in the G Division. It was in his training. He had been a clerk in a Belfast mill before joining the police and he brought the disciplines of modern industrial practices with him. Swallow sometimes worried about Mossop's health. He met the height requirement for the police, but he was thin as a broom handle. Was there an illness or a disability in childhood? Swallow wondered but he never felt it right to ask.

Notwithstanding his delicate physique, Mossop was energetic. He was as organised in his personal life as in his police work. Still in his thirties, he lived with a cheerful wife and four lively children in rooms over a poulterer's in Aungier Street. But over and above his competence in record keeping, Swallow liked him for his irrepressible optimism. Sometimes, especially in the fallow stages of an investigation, it was what kept a G-man going.

A Dublin Fire Brigade ambulance was drawn up next to the police side-car. The photographer had set up his heavy field-camera on its tripod and had taken close-up pictures of the bodies.

When the medical examiner had finished, the ambulance crew would take the remains to the City Morgue at Marlborough Street, but for now the two attendants sat shirt-sleeved against the trunk of a massive beech. The ambulance horses stood tethered beside them, men and beasts sharing the tree's shade.

'I'm sorry it's taken me a while,' Lafeyre apologised. 'I had an early patient with an acute appendix in the surgery. Once I got her down to Mercer's Hospital I got here as quickly as I could.'

Swallow knew that Lafeyre had to attend to his private practice as well in order to make a living. The post of medical examiner for Dublin was a part-time one, and Lafeyre ran his main practice from the house at Harcourt Street that he had bought with savings from his African tour.

The authorities provided him with a small office in the Lower Yard at Dublin Castle, close to the Army Medical Office, while he used the facilities at the Marlborough Street morgue for post-mortem examinations. He moved constantly between the three locations.

He hefted his examination bag from inside the brougham. 'The message said it's a dead man and a child.'

'Don't worry about your timing, Doctor. We didn't have any other great plans for the day,' Stephen Doolan said with an attempt at black humour. 'When you see what's above there in the trees you'll understand why.'

Swallow saw Doolan's eyes suddenly fix in alertness. The uniformed sergeant nodded to a point somewhere over Harry Lafeyre's shoulder.

'You take the doctor over to the scene, Joe, and I'll deal with these gentlemen here.'

Swallow followed Doolan's gaze to where two Ringsend cars, Dublin's inexpensive equivalent of the hackney cab, were clattering along the Acres Road from the direction of Chesterfield Avenue.

Even at this distance he could recognise some of the pressmen. The news had obviously reached the *Freeman's Journal*, the *Evening Telegraph*, and *The Irish Times*. In all, the two Ringsend cars seemed to be carrying seven or eight pressmen.

'You go ahead,' Doolan said. 'I'll slow these fellows in their gallop.'

The sergeant walked forward to meet the coming cars, right hand raised to arrest their approach. Doolan was good at that sort of thing, Swallow reflected. With the added height of the police helmet over his bearded features, he was an impressive 6 feet and 9 inches. Even a car load of news-hungry reporters would hesitate to challenge his authority.

'A policeman mightn't need a lot of brains in every situation,' Doolan liked to quip, 'but he needs a certain amount of *altitude*.'

Swallow, Mossop and Lafeyre strode to the copse of trees.

Now it was Swallow's turn to lift the grey blanket from the adult body between the beeches. The heat of the morning had accelerated the processes of decomposition and the skin, waxen white earlier, was beginning to tinge with faint green and blue. Swallow could see that armies of small woodland insects had gathered where blood had spattered on the mossy earth. Some had already begun to explore the corpse. Buzzing summer flies began to land on the face and skull when the blanket was lifted.

Lafeyre surveyed the destruction to the face and skull. He squatted silently beside the body and reached out to touch the right arm, replicating Swallow's test of some hours previously. This time the arm moved a little.

'Rigor mortis is passing,' he said. 'Allowing for the warmth of the day, I'd estimate he's dead perhaps 12 hours. Say about 10 o'clock last night, give or take an hour.'

Pat Mossop's pencil scratched the details in the murder book.

Lafeyre got to his feet and nodded to the smaller form under the second blanket.

'That's the boy, I assume.'

Swallow lifted the second blanket. Lafeyre squatted again and pushed at the small, clasped hands with his forefinger. The tones of the skin had deepened in places to a bluish mottle. The hands moved a little in response to the examiner's pressure. Lafeyre put his right hand under the child's head, raising it sufficiently to see the back of the skull.

'Grim bloody work by somebody,' he said after an interval. He turned back to Swallow.

'How much have you learned? Any idea what happened?'

Doolan's searching constables had found wheel-marks and hoof-marks leading along the track from Chesterfield Avenue and ending perhaps 10 yards from the edge of the copse. From there, they led across the grassy verge towards the Chapelizod Gate. A carriage had arrived from the direction of the city and then left through the gate. Beyond that, the searches had yielded nothing so far.

'Not really. And no scrap of identification. If there were any valuables like a watch or a purse they're gone. We're taking plaster casts of a set of wheel-marks and hoof-marks. It looks like a sizeable carriage but it was drawn by just one horse.'

Swallow gestured to the woodland floor around them.

'The ground here under the trees is too dry to get anything like decent footprints. They're doing house-to-house inquiries now in the village and the cottages, but we've no witnesses so far. We've interviewed the park-keeper but I don't think he's involved.'

Lafeyre grimaced. 'Not much that's helpful in any of that.'

'Nothing. What do you make of it?' Swallow nodded towards the bodies.

'Someone did a hacking job on the faces. I'll need to get them to the morgue to have a look with the microscope. I should be able to tell you what might have been used. But it looks like a knife, maybe 5 or 6 inches of blade and none too sharp.'

He pointed to the circular wound on the man's left temple.

'At a good guess, that's our cause of death. The same for the child, I'd say. There's been little enough bleeding, as you can see. There aren't any defensive wounds on the hands either. So I'd hazard that the mutilation on the faces was done post mortem – for which small mercy you might be grateful. Have you looked at the wounds?'

Swallow nodded. 'They look like bullet entries. But there aren't any exit wounds.'

Lafeyre drew a brass-rimmed magnifying glass from his bag and leaned forward across the body, scrutinising the blackened cavity on the man's forehead.

'It's impossible to say. There's probably a slug in there, perhaps from a very low-velocity weapon. I won't know until I can do a probe later.'

He dropped the glass into the bag and got to his feet again. He turned his back to where Doolan and the other uniformed police were standing, some 20 or 30 yards back. He dropped his voice.

'How're you going to handle this with our friends of the press?' He jerked a thumb towards where Doolan stood with the reporters.

'I haven't much to tell them. This isn't your run-of-the-mill brawl. We've no witnesses. No motive. No weapon. We don't even know who they are, for God's sake.'

'Well you're going to have to present yourself as knowing more than you do,' Lafeyre said quietly.

The sound of raised voices drifted across the grass. Swallow turned to see Doolan raise his arms as if entreating the reporters to be patient. Two or three constables had moved to position themselves beside their sergeant as if anticipating an attempt by the pressmen to sweep past him to the crime scene.

Swallow knew what Harry Lafeyre was worried about. Most of the Dublin press had developed a taste for the outrageous and the blood-thirsty. It had been stimulated by the brutal knifings of Cavendish and Burke five years previously. Three months later it had been reinforced by the massacre of five members of one family – the Joyces – in the remote Maamtrasna district of Connemara.

The newspapers were filled with daily accounts of shootings, burn-ings and rioting across rural Ireland as a desperate but now inflamed tenantry fought the landlords and their agents for control of their farms with the police caught in the middle.

The beleaguered Dublin Castle administration had determined to break the Irish National Land League, inspired by the charismatic, one-armed Michael Davitt from County Mayo. When key nationalist members of the Westminster Parliament initiated what became known as the 'Plan of Campaign,' many of Davitt's supporters took it as a prompt to adopt stronger methods of direct action.

The 'Plan' was effectively a powerful rent boycott, targeted on key landlords. The Government declared it a 'criminal conspiracy.' Police and troops were sent in to break it. The tenants and smallholders resisted.

At the same time, the Castle sought to undermine the 'Home Rule' movement. Driving for Irish political independence, it was championed by the Wicklow landowner and leader of the Irish Party at Westminster, Charles Stewart Parnell.

A 'Home Rule' Bill for Ireland, sponsored by Prime Minister Glad-stone, had been defeated two years previously, leading to the downfall of the Liberal Government. But Parnell had not abandoned the strug-gle, and the authorities knew that when the circumstances were opportune there would be a renewed push to challenge the writ of the Westminster Parliament.

A case like this would offer a newsworthy if ghastly variation on the nightly toll being reported from the countryside. The Dublin police had largely escaped the criticisms being levelled against the RIC. But a case of extreme violence like this would be ideal fodder for newspapers seeking to outdo each other in their sense of outrage.

Swallow strode out of the copse to the group of reporters. Seeing him approach, they turned their focus from Doolan. They were already shouting questions before he reached them.

'Who's the dead man, Joe?'

'How old is the child?'

'We've been told it's a brutal case. Is it true?'

'Have you any clues at this stage?'

'Can we come up to have a look?'

Swallow placed himself beside Doolan and raised his hands to still the cacophony.

'I can't answer everyone at the same time… if you'd please be quiet, I'll tell you what I can. I can't say much to you that you can attribute officially to the police. If you want the official position on anything, you know where the Commissioner's office is in the Lower Castle Yard.'

There was an impatient murmur and Swallow heard a swear word. He knew that no journalist ever got any useful information about anything from the Commissioner's office. His invocation of higher authority was a formula to cover his own back.

'First, there's no question of anybody being let up there. There's a dead man and a young boy in the copse. We don't know who they are and we don't know what happened to them. I can tell you the man is probably in his twenties, maybe a bit more. The boy could be 8 or 9 years old.'

'Is it true they're completely unrecognisable?' The question came from Andrew Dunlop, *The Irish Times*'s man. Swallow knew Dunlop for a solid, if persistent, news reporter.

'The bodies aren't a pleasant sight, but I'm confident we'll establish who they are,' Swallow said.

'Who found them and when?'

It was the *Evening Telegraph*'s reporter, Simon Sweeney.

Always fashionably dressed and well groomed, Sweeney was more polished and better spoken than most of his press colleagues.

Swallow had heard that he was the product of an expensive private education and had graduated from Trinity College. Had he not known the young reporter's avocation he might have taken him for a solicitor or a bank official.

Swallow detailed the sequence of communication from when the park-keeper's dog had led his master to the copse in the early hours. The journalist jotted the details in his notebook.

'Have you established the cause of death, Sergeant?' *The Irish Times*'s man asked.

'That's a matter for Dr Lafeyre, the medical examiner, to determine. At this time we don't know.'

'You don't seem to know very much at all, do you?' The tone was sarcastic and hostile and it was more of a comment than a question. It came from Irving, the correspondent for the *London Daily Sketch*. Swallow and he had clashed many times in the past.

'That's sometimes how crime investigations work, Mr Irving,' Swallow replied evenly. 'We're in the very early stages of this one. As I said, I'm confident we'll know a lot more as we go on.'

Irving sneered. 'You were just as confident about the Elizabeth Logan murder. Were you not, Mr Swallow?'

Swallow felt himself flush. Elizabeth Logan was a prostitute whose body had been found on Sandymount Strand a year previously. The early identification of a suspect had proven to be ill-founded. Swallow knew that his handling of the case had not been the high point of his career.

His face registered the surge of irritation. Sweeney shot a warning look at his colleague.

'Leave it alone, Irving,' he hissed, jabbing his pencil towards Swallow.

'It does sound as if you've got nothing much to go on at this stage, Sergeant,' Sweeney said sharply. 'Why would anyone shoot a man and a child? Isn't that most unusual? Maybe it was a robbery?'

Swallow seemed to hesitate, as if considering something that had just occurred to him.

'Every murder case is unusual, Mr Sweeney. And no, I don't have any idea about motive at this stage. It would be helpful if any of your valued readers were aware of a man and a young boy gone missing. If that were to be so, the detective office at Exchange Court would be glad to hear from them.'

Sweeney sighed with irritation.

'Is that all we get for being out here at this hour of the morning?'

'I didn't ask you to be here at all, Mr Sweeney,' Swallow snapped. 'And I've been here myself from an even earlier hour.'

He forced himself to what he hoped was a smile. 'Now, gentlemen, if you don't mind, I have my work to do and I imagine that you have printing deadlines to meet.'

Half an hour later, when the pressmen had departed, the ambulance crew went into the copse with two canvas stretchers and took the bodies to Lafeyre's morgue at Marlborough Street.

A constable from Kilmainham had taken the plaster casts from the wheel-marks and hoof-marks on the dirt track and would bring them to the detective office. The police photographer had already departed.

Doolan's parties of constables, under Detectives Mick Feore and Tom Swift, were continuing their door-to-door inquiries.

Swallow knew there was little more that could be done to further the investigation on the site. Two constables would remain on duty at the copse to deter sightseers and to preserve the scene in case further examination might prove necessary once Harry Lafeyre's examination had been concluded.

He walked back to Pat Mossop, who was finishing his notes in the murder book.

'Set up a crime conference for 11 o'clock in the morning at Exchange Court. And notify the City Coroner that we have two deaths by misadventure, an unknown man and a male child. Advise him that when we have causes of death confirmed by Dr Lafeyre we'll be asking him to set up an inquest. '

He queried Lafeyre.

'When can I expect to have the post-mortem reports?'

'I've got patients at Harcourt Street until about 5 o'clock, but I'll try to get working on them this evening. I'll have something by tomorrow morning. Say 9 o'clock. Once I've got that completed you'll be able to notify the City Coroner to get a jury together for the inquest.'

Almost a full day would be gone, Swallow reckoned. The bureaucracy of violent death moved at its own pace. But there was little point in protesting. Harry Lafeyre had a practice to look after. He had to earn a living too.

Mossop read Swallow's mind.

The Book Man tried to be positive, as was his wont, in the guise of humour.

'Ah, I know what you're thinking, Boss. But sure, jam tomorrow is better than no jam at all?'

FOUR

When Swallow reached Exchange Court the parade room was empty. All available G-men were engaged on crime investigation or on surveillance, monitoring individuals around the city who might be intent on mischief in the days leading up to the Jubilee.

Two young men hurried out of the detective office as he arrived. They brushed past him, talking in loud, angry tones. Swallow caught the whiff of alcohol.

An overzealous constable had taken them into custody outside a public house on Nassau Street, where he heard them attempt a drunken rendition of *The Minstrel Boy*. They might be Fenian agents from America, he thought. It turned out they were two Canadian students from Trinity College, celebrating examination results.

The duty sergeant was taking a statement from a commercial traveller from Antwerp who had been relieved of his wallet, his watch and his trade samples during a night's socialising. He remembered meeting a young lady in Grafton Street sometime before midnight, but he had no clear recollection of how he had ended up in 'Monto,' the city's red-light district on the other side of the river.

Officially, the G-Division detective office was in Dublin Castle. But this was an administrative conceit. Exchange Court was a blind, sunless alley on the northern flank of the Castle proper. Incongruously, its nearest neighbour was a pet shop, specialising in exotic species where the alley abutted onto Dame Street.

Swallow was glad to be out of the glare of the sun, even if the grimy corridors of the detective office were airless.

A couple of G-men queried him as he made his way to the crime sergeants' room that he shared with four other officers of his own rank. The grim news from the Chapelizod Gate had travelled quickly. Violence and sometimes murder were not unknown in Dublin, but even the hard men of the G Division were shocked by the reports coming in from the crime scene.

His first task was to brief his boss, Detective Chief Superintendent John Mallon.

John Mallon was at the height of his reputation. The G Division's chief was reputedly more influential than the head of the force, Commissioner David Harral. It was said that Chief Secretary Balfour considered him more important to the success of government policy in Ireland than the Security Secretary – or the Assistant Under-Secretary for Security, to give him his official title.

His work on the Cavendish and Burke murders had put his reputation beyond argument. Now aged 55, he had the option of retirement on a full and generous pension. But it was clear that Mallon preferred to hold to his career and his place at the centre of the country's security apparatus.

His masters in the Dublin Castle administration wanted to hold on to Mallon too. It was understood in administrative circles that he would probably go beyond his present grade of Detective Chief Superintendent to the Commissioner ranks. In the order of things at Dublin Castle, that sort of progression for the son of a poor Catholic farmer from County Armagh would be without precedent.

Each day and night brought Mallon's office a tally of shootings and burnings from around the country. There were confrontations between the constabulary and the tenantry at public meetings. Burnings of landlords' properties were reported nightly. Judges, magistrates and landlords were under constant threat and could operate only under armed protection. The Royal Irish Constabulary itself was stretched to breaking point and required reinforcement from the military in many areas.

The action in the land war was on the farms and in the rural areas, but it was planned and directed by men who lived and worked in the city. While the rural police and magistracy were the administration's front-line defence against the agitation; they too were directed from the city; from Dublin Castle, to be precise.

Balfour privately acknowledged that four decades after the ravages of the Great Famine, the lot of the Irish smallholders was still indefensible. In England and Wales the poorest farmers and their families lived securely in the ownership of their properties. In Ireland, by contrast, families still worked the land without security of tenure, while struggling to pay high rents to English landlords or their Irish agents.

The potential fusing together of the land campaign with a renewed demand for Home Rule was a constant threat. It was the Westminster government's worst nightmare.

Shortly after the murders of Cavendish and Burke, Parnell had founded the Irish National League to advance both aims, and for a time he and Davitt had made common cause. Although Parnell denied it vigorously, the constant threat of Fenian violence lay behind both demands. Much to the relief of the authorities, however, Parnell had more recently stepped back from the alliance.

The new Chief Secretary's approach was two-pronged. He pushed legislation through Parliament giving the police and the courts sweeping new powers to counter terrorism and to break the League's 'Plan of Campaign.'

The 'Plan' was reducing many of the once-powerful landlords to penury. At the same time, Balfour wanted to accelerate the purchase of land by the tenant farmers. His policy was to achieve this with a scheme of generous loans and grants.

But the processes of reform were slow. If it was to contain the threat of social and political breakdown, the administration desperately needed quality intelligence with which to direct its police forces and its legal machinery. And John Mallon was the master of intelligence gathering.

The clerk in Mallon's outer office was shocked at what he had already heard of Swallow's business during the morning.

'The chief was expecting you, Sergeant. Jesus, it sounds like a terrible affair at the Chapelizod Gate. Do you know what it's all about?'

'A bad business but it's early days,' Swallow said non-committedly. He had learned that the one person to whom he should not drop information was his boss's clerk. It was rarely passed on without some inaccuracy or distortion.

'He's not here,' the clerk explained. 'He's been called to a meeting with the Chief Secretary. He got the report you sent earlier from Kilmainham. He said you're to complete whatever you have now and leave it here for him. We'll get it to him before he finishes this evening or we'll send it across to his house later.'

Swallow was familiar with Mallon's procedures. If an urgent crime report was ready he wanted it delivered to wherever he might be, whether on duty or otherwise.

In earlier years, the Castle's messengers were frequent callers at Mallon's home on the North Circular Road. But since his promotion to head of the G Division, he and his family had the privilege of being accommodated in a house in the Lower Yard of the Castle. A few steps across the Yard and Mallon could be back in the office at any hour, day or night. Urgent information or documents could be in his hands literally within a minute of their arrival at Exchange Court.

Swallow retreated to the crime sergeants' office. He spent two hours trawling through the files of the official police publication, *Hue and Cry*, to see if any incidents or reports might indicate some connection with the double murder. Then he went through the missing-persons file and the daily report on goods deposited in the city's pawn shops. Nothing out of the ordinary suggested itself.

Late in the afternoon he began to put together his report of the day's events on a battered Remington typewriter. It was one of the DMP's acquisitions from the brief expansion of its resources in the aftermath of the Cavendish and Burke murders.

He had taught himself to use the machine. He enjoyed the sharp action and counteraction between key, hammer and paper. He saw it as a mechanical evolution from the process of creating images on a pad with the point of a lead pencil.

He made four copies, interleaving the foolscap sheets with carbon paper. One would go to the Detective Chief Superintendent's office, one would go into Pat Mossop's murder book, one would be circulated at the crime conference in the morning and one was for his own use.

By the time he finished, the heat had abated and it was evening. He had been on continuous duty for 21 hours without rest. He was tired and frustrated with no investigative results to show for his efforts.

He left the detective office shortly after 7 o'clock for Maria Walsh's. He turned out of Exchange Court to pass the Cork Hill Gate of the Castle where the statue of blind Justice topped the archway with her back to the city – a directional bias that was the subject of much sarcasm among Dubliners.

He passed Christ Church, crossing the corner of Nicholas Street into High Street and on to Cornmarket. It seemed as if every tenement family had come out to breathe the evening air on the steps and pavements. Humid though it was outside, it was doubtless healthier than inside where a score of people might inhabit a couple of rooms. The odours of unwashed bodies, rancid food and human waste, smells never absent from the poor streets of Dublin, hung heavily in the air.

On the steps of a tenement house where High Street merged into Thomas Street, a knot of people had gathered around a young man who was slowly reading aloud from a copy of the *Evening Mail*.

From the rapt attention of the group and the expressions on their faces, Swallow knew that the young man was relaying the details of the morning's horrors from the Chapelizod Gate. He saw a woman bless herself and heard another mutter, 'Jesus, have mercy on them...'

Maria Walsh's public house stood on Thomas Street. It faced the Church of St Catherine that locals pointed out as the execution place of Robert Emmet in 1803. Tradition in the family had it that Maria's great grandfather had witnessed the young revolutionary's end.

A narrow alley ran beside the house. He let himself in by the side door giving onto the alley and climbed the back stairs that led to the living quarters. Notionally, Swallow was the tenant of a sizeable room on the first floor with a window looking out to the street. He had use of the parlour and his meals, when his duty hours permitted, were served in the dining room by Maria Walsh's housekeeper, Carrie, or by the day maid.

The relationship between Joe Swallow and Maria Walsh had developed slowly and was still ambiguous.

She had been married at 20 and widowed at 25. Her merchant sailor husband, William Walsh, lost when his ship went down with all hands off the Welsh coast on a January night in 1882, was still a presence in the house when she rented the room to Swallow two years later.

An oilskin deck coat hung in the return hallway. A scale model of a three-masted clipper ship stood on the mantle shelf in the dining room. Occasionally an opened drawer would yield a tobacco tin or a navigation chart. And she kept her married name, reverting to her maiden name, Grant, only for legal purposes concerned with the running of the public house.

It was not that Maria particularly needed the money. The public house into which she had been born and which she inherited from her mother did good business. And it was her home. The name over the door, 'M & M Grant and Son' referred to her long-deceased grandfather and great grandfather. But the emptiness and the silence at night when the last of the customers had gone were painful. And there was always a vulnerability about a house without a man, even a lodger.

When Swallow answered her advertisement offering accommodation in the *Freeman's Journal* he did not reveal that he was a policeman, only that he worked 'in an office near Dame Street.' She learned of his occupation six months later when an off-duty constable from the D Division station at the Bridewell recognised him in the bar one evening. The constable nodded the briefest of salutations and fled to find a hostelry where he might drink without finding himself under the eye of a G-Division detective sergeant.

For more than a year the widow and the bachelor policeman were wary. Relations were amiable but always formal. The irregularity of his duty rosters and her hours of attendance at the bar meant that meals were rarely taken together. When it happened that they could converse over a meal it was 'Mrs Walsh' and 'Mr Swallow.'

But gradually the barriers came down. The turning point had been the night that a drunken attendant from the nearby St Patrick's Hospital for the Mentally Ill had made a lewd remark to Maria within Swallow's hearing in the bar. The policeman first asked him to apologise, and then to leave. When the man struck out, Swallow put him in an arm lock and threw him into the street.

Later, he and Maria talked long into the night in the parlour upstairs. The house had fallen gradually quiet as the young apprentice barman finished clearing up downstairs before retiring to his room at the back of the house.

He told her of the other life he might have had as a doctor, were it not for the excesses of alcohol. She opened up about herself. The Grants had educated their daughters to a high standard for young women in their time and circumstances, with a finishing year in a convent school near Bordeaux. She had developed tastes in reading – Jane Austen, the Brontës, Charles Dickens and an Irish woman writer that Swallow had never heard of, Maria Edgeworth. She played the piano well. Taking over the running of Grant's had been an inherited duty that she felt she owed to her family.

They heard Tess, the maid, climb to her space on the top floor under the attic. A little later the thump of a closing door told them that Carrie, Maria's housekeeper and cook, had turned in for the night too.

When the house was quite still, Maria took him to her room and to the big bed with its crisp linen sheets and deep pillows where she had slept alone for almost three years.

After that night, his own rented bedroom was maintained as a genteel fiction. The day maid changed the unused sheets at intervals and filled the pitcher that stood on the sideboard with fresh water each night. From time to time, Swallow would use the room for a quiet nap or to change his clothes when he came off duty. Occasionally, if he had worked through the night and if it was close to her rising hour, he would sleep there for fear of waking Maria.

Swallow knew the relationship could go a long way, even to marriage, if that was what he wanted. But he hesitated to commit. Sometimes he felt that the impulses that caused him to squander the potential of a medical career would also prevent him from making a success of a permanent relationship. The arrangement with Maria was at once convenient and uneasy.

By now, he knew she would be downstairs, ready to supervise the night's business, moving regularly to and fro between the public bar and the select bar and looking in occasionally at the snugs where the women came in twos and threes for their glass of port wine or bottle of stout.

M & M Grant and Son was a respectable establishment. The sign saying 'Select Bar' meant what it said. The tinkers and hawkers and beggars, of whom there was a multitude in and around Thomas Street, knew that there was no welcome for them there. The clientele at Grant's comprised skilled Liberties tradesmen, clerks, brewery men, honest labourers and employees from the South Dublin Union workhouse. Sometimes there were young doctors from St Patrick's Hospital or lively students from the Metropolitan School of Art, which was located just down the street.

The clientele liked Maria. Her uniform for work was invariably a severe black or dark grey dress with high, ruffed collars and buttoned cuffs. She wore her blonde hair drawn in a French coil at the back, setting off her high cheekbones and bright blue eyes.

She knew all of the regular clients by name. As befitted her status as licensee and proprietress she did not serve drink or clear empties from the bar or tabletops. She did not handle money in the bar. She did not deal with spillages or broken glasses. All of these tasks were the responsibility of the barmen. Maria Walsh was a dignified, watchful presence in a well-run establishment where patrons and staff alike expected to be treated with courtesy and politeness.

Later, Swallow would go downstairs and fall into his role as Mrs Walsh's collaborator, clearing the bar of stragglers and then, in the privacy of the upstairs parlour, helping her to count the day's takings. It was highly irregular, of course, for an officer of the Dublin Metropolitan

Police, much less a detective sergeant of G Division. But then, there was nothing that was regular in the relationship between Joe Swallow and Maria Walsh, widow and licensed publican.

But first, he would sleep. He went to the big bedroom at the back of the house. It was quiet and cool, in contrast to the warmth of the evening outside. He took off his boots and his suit, sweaty after the long day. He unbuckled the shoulder-holster with the heavy DMP-issue Webley Bulldog revolver.

Then he dropped into the big double bed and closed his eyes. When he slept, he dreamed. He was with his father, walking across the fields to stare at the grey bones of people who had died 4,000 years ago. But when they got to the place where the farmer's plough had opened the burial chamber, the body nearest the edge of the pit had the face of a young boy with no eyes.

FIVE

When Charlie Vanucchi and Vinny Cussen pinned the black crepe with Ces Downes's death-notice on the door, the word was whispered through the streets and the courts and in the public houses on Francis Street.

It spread to other public houses and into the tenements in Meath Street, Thomas Street, the Coombe, in Patrick Street, in James's Street and in Pimlico.

Then it travelled along the narrow streets around the *Dubh Linn*, or 'Dark Pool,' where the Vikings once moored their longboats, and from which the city had taken its name.

Within the hour the death of Ces Downes was known in Smithfield and Stoneybatter across the river and in the alleys and courts where the prostitutes plied their trade, around Mecklenburgh Street and Montgomery Street and the Gloucester Diamond. A little later the news was in most of the small village communities that ringed the city, Irishtown, Ringsend, Drumcondra, Dolphin's Barn and Inchicore.

The constable who had been placed where Francis Street meets the Coombe to watch Ces Downes's house left his post and marched at the double to his station at Kevin Street to report the putting out of the mourning crepe.

The sergeant at Kevin Street telephoned it to the night inspector at the DMP headquarters in the Lower Yard of Dublin Castle. He considered it of sufficient import, in turn, to send a short, written note to the Commissioner's personal office to be read in the morning.

Then he used the ABC – the force's internal telegraph system – to notify the shift sergeants in the other DMP divisions, out as far as the F Division at Kingstown.

Within a quarter of an hour the news had reached the offices of the *Freeman's Journal* and *The Irish Times*. The night shift on duty at the Fire Station at Winetavern Street heard of it. So did the cab drivers waiting with their cars for hire outside the fashionable hotels, the Shelbourne, the Imperial and the Royal Hibernian.

The Canon of the parish Church of Saint Nicholas of Myra on Francis Street heard it as he sat to his supper of Boyne salmon. He interrupted his dining to despatch a servant with a note to inform His Grace the Archbishop of Dublin, Dr Walsh, at his home on Rutland Square.

The sentries at Marlborough, Richmond, Royal and Beggar's Bush barracks knew it. The coal-stokers tending the furnaces at the Alliance and Dublin Gas Company beside Sir John Rogerson's Quay heard it. When the fishermen came into Ringsend on the high tide just before midnight, they heard it from the women waiting to gut and box the night's catch.

Joe Swallow heard it when he came down from the back bedroom to help clear the bar in Grant's for Maria Walsh, shortly after 11 o'clock. He had slept for perhaps two hours after which he had washed, shaved and put on a fresh white shirt and collar. At some point while he slept he had become aware of the bedroom door opening and closing. He knew it was Maria checking that he had come home.

The sleep was not long enough to refresh him fully, and his dream of burial pits and a dead boy left him disquieted. But he examined himself in the mirror and reckoned that he was fit to be seen.

He sensed a different atmosphere from usual as he entered the bar, now smoky and muggy, towards the end of business in the hot summer's night. The clientele knew to a man that he was a 'Peeler,' a 'Bobby,' a *'polisman.'* And they knew that he had been at work for the day on what was undoubtedly one of the most shocking crimes of recent years in Dublin city.

He had many times experienced this sensation of being apart. When he came from a bloody crime scene or from immersing himself in a situation where violence or evil were involved, it was as if he carried some of it with him. It seemed to cut him off. People could sense it on him. He could sense it himself. It set up an invisible, intangible barrier between him and other people, even in a crowded room.

Perhaps the pitch of the talk was quieter than usual, the eyes more watchful. Somewhere across the house he heard his name whispered. Maria stood near the bar, surveying the room and supervising the two young barmen working the taps to draw the last few pints of the night.

Pride of place on the wall behind the bar had been accorded to one of Swallow's watercolours. It was a view of the river at Islandbridge, one of his earliest efforts. Every time he looked at it now he saw a naive reduction of blue water and green foliage. But Maria said she liked it, and she had it professionally framed.

Now she glanced warily at Swallow. She sensed the changed atmosphere of the evening too. He nodded a muted, almost invisible response. They had developed this silent sign language for the hours when the bar was open and filled with customers.

An old Dublin Militia sergeant, toothless and crooked, tried his luck for a free drink before the bar closed, tugging at Swallow's sleeve as he passed by.

'Th' oul wan, Downes, is gone. Ah, but she led yiz a merry dance before goin' to the Devil this night. Isn't that right, Sor?'

'Aye, I heard all right that she's gone.'

There was no good reason for Swallow's lie, beyond a policeman's instinctive inclination to maintain an advantage. The old soldier hobbled after him as he went towards the bar. He lifted the hinged top and stepped into the serving area.

Swallow felt a twinge of guilt at stealing the pensioner's bit of news.

'You'll have one on the house for her.' He poured a half whiskey into a tumbler and pushed it across the counter to the militia man.

Thus the news of the passing of Pisspot Ces Downes, on the 17th day in the month of June 1887, spread out over the city in a susurration, from public house to public house, from police station to police station, from street to street.

Many tales of Pisspot Ces, her cruelty and her cleverness, some true, more probably untrue, were told and retold as the night settled on the city, spread out around the great, dark platter of Dublin Bay.

Saturday June 18th, 1887

SIX

Dublin's northerly latitude and prevailing westerly airflow ensure that it rarely enjoys any sustained elevation of barometric pressure or more than a few successive days of sunshine. When that pattern is broken the citizens are likely to take it as an aberration, an unnatural occurrence. Deprived of the rain and damp as their daily topics of grievance they turn irritable and fractious.

They had growing reason for doing so in the third week of June 1887 as humans and animals alike grew increasingly uncomfortable in the unaccustomed and unremitting heat.

A postman in Fitzwilliam Street collapsed and died on the third day. In Sackville Street and College Green the horse troughs, although now connected to the Vartry water supply from the mountains, started to run dry. Drivers and cabmen took buckets to the river with long ropes and drew green Liffey water that they sluiced over their suffering beasts to cool them.

On St Stephen's Green, where the new steam trams ran to Blackrock and Ball's Bridge, the metal tracks expanded in the heat to such an extent that locomotion was impossible for a time in the afternoon. Half a dozen of the double-decked vehicles stood immobilised outside the Shelbourne Hotel and the University Club until after 6 o'clock, when the steel would retract to its normal dimensions in the cooler temperatures of the evening.

The newly developing suburbs in the townships of Ball's Bridge and Rathmines and beyond had their own running water from the Vartry reservoir. Their sewage and waste were carried to the sea in a complex labyrinth of subterranean channels and pipes.

But in the poorer quarters of the city, marked out by the health authorities as Dispensary Districts B, C and D, the air grew thick as the human waste that accumulated in thousands of dry lavatories baked and stank in the heat. In the courts and alleys of the Liberties many of the communal water taps ran to a trickle or dried completely. It was not to be wondered at that the atmosphere had grown heavy and wearying in the days before Pisspot Ces Downes died.

Swallow rose before 7 o'clock. He washed and shaved in what was still notionally his rented room over Grant's. Appearances and convention required that he would complete his morning ablutions here. Each evening Tess, the housemaid, dutifully put out a towel, a basin and a ewer of fresh water on the dressing table where he had his razor, brush and soap.

He was careful, slow and thorough with the blade. Even though beards or moustaches were fashionable, and were permitted even to uniformed policemen, he preferred to go clean-shaven. He believed it helped to make him seem younger than his years.

He had slept fitfully even after three Tullamores in the parlour over Grant's with Maria when the bar had closed. He had described the scene where the man and boy had been found by the Chapelizod Gate. She had grown accustomed to Swallow's recitations of the grim business he frequently encountered in his work, but on this night she could sense his particular distress and apprehension.

It would be a long Saturday. He would have to report to Detective Chief Superintendent Mallon in the Castle. Then he would be briefed by Harry Lafeyre on his post-mortem examinations. At 11 o'clock the other officers engaged in the case would assemble at Exchange Court for the conference arranged by Pat Mossop, the Book Man.

Swallow took a breakfast of oatmeal porridge in the kitchen, washed down with a mug of milk. Then he stepped out into Thomas Street to walk the half mile to the Castle.

Few Dublin tradesmen or deliverymen would stir onto the streets before nine o'clock. Businessmen and professionals considered it improper to be at their offices or consulting rooms before 10 o'clock, even on Saturdays, when they would generally end the day's work at lunchtime. The streets were quiet, apart from a couple of early horse-drawn trams serving the routes in and out from the villages of Inchicore and Kilmainham.

Notwithstanding the paucity of custom, a news vendor was at work on the corner of Francis Street, surrounded by stacks of the morning newspapers.

His billboards screamed the gory details of the murders in the Park. 'MAN AND CHILD IN GHASTLY PARK ATROCITY,' said the *Freeman's Journal* poster.

'DREADFUL MURDERS DISCOVERED,' proclaimed the *Daily Sketch*.

'TWO BODIES IN PHOENIX PARK,' *The Irish Times* reported more soberly.

Entering the Castle's Lower Yard from Palace Street, he passed the military picket at the gate. He pitied the soldiers facing the heat of the day ahead in their heavy uniforms and boots. He went past the gothic apse of the Chapel Royal to the brick-fronted building that housed, among other departments, the office of the chief of detectives of the Dublin Metropolitan Police, John Mallon.

The Lower Yard was decidedly the less favoured and less desirable area of the vast, administrative sprawl that was Dublin Castle. Its buildings were dowdy and poorly maintained by comparison with the fine State Apartments of the Upper Yard. That was where the high functionaries and officials of the administration, led by the Chief Secretary, were accommodated and where the Viceroy, the Queen's deputy, took up residence with his family during the 'season' when Dublin society showed itself off.

The formal rooms, which were opened for the 'season' from February to March, were palatial. From the classically proportioned St Patrick's Hall to the lofty Throne Room, they were a regal presentation of gold and gilt, luxurious carpets and drapes, fine furniture and works of art.

It was understood that the current Viceroy, Lord Londonderry, never spoke to his wife, Lady Theresa, because of some alleged infidelity with a Westminster politician.

Swallow believed that the reports of their estrangement were not without foundation. He had been posted on protection duty at the State Apartments during the 'season' gone by. From the required discreet distance under the palm fronds, his Webley Bulldog sitting in its shoulder-holster, he had watched the viceregal couple preside over a score of balls, levees and receptions without a single word passing between them.

When Swallow arrived at Mallon's office his clerks were already at work and there was tea brewing in a tin pot in the outer office. He took a vacant chair to go through his typed report of the previous evening.

He had been through the routine many times. The Detective Chief Superintendent would come through a private door, bypassing the outer office, sometimes as early at 7 o'clock. The night's reports from each of the Metropolitan Police's seven divisions would be on his desk, starting with the G-Division report on crime and security.

Some time before 9 o'clock, Swallow, or whoever might be in attendance with a crime report, would be shown in to the inner office. Mallon might have read the investigating officer's report the previous night or perhaps earlier that morning, but it was certain that he would have read it. Pencil marks along the margins would indicate where he had picked up an inconsistency or an incongruous detail.

Although separated by rank, there were empathies in their relationship. Swallow's background was in County Kildare, where his family had run their public house for three generations. Mallon was a farmer's son from Armagh. Both were countrymen, rooted in the values and conventions of rural Ireland, and both were Catholics in an organisation where preferment almost invariably went to Protestants and, in particular, to those who were members of the Worshipful Society of Free Masons.

Mallon had almost 30 years' service. His ascent to the rank of Chief Superintendent and head of G Division ran against all the odds. Swallow's advancement to Detective Sergeant was a good deal less noteworthy, but even in the lower supervisory ranks he was in a minority as far as religious affinity was concerned.

Mallon was seated as usual behind his oak desk. The chief of G Division was an impeccable dresser. While most G-men favoured serviceable tweed or serge, Mallon liked fine woollen suits, well cut by a Duke Street tailor, set off with high, formal collars. His beard, now showing grey, was neatly trimmed. The sandy hair also starting to silver was expertly barbered and neatly combed.

Swallow did not smoke. He felt himself invariably assailed by the tobacco fumes that permeated the air of the police offices and public places. But Mallon did, incessantly. The dark timbers and furniture of his office retained the impregnated odour of tobacco exhaled by the chief of detectives and his predecessors down the decades. No amount of painting or redecorating seemed to diminish or dilute it.

To Swallow's dismay, Mallon was reading the *Daily Sketch* rather than the copy of the crime report that he had been sent the previous evening. When he raised his eyes from the newspaper to glare across the desk, Swallow feared the worst.

Mallon threw the folded newspaper on the desk in front of Swallow.

'Not a great advertisement for the second city of the Empire or its police force as we mark Her Majesty's Jubilee, is it?'

Swallow remained standing. He saw that Irving's report on the discovery of the bodies inside the Chapelizod Gate occupied the lead column of the main news page.

'Read it,' Mallon commanded in his sharp Ulster accent.

Swallow took up the newspaper. Irving's report ran the length of the broadsheet page in a single column.

TERRIBLE MURDERS IN THE PARK
Police have no clues
BODIES WITH MUTILATED FACES

The terribly mutilated bodies of a man and a young boy were found yesterday in the Phoenix Park by the Chapelizod Gate. Witnesses who have seen the man's body say that much of the head had been cut away or mutilated beyond recognition.

The gruesome find was made by a park-keeper shortly before 6 a.m.

Detective Sergeant Swallow of G Division was at the scene later. He told the Daily Sketch *that he did not know who the man or child were or what had happened.*

He said that the police would investigate this case slowly. But he was confident that in time he would have important clues.

The Sketch finds it curious that the attitude of the police should be so indifferent in a shocking case of this nature.

Dublin's good name has scarcely been regained after the appalling murders of Lord Frederick Cavendish and Mr Burke. The police have been increased in numbers and strengthened with new powers, yet have failed to prevent another brutal crime from being perpetrated...

The rest of the report detailed the searches that had been conducted by Doolan's uniformed officers, and the fact that the bodies had been removed to the morgue after examination by Dr Henry Lafeyre.

Swallow put the newspaper on the desk.

'There's more here.' Mallon pointed to copies of the *Freeman's Journal* and *The Irish Times* at the end of the desk. 'It's not as bad. But it's not good either.'

He gestured to the chair beside Swallow.

'This is a shocking case. It's savage.'

He waved a sheet of paper with an embossed crown.

'The Lord Lieutenant's secretary sent down a note. Lady Londonderry and the ladies at the Viceregal Lodge are in fear for their lives. They won't walk outside in the garden. Even the pick-up girls along Grafton Street stayed indoors last night. We're going to be expected to clear it up damned fast. But my immediate problem is what's in these rags. Tell me something positive I can bring to Commissioner Harrel.'

Swallow sat. 'With your permission, Chief, what's in the *Sketch* is a complete misrepresentation of what happened. I didn't say those things.'

Mallon raised his eyebrows. 'I'm sure you didn't, Swallow. If I thought you did, I'd probably resign in despair myself. What I want to know is why you talked to the reporters at all if the case is as bleak as it looks.'

'There wasn't much choice. It was out in the open space of the Phoenix Park so I couldn't very well chase them off or have them arrested. Seven or eight of them arrived on a couple of cars. We had difficulty enough keeping them away from the scene. That report in the *Sketch* is by Irving. He's hostile to the police in general and to me in particular.'

The Chief Superintendent nodded. 'I know Irving. He's a poisonous creature.'

'I didn't say we had no clues,' Swallow pointed to the headline. 'And I didn't indicate any lack of urgency or seriousness. What I said was that crime investigations often have to move slowly.'

'The truth is,' he added, 'if we don't get an early identification of the victims, this case has the potential to turn into a nasty problem. I asked the reporters to put an appeal out to their readers to see if they can tell us anything.'

Mallon sighed. 'Well we won't get much response from the general public in dear old Dublin. My problem is going to be with the Commissioner and the Security Secretary. What Irving has you saying is that there's no real concern about this case and that you'll take a leisurely run at it. They'll make a big thing of all this, you know.'

'There surely has to be some sense of proportion, Sir, even in the newspapers. This is an appalling case. But isn't it true that crime rates here are lower than in other cities?' Swallow asked hopefully.

'Of course, that's true for the city here. But once you go outside Dublin it's pretty well open warfare between the police, the Land Leaguers, the remnants of the bloody Fenians and God knows who else. Nobody will give evidence in court. They've had to suspend trial by jury. No policeman is safe. They live like a garrison under siege. We have it easy here in the city by comparison.'

Swallow knew from the daily newspapers that the picture painted by Mallon was accurate. The unarmed Dublin police operated much like police forces in any British city, with only the men of G Division carrying guns. In contrast, the Royal Irish Constabulary, covering the rural areas, was heavily armed. Even his home county of Kildare had seen burnings, attacks on police stations and evictions.

Mallon rose and walked to the window. He looked out into the Lower Yard, already filling with sunshine.

'There's nothing political about this case from what you've told me. Is that right, Swallow?'

In Mallon's view of the world, Swallow knew, anything that was 'special,' touching on politics, subversion or state business had absolute priority. In the lexicon of G Division, everything else was classified as 'ordinary.'

Mallon saw the threat of subversion everywhere. There were rumours of another Fenian rising. Any threat of political destabilisation was taken seriously. Anything else, even a gruesome double murder, was a lesser priority.

Just a few months previously, *The Times* of London had published letters alleged to have been written by Parnell intimating that he was complicit in the murders of Cavendish and Burke. Parnell had sued the newspaper for defamation and demanded an independent commission of inquiry into the allegations.

The Tory government at Westminster and the Irish administration at Dublin Castle were obliged to appear as disinterested parties in the clash between the Irish leader and the newspaper, but in reality they were striving with all their resources to discredit Parnell and to find evidence to vindicate *The Times* in its supposed revelations.

Teams of secret police agents had been formed in Scotland Yard and at Dublin Castle to assemble evidence against Parnell by fair means or foul. Their task was to provide proof that Parnellism and violent Fenianism were at root a single movement.

The men who made up the new squads were not part of the regular police establishment or structure. In Dublin, they reported directly to the Assistant Under-Secretary for Security in the Upper Yard of the Castle. They were shadowy figures, for the most part English and Scottish. They were billeted in out-of-the-way hotels under assumed identities. Even within the Castle walls they did not socialise or move about openly. Their food and drink was brought in to them at their offices. They came and went usually under cover of darkness.

These were days of uncertainty and disquiet for the regular police officials at the Castle, especially for senior men like John Mallon, whose job it was to ensure the security of the administration.

Swallow preferred to keep his distance from the political end of G Division's work, but that was not always possible, as with the Cavendish and Burke murders. For a G-man, political work could sometimes provide a swift upward route in the promotion stakes. Conversely, a simple error in judgment in dealing with security issues could also destroy an officer's career.

'Yes, Sir,' Swallow was emphatic. 'These murders are ordinary. There's nothing that's political so far in the case.' He hoped he was right.

Mallon nodded. 'Good. We don't need even a hint of political trouble. We have the Queen's grandson, Prince Albert Victor, coming here in little more than a week to mark the Jubilee. The government wants a warm Irish welcome for him – a full civic reception, spontaneous outpourings of loyalty, young women throwing bouquets of flowers – that kind of thing.'

'I'd have thought the Queen might want to come herself, Chief,' Swallow said tentatively. 'She hasn't been here for what… 25 years or so?'

'26 years, to be precise,' Mallon replied. 'More or less since her husband died. It may be that London thinks we couldn't guarantee her safety. Officially what I'm told is that she remains displeased with the Dublin Corporation because it wouldn't issue a formal statement of congratulations when the Prince was born 23 years ago. You'd think these things would be left in the past.'

For a brief moment Swallow thought he saw Mallon smile. If he did, it was gone instantaneously.

'Anyway, he's coming whether we like it or not. We can't afford to have anything disruptive going on.'

'I know that, Chief.'

Swallow was indifferent to the prospect of a royal visit. It held no interest for him one way or another. But it was safer to express himself with more certainty to Mallon.

'You can be sure the whole force will be on top form, Chief. And there's hardly any of the politicals or subversives now that we don't have tabs on in G Division. Isn't that the case?'

The question was rhetorical. He did not expect an answer from Mallon, but he thought the Chief Superintendent would want him to sound confident.

Mallon's nod was ambiguous.

'We'll leave it be, Swallow. I'll have to deal with this business of the newspapers and I'll try to keep you out of trouble. I imagine the Commissioner will want some explanation about the newspaper details. I'll try to reassure him. Mind you, he won't have forgotten that you still have the Elizabeth Logan murder on your books.'

Swallow fought down a surge of frustration. It was grossly unjust, he told himself, that a successful record over many years appeared to count for so little. But to argue with Mallon would only make things worse. He knew that the Chief Superintendent was probably his best ally at this time.

'Yes, Sir. Thank you.'

He seethed silently.

'Now,' Mallon resumed his seat and reached for his copy of Swallow's crime file, 'tell me about the investigation plan.'

Swallow took the detective Chief Superintendent through the events of the previous day. He started with the call out and his visit to the scene inside the Chapelizod Gate. He described the wounds to the dead man and boy, the mutilation of the faces, their clothing and the position of the bodies. Then he detailed the search procedures that had taken place under Doolan's direction.

Mallon sat silently throughout, turning the pages of the crime report in parallel with Swallow's narrative. When they had reached the end of the last page he closed the file and nodded at Swallow.

'You've done everything that could have been done at this stage. Now, you've been known as a good detective because apart from an organisational mind you've got instinct. So what does your instinct tell you about this business?'

Swallow was familiar with Mallon's technique. Every case was first analysed clinically, each particle of evidence tested and examined separately. Then the investigator was invited to let his imagination loose on the problem. It put Swallow in mind of an African tribe he had once heard about whose custom was to discuss every issue twice before coming to any important decision – once sober and once drunk.

'I think this is going to be a difficult case, Sir. It could be a very slow one. There was nothing casual or spontaneous about what happened here. The killings were planned, and I'd guess that the mutilation of the faces was deliberately done to prevent identification. Unless we get a good break we're a long way off cracking it. We don't even know who the victims are.'

Mallon grimaced. 'I don't disagree with any of that. But I want you to go a bit further. Speculate for me. Give me a possible motive. Tell me what sort of man the victim was. How did the poor child come to be involved? What might we be dealing with here? We don't get many jobs as bad as this one, thank God. What's the feeling in your gut?'

Swallow sensed danger. If he responded as Mallon asked, he would leave himself open to an accusation of jumping to conclusions, of working to a set of preconceptions. He opted for caution.

'I can't do that just yet, Chief. Maybe when I have Dr Lafeyre's report later this morning I'd feel a bit more confident about putting out a theory. I don't want to be back in here to you with two different stories.'

Mallon grimaced again, this time with a hint of knowing. 'You're probably right, Sergeant. It's too soon. When does the medical examiner plan to give you his reports? And who have you got on the case with you?'

'Harry said he'd have his reports early this morning. I'm going to see him after this. And I've got Mossop as the Book Man. Swift and Feore led the uniformed inquiry teams at the scene.'

'They're good men,' Mallon nodded. 'Hang on to them if you can. We'll be stretched over the next few days with the Jubilee. And we've a big surveillance task with the politicals coming up to the prince's visit. On top of all that we have Ces Downes's death… with unpredictable consequences.'

'Yes, Sir. I know that Ces Downes died last night. It'll be interesting to see who comes out on top now, Charlie Vanucchi or Vinny Cussen.'

Mallon gathered his files and stood from behind the desk.

'God knows what they'll do to each other in order to get control of her business,' he said. 'Not to mention what Vanucchi and Cussen will do to get hold of whatever money she put away.'

'Do you think she had much of that, Sir?'

'Hard to say,' Mallon mused. 'We know she did a lot of business through McGloin, the solicitor. He's not too particular about where his clients get their funds from. And he doesn't entertain people who have no money.'

Every G-man knew Horace 'Fish' McGloin, so called because of his slippery nature. He operated his law practice from a dingy one-room office over a public house on Essex Street, by the river. It was the first port of call for many a crook seeking advice on what to do with the profits of crime.

The strengthening sun had started to form a golden rectangle on the carpet under the high-paned window.

'I'm due at the Commissioner's office,' Mallon said.' I'll do what I can on the newspaper problem. With any luck – from your viewpoint – he'll be more exercised over what's going to happen with the Jubilee and the royal visit. Come, I'll walk down to the Yard with you.'

They went down the narrow stairway leading from Mallon's office to the Lower Yard. As they reached the ground floor, Mallon turned to look Swallow directly in the eye.

'What's this I've been hearing about your off-duty activities?'

Swallow's heart sank. He lived in constant anxiety that someone, some day, would lodge a complaint about his unorthodox domestic arrangements with Maria Walsh. They violated at least three canons of the DMP code of discipline: being domiciled with a woman who was not his lawful wife; lodging in premises licensed for the sale of intoxicating liquor and participating or assisting in the operation of a commercial enterprise without permission.

If a disciplinary inquiry found that he was in violation of even one of the three he could face a censure that might range from a loss of pay to dismissal.

'I don't know… what have you been hearing, Chief?' he replied in what he hoped was an even tone.

'I hear you've become a painter. That you're showing a talent with watercolours.'

Swallow felt a surge of relief. 'That's not quite true, Sir. I'm an amateur, but I find it helps to relax me when I'm not on the job.'

'That's good, Swallow. Everyone needs to focus on a hobby or something outside of their job, even if it's only growing flowers in a window-box.'

They walked across the sunlit Lower Yard to the steps of the DMP Commissioner's office.

'I hope you get a good result on this quickly, Swallow,' Mallon said. 'I'm thinking of your own good. You know, a policeman's luck can run out too. I wouldn't want to lose you from G Division, but if this doesn't come right for you there could be worse things than going to Dalkey or Blackrock in uniform. You're an educated man – more or less. You could move up the ranks with a bit of study. You'd have regular hours and a hell of a lot less strain out there in the suburbs.'

He moved up the steps. 'Good luck, Sergeant. Keep me informed.'

Swallow believed Mallon when he said he was thinking of his best interests. Mallon saw Swallow as one of his own. He wanted him looked after. The chief of G Division would not want to see a hardworking officer disadvantaged just because his luck had turned.

Even so, there was something in what Mallon was saying about the attraction of a job in coastal Dalkey or leafy Kingstown and maybe a lift up to inspector or even to superintendent. Swallow could never understand why Dalkey in particular, a pretty and peaceful fishing village at the extremity of the F Division, should be viewed as a punishment station by the authorities.

Mallon was right. There were worse places than Dalkey. But there was an issue of pride here too, of self-respect. If he went that route, Swallow thought to himself, it would be because he wanted to and in his own time, not because some reporter alleged that he couldn't crack a dirty case.

His momentary alarm at the possibility of being challenged on his domestic arrangements had now receded. He checked his pocketwatch. If there was to be any decency in the day, perhaps Harry Lafeyre's post-mortem reports would provide him at least with a starting point for the investigation of the murders at the Chapelizod Gate.

SEVEN

Immediately he had parted with Mallon in the Lower Castle Yard, Swallow sensed that there was a problem.

Harry Lafeyre's carriage should have been standing in the stable yard behind the DMP building. It wasn't there. That meant that Lafeyre would not be in his office as arranged to brief Swallow on his post-mortem examination.

Swallow was a few minutes late. Lafeyre was usually punctual, and he had been left in no doubt that the investigation of the double murder by the Chapelizod Gate was a priority. If he was not at his office as arranged either something must have gone wrong with the post-mortem schedule, or some medical emergency had taken priority.

Doctor and detective had worked together on perhaps a score of difficult homicides. Not all were murders, for murder was not a very frequent occurrence in Dublin. Some were suicides, others deaths by misadventure. Most of them started as a mystery, a blank sheet upon which they worked hand-in-hand, methodically and patiently, filling in the empty spaces, gradually converting the unknown into the known, building comprehension where once there had been mystery.

Harry Lafeyre was from a Huguenot family in Queen's County. He had followed his medical degree at Trinity College with a diploma in medical jurisprudence at Edinburgh, studying under the celebrated Professor Alfred Taylor. After that he enrolled for a three-year tour as Medical Officer to the Cape Colony Mounted Police. It was a decision that puzzled and hurt his father, a second-generation country doctor whose hope it had been that his son would come home to continue the family practice.

For a time, Lafeyre once told Swallow, he had thought he would make his life and career in Africa. Athletic and adventurous, he relished the outdoor life on the *veld*. He became a skilled horseman and a crack shot with the smooth-bore game rifle.

But when an affair of the heart involving the daughter of a district Commissioner went wrong he learned that Africa could be a very lonely place. He decided to return to Europe. When he did so, it was to Dublin.

His part-time services had been engaged by the Castle authorities. Lafeyre was a rare combination of talents and qualifications: a doctor, a crime examiner and a man with experience of police work. The civil servants in the Castle knew a bargain when they saw one. He was put on a modest retainer that supplemented the private practice he embarked upon from his house-cum-surgery in Harcourt Street.

In addition, he had been appointed as a Justice of the Peace. It gave him the necessary authority to issue warrants when his examination might require a search of premises or a seizure of evidence.

Six months ago, he and Lily Grant had announced their engagement to be married. Maria Walsh had introduced him to her younger sister when Swallow and the medical examiner were having a quiet drink in the parlour after a late-night post mortem. Lily had finished term at her college and had come to stay for a few nights with her older sister before travelling to England to enrol in a summer painting course.

Swallow found himself cheered by their company. Lily's training in art and his amateur enthusiasm gave them a point of common interest. She and Lafeyre made a lively and attractive couple. There were times when Swallow envied them the clarity of their intentions with a marriage date fixed for the springtime of the year ahead.

Joe Swallow's formation had been different. His family's public house drew its clientele from the army and from the racing business. The Curragh Camp was one of the largest military installations in the British Isles, and some of the finest bloodstock in the world was bred and trained in the countryside around Newcroft.

Business was solid in Swallow's childhood years. There was comfort and relative prosperity, even though the starvation and disease that came in the aftermath of the Famine had devastated villages and townlands just a few miles away. His parents' ambition was to make Joseph a doctor. With hard work and prudent management there would be enough money to achieve it.

Then he wasted two years of his life and a great deal of their savings in the public houses and music halls around the Catholic University's Medical School. When the money ran out, and when the illness that was to end his father's life was diagnosed, his options were few.

He thought about the army. He considered America. Then he heard that the Dublin Metropolitan Police was recruiting.

Unrest over poor pay and harsh conditions had come to a head a few years previously. Dublin's police were notoriously badly paid. Basic pay trailed well behind any tradesman's wages and the families of married constables often lived in want.

Some policemen resigned to try their luck with English or Scottish forces. Others were disciplined by the authorities and forced to resign. When the Commissioner got clearance to start filling vacancies, pay rates were improved with the aim of forestalling any further trouble.

Joe Swallow had the height requirement and the chest measurement. He went on the dry, staying away from alcohol for a month before sitting the written tests at the Kevin Street depot. After that, he was in. While he continued to enjoy his drink, it never again became an obstacle to completing his work.

On the contrary, Swallow's work had become his life. From regular and heavy alcohol abuse, he changed to become a driven police officer. Long and irregular hours of work had taken the place of the extended drinking sessions. There was little time for a social life and none for seeking out romance or a life partner. He would be 43 at his coming birthday. He knew he did not have all the time in the world.

Perhaps Lafeyre's assistant, Scollan, was in the office already, Swallow surmised. There might be a message. Or Scollan might have some knowledge of his master's whereabouts. He set out towards the medical examiner's office when he saw Scollan turning Lafeyre's carriage across the cobblestones of the Palace Street Gate.

Swallow reached the office door just as Harry Lafeyre stepped down from the brougham. He could see from the medical examiner's grim expression that the news was bad.

'We'll go upstairs,' Lafeyre said tersely, striding through the door towards the rickety wooden staircase.

On the first landing he flung open a heavy door, layered with generations of cracked paint. The words '*OFFICE OF THE CHIEF MEDICAL EXAMINER*' were stencilled across the upper panels.

'We'll have some tea if you please, Scollan,' Lafeyre called over his shoulder as he led the way into his inner office.

Lafeyre gestured Swallow to a chair at the end of a trestle table. He was already perspiring in the heat of the morning. He removed his jacket and threw it expertly to catch the arm of a coat stand against the wall.

'My God, that's a day when one should be a free man, not stuck in a hole like this,' he said without pleasure.

Perfect rectangles of blue sky shone through the 12-paned windows that gave out onto the Lower Yard behind Lafeyre's desk. Swallow, though, was not in a mood to hear about the weather.

'I got up here as fast as I could,' Lafeyre said. You won't want to hear what I've got to tell you. I take it you've been in with Chief Mallon?'

'Yes, I've just left him.'

The medical examiner groaned. 'Oh Jesus, I'm sorry.'

'Will you for God's sake tell me what the problem is?' Swallow asked sharply.

Lafeyre raised his hand as if to calm him. 'I couldn't make a start on the post mortems last evening as I promised. The blasted electricity at Marlborough Street failed. The light from the gas is so poor that I thought it better to hold off until this morning, so I arranged to start as early as I could.'

He paused. 'I knew you were meeting Mallon. I hoped I'd have some report for you before that. But... something very unexpected emerged... I stopped the examination right away and got here as quickly as I could. We've made fools of ourselves – I as much as you – more so, indeed.'

'Will you for the love of Jesus tell me what you're talking about?' Swallow said, apprehension now giving way to alarm.

Lafeyre raised his hands in exasperation.

'It's the dead man, Joe.' He paused. 'It isn't a man. It's a woman.'

Swallow felt sick.

He heard himself, just moments ago, describe to Mallon what he had seen inside the Chapelizod Gate. He saw himself with the reporters in the park. He saw the headlines of the newspaper reports, based on what he had said. He saw Mallon with Commissioner Harrel trying to put distance between his detective sergeant and the warped prose of the *Daily Sketch*.

He was destroyed.

'A woman?' he repeated. 'Are you telling me what we saw up there by the Chapelizod Gate was a dead woman – not a dead man?'

'Yes. It's not a mistake that a trained physician will easily make when the clothing is cut away,' Lafeyre said in sarcasm.

'But it's a mistake that might occur when a woman has disguised herself in a loose-fitting man's suit, when her hair is short and when the face is effectively destroyed. You were fooled, so were the others, so was I.'

'Jesus Christ.' Swallow tried to bring the scene back in detail in his mind's eye. 'I thought he was small and slight. But I never thought...'

'I know,' Lafeyre said sympathetically. 'I wish I'd been able to get to you before you reported to Mallon. It's bad enough to have given the pressmen a wrong steer. I know they'll have a field day with it.'

It would be more trouble to add to the trouble he had already, Swallow reflected gloomily. His credibility with Mallon was already, if unfairly, damaged. This could undermine it completely.

It also added a bizarre new twist to the investigation. What was a woman doing dressed as a man, with a child, in the Phoenix Park, both now dead? He tried to imagine some set of circumstances that might fit with the facts as he was hearing them anew. Was it a charade, a disguise perhaps? Did the dead woman choose to wear a man's outfit or was she forced to do so? Were they her own clothes or did they belong to somebody else?

'Christ, this is bad. How am – how are *we* – going to explain this? The G Division's celebrated crime detective and the city medical examiner can't tell a man from a woman when there's a corpse lying out in front of them?'

Lafeyre nodded to the clock on the wall.

'You've more than an hour before your crime conference. We'll go back to Marlborough Street. I'll get a good start on the post mortems in that time. By 11 o'clock you might have something more that you can tell them. And maybe something to stave off Mallon's anger.'

The office door opened and Scollan entered carrying a tray with an Indian-style tea service. It was one of Lafeyre's souvenirs from the Cape Colony. He set it down, scowling, on the trestle and made to shuffle away.

'We won't take that tea now, Scollan,' Lafeyre told him. 'We're going back to Marlborough Street immediately.'

'Was it a tough meeting with Mallon?' Lafeyre asked as the carriage turned out through the Palace Street Gate. 'You didn't seem to be the happiest man in Dublin even before I opened my mouth to you.'

63

Swallow nodded.

'There's a lot of bullshit in the newspapers this morning. I'm quoted by Irving in the *Sketch* as saying I have no clues and that I'm not concerned about this case. You were there, Harry, you heard what I said and it wasn't anything like that.'

'I don't read the newspapers to find out about anything I'm involved in myself. They say that anything you read in the newspapers is right unless it's something you actually know about.'

Swallow chuckled mirthlessly.

'That puts it well enough. Mallon says there'll be trouble with the Commissioner over it. He'll do his best to dampen it down, but he's getting pressure on all fronts. There's the Jubilee and a bloody royal visit next week. Anything could happen with the politicals when that's going on. And you probably know that Ces Downes died last night.'

'Sure, those are problems,' Lafeyre replied, 'but they're not your immediate problem. Your immediate problem is a dead woman and child in the park, murdered and with no identification.'

'And the fact that for the first 24 hours of the investigation I thought the woman was a man. Jesus, it sounds brilliant, doesn't it?'

'There's some good news,' Lafeyre said. 'Or at least there's something that might help to explain our way out of the mistake. The photographer developed his prints from the scene last night and left them at the morgue for me this morning.'

He took a manila file from his bag and brought out two photographic prints of the dead man – or woman, as it now turned out to be. One showed the body, lying under the beech trees. The other was a facial close-up, taken from directly above. The clear, circular hole showed black against the grey bone and gristle where the skin had been slashed and torn.

'It's impossible to tell from either picture what sex this person was,' he said emphatically. 'One could only make assumptions from the clothes. I'll warrant that if you showed that picture to any witness, including John Mallon, they'd say it was a man. Unless someone examined the body under the clothing they couldn't know. And remember, we followed proper procedure in not disturbing the clothing at the scene.'

He handed the file to Swallow. 'There's three sets of photographic prints here. I've kept one for my own records.'

It was a fair argument, Swallow acknowledged, sensing for the first time a small degree of relief.

Scollan rattled the carriage across Carlisle Bridge. The river was low, sucked out into the bay by the morning ebb tide. Screaming gulls swooped and pecked for nourishment on the brown mud and along the slime-covered embankment walls. They drove up Sackville Street towards the Nelson Pillar, encircled by the flower-sellers with their baskets, before the brougham swung down Talbot Street to its junction with Marlborough Street.

The City Morgue was a three-storey building that had once served as a schoolhouse. Its thick foundation walls of Wicklow granite, augmented by ice-blocks brought in during the winter, served to maintain low temperatures in the basement where cadavers would await examination or claim by relatives for burial.

Detective Pat Mossop, the Book Man, was climbing the steps to the building with the murder book under his arm just as Swallow and Lafeyre arrived.

Swallow told him what he had just learned from Harry Lafeyre.

'Jesus, Boss.' Mossop ran his fingers through his thin hair. 'I'll be put to the pin of my collar trying to put a version of this down in sensible English. And it means we'll have to brief the inquiry teams again. Now we're looking for information about a *woman* and a child – not a man and a child.'

Swallow shrugged.

'We know now that the victims are a woman and a child. But to anybody who might have seen them – any witnesses – they probably seemed to be a man and child. Just as we thought they were at first. We don't know at what point or where she took off her female clothing and put on her disguise.'

'So we don't know what gender the victim might have seemed to be at any given time,' Mossop ventured. 'I suppose she must have left her own clothing and maybe other effects somewhere. If we could find that we'd have a start, wouldn't we?' His voice trailed off as he realised that he was building on thin air.

Lafeyre beckoned to the detectives from the door of the examination room. He led the way to where the two bodies lay on steel tables, draped in white sheets.

Four steel examination tables stood against the wall under a battery of electrically powered lights.

The medical examiner had wrung the cost out of the Under-Secretary's office in Dublin Castle. 'What one smells may be as important as what one sees in a post mortem,' he had argued with the senior accounting clerk who had challenged the cost. 'The fumes from the old gas-burning lights negate the olfactory senses – you can smell nothing.'

The clerk, who saw himself as a moderniser, accepted the argument and approved the outlay.

Two bundles of clothing sat on a side table. Swallow recognised the man's jacket and trousers from the park. All the items had been labelled and tagged by Lafeyre's assistant. The child's trousers and jacket and the light shoes he had been wearing made up the smaller bundle.

Lafeyre tied a rubber apron at the neck and waist and began the examination of the woman's body. Under the strong electric light Swallow saw that she had been well nourished and healthily formed. The pallor of death seemed to add years to the face, but the smooth limbs and torso were those of a young woman in her physical prime.

Lafeyre or Scollan had cleaned the bloodied face so that in spite of the knife wounds Swallow could begin to imagine her as she might have been in life. The features would have been handsome and regular, the skin smooth. The lips were firm and well-formed. Swallow could imagine a lively young woman smiling or laughing with her son. He felt his anger stir at the destruction, the waste of beautiful life.

Pat Mossop opened the murder book and started to write as Lafeyre began his commentary.

'The time of death, judging by the degree of rigor mortis when I examined the body, I'd say was around 10 to 12 hours previously. That's roughly between, say, 10 p.m. on Thursday night and early on Friday morning. But I can't be any more certain. The warm night could perhaps slow the process.

'Cause of death was the wound to the temple. This one… it certainly looks like a bullet entry, but it's an unusual bullet...'

'What's that supposed to mean?' Swallow asked.

'I'll try to tell you in a moment. First, let's see the damage.'

He indicated to his assistant who stepped forward with a heavy steel saw to section the skull. After a few minutes of noisy work he put away the implement and removed the forward section. Almost like quartering an apple, Swallow thought.

Lafeyre took his magnifying glass and a steel spatula with which he probed the now-open skull.

After a moment he put down the probe and took up long, surgical tweezers which he inserted into the open cavity. A few seconds later he withdrew the instrument and deposited a flat-headed lead slug into a small, steel kidney dish.

He resumed his narrative for Mossop.

'The diameter of the wound on the right frontal lobe is six tenths of an inch. The wound penetrated three and a half inches into the brain so death would have been instantaneous.

'At the extreme site of the wound I have located and withdrawn a bullet. It is a little distorted but not flattened. It appears to be of a medium calibre with a flat point. I would estimate it to be a .38 or .32 calibre.'

He reached for a small glass bottle on a shelf behind him and held it by thumb and index finger in front of Swallow and Mossop. It was filled with a clear, pinkish liquid. Then he swabbed the wound and the eye sockets with small pieces of linen and placed them on a series of glass slides on the table. He watched and waited for perhaps a minute. He turned to Mossop as if to ensure the book man was getting all the details he needed.

'I've swabbed the wound and I've tested the swab for the main kinds of gunpowder or ballistic propellant. It's a simple alkali test. After three tests without a reaction, I got this. The colour confirms the presence of nitro-cordite.'

'Nitro-cordite?' Mossop repeated. 'Didn't they use it for muskets?'

'Yes. And it's still used today, but only in low-charge ammunition where the bullet isn't intended to travel very far. Nitro-cellulose is used nowadays for longer range and greater force.'

'I don't understand,' Swallow interjected. 'Who would use that sort of ammunition and why?'

'I think I know of some uses for it,' Pat Mossop said. 'It's sometimes used in shooting ranges for target practice, for example. There'd be a danger if the bullets carried too far so the manufacturers reduce the amount of propellant.'

'That would tally with the use of flat-pointed slugs,' Lafeyre agreed. 'They make for a neatly punched hole in the target, plainly visible.'

Lafeyre replaced the bottle on the shelf. 'It makes sense of what we're looking at here. There's no exit wound on either victim, yet the presence of nitro-cordite on the skin tells us the shots were fired at very close range, maybe even with the weapon pressed up against the victim's temple. The nitro-cordite powder is actually burned into the skin. A standard .32 or .38 bullet fired into human tissue, even bone, would usually go straight through and out the other side. That hasn't happened here.'

Swallow absorbed the information, framing immediate questions in his own mind. 'What about the other wounds? What do we know about the injuries to the face apart from the bullet wound?'

Lafeyre turned back to the woman's corpse and worked with his magnifying glass, peering at the wounds from different angles.

'I looked at these earlier with the microscope. It was done with a middle-sized knife, maybe 5 or 6 inches long, smooth-edged rather than serrated. Not too sharp, either. The cutting pattern was rough, almost random.'

Swallow was silent for a moment, staring at the blue sky through the morgue's paned windows. 'Brutal,' he said quietly.

'That's a fair enough description. But if you're looking for any mercy here it's the fact that they were killed before they were mutilated. There was very little post-mortem bleeding in spite of the repeated stabbing or slashing with the knife. And there are no defensive wounds on the hands that you'll generally get if someone is attacked with a knife.'

Lafeyre signalled to Scollan, who took a heavy brace from the shelf. Lafeyre expertly slipped the knife under the breast bone, then the assistant inserted the brace. The ribcage came apart with a harsh snapping sound to reveal dark lungs and a red-yellow cardiac sac.

Lafeyre probed the lungs and the area around the heart for a few minutes. He took a scalpel and, in one swift, slicing movement, opened the woman's stomach. A hiss of foul gases floated across the room, making Swallow and Mossop blanch.

Lafeyre plunged his spatula into the stomach and started probing and testing. He took small samples and placed them in various glass tubes, adding chemicals and noting reactions. Then he laid down his implements.

'The heart and lungs look healthy. There's nothing out of the ordinary in the stomach or other visible organs. If there was anything like a poison ingested it would show up. I think I can say with certainty that she died of the gunshot and that alone.'

'Anything else that might be helpful?' Swallow asked.

'Well, there's one possibility that might help in identification,' Lafeyre said.

'There's a tumour or cyst under the skin behind the right eye and a smaller one near the left eye. At a guess I'd say it's some sort of inherited condition. The one behind the right eye was partially exposed in the mutilation of the face. It would probably have caused a protrusion or swelling of the eye itself. It might have been quite noticeable. Do you remember anything from your medical classes about a condition known as Grave's Disease?'

'A bit,' Swallow said. 'Graves was a Dublin doctor, I know, quite celebrated in his time. The condition causes the eyes to swell.'

'Not bad,' Lafeyre smiled. 'You must have been at least half sober in one or two of your medical lectures. These cysts might mimic the symptoms.'

He gestured to the woman's body.

'I think she could have had somewhat prominent eyes, bulging if you like. It might have been noticeable.'

Swallow nodded. 'A distinctive thing like that might help us to identify them, or at least trace their movements. What about the child?'

They moved to the adjoining table. The child's face too had been cleaned of blood and dirt, but the hair was matted above the dark spaces where the eyes had been. Swallow saw a terrible sadness in his expression. His instinct told him now that the woman was first to be killed. The boy had seen his mother shot.

On a signal from Lafeyre, Scollan sectioned the child's skull as he had done with the woman, then the medical examiner probed the wound with the surgical tweezers. Within a minute or two the probe located the bullet that had killed the boy. Lafeyre dropped the small, distorted slug into another kidney dish.

'It looks to me to be the same calibre as for the woman. It's probably .38.

'The knife wounds also follow the same pattern,' he said after a few minutes of further probing. 'I'll test again later for gunpowder, but I imagine it's the same nitro-cordite. You can see the burning on the skin where the weapon was fired at point-blank range.'

He spent another ten minutes examining the boy's body with his magnifying glass before signalling to Scollan to replace the sheets over the two corpses.

'There's nothing of significance apart from what I've recorded. He was a healthy young boy, quite well-nourished. I'd say 8 or 9 years old. No signs of illness. No scars.'

Lafeyre, Swallow and Mossop withdrew to the office. Lafeyre removed his rubber apron and indicated to the detectives to take seats at the work desk.

'Let's go through things one at a time,' Swallow suggested, 'as though we're starting from nothing.'

They had done this many times, on many cases, detective and doctor. They went back to basics, sieving the questions, examining and re-examining what might appear to be obvious, testing theories and possibilities against each other's judgment and knowledge.

Lafeyre steepled his fingers and indicated to Mossop, who began to scribble quickly.

'All right, first we'll describe the woman. She was a healthy female, apart from the two small cysts that I've mentioned. She was aged about 25 to 30 years, I'd guess. She was 5 feet 6 inches tall. The corpse weighs 7 stone and 12 pounds. No signs of illness or surgical scars. There was some decay on the teeth. She had a good head of hair, dark, healthy but cut short. No colourant or dye used.'

'There's nothing of significance in the contents of the stomach. She'd eaten maybe three or four hours before she died. Some sort of vegetables, certainly potatoes. I'd think some oatmeal bread too. I've tested for alcohol and found none.'

He paused. 'I can tell you also that the woman experienced at least one delivery, maybe more. But that wasn't very recently. It was a number of years ago. At a guess, she could have been the boy's mother.'

Swallow made a sour face. 'What did you think about her? Tell me her life story.'

Lafeyre shrugged.

'My acquaintance with her has been too brief for that, but I'll take a bit of a leap in the dark. From the state of her hands, I'd say she was a servant, or perhaps a shop assistant or maybe she did light work in a mill. Her hands weren't used for labouring or farming. She was a city woman rather than, say, a farmer. She wasn't very muscular so I don't think she would have been fit for that sort of life anyway.'

'Was she Irish?' Swallow asked.

'Maybe, there's nothing to indicate one way or another.'

Mossop continued to write as Swallow summarised.

'So, we know we have one female victim of about 25 to 30 years of age, maybe a servant or a shop assistant or a mill worker. Shot to death with a low-charge, medium-calibre slug. We have the second victim, a male child, killed in the same way. We have the faces of both victims extensively mutilated, probably with a knife. And we have the bizarre dimension that the woman was masquerading as a man.'

Lafeyre nodded. 'That's a fair summary. Can the clothing or footwear tell you anything about their identities?'

'Not a lot. The man's clothing worn by the woman could be bought in any city or town here or in England, I'd say. There aren't any tailor's or manufacturer's labels. The boy's clothing is much the same. The shirts could have come from any cotton factory. The boots show some repair work. There's nothing of much help there. So what do we know – or what can we speculate – about the killer, or killers?'

Lafeyre shrugged again.

'Whoever did the killing might have been somewhat bloodstained. The shots were fired at very close range so spattering could be expected. The knife wounds were inflicted post mortem so there wouldn't have been any great gushing or effusion of blood even from the deep wounds. The killer or killers would probably have picked up some stains, but they wouldn't necessarily have stood out with blood all over their clothing.'

'You've placed the death some time late on Thursday night or early on the Friday morning,' Swallow said. 'There'd still be people on the streets in the village or on the roads up to midnight. A bloodstained man would probably be noticed... unless he was in a carriage. So give me a medical opinion. What sort of sick person would do those things to a woman and child?'

Lafeyre shook his head.

'You know there doesn't have to be any sickness involved. When the motivation is strong enough, certain men – or women – won't be held back by any barriers or restraints. So let me turn the question back on you. You tell me, have you any idea as to what sort of motive we might be dealing with here?'

Swallow pushed back his chair, rose, and paced across the room.

'I doubt that it was a robbery even though there was nothing of value left on them. They were left with just the clothes they were wearing. I don't think they were taken by force to the park because there were no signs of a struggle, or restraints or ropes or tearing of the clothing or anything like that. I think they were lured there, or they met somebody by arrangement there.'

'That's plausible,' Lafeyre said. 'There may have been some sort of rendezvous for sexual purposes? But does that make sense with the child present?'

Swallow crossed the room again.

'I just don't know. God knows, anything is possible, even that. But there is no sign of any sexual assault or sexual activity. One thing is clear, though. The killer or killers came prepared. There was a gun and a knife. It wasn't that the victims' heads were battered with a rock or a stick that just happened to be around at the scene.'

'So I put your own question back to you again,' Lafeyre said. 'What motivates a person to do those things to a woman and to murder an innocent child?'

'It could be an urge to take revenge for some reason,' Swallow said. 'But if a killer simply wanted to inflict maximum destruction, perhaps for vengeance or in a demented rage, wouldn't he mutilate other parts of the body too? It's possible that the face may have been mutilated and the effects removed to prevent identification.'

Lafeyre nodded. 'That's credible. It could also be consistent with the eyes being damaged. There's a myth you'll sometimes encounter among criminals that when a person dies violently the last sight he or she sees is somehow recorded in the pupils of the eyes. It's complete nonsense of course, ignorance. But cutting at the eyes might be a misguided precaution by a killer against identification.'

'Not much to show after 24 hours' work, is it though?' Swallow said bleakly.

At that moment Pat Mossop called from across the room.

'Boss, there's something here you'll want to see.'

He was holding two small pieces of buff-coloured paper. He placed them side by side in the palm of his outstretched hand.

'We've got the return halves of two sailing tickets, an adult and a child. They're for the mail packet from Kingstown back to Holyhead.'

'Where were they, Mossop?'

'I found them in the sole of the woman's right boot, Boss; there's a sort of loose canvas lining.'

For the first time since he had seen the victims at the Chapelizod Gate, Swallow allowed himself to feel a small twinge of optimism. Whoever had cleared away the dead woman's personal effects had missed the tickets. They had almost certainly been concealed for safety. He could see that the stubs bore serial numbers.

He began to visualise a likely trail of important clues. The woman and child had crossed the Irish Sea from Wales and the return tickets indicated that they planned to return. The mail packets sailed up to three times a day, but the serial numbers should indicate when they had travelled and on which crossing. There would have to be eye-witnesses, descriptions, maybe a swift identification of a suspect.

'Bloody well done, Mossop,' Lafeyre said.

Swallow nodded. 'Get the details off. First get them to the detectives at the passenger pier in Kingstown. We need to establish on which date those tickets were issued. Then they should start questioning everyone on the cross-channel packets who might have seen a man and a child, or indeed maybe a woman and a child on that date. We don't know at what stage she disguised herself. The prominent eyes and the short hair that Dr Lafeyre mentioned could be significant. They'd have been apparent whether she was passing herself off as a man or a woman.'

Detectives attended every sailing at the mail-packet pier, watchful for suspicious travellers whose activities might be of interest to the authorities. They would be more than normally vigilant because of the imminence of the Jubilee celebrations and the pending royal visit. There was a good chance, Swallow knew, that the victims would have been spotted by policemen trained to remember detail and to note anything out of the ordinary.

'So what do you do next?' Lafeyre queried Swallow.

'I've got the crime conference shortly at the Castle. We'll see what the search teams came up with out around the murder site. We'll get to work on the clothing and the boots. We'll have a look at the plaster casts from the tracks in the park. The width of the carriage wheels should give us some sort of indication what kind of vehicle it was.'

He paused. 'And I've to tell Chief Mallon that my dead man is really a dead woman.'

'Is there anything more I can do? Or can I sign off that you're satisfied with the examinations?' Lafeyre inquired. 'The Coroner needs to get on with an inquest and I need to arrange the burial.'

Swallow thought for a moment. 'There isn't much point in keeping them above ground at this point is there?'

'I don't think so. I can't retain the corpses for very much longer anyway. The hot weather has raised the numbers of sudden deaths and quite a few of them are coming my way. I'll get Scollan to make the arrangements.'

Swallow's mind briefly flashed to the paupers' sections of the Prospect Cemetery at Glasnevin, where the unknown woman and the child would be buried.

'Yes, I'd be grateful if you would.' He turned to Mossop.

'Prepare a note for Chief Superintendent Mallon. Inform him that there's been a misunderstanding about the gender of the deceased adult but that this has been clarified after examination by Dr Lafeyre. Also advise him about the tickets for the Holyhead crossing. Tell him that I'll be working late tonight at Exchange Court but if he needs me to brief him I'll attend at his house. Otherwise I'll have a full report for him on Monday morning at Exchange Court.'

Mossop scribbled Swallow's instructions. 'Sure, Boss. And what's the second thing?'

'Make sure that Swift and Feore and the rest of the search teams know that we're now looking for information about an adult of either gender and a child rather than a man and a child. Put the same information out on the ABC telegraph to all stations, but make sure Mr Mallon knows this before anyone else.'

Swallow knew that once the information went out on the ABC every journalist in Dublin would hear of it within minutes. The last thing he wanted was for John Mallon to learn the news from a Saturday evening newspaper.

Swallow stood up to leave.

Lafeyre stood too. 'There's one other thing I could do that might just help in this case. It would be a bit of an experiment, but it can't do any harm I'll venture.'

He reached to the bookshelf behind his desk and drew down a cloth-bound volume.

He turned the book towards Swallow so that he could read the title on the spine.

Identification After Death.
By Professor Lazlo Hiss, MD, B.Ch, FCSV.

Lafeyre opened the book.

'This Professor Hiss is the leading expert in his field. He's based at the University of Vienna. He's making some very challenging predictions about human identification both before and after death. He's arguing, for example, that one day we will be able to identify each human being individually from what he calls the "fingerprints." Those are the distinctive marks on the surface of the skin at the fingertips.'

He shrugged his shoulders.

'Personally, I think that's probably a long way off, if it ever happens. It seems indeed that we all have different fingertip patterns, but how could we construct a system for the recognition of each individual one? What might be of some help in this case is the technique that Professor Hiss has devised for reconstructing a face from a human skull.

'See here,' he flicked four pages of full-sized photographs. Each showed a grotesque but distinctively recognisable human face.

'Hiss devised techniques based on cranial and facial measurements that enable him to build up a face in wax or plaster on a skull. He's successfully identified several people whose features were destroyed, the majority by fire. Obviously, the more of the original tissue, muscle and so on that survives, the more accurate will be the result.'

'So what are you planning?' Swallow asked doubtfully.

'I think I should have a try at rebuilding the woman's features. I'll take a plaster cast before I hand over the remains to the undertakers. Then I'll start building over the muscle and the facial frame with plaster of Paris. If I'm even partially happy with the results, we'll have a face we can photograph and circulate. What do you say?'

Swallow fingered the book. It brought back recollections of student days, when he dozed over his medical texts, waiting for the next postal order to arrive from home to enable him to resume his entertainments in the pub and music hall.

'It isn't even as simple as that, Harry, is it? If you try this technique you're going to have to reconstruct the face of a woman who managed to pass herself off as a man.'

Lafeyre shrugged. 'True enough. I can but try. There's sufficient of the skin and muscles still there to enable me to get a good likeness. And apart from the bullet wound the bone structure is intact.'

Swallow knew he needed something to extricate himself from the humiliation he would suffer when he would report to Mallon.

'We've got a saying in my part of the country,' he told Lafeyre. '"When all fruit fails, welcome haws." I say get on with it, as quickly as you can.'

EIGHT

The briefing of the Chapelizod Gate investigation team got under way in the Exchange Court parade room a few minutes after 11 o'clock.

Swallow and Mossop took their places at the top of the room just in time to forestall a rising murmur of complaint about the heat and the lack of air.

Detective Officers Tom Swift and Mick Feore sat on two cane chairs beside the window, hoping for a current of cooler air from the alley outside. Stephen Doolan stood beside them, running an index finger under the high collar of his uniform to achieve some relief from the perspiration.

A dozen constables were scattered around the room, some perched on desks with their helmets beside them. Others leaned against the wall, thumbs hooked in their belts. One overweight, bearded officer had a red pocket handkerchief clamped to his sweaty forehead.

Swallow scanned the room. He knew all the older men by name. The younger ones, he thought, all looked alike: fresh-cheeked country lads. Some of them, he reckoned, were probably not yet 20.

'For those of you who don't know me, I'm Detective Sergeant Joe Swallow. First, I'd like to thank you all, starting with Sergeant Doolan, for your work to date. I know you put in a long day yesterday on house-to-house. It's hard bloody slog-work but it's essential. Now, let me tell you what we know in outline about this case, then I'm going to ask for reports.'

Notebooks were opened around the room. Pencils were poised.

'First, there's been a development that nobody can be very pleased about, least of all me. There's been a mistake in the identification process. It turns out that what we believed to be a dead man is in fact a woman.'

Heads shot up all over the room. There were mutters of surprise and one or two low whistles.

'I'd like to explain why we didn't know this until Doctor Lafeyre started his examination at Marlborough Street this morning.'

He paused.

'The best procedure in an investigation is not to interfere with a scene or in particular with a body until the medical examination is over, the photographs are taken and so on. That's what we did. The woman was well disguised, wearing a man's suit and hat and with close-cut hair. It's unfortunate that the doctor wasn't able to do his examination any sooner. The electric lights failed at the morgue and he couldn't start until this morning. As soon as he realised the mistake he notified me.'

One or two young constables laughed nervously. Was it some sort of joke or a test? Swallow's expression told them otherwise. There were a few more exclamations and then the room fell silent.

'The adult victim was a female, generally healthy, aged perhaps 25 to 30 years. She was 5 feet 6 inches in height. Dr Lafeyre found two cysts or tumours around the eyes. That might have caused some bulging of the eyes, making the sufferer look as if they are staring hard. That might be useful in identification if we can find any witnesses. The doctor says it would have been quite noticeable.

'Dr Lafeyre weighed the corpse at 7 stone and 12 pounds. He found no other signs of illness or distinguishing scars or marks. She was dark haired, adequately built. The examination shows that she gave birth, at least once, maybe more than once, but it wasn't recently and was probably some years ago. It's possible but not certain that they were mother and son, according to the medical examiner.

'The child was a male, also healthy. No distinguishing marks. He was perhaps 8 to 9 years old, dark haired also.

'We do have one lead that may help us. Equally, it could throw the case open so wide that we'll never get to the bottom of it. We believe that the woman and child crossed from Holyhead on the mail packet some days ago. If they did they probably reached Holyhead on one of the railway routes from England.'

Swallow paused while pencils translated the information into notebooks.

'We've got the men at the mail-packet pier checking with the crews and we're arranging to get the English and Welsh police and the Railway Police on the job as well.

'Some of you saw the mutilation to the faces. The rest of you have heard about it, I'm sure. Pat Mossop will go through the medical details in a moment. Let me just say they weren't an attractive sight and that at this point we still have no identification.

'Dr Lafeyre has put the time of death at perhaps 10 to 12 hours before he examined the bodies at the scene. So that would place death at, say, between 10 o'clock on Thursday and early on Friday morning. He confirms the cause of death in both cases as a severe wound to the skull and brain caused by gunshot.'

Swallow pointed an index finger to the frontal lobe above his own left eye.

'Just here. You can see them in the photographs, round as a sixpence. They're entry wounds from a medium-calibre bullet. Dr Lafeyre recovered them. They're .38 calibre and I'll have possession of the two slugs. He found traces of cordite powder suggesting the use of low-propellant ammunition such as might be used for target practice. That would accord with the fact that the bullets didn't exit the victims' heads.'

A murmur ran around the group. Pencils flew across notebook pages.

'These murders were premeditated and planned. This wasn't a case of someone being beaten to death with a weapon of opportunity. Everything that could assist in identification of the woman was removed. It seems likely that the mutilation of the eyes and face was a further effort to prevent or delay identification as well.

'That's the essence of it. We've no witnesses that I know of. We've got nothing to indicate a motive. We don't know why they were killed or even who they are. So it's going to be a steep, uphill climb, I'm afraid,'

He turned to Stephen Doolan. 'Will you take up from there, Stephen?'

Doolan stood, taking a large notepad in his hand.

'The bodies were reported to the police station at Chapelizod by a park-keeper. We organised ground searches at the scene. They came up with nothing of immediate significance. We have a few buttons and matchsticks. We located a set of wheel-tracks and some hoof-marks where a carriage appears to have come off the dirt track leading from Chesterfield Avenue. We took casts and measurements.'

Doolan nodded to a middle-aged constable across the room. 'Would you tell us about the wheel-tracks, Matt?'

Constable Matt Culliton was one of the DMP's specialist officers who supervised the city's carriages and hired cars. He read from his notebook.

'The ground was too dry to take any impression of depth from the carriage, but I have a measurement of the wheel span at 6 feet and 6 inches. So it was a big vehicle, like a brougham or a clarence. It wouldn't have been a side-car or a Ringsend Car.

'The hoof-marks show just one horse drawing the vehicle, so it would have been moving fairly slowly. You wouldn't get much of a gallop even out of a strong animal drawing that kind of weight on its own.'

'Thanks, Matt. Maybe that narrows it a bit.' Doolan turned a page on his notepad.

'The house-to-house inquiries got under way fairly quickly. In some places we were out of DMP jurisdiction, so we had RIC men accompany us. We did every cottage and farmhouse between the Chapelizod Gate and the village in one direction, and every building between Chapelizod Gate and the Strawberry Beds in the other direction.

'Mostly people hadn't heard the news at all. Nobody had information on any unusual activity. Nobody reported strangers passing through. Nobody heard any shots. That might be because of the low-propellant charge making less of a bang than conventional ammunition. We wanted any sightings of people with bloodied clothing, or people looking to change their clothing, that kind of thing.

'So apart from the wheel-marks and hoof-marks, the inquiries on the scene haven't yielded anything,' he said. 'We're putting on night patrols and rising patrols starting at 5 a.m. with the RIC. They'll stop and question everyone moving in the area. It's possible that some night workers or early risers might have seen something that could be useful.'

A glum silence hung across the room. There were no fish of any significance in the investigation net.

Swallow nodded to Pat Mossop.

'Will you go through Dr Lafeyre's report for us please, Pat?'

Mossop detailed the injuries to the faces of the dead woman and child and Lafeyre's comments on the contents of the woman's stomach. He described the lividity marks on the underside of the bodies by which Lafeyre had confirmed Swallow's original conclusion that they had been killed at the copse of trees and that the bodies had not been moved after death.

He repeated Lafeyre's conclusions about the weapon that had fired the fatal shots, then he briefly set out the details of the dead boy.

When he had finished, the silence again enveloped the room.

'Well, it's not great. But there's enough to get started on,' said Stephen Doolan, getting to his feet. 'Tell us what you want done now.'

'There are a few obvious things.' Swallow said. 'There isn't anybody on the missing persons list that's an immediate match, but we should have all divisions checking boarding-houses and hotels for guests who haven't returned. They came in from Wales so we have to assume they were somewhere around Dublin for a time. There were no personal effects left with the woman's body, so it's possible something unusual might turn up in one of the pawn shops, maybe a watch or a ring or some jewellery.'

His mind went back momentarily to the scene by the Chapelizod Gate and the two bodies stripped of anything that might help to give them names or identities. It added a particular dimension of obscenity, almost as if the victims had been left naked.

'Extend the house-to-house inquiries to the streets around the main park gate leading to the city as well. We've checked the exit through the Chapelizod Gate, but the carriage could have come in through any of the gates to the park.'

He gestured to Matt Culliton, the constable who had measured the carriage-tracks.

'Go across to Hutton's, the coach-makers in the Coombe, and see if you can get a precise match for that wheel span. They might be able to tell you a bit more about the make, weight and shape of the carriage we're looking for.

'We'll get a general request out to all stations, including the RIC, to see what can be got out of local informants. As you know, any scrap of information, no matter how insignificant, comes back to the Book Man.'

Swallow saw Mossop's narrow shoulders droop.

The mood was gloomy. Pat Mossop was an incurable optimist. Swallow knew that when the cheery Belfast man lost heart it was a serious sign. He thought for a moment about telling the conference of Lafeyre's proposed experiment in constructing a face on the dead woman's skull, but on balance he decided against it. It would raise hopes unreasonably. Harry Lafeyre might believe in Professor Hiss and his techniques, but with the fates running hard against him, Swallow was not going to allow himself to fall victim to reckless optimism.

NINE

By the time Lafeyre had completed taking the dead woman's facial casts, the second day-shift of the Dublin Metropolitan Police were well into their tour of duty. It would stretch from 2 p.m. until 10 o'clock in the evening.

With no investigative leads worth talking about, Swallow tried to take some comfort from the fact that the not inconsiderable resources of the city's police system were now focused on the murders at the Chapelizod Gate.

Singly or in pairs, constables and sergeants worked their beats or manned their fixed posts. Every officer had the details of what was now being described as a dead woman and boy. Across the city, under the hot June sun, ladies and maids, cab drivers and tram conductors, pawnbrokers and porters, holiday-makers and visitors to the city were quizzed.

Had anyone's attention fallen, for any reason, on an adult with a child? Did anyone know, perhaps, of a father or mother and child now missing from home? Was there any suspicious activity that might be linked to the brutality that had been discovered at the Chapelizod Gate of the Phoenix Park?

At the mail-packet pier at Kingstown, the G-Division detectives who monitored each sailing began the questioning of crew members who had worked the crossings from Holyhead in recent days. In the shipping company's office, behind the pier, a sergeant sat beside a senior clerk who had started ploughing though the receipt books in order to establish the date when the tickets found in the murder victim's shoe had been used.

Late in the evening, as he sat at his desk at Exchange Court, it struck Swallow that with Harriet's examinations over he still had no opportunity to find out how she had fared. She would wonder why he had not come to the training college on the previous afternoon, as arranged. On the other hand, he knew she would not be alarmed. She had become accustomed to the unpredictability of her brother's work.

Almost at the same moment, he remembered that they had an arrangement to meet on Sunday evening at the Royal Hibernian Academy.

Harriet was planning to travel into the city to attend the opening of an exhibition of new works by the artist Stella Purcell. It was one of dozens of events timed to coincide with the run up to the Jubilee.

Swallow was looking forward to the exhibition. Miss Purcell's portraits were highly regarded. He also hoped the occasion might provide an opportunity to learn a little more about his younger sister's friends and the company she was keeping.

He calculated that if he pushed hard on the investigation he would be in the clear to keep the rendezvous at the Academy. Otherwise, it was a question of sending an early cancellation telegram to Harriet at the training college. But it was important to talk to her. He worked through the afternoon, reviewing Pat Mossop's notes in the murder book and turning over every detail of Harry Lafeyre's post-mortem reports.

Some time after 8 o'clock, with Exchange Court virtually empty of personnel, the duty constable at the ABC telegraph room brought him a message. It originated from the sergeant who had been sent to the mail-packet office to oversee the checking of the victim's tickets.

The tickets had been tracked by number. They were issued at the sales office at Holyhead on the previous Wednesday. The time of issue was estimated at half an hour before the departure of the Kingstown mail packet at 9 a.m. And it was 15 minutes after the arrival of the morning train from Liverpool via Chester. The timings made it likely, although not certain, that the woman and child had travelled from Chester, and possibly from Liverpool.

At least it narrowed the immediate field of survey, Swallow reflected. They had a particular train and a particular mail-packet crossing on which to concentrate in the search for possible witnesses.

'Ensure officers questioning crews have this information,' he telegraphed in response. 'Seeking reports of either man or woman, aged about 25 to 30, and boy, 8 to 9 years. Details also to British

Railway Police for circulation to railway staff, ticket inspectors, porters etc. on lines to Holyhead.'

He left his desk shortly after 9 o'clock and stepped out into Exchange Court. The heat of the day caused the alley to stink even more than usual and there was no stirring in the rank evening air. The oppressive atmosphere did little to raise his spirits as he set off to pay his respects to the dead.

TEN

Swallow had grappled with the question of attending Ces Downes's wake as he worked through the afternoon at Exchange Court.

In keeping with Dublin tradition, the dead woman would be laid out at her house in Francis Street. There would be a bedside vigil until the corpse would be brought to the church or taken directly for burial. Since the city authorities did not allow the cemeteries to operate on Sundays it would be Monday before the mortal remains of Cecilia Downes would be put in the earth.

Part of his brain told him to stay away. It would be a gathering at which drink would flow freely. Every significant criminal in the city would make it his business to be seen there. There would be tensions and bad temper, and perhaps worse.

The other part of his reasoning told Swallow that with so many of the city's criminals gathered together, Pisspot Ces Downes's wake would be a likely place to pick up whatever whispers might be going about in connection with the murders at the Chapelizod Gate. On balance, there was possibly more to be gained than risked in going to pay his respects.

There was also the fact that he had known the dead woman over most of his 20 years as a crime detective. It was not as if there was any affection or respect in the relationship, but the principles governing attendance at Irish funerals did not take account of such considerations. Even a slight acquaintance with the deceased generated an obligation to put in an appearance.

He walked past Christ Church into High Street and Cornmarket and then turned into Francis Street. Crossing the junction with Swift's Alley he could hear raised voices drifting up the street from where groups of mourners had spilled out from the house onto the pavement. As he drew nearer, a wave of tobacco smoke, sweat and alcohol came up at him on the clammy evening air.

From the moment that her death had been announced, the superintendent of the A district had assigned a pair of men to watch Ces Downes's house from a discreet distance. Swallow saw the short capes and the blackened night badges of the two constables in a shop doorway across the street.

He anticipated the noisy chorus of recognition as he drew closer to the drinking mourners. In the evening dusk he could make out that there were perhaps 30 people on the street, gathered in small groups.

'Ah sure, Sergeant Swallow, is it yerself?'

'Good man, Joe, ye've come to do the right thing by poor oul' Ces.'

'G'wan inside there, Misther Swalla'… and get yourself a drink for the night that's in it.'

There was hardly one of them that he could not name. These were not the decent hard-working people he knew across the Dublin Liberties who struggled hard to make a living and to raise their families well. These were not the tradesmen, the shopkeepers, the brewers, the weavers, the tram workers, the cabmen, the stokers, the stall-keepers or the general labourers who underpinned the economy of the city.

These were brutalised, cunning and dangerous criminals. He detested them all. They were knife men, robbers, prostitutes, house breakers, pimps, receivers, burglars and petty thieves – the detritus of the city's slums. Some of them had done jail time on his evidence. He recognised hard men who had come at him in the past with fists and, in one instance, with a stiletto. Swallow's baton strike was faster. The man never fully recovered the use of his right hand.

He nodded a terse acknowledgment in return and stepped through the open front door into the hallway of the house.

Vinny Cussen stood at the foot of the stairs with half a dozen of his gang around him. Swallow recognised Tommy 'Tiger' McKnight, one of Cussen's principal strong men in the group. There were guffaws and curses. The air was thick with smoke and the smell of drink. Cussen stepped out of the group, attempting a welcome that he hoped would be suitably sombre. He thrust his hand out to grasp Swallow's.

'Yer welcome, Mister Swallow, Ces would've been pleased to see you here… yer welcome.' He beckoned with a nod to a young girl standing across the hallway. Swallow guessed from her features and her colouring that she was probably Cussen's daughter. 'You'll have a little somethin' wet before you go above to see her.'

On cue, the girl disappeared into the room that was apparently being used as a dispensing area for the mourners' refreshments. She reappeared a moment later with a half-full beaker of whiskey and a jug of water.

'Ye'd generally take a little water in that, Mister Swalla, 'if I recall your preference,' Cussen said amiably. 'It brings out the flavours of the malt, don't it?'

Swallow raised the glass and drank. It was smooth, mellow whiskey: Tullamore, his preferred choice.

'Here's to your health, Vinny.' He sipped again. 'I thought I should stop by. Ces Downes gave us plenty of hard work down the years. But I won't hold that against her in eternity. May the Lord have mercy on her soul.'

Cussen laughed nervously. 'Ah, I know, I know. But all the lads would be glad to know that ye wanted to see her at th' end. They have the prayers still goin' in the room. Will you make a visit above?' He pointed to the landing.

He nodded. 'I'll do that now, Vinny.'

'See Sergeant Swalla' to the upstairs, Tommy,' Cussen told McKnight.

Swallow declined the offer of an escort. If he were to encounter a helpful source of information somewhere around the house he did not want Cussen's strong man in earshot.

'That's all right, thanks, Vinny. I think I'll be able to find my own way up.'

He climbed the stairs, glass in hand. At the turn of the banister he met Charlie Vanucchi. Vanucchi's lurching downward progress indicated that he too had an amount of drink on board. The sallow, Neapolitan features were blotched where the alcohol was showing through.

He succeeded in focusing on the face coming up the stairs against him. 'Ah, Misther Swallow… you… you're comin' to say goodbye to Ces.' He formed a smile.

As with Vinny Cussen, Swallow chose his words carefully. He was required to be formal and polite, but he could not bring himself to offer sympathy or to express regret.

'I am, Charlie. May the Lord have mercy on her.'

Vanucchi nodded to the drink in Swallow's hand. 'I'm glad ye were offered the hospitality of the house, Sergeant. That's what she would have wanted.'

'You needn't worry, Charlie, Vinny Cussen below saw me right on that,' Swallow said, raising his whiskey glass.

Vanucchi's face darkened in anger.

'That drink you're havin' is from me, not Vinny Cussen, Sergeant Swalla' – and yer very welcome to it. But it's me… it's Charlie Vanucchi… that's bought and paid for the hospitality here this night… and last night… and tomorra'. That's… wha' Ces would've expected of me.'

He raised his voice. 'I was workin' with Ces Downes for many a long year before that bastard Cussen was ever seen around Francis Street.'

Silence fell along the stairway as Vanucchi's shouted words dropped into the hallway below. At the end of stairs, Vinny Cussen swung around. He glared up at his rival and at Swallow. Then he put his right foot on the bottom step. Tiger McKnight stood behind him, a vicious look in his eyes. Swallow thought they would charge up at Vanucchi.

'Fuck you, Vanucchi!' Cussen shouted. 'Fuck you. I've put me hand in me own pocket for proper whiskey for the likes o' Sergeant Swalla'. I wouldn't insult the man by offerin' him the bootleg piss you're after puttin' in here.'

He moved a step higher on the stairs and pointed a finger at Vanucchi.

'I hear you talkin' about how ye worked with Ces Downes all these years gone by. You've done sweet fuck all, Vanucchi, since ye were a kid robbin' apples off old women in the South City Market. Any work that was done here was done be meself and these lads here. Yer all talk and no bottle.'

He extended an arm to his companions, in the style of a classical orator, inviting them to give voice to their support. There was a chorus of muttered agreement from the four or five men gathered around him in the hallway.

Charlie Vanucchi was not going to back down from the challenge. He moved another step down the stairs.

Swallow cut in front of him.

'Go back upstairs, Charlie, like a good man. There's no need to dishonour Ces's memory, with her up there still being waked in her own house. Do you hear me?'

In spite of the alcohol dimming his brain, Vanucchi registered the hard edge in Swallow's voice. He hesitated for a moment and then slowly turned back up the stairs without a word.

'There's the brave fuckin' man now, hidin' behind the bobby,' Cussen called from the hallway below. 'What did I tell ye, lads, all fuckin' talk?'

Swallow swung around to face Cussen. 'You cool down too, Vinny,' he said angrily. 'Charlie's walking away here for the right reasons. You should do the same now yourself. There's a dead woman upstairs and she's entitled to a bit of respect from the two of you.'

Cussen scowled and turned back to his men. The buzz of talk picked up again across the hallway and along the stairs. Swallow continued his climb to the third floor.

At the top of the stairs, he was surprised to discover that conditions on the third floor of Ces Downes's house contrasted dramatically with those on the lower floors.

The broken boards and tattered furniture gave way to well-carpeted rooms. Most of the plasterwork on the downstairs ceilings had long broken away, but on the upper floor it seemed to retain much of its original detail. Doors, wainscoting and window frames were well preserved and neatly painted. Half a dozen paintings of hunting scenes hung in gold-leaf frames on the walls of the corridor.

He looked around for any sight of the two dogs that supposedly roamed the top floor. There was no sign of them. Swallow could hear the cadences of the prayers for the dead drifting from the front room across the corridor.

He stepped into the room. Half a dozen women sat around the big brass bed, most of them with rosary beads twined in their fingers, making the responses to the prayers. The blinds were down and four wax candles were burning in tall brass holders, one at each corner of the bed. The dead crime boss, laid out in a white satin habit, looked smaller than she had in life and utterly harmless, Swallow thought.

A youth silently pointed him to an empty chair against the wall. He felt awkward with the whiskey in his hand, but there was no shelf or table upon which he could safely place it. He reckoned it was better to sit and hold on to the glass.

A white-haired priest, a purple stole around his neck, knelt near the top of the bed. Candlelight flickered off his face and across the pages of the book he held out before him. Intoning the 'Glory be to the Father,' he brought the prayers to an end. He closed the book, blessed himself and rose stiffly to his feet.

As the priest started slowly across the room, Swallow realised that under the ceremonial vestments he wore the brown habit of the Franciscans. It took him a moment to recognise Father Laurence, the friar who had attended the previous morning to administer the late rites to the murdered woman and child inside the Chapelizod Gate.

The friar nodded in recognition. Swallow nodded back and then rose from his chair, stepping after him to the corridor outside. Father Laurence extended his hand in greeting.

'I didn't expect to see you again so soon, Sergeant,' he said. It was a soft accent from the South; Cork, or more likely Kerry, Swallow guessed. 'But I suppose I shouldn't be surprised to find you here. I know that Ces Downes was no stranger to the police.'

Swallow laughed quietly. 'That might be one way of putting it, Father. But if you'll allow me to turn that comment around, I didn't realise either that she was known to the church. I always thought she kept away from religion.'

The friar smiled. 'Well, that's partly true. She wanted nothing to do with the priests of the parish. She avoided the local clergy here in Francis Street. I remember she used to rail on about well-fed bishops and monsignors, but she always seemed to be comfortable with us. I think she felt that humble mendicants weren't a challenge or a threat to her. She had friends among our community, you know. In fact, my understanding is that she bequeathed this house to us – to the Franciscans…'

His voice trailed off. Swallow realised that Father Laurence was eyeing the whiskey glass in his right hand. He took the cue.

'Would you like to have a drink, Father? We could go below to the room. They have a decent whiskey at least.'

The friar's eyes lit up. 'Well, that's a very good idea, Sergeant. But you'll have to… ah… order for me though. I can't really be seen going into the room myself… a holy priest, looking for whiskey, can I?'

Swallow laughed. 'I'll do what I can to protect your reputation, Father.'

He led the way down past the mourners on the landings and along the stairs. There was no sign of Vinny Cussen or Charlie Vanucchi, but Swallow saw the girl that Cussen had earlier told to fetch his own drink. He caught her eye, raised his glass and pointed to the priest. Someone in the hallway called to her, 'Kate', but she ignored the call. She nodded and turned into the room, emerging almost immediately with a tumbler of whiskey that matched the one she had procured for Swallow.

'We might find a bit of quiet at the back of the house,' Father Laurence said, moving down the passageway.

They found a bench seat outside what would once have been the kitchens.

The friar raised his glass and touched it lightly against Swallow's.

'Good health, Sergeant. As I was saying, Ces Downes was a regular visitor to the friary. She was a complex woman, you know. I think people like the police only saw one side of her, but she suffered terrible injustices in her own life too. So she knew the pain that people can feel when they believe the whole world is against them… and sometimes maybe they feel that God is against them too. I can't say any more, but I can say that.'

He took a mouthful of the whiskey and smacked his lips appreciatively.

'Ah, God bless that man Dan Williams below in Tullamore. "Tullamore Dew," they're starting to call this now. He'll surely find salvation on account of his good works on Earth if nothing else.'

Swallow found himself wondering at the friar's apparently developed knowledge of the distilling industry.

The friar put his hand to his forehead. 'Oh, I'm sorry, Sergeant. I've probably offended you. That's a stupid thing to have said.'

Swallow laughed. 'Not at all, Father. I'm of the same flock as yourself, you know.'

'I took the name 'Swallow' to be Protestant,' Father Laurence said in a tone of relief. 'Where's it from?'

'My people have been around South Kildare for as far back as we can trace it,' Swallow said. 'Somebody said it's probably French, from the word '*soie*,' which means silk in French. Maybe my ancestors were silk merchants.'

'It's a funny world,' the friar laughed. 'Here's the progeny of a French silk merchant, a policeman and an officer of the Crown, drinking whiskey along with a mendicant friar and a house full of criminals.'

'It's more complicated than that, Father,' Swallow grinned. 'My grandfather on my mother's side carried a pike with the United Irishmen in 1798. So there's the grandson of a rebel sitting beside you too.'

'Did that ever cause you… any… difficulty, you know, being a policeman with a rebel family background? It's a bit of a contradiction,' the friar asked tentatively.

Swallow tried not to let his irritation show.

'Never gave it a moment's thought, Father,' he lied. 'If the United men had won they'd have set up their own police force too. And it mightn't be as civilised as the DMP.'

'So, where do you worship, Sergeant? I always like to know where people go to talk to God.'

'When I do it at all, I like to do my praying over with the Carmelites in Whitefriar Street. But my conversations with God are usually one way. I'm not sure he has a lot to say to me.'

The friar smiled. 'It's usually a matter of listening. God can make himself heard without speaking… if you know what I mean. Whitefriar Street is a good place to hear him, I'd say. They're good men, too, the Carmelites. I wouldn't hear a word against them. And they have the bones of St Valentine over there. I'm afraid the poor Franciscans can't compete with that.'

The priest's expression grew serious. 'That's a terrible, terrible business you had to deal with in the park yesterday. I've seen shocking sights in my time, but I don't know if I've ever had to attend at a more dreadful thing. The whole city is shocked by it. It's hard to imagine how anybody could do such a thing to a woman and an innocent child.'

'It is, Father,' Swallow said quietly. 'I'm sorry that we had to keep you waiting. We have to keep the scene clear until the experts have done their work.'

The friar waved his hand dismissively. 'Ah, not at all… I understand that, of course. You have to do your particular duty. Tell me, have you any idea of what happened or why? Or if you think you know who did it? Do you know who they were, the poor creatures?'

'We're making slow enough progress,' Swallow said. 'We'll need all the help we can get.'

Father Laurence drank from his whiskey glass.

'Then there's this strange business of the woman being dressed in a man's clothes? You know, when I administered the last rites I thought it was a man. Then I saw in the evening newspapers that you've discovered it was a woman, disguised as a man. But I could see how the mistake might have been made in the first place.'

'That's true, Father. It wasn't until the medical examiner got to work on the remains that he realised it. I saw them there in the trees and I took the adult for a man. And whoever killed them went to a lot of trouble to make sure they won't be easily identified.'

Charlie Vanucchi appeared out of the back room, an open bottle of porter in hand.

'We were just saying here, Charlie, isn't that a dreadful business above in the park by the Chapelizod Gate?' Father Laurence said. 'It's terrible to think of a woman and child ending like that.'

If Vanucchi heard what the priest had said he gave no indication of it. Swallow realised that he was quite intoxicated.

'I'd jus' like to say thank you, Father, for comin' over here... to say... to say the prayers over Ces. She wasn't one for much religion but she had a great regard for the Francis... Franciscan fathers.'

'Did you not hear what the reverend father said there, Charlie?' Swallow probed. 'He said it was a terrible deed done in the park to that poor woman and child.' He paused. 'Is there any word about it around the city?'

Vanucchi's eyes narrowed. He rallied what remained of his coherence to reply.

'None of my lads... knows anythin' about that. There isn't one man that that could have anythin' to do... with the killin' of an innocent woman and child.'

He raised the bottle to his lips. 'If you're lookin' for criminals, Mr Swalla', you know very well there's no shortage of them around here. But not for that kind of business.'

He called to his daughter. 'We'll have another drink... here, Kate. Drinks for Father Laurence and for... our friend... Sergeant Swallow.'

Sunday June 19th, 1887

ELEVEN

Swallow hated the uselessness of Sundays when he was trying to pursue an investigation. Offices and businesses were closed. People could not be found where they were supposed to be. Police divisions worked on half strength. No official mail was delivered. The investigation of crime was brought to a shuddering halt.

Maria usually walked to the 9 o'clock Sunday Mass at the parish church of St Nicholas of Myra in Francis Street. The Grants were a Church of Ireland family, but Maria had embraced her late husband's Roman Catholic faith when they married. And she was a dutiful Catholic.

Even if Swallow wanted to, it would have been unseemly and foolish for him to accompany her to Mass. The last thing either of them needed was an anonymous note to the Commissioner citing him for the scandal of living on licensed premises with a widowed woman and then having the gall to walk her to church.

His head ached from the whiskey of the night before, and for a while he thought about sleeping in to allow the effects of the alcohol to wear off. But the sounds of Carrie, the housekeeper, bustling around in the kitchen penetrated from downstairs. Finally the banging of pots and the rattle of crockery defeated the urge to sleep and he decided to face the day.

Swallow preferred the Carmelite friary on Whitefriar Street because it was unlikely that he would encounter any of the immediate denizens of Thomas Street there. There was a Mass at 10 o'clock, he knew. He felt he needed the quiet and a little time for reflection.

He decided to avoid walking through Francis Street where there was a probability that he would encounter stragglers from Ces Downes's wake. He took a somewhat longer route via Nicholas Street, flanking St Patrick's Cathedral and passing through Bull Alley and Golden Lane.

One of Sunday's mercies was that none of the big newspapers published. There was no *Freeman's Journal* or *Irish Times*. But there was a *Mercury*. He bought a copy at a newsboy's stand by the Cathedral.

The developments in the Chapelizod Gate murders were relegated down the news page, yielding place to a report on the shooting of two rioters by police in County Limerick.

The *Mercury* did not make anything of the mistaken gender of the adult victim at Chapelizod Gate. It reported that the police were investigating the deaths of a woman and child. It mentioned Swallow's name and stated that Dr Lafeyre had visited the scene, but that was all.

He felt relieved that the murders seemed to be out of the limelight, even a little. But the strengthening morning sun and the tolling of the St Patrick's bells hammered into his whiskey hangover.

The church at Whitefriars Street was crowded and noisy with squalling children, denying him his anticipated hour of quiet. The sermon delivered by a mumbling Carmelite was a deadening account of the life of a martyred Pope of the Sixth Century.

After his unsuccessful attempt to find spiritual solace, he took the route down Wexford Street and Aungier Street to the Castle.

Pat Mossop was at work in the otherwise deserted Crime Sergeants' office. Swallow knew from the experience of previous investigations that the wiry, energised Belfast detective stayed with the job when there was work to be done whether it was a Sunday or any other day.

The Book Man had spread his files across two desks. Swallow knew that Mossop was not surprised to see him either, even on a Sunday morning.

'The last of the house-to-house checks should have been done this morning, Boss,' Mossop volunteered. 'They have a few small streets around the back of Chapelizod village and a couple of farm cottages that they had left to cover, but there's nothing of significance in so far, I'm afraid.' He gestured to a sheaf of reports on the desk in front of him.

'Is Stephen Doolan out with the teams himself?' Swallow asked.

'No, Boss, he's on a rest day. He's got interested in some new crowd that want to build up traditional Irish games. They're the "Gaelic Athletic something-or-other." So he's gone off with them to train some young fellows out in County Wicklow. Mind you, I think they don't want policemen at all, so Stephen hasn't told them he's a DMP man.'

Swallow was momentarily angry for Doolan's sake. He knew that the recently-formed Gaelic Athletic Association had declared that policemen and military were not to be admitted to membership. It was a cruel exclusion for individuals like Stephen Doolan who considered himself as good an Irishman as any. He could speak the Irish language from his childhood in West Cork. He was accomplished in Irish dancing. He was a powerful athlete. The greater loss, Swallow reckoned, was the GAA's. What sort of national movement would start by emphasising differences among Irishmen, he wondered? He put the issue from his mind.

'Nothing in from England? From the cross-channel packets or the railway?'

Mossop shook his head. 'Not a thing, Boss. But you know yourself they won't have any clerical staff on a Sunday, so the earliest we might get something would be tomorrow, I'd say.'

Swallow glumly accepted Mossop's verdict, but he resented it. God could hardly have intended that the Sabbath would shut down a double murder investigation. He told Mossop to put away the murder book and to go home to Mrs Mossop and the children.

His sense of depression deepened as he made his way back to Maria Walsh's.

Carrie, the housekeeper, had prepared a Sunday dinner of roast beef with boiled potatoes and fresh vegetables, to be served by Tess, the housemaid. After the main course there was a blancmange. There was a bottle of claret. Swallow drew the cork and poured a small glass of wine for each of them.

A first-floor room over the public house had served for many years as the Grant family dining room. Swallow liked it for its spacious quiet. Muslin curtains filtered the strong sun. The dark mahogany dining furniture was cool to the touch after the heat of the morning.

But the conversation was difficult. They left the wine untouched after the first glass. When the meal was finished, and Tess had departed to spend the afternoon with her own family, Maria started to probe him. It was clear that his spirits were down.

'You're in very poor form, Joe. Is it the murders?'

He saw little point in prevaricating. Maria knew him too well to accept a plea that he was just tired. Swallow had learned that when she asked a serious question she was not content with anything less than a serious answer.

'Yes, it's the murders. I just can't get the boy in particular out of my head. The mind doesn't want to imagine what happened to the child, what he saw and felt in those last few moments. And we're not getting to the bottom of the case nearly quickly enough. I don't even know who they are.'

'But it's only been what, two days?'

'Yes. But it's a long time for a killer who could do that kind of thing to be out there at large.'

'Do you think other people might be in danger; other women… other children?' she asked.

'I don't know, maybe. Anybody who would commit that sort of crime must be a risk to others as well. If someone can commit an act so brutal once – or twice – they can do it again.'

Maria had seen him deal with the burden of an investigation that did not appear to be going anywhere before, but she sensed that there was more to it this time and that it was not just the ghastly circumstances of these particular deaths.

She took his hand across the table.

'I can see that it's affecting you,' she said. 'Are you under a lot of pressure? Does Mr Mallon think this case should be moving more quickly for you?'

He shrugged. 'Ah, Mallon isn't the worst. But he's under pressure too, between the Land League and Parnell and now this bloody royal visit coming up next week. He expects me to keep the books clear on things like this. And I have to be honest. I know my own success rate hasn't been the best in recent times.'

She had heard him talk in similar terms a few months previously about the Elizabeth Logan case.

'I don't think they can expect that you'll solve every single crime you have to investigate,' she said. 'Some things just can't be known and never will be known. I'm sure that's the case in every walk of life, not just in police work.'

He was silent for a moment. 'Sometimes I think that maybe I'm not as sharp as I was. And maybe the criminals are getting smarter. Whoever murdered the woman and child knew how important it was to remove anything that could help to identify them. If we can't establish who they are then the chances become very slim of ever finding out who killed them.'

'You don't have to stay with it, you know,' she said. 'You've got more than 20 years' service so you could take your pension. And if you were out of the job we could run this place together without having to worry about rules and police regulations.'

'I know what you're saying,' he responded. 'But it's your business, your home. It's been your life. It's one thing for me to help out a bit now and again like I do, but I'm not sure how it would be if we were thrown together, working all the long day and night in the bar below.'

'I wouldn't want you to come in as some sort of hired help, Joe.' There was a sharper edge to her words. 'You know that. And if you didn't like it here, I'd be willing to put family loyalty aside, sell the place and set up somewhere else. We could make a completely new start with a new house and a new business. We could move out of the city, to some place by the sea maybe, Howth or Kingstown or Blackrock. We could even go down to your family place in Newcroft.'

Swallow knew that Maria was making a generous and attractive offer. She was attached to the business that had been in her family for four generations. She was offering, if necessary, to sell it on so they could make their lives together. It was as good an offer as he was likely to get, he knew. And it was not the first time that Maria had put it forward.

He wondered if it really was what she would want in the years ahead. The gap in their ages was not unbridgeable, but it was a factor if there was to be a family. He would not be a young father. But she was still of an age at which she would very likely bear children.

Oddly, although she had never mentioned marriage, they had talked about children. Sometimes, when she seemed to be immersed in a book she would look up and read a passage aloud to him. More often than not it was about the interactions between family members, brothers and sisters, parents and children.

She had told him once how she would like to have a little boy and a little girl. She even had names in her head, she told him, one night after the bar had emptied and they sat together in the upstairs parlour.

'And what about you?' she had asked. 'Would you like to have children, a new generation coming up behind you?'

He had searched around for the right words with which to answer. The truth was that he had not really thought about it. He had a happy childhood in Kildare, but he sometimes doubted if he could provide an equally happy upbringing for any children of his own. On the other hand, some of the most contented colleagues he knew in G Division were good family men.

Maybe Maria was right. Perhaps it was time, he thought, to put police life behind him and to take the opportunity of happiness, a settled life, reasonable security and the company of a strong woman he knew he loved.

But was this the right time and were these the right conditions in which to do it? Why would he step away from the job to which he had devoted the best years of his life? Why would he stop doing what he was still reasonably good at, in spite of the long hours, the unpredictability and the arcane disciplinary code? Why would he make room in G Division for some time-server who thought he could be a detective sergeant because he was a Free Mason or knew somebody who was?

'I'll think about it again,' he said, placing his free hand on hers. 'I know I said that before. And I know that you've been very patient about things. But I have to follow this case at least to the point where I can see if it can be cleared up. Something like this can't just be put away in a file and forgotten about.'

She sighed and stood from the dining table.

'I know you so well by now and I can see that you're burdened. I don't see the same spark, the same enthusiasm that I saw even a year ago. You'll do your duty and that's one of the reasons I love you and respect you. But I ask you, please don't make the mistake of thinking that you can forever put off choosing.'

Later, they walked from Grant's to Christ Church, down the dropping curve of Fishamble Street to Wood Quay and across the river by way of Essex Bridge.

In Christ Church yard a platoon of schoolchildren carrying Union flags picked their way around the headstones and memorials. A young teacher, her features hidden under her parasol, was calling out a narrative about the Viking kings and Norman knights whose bones lay underfoot.

Dublin was usually quiet on a Sunday afternoon, but on this particular day there was an incipient sense of fiesta. Red, white and blue bunting hung from the lighting standards. Shop windows were decorated with photographs of the Monarch and her deceased consort,

Prince Albert. Many of the more prominent business houses hung out floral decorations and wreaths.

They had to step nimbly to the pavement crossing Wood Quay to avoid a cycling party of young men and women, seven or eight in all, laughing and calling to each other on their safety bicycles. The women wore colourful summer hats decorated with flowers and ribbons, and the young men sported blue and white blazers. Swallow guessed they were bound for a garden party or something such, perhaps at one of the boat clubs along the Liffey at Islandbridge.

There was time to put down in the afternoon before the opening of the exhibition at the Royal Hibernian Academy.

They took a tram to Sandymount to get the cooling benefit of the sea air as a relief from the heat of the city. They walked far out across the wide, rippled sand almost to the water's edge. There was white foam and strong-smelling seaweed on the low tide.

Across the bay, the coastline of Sutton and Howth reminded Swallow of a Mediterranean scene by Monet. He had never seen the original, of course, but he knew a colour plate copy that hung in the grill room in Jury's Hotel.

Swallow was conscious of his increasing tendency to frame everyday scenes within his artistic experience. He found himself relating people and events to the images he absorbed in the galleries or in books. It was a soothing indulgence, but sometimes he worried. Was it healthy? Could it signify some sort of retreat from reality?

They made their way back to the city centre on the same tram, crowded on the upper deck with joyful, shrieking children and tired parents, returning from the fun of paddling in the sea or sitting in the sun.

The Royal Hibernian Academy on Lower Abbey Street was alive with activity by the time they got there. Suited gentlemen and ladies in bright summer dresses and colourful hats climbed down from carriages at the steps of the building, where they were greeted by a frock-coated official. A splash of red and gold among the crowd signalled the presence of army officers with their ladies.

Three or four constables stood a few feet from the door, eyes scanning the visitors and a small crowd of onlookers that had gathered. Some notables were to attend the opening, Swallow reckoned. There was always the nuisance of beggars from the nearby tenement streets to be dealt with.

One of the constables recognised Swallow and nodded a wordless acknowledgement. As a security precaution, G-Division detectives were not saluted in public. It always struck Swallow as pointless since every G-man's face was well known to the capital's miscreants.

The strains of a string quartet floated through the open door into the warm evening air. Swallow nodded back to the policemen and steered Maria into the foyer behind the frock-coat, nimbly lifting two glasses of Hock from the tray held by a waiter inside the door.

He knew that the main exhibition would be in the extension at the back of the building. Wineglass in hand, he negotiated a path for them both through the crowded ante-hall towards the high-ceilinged room where Miss Purcell's most recent paintings were hanging.

As he led Maria in, elbowing his way through the guests, there was a faint cheering and clapping from the front door occasioned by the arrival of the dignitaries. Two well-dressed men, both wearing the silk top hats that were the definitive mark of position, were flanked by officials of the Academy, clearing a pathway through the crowd.

He recognised the taller of the two. He was perhaps 50 years of age with dark hair turning to grey. He was well-featured, clean-shaven apart from a dark moustache, with a pleasant smile and the easy, confident carriage of a man who considers himself safe against the world. It was Thomas Fitzpatrick, a senior nationalist Alderman of the City Corporation.

The Dublin Corporation was long wrested from the traditional control of the Protestant business classes. As senior Alderman, Fitzpatrick was in line to become Lord Mayor. He was reputed to be one of the wealthiest Catholic businessmen in Dublin. Swallow had read somewhere in a popular newspaper that, although various Dublin matrons had sought to match him over the years with their daughters, he had remained unmarried.

Swallow had never met Thomas Fitzpatrick or spoken to him, but when threats had been made against his life by a Fenian splinter group he had done protection duty at his house on Merrion Square.

Fitzpatrick's wealth was inherited. Swallow knew that his late father had built a fortune exporting Irish cattle to feed Her Majesty's forces overseas.

Fitzpatrick senior had been one of the earliest of his faith and political persuasion in Dublin to achieve significant wealth. His son followed in his footsteps into business and politics. He was a director of the largest cattle-exporting company in Ireland as well as sitting on the boards of half a dozen other leading commercial companies, including newspapers, hotels and retail stores.

Thomas Fitzpatrick was also a patron of the arts. He had contributed to the city's cultural institutions such as the National Museum and the National Gallery.

The second man was younger, with a neatly trimmed beard, shorter in height and somewhat overweight. Swallow recognised him as Howard Smith Berry, the Assistant Under-Secretary, assigned to the Castle from London a year ago with responsibility for security. Swallow had never met him either, even though he had seen him on occasions when business brought him to the Castle's Upper Yard.

Knowledgeable Castle officials understood him to be more influential even than his immediate boss, Sir Redvers Henry Buller, the Under-Secretary. It was said that he was considered a shade too sympathetic to the Irish National League by the government at Westminster. Security issues were now paramount. The Security Secretary, as his title was abbreviated, was pre-eminent in influence among the Castle bureaucrats.

He led Maria through to the main exhibition. Taking two catalogues from a stand, he gave one to Maria and started a circumnavigation of the room.

Miss Purcell specialised in portraits of the aristocracy and persons prominent in the administration. It was said that she could command an astonishing 50 guineas for a commission. Swallow recognised the framed features of a judge before whom he had once given evidence. There were images of military men and aristocratic-looking women in the adjoining frames.

Stopping in front of the image of a robed and mitred archbishop, he thought ruefully of his own amateur dabblings on leave days. With practice, he would improve on his seascapes and still life, he knew. But to capture a human face so perfectly, with the character and the soul shining through, was a talent to which he knew he could never aspire.

'I'll wager that this is a good deal more pleasant than crime work,' a bantering voice said beside him.

It was the *Evening Telegraph* reporter, Simon Sweeney. He was turned out for the warm evening in a smart, lightweight suit, a silver-topped cane in one hand and copy of the exhibition catalogue in the other.

'Mr Sweeney,' Swallow acknowledged the greeting. 'You'll have to understand that policemen can have an artistic side too. I'd like to introduce you to a friend of mine, Mrs Walsh.'

Maria smiled when Sweeney bowed. 'I'm enchanted,' he said, 'and very glad to see that a hard-working detective can have such delightful company on an occasion like this.'

He turned back to Swallow. 'I wouldn't doubt that you had an artistic side, Sergeant. But until you introduced me to the charming Mrs Walsh, I thought you might be on duty, what with the day that's in it and the presence of these important dignitaries.' He gestured with his catalogue towards the party of guests now advancing across the lobby.

'I'm here to discharge a family commitment,' Swallow answered. 'But as it happens, I do admire Miss Purcell's work.'

'And what about you, Mr Sweeney?' Maria asked pleasantly. 'Are you a man who appreciates the arts?'

Sweeney smiled self-deprecatingly.

'I'm a bit like Sergeant Swallow, Mrs Walsh. I'm just an admirer. But in fact I'm working here this evening. I'm a member of a species that Mr Swallow doesn't much approve of, the press that is. I have to cover Alderman Fitzpatrick's speech. Then I go on to a dinner being given by the Lord Mayor for Mr Parnell at the Mansion House. The press has to provide a full record of public events.'

Swallow could not resist the opportunity for gentle retaliation.

'Well, I guess the Lord Mayor's dinner will be a good deal more pleasant than visiting crime scenes at dawn.'

'You shouldn't misunderstand, Sergeant. Journalists work hard at these events. What people like Fitzpatrick say at this time can have consequences. It's not more than a few months since the whole balance of power at Westminster rested on the Irish members. And who knows when that might be so again? Misquote one of the politicians or miss an important point in what they say and your head is on the editor's chopping block.'

'With any luck the speeches mightn't be too lengthy,' Swallow ventured hopefully, 'and we can all enjoy the exhibition. I doubt that this is an occasion for making important political statements.'

'I wouldn't be optimistic,' Sweeney grinned. 'It's going to be a week of long speeches. I imagine the police will be at full stretch too. Speaking of which, that's an extraordinary development in the Chapelizod Gate inquiry. How on earth did you take a dead woman for a dead man?'

Swallow felt himself growing irritated. 'I'm not really going to discuss that with you here. Not in the presence of a lady. You can use your own imagination.'

Sweeney looked concerned for a moment.

'Of course. I apologise, Mrs Walsh. That was very thoughtless of me.'

He turned back to Swallow. 'So has there been any progress on the cases? The whole city seems to be terrified. We heard that the Lord Lieutenant has asked for extra protection at the Viceregal Lodge because Lady Londonderry and her ladies are in mortal fear.'

'You can inquire of course, Mr Sweeney, but I can't tell you anything,' Swallow retorted. 'And if there's extra protection being put on at the Viceregal Lodge I wouldn't know about it.'

'Joe, over here.' He heard his name being called by a woman's voice from across the room. 'Joe, Maria, hello.'

It took him a moment to realise that the smart-looking lady in the green summer dress calling his name was Harriet. He had to adjust from the childhood image of his younger sister to that of a 21-year-old, grown woman.

Harriet was waving from beside a window giving out onto the rear of the building. Swallow saw that she was with a group of four or five young people, all talking animatedly, wineglasses in hand.

'Will you excuse us, Mr Sweeney,' he said. 'Mrs Walsh and I have to meet someone.'

They crossed to where Harriet stood. She kissed them both on the cheeks and greeted them in Irish.

'*Dia daoibh, tá súil agam go bhfuil sibh go maith.*'

Swallow hoped his irritation did not show. He disliked the conceit that was becoming commonplace with Irish nationalists of greeting others in a language that they could not understand.

When neither he nor Maria responded, Harriet said tersely, 'It means 'God be with you both. I hope you're keeping well.'

She turned to her companions. 'I'd like to introduce you to my brother, Joseph, and to his friend, Mrs Maria Walsh.'

Swallow was relieved that at least she had the wit on this occasion not to use what she claimed was the Irish language form of his name. When she introduced him previously as '*Seosamh*' he had been angry.

She smiled at Swallow and Maria.

'I'm very glad you could come. Now, I'd like you to meet my friends.' Harriet nodded to two young men. 'This is Mr John Horan and I believe you have met Mr James – *Seamus* – O'Donnell already.'

Swallow recognised O'Donnell as the young man he had encountered previously with Harriet in the coffee shop. He was perhaps 24 or 25 years of age, not tall, slightly built, with a full, dark moustache and prematurely thinning hair. His suit was damp with perspiration from the heat of the crowded room.

There were polite nods from the two men and more greetings in Irish.

'I'm sorry I didn't get to call yesterday as I had hoped,' Swallow told Harriet. 'I'm involved in a serious investigation and I had to drop everything else. But what I really want to know is how did the examinations go?'

'Oh, they were fine, Joe. It wasn't pleasant being locked indoors with this wonderful weather outside.' Harriet grimaced. 'I read about those dreadful murders at the Chapelizod Gate and I knew you were involved in the inquiry. Your name was in the newspaper.'

She waved a hand at the others. 'My brother is famous you know,' she said.

O'Donnell raised his wineglass mockingly to Swallow and Maria. 'Oh yes, we know all about the great Sergeant Swallow, doing England's work in Dublin Castle.'

Swallow saw Maria's face flush in anger. Harriet looked momentarily embarrassed but said nothing.

O'Donnell took a noisy gulp from his glass. Swallow realised that the young man was more than slightly drunk. He decided it was best to laugh off the clumsy attempt at provocation.

Swallow grinned. 'Well, Mr O'Donnell, we all have to earn a living. Even if in my case it's not a particularly good one.'

'Oh, I wouldn't say that. There's a long tradition attaching to your kind, Sergeant Swallow, of selling their country for 30 pieces of silver.'

The insult was delivered with a leer. Now Swallow flushed too. He retaliated.

'I'd be interested to know what it is you do yourself for a living, Mr O'Donnell. It isn't a whole lot, I'd say.'

Without waiting for an answer, he turned to Harriet.

'Maybe it would be best if we went to the other room to talk about family matters for a few moments and then you can rejoin your friends?'

'Oh, I'm not sure… Seamus wants to make a protest about Fitzpatrick and the Assistant Under-Secretary.'

Swallow's sense of danger activated. 'He wants to do what?'

'There's going to be a protest about Irish art being exploited for England's empire.'

At that moment, Thomas Fitzpatrick and Smith Berry started to cross the room, preceded by the official who had greeted them at the main door.

The group made its way to a dais from which the Alderman would speak. As Fitzpatrick mounted the steps, Swallow realised that half a dozen young men had emerged from the crowd to form a semicircle around the low platform.

Fitzpatrick smiled, and raised one hand to acknowledge the audience. With the other he went to draw his script from an inside pocket. The hum of conversation around the room dropped.

On cue, two of the young men sprinted up the steps. One made to grab Fitzpatrick's script, but the older man's reflexes were surprisingly fast and he fended off his attacker with a palmed hand.

The second young man threw himself forward, using his body weight to propel Fitzpatrick towards the edge of the platform. An Academy official went to pull the assailant away, but a third man who had leaped to the platform felled the official with a fist to the side of the head.

Fitzpatrick was agile. He recovered his balance and stepped nimbly to the floor. Two or three Academy staff members immediately formed a protective phalanx around him.

'Get out of the room now,' Swallow told Maria. 'Go outside and wait for me. There's trouble here.'

As she moved away, he saw O'Donnell climb the steps of the dais. He turned to face the audience, arms outstretched dramatically.

'You have no reason to celebrate British art or the Jubilee of the British Queen!' he shouted. 'The British Queen and British art should be kept in Britain and out of Ireland. We want Irish art that reflects Ireland's character. Let Thomas Fitzpatrick support Irish art if he wants to.'

The other young men who had gathered around the dais began to chant in unison.

'Down with British art. We want Irish culture for the Irish people.'

'No British Queen while the Irish are denied their farms.'

The felled Academy official was on his feet now. He aimed a retaliatory blow at the young man who had hit him. He fell forward, knocking hard against the Security Secretary who staggered against the side of the platform.

Swallow pushed forward through the crowd and placed himself in front of the Security Secretary. A booted foot cracked against his ankle and he fell forward into the melee.

Something solid hit his wrist. He saw a hand reach past him as if grabbing towards Smith Berry and he punched hard and upwards towards where he estimated its owner's head should be. A shock ran the length of his arm as his fist connected with an unseen face.

Then strong fingers closed around his throat from behind. He struck backwards with his elbow but failed to connect. The clamp around his throat tightened. His lungs sought air but there was nothing. He felt himself weakening.

Suddenly, the pressure eased. He squirmed and turned to see Simon Sweeney with a headlock on the man who had been throttling him. The journalist pushed the man to the floor and then brought his cane down hard across his face. Swallow saw blood spurt from his assailant's mouth and nose.

Another man lunged at Smith Berry. Swallow got to his feet and threw his right arm around the attacker's neck and seized his left arm at the wrist. He shoved it high up the man's back and heard a gratifying shriek of pain.

There was a sharp whistle-blast. Swallow saw uniforms and realised that the constables from the street had arrived. Two of them placed themselves in front of the Security Secretary. Another helped Thomas Fitzpatrick to his feet, assisted by Sweeney. Between them the constables and the journalist half pushed, half pulled the two men from the ruck and out the door to safety.

Swallow realised that his prisoner was James O'Donnell.

One of the constables, who was struggling to hold O'Donnell's friend, Horan, shouted, 'Gun! This fella has a gun!'

The constable grasped his prisoner's wrist. Swallow could see that Horan was trying to pull a revolver clear of his jacket pocket with his other hand.

Another policeman saw the butt of the weapon and went to wrestle it from him. There was a deafening bang as a shot discharged into the floor.

The constable holding Horan hit him hard with his fist on the back of the head. He sank to the ground, the gun clattering to the floor beside him. The officer grabbed the weapon and handed it to Swallow.

Swallow recognised it as a *Reichsrevolver*, Prussian army issue. He broke it open. All six chambers were loaded.

Another constable snapped handcuffs onto Horan and then ran his hands over O'Donnell's clothing.

'This fella's clear now. There's nothing else here.' He closed another set of handcuffs around O'Donnell's wrists.

The room was filling with uniforms. Two or three of Swallow's immediate colleagues from G Division had arrived as well.

He was breathless from the struggle on the floor. Darts of pain shot along his right leg, but there was no difficulty putting his weight on it. It would be bruised and sore, but there was nothing broken, he reckoned.

He realised thankfully that Harriet too had disappeared. He turned to a uniformed sergeant.

'We need a car to take these two fellows to Exchange Court. Arrange for them to go in separate cells in the Lower Yard. We have a lot of questions to ask them.'

O'Donnell glared defiantly, his hands cuffed behind his back. 'You can ask all the questions you want, Swallow. As Irishmen we defy your so-called authority.'

Swallow fought hard to maintain his self-control.

'I'm not sure you understand how much trouble you're in, Mr O'Donnell,' he said as evenly as he could.

He pointed to Horan. 'You're engaged in a common enterprise with your friend here. That gun might just as easily have been in your pocket as far as the law is concerned.'

O'Donnell leered again. 'So what about your sister then, is she in trouble too? Or will her brother the G-man look after her?'

Swallow wanted to hit him. Instead, he forced a cold smile.

'We don't need to talk about my sister now, Mr O'Donnell. We're going to spend a long time talking to you. If you have any brains at all, and I'd say there's a serious doubt about that, you'll need to start using them.'

Monday June 20th, 1887

TWELVE

The two Grand Canal bargemen had been at work an hour before dawn, feeding coal and slag into the plate-iron burner under the steam engine until it rumbled and hissed at an even, steady pace.

Monday saw the sixth day of the heatwave.

They cast off from their berth in the Grand Canal Dock before 5 o'clock and nosed their squat, graceless vessel into the first lock as the sun rose. The first light caught the headlands that define Dublin Bay: Killiney, Dalkey and Howth. Then it spread across Kingstown, Blackrock and Sandymount Strand, touching the roofs and windows of the coastal houses.

The stopman at the tiller saw it catch the rooftops along Clanwilliam Place as the master opened the valve to engage the single-stroke engine that would power them on their voyage to the middle of Ireland. Theirs was the first barge of the day, bound with a cargo of Yorkshire malt for Shannon Harbour.

At four miles an hour – if the locks operated well – they would be at Tullamore by nightfall. That was a pleasing prospect. The public houses by the harbour had a welcome for bargemen with money in their pockets. There was music with fiddles and squeezeboxes and dancing and some not-too-particular women in one or two of the taverns around the town. If they failed to make good time, it would be the misery of Phillipstown for the night, a grey little place that no bargeman had anything good to say about.

A person walking the line of the Grand Canal from the Dock to the hotel at Portobello will scarcely notice the rise in the ground. It is a distance of about two miles from where the canal joins the estuary of the

Liffey and the ascent is no more than 60 feet above sea level. But the climb means that a vessel's upward progress along this stretch of waterway is dependent upon the navigation of no fewer than six locks.

First, the lower gates open outward and the barge nudges forward into the lifting chamber. Then the gates swing shut behind and the forward gates are winched open to allow the rising water to flood into the chamber, taking the barge to the level of the next section of the canal.

It is a skilled task both for the boatmen and the lock-keeper. If the forward gates are opened too quickly, the force of the flow can turn a vessel so that it wedges transversely between the granite walls of the lock. The bow must be kept forward, using tiller and gaff and, if the winds are high, securing the craft with heavy-duty ropes. A careless bargeman, or a lock-keeper who is too hasty, courts catastrophe.

Neither the master nor the stopman nor any of the lock-keepers that morning were other than conscientious about their tasks. They were careful, watchful and methodical. The uncommon heat of recent days had created the inevitable hazard of young children swimming, diving and jumping in the canal. It was only at the sixth lock, at Portobello, that the stopman at the tiller took his eyes off his forward task and turned his back to a morning breeze that was more imagined than real in order to put a match to the pipe he had filled a while earlier.

As he dropped the spent match in the canal, his eye caught something dark below him in the water by the tiller blade. He leaned backward across the safety rail and peered down into the murkiness. Then he raised his hand and shouted against the thud of the engine and the roar of the water tumbling into the lock.

'Lads... hold on... there's somethin' down here...'

Neither the master nor the lock-keeper heard him the first time.

The stopman pounded the barge's metal hull with a steel-tipped gaff and roared.

'Stop th' engine and shut the bloody gates! There's a body!'

His companion put the boiler lever to the neutral position and stepped back along the deck, impatience and irritation on his face.

'What's the problem, Dickie? We're makin' slow enough ground as it is.'

'I'm tellin' ye, there's a body, a woman I think, caught down by the tiller blade. Stop th'engine!.'

The master, in turn, grasped the safety rail and craned his head down towards the green surface of the canal. He too saw the red of the woman's clothing refracted through the water and the flow of her dark hair, streaming out behind the tiller blade.

Drowned bodies are no novelty to bargemen. His groan was the frustration of knowing that the schedule of the day was lost.

'Ah Jaysus, fuck it… fuck it… how did she get there?'

He stepped back to the engine house and angrily rammed the shut-off valve home, killing the power. The lock-keeper, measuring the scene with an experienced eye, hauled to reverse the greased wheel that drove the levers on the gates, shutting the water flow.

Morning birdsong filled the vacuum created by the silencing of the engine and the stopping up of the waterfall.

They used the berthage ropes and the gaffs to move the barge back out of the sixth lock and ran the ropes to an elm tree along the grassy bank. Here, a man could get down to the water level in safety even though he might risk a partial wetting in the reeds.

As the senior man, it fell to the master to don the India-rubber waders supplied by the company and to splash out through the shallows. He pushed the gaff before him to probe the water under the tiller blade. The gaff's hook caught the woman's clothing in the second thrust and he hauled heavily on the long, birch staff.

The body came away from the tiller blade, leaving a half-petticoat showing a dull, ragged red in the water. The others grasped the staff behind the master and between them they drew the weight in through the reeds to the canal's earthen bank.

It was not yet 7 o'clock. There were no passers-by, and the only sounds were the lapping of the canal water and the birdsong. They saw that the woman was young, in her twenties. Her long, dark hair was matted with sedge and weed. The face and the head were badly marked with blue and black abrasions that might have come, the men knew, from the turning of the tiller blade or the impact of the granite walls in any of the six locks they had traversed in the past hour.

They both saw that the skull above the left temple was badly gashed. The skin peeled back in a V-shaped flap, upwards across the forehead, showing white bone, splintered and broken.

There would be no Tullamore tonight, or even Phillipstown.

The master wiped his hands on his trousers and shook his head.

'Ah, fuck it… this is dirty work. We're here for the day… fuck it anyway…'

He turned to the lock-keeper.

'Do ye know where to find a bobby at this hour of the mornin'?'

'I do, surely. There's nearly always one on the beat, 'cross by the Portobello hotel.'

'Well, go and get him, like a decent man. Ye can tell him he's got work to do… for a change.'

THIRTEEN

The uniformed divisions of the Dublin Metropolitan Police worked an eight-hour, three-shift system, known as 'the regular.' Some G-Division men also worked 'the regular,' ensuring that armed detective support was available around the clock for the uniformed divisions.

But for the most part, G-Division officers worked what was called 'inquiries shift,' a period of duty that could be anything from 8 to 12 hours, as determined by the workload of the day and at the diktat of the shift inspector or senior sergeant.

Four detective sergeants and a score of detective officers had assembled for the inquiries shift. At 10.30 they would meet in 'parade' to be briefed on the city's crime tally from the previous night and to be assigned their day's duties.

By the time the day room had filled for parade, the sun had already begun to raise blisters on the lead paint of the window frames. Although the sash windows had been fully opened along the length of the room, the air was already fetid and humid. The detectives jostled for sitting space on desks and tabletops where there might be a draught of air. Jackets were draped across knees and collars were unbuttoned. There was a heavy odour of perspiration and stale smoke.

Swallow had worked at Exchange Court until after midnight on Sunday completing his report on the incident at the Royal Hibernian Academy. A couple of G-men questioned James O'Donnell and John Horan separately, but without significant success. Neither man was prepared to answer any questions beyond giving their names, addresses and occupations.

That neither prisoner was forthcoming at this stage did not surprise or dishearten the G-men. The 'politicals' were always like that at first.

Under Balfour's Coercion Act, the G Division could hold them more or less indefinitely in police custody without bringing them before a court or lodging them in prison.

It suited investigating officers to hold suspects in close proximity while preliminary questioning was going on. Shuttling forward and back to one or other of the prisons was time consuming, and there was always the risk that suspected persons might establish contact with other inmates in prison and thus be fortified in their resolve to resist interrogation.

There were no such risks in the cells in the Lower Yard behind Exchange Court. After a day or two, the dankness, the inedible food and the attentions of vermin usually persuaded prisoners to start talking to their captors.

The G Division's intelligence files linked the two men to a splinter group calling itself the 'Hibernian Brothers'. It saw itself as providing armed support for the actions of the Land League, even though the newly aligned National League publicly dissociated itself from violent action.

Horan, the intelligence recorded, was employed by the post office. O'Donnell described himself as a student and part-time journalist, but the files did not offer any details of where he studied or where he plied his supposed trade.

Swallow was secretly relieved that the two suspects had elected to stay quiet for the moment. The less said about Harriet and her friends the better.

He knew that as soon as he could get an hour or two, he had to talk urgently to his younger sister about the dangerous waters in which she was moving. He was angry and worried. With luck, he calculated, there would be a safe interval before one or other of the prisoners would want to talk in the hope of saving their own skins.

Swallow knew the pattern. Initial defiance would begin to fade after a few nights in the cells where they would be held in isolation from one another. Some time after that, the prospect of 10 or 15 years in a prison cell would inevitably cause someone to rethink the policy of non-cooperation.

For the moment, though, he had to deal with other matters.

'Duck' Boyle was the detective inspector in charge of G Division's inquiries shift this morning.

If there were moments still when Joe Swallow bitterly regretted the failure of his medical career, they usually occurred in the days or nights when Boyle was rostered to run the detective office.

Shortly before 10.30, Duck Boyle was standing in the centre of the parade room, a bundle of files under one arm and a sheaf of incident reports clutched in his right hand. Perspiration rolled down his florid face, coursing along the fleshy rolls of his squat neck and forming into patches of dampness on his shirt and waistcoat.

'Holy Mother of Christ,' he waved the sheaf of incident forms at nobody in particular. 'What was going on last night in this bloody city? How're we going to deal with all this? Jesus, we'll all be on the transfer list.'

In Swallow's estimation, Boyle embodied police bureaucracy at its worst. His sole object was to keep the books and the records accurate, proofing himself against any possible reprimand or mark of disfavour from higher authority. Weighed down with volumes of regulations and green cloth files, he scuttled around the detective office in a curious, waddling gait, as fast as his short, corpulent frame would allow, earning himself the soubriquet 'Duck' or 'Duckfoot.'

The contempt in which Swallow and most of his colleagues held Boyle was compounded by his being devoid of detective skills. Rumour had it that he was the landlord of half a dozen tenement buildings around the city, the management of which occupied most of his energies and all of his intellectual capacities.

His appointment to the G Division was a mystery. As far as was known, Boyle was not a churchgoer and he swore like an artillery man. It was said that his advancement was effected through his brother, a Church of Ireland canon and reputedly a man of influence in the corridors of power.

'That bloody canon must have had a lot of pull to get Duck into the G Division,' Stephen Doolan observed one evening as he and Swallow worked their way through a few pints in a public house at the South City Markets, neighbouring the Castle. 'The shagger couldn't track an elephant in snow.'

'The whole city seems to have gone berserk last night,' Boyle was shrieking as he stabbed a pudgy finger into the sheaf of incident forms. 'How in the name of God are we going to deal with all this?'

His voice rose a further octave when he saw Swallow coming into the office. 'Swalla', you took your time gettin' in, didn't ye? And the whole city of Dublin bein' swept be crime an' depredation.'

Swallow had learned that the best method of defence with Boyle was to attack.

'I haven't been sitting around idle,' he said sharply. 'I've already been over to talk to Chief Mallon. I've been down to the morgue with Dr Lafeyre. I'm to parade here at 10.30, before getting on with the murder investigations,' Swallow said. 'I believe it's there in the orders for the day.'

He nodded to the sheaf of papers in Boyle's hand and glanced at the wall clock. 'It's two minutes to the half hour.'

'Jesus,' Boyle wailed. 'That's a great attitude and we facing a bloody epidemic.'

He waddled to the trestle table running across the centre of the room and began to fling down the incident reports, one after another.

'We have two dead bodies last Friday at the Chapelizod Gate and then we learn that havin' spent a full day investigatin' them as a man and a boy, Sergeant Swalla' finds out that the man is a woman.' He shook his head. 'Jesus… could you believe it? Six breakin' an' enterin' in the A Division, four shops along James's Street and two private dwellin's in the Coombe. Murtagh's public house in Pimlico half burned out with a bucket of oil flung through the window. Two Fenians of some sort arrested for attemptin' an assault on the Assistant Under-Secretary and Alderman Fitzpatrick and for possession of a loaded German revolver. It seems as if Sergeant Swallow was on the spot in that particular incident so he hasn't been altogether wastin' his time.'

He paused to glare around at the detectives. They tried hard to give an impression of shared outrage. He hurled three more incident reports to the table.

'There's four serious assaults, two men across the river in Mecklenburgh Street and two men in Rutland Street. There's one victim critical in the Meath Hospital with his skull broke' open and another in Doctor Steevens' with an eye gone. I remember when Sunday was supposed to be a day of prayer and reconciliation.

'And…,' he threw the remaining papers on the table, 'there's fears bein' expressed by Lady Londonderry about intruders in the grounds at the Viceregal Lodge… the bloody Viceregal Lodge, no less.'

Swallow acknowledged to himself that it was an unusual night's toll.

'Then, as if we hadn't anythin' else to worry about, we're goin' to have to watch the gangsters at Ces Downes's removal and funeral today. The scum will be full a' drink and ready for fight over whatever she left behind her.'

Boyle slumped his shoulders like a man who had finally calculated the certainty of defeat in the face of overwhelming odds.

'Meanwhile,' he intoned wearily, 'the crack detective of the Dublin Metropolitan Police can't even put a name to the poor woman found murdered with her child dead beside her. Mind you, I suppose at least we know the gender of the deceased at this stage.'

Swallow winced inwardly at the jibe.

Tony Swann, a detective who specialised in organised criminal gangs, chimed in cheerily from a window-ledge, 'Ah hell, Inspector, it's not the end of the world. Sure we've a full unit here and the day is long.'

One of the curiosities of the detective branch was that it counted half a dozen men among its ranks whose names were ornithological synonyms. In addition to Swallow and Swann it had Wren, Crowe, Pigeon and Swift. A uniformed superintendent who fancied himself as a wit once dubbed G Division 'the birdie club.' It did not go down well with John Mallon.

'Speak when yer spoken to, Swann,' Boyle hissed. 'Don't be tryin' to make light of things. Ye might bear in mind that the detective unit from College Street is out on them breakin' and enterin' cases. We'll get no help off them today.'

'Swann's right,' Swallow said. 'We can deal with things by dividing them out sensibly. Let's have a look at the incident reports and see if we can get a grip of what's going on.'

He scanned the forms thrown on the table by Boyle, drawing the reports on the assault cases together. He recognised the names of the assault victims and saw the pattern at once.

The two men badly beaten in Rutland Street were runners for Charlie Vanucchi. One of the victims of the attack in Mecklenburgh Street was Tommy 'Tiger' McKnight, Vinny Cussen's right-hand man, and Murtagh's public house in Pimlico was a favoured drinking haunt of Cussen's gang.

The turf war between the Cussen and the Vanucchi factions had broken out already. Boyle might have stared at the sheets for a month and not seen the connections. Swallow reckoned it was better to deal with it diplomatically.

'I've got a couple of good informants across the river in the C Division right now, Inspector,' he said. 'They know what's going on. Put Swann on it, I'll give him the names of my contacts and let him look after these assaults. That'll cut the workload.'

Swallow's solution had been put forward mildly and pleasantly, but Boyle was not going to be pacified.

'You won't tell me how to run me unit, Swalla" he snarled. 'I'll decide who does what.'

Swallow shrugged his shoulders. Behind Boyle's back he saw Tony Swann raise his eyebrows towards the ceiling. The door opened and the constable operating the ABC telegraph in the Lower Yard put his head into the room.

'Urgent crime report here for the duty inspector.'

He handed a manila folder to one of the detectives who passed it across the room to Boyle. He read it silently for moment.

'Jesus, have mercy. Is there no end to it?'

He waved the folder in front of him. 'Now there's a dead woman in the canal by Portobello Bridge. The sergeant at Lad Lane says there's signs of foul play.'

He jerked his head towards Swallow.

'Swallow, you can get up to Portobello and see about this woman. She's up there on the canal bank with a couple a' constables holdin' the scene. There's a director of the Grand Canal company on the tele-phone to the Commissioner's office, roarin' to get his feckin' boat under way. Ye'd think it was a voyage t'Austhralia they were at.'

For a moment Swallow thought about protesting the instruction to attend the scene at Portobello.

He had his hands full with the Chapelizod Gate inquiry. If he protested, though, it would invite further vituperation from Boyle. It was easier to go along with it and hope that it was nothing too complicated.

'I've got a conference on the Chapelizod Gate case so I can't get to Portobello until maybe 12 o'clock,' Swallow interjected as Boyle began to hand out the incident sheets to the detectives.

Boyle waved his pencil at two officers perched on the window-ledge.

'Officer Feore and Constable Collins, you'll do the assaults.'

Mick Feore combined intuition with valuable experience built over his years of service. Collins was a neophyte, just newly arrived from uniformed duties. Although he worked in plain clothes he was not yet formally appointed as a detective.

'Seein' as I'm the senior man, naturally I'll g'up to the Viceregal Lodge with Tony Swann and Pat Mossop. I'll want to check that all the protection posts are manned and to reassure the household that they have nothin' to fear,' Boyle announced.

He waved the pencil again, pointing to Swann and to Mossop who had been sitting quietly, his murder book on his lap, on a low filing cabinet near the windows.

The whole unit knew that Boyle would want to do the job himself at the Viceregal Lodge on the off chance that he might ingratiate himself with some minor official. In taking along two experienced officers – Swann and Mossop – he would minimise the risk of being exposed in the event of encountering any problem.

'I've told you that I've got a crime conference here,' Swallow said, 'and Pat Mossop is the Book Man on the murders, so I can't release him to work with Collins on the assaults.'

Duck Boyle stood stock still.

'Don't cut across me, Swalla',' he hissed. 'Ye can get somewan else for Book Man. I'm the man who decides th'orders o' the day.'

There was silence across the detective office.

'I'm not contesting that, Inspector,' Swallow was precise and respectful. 'But Chief Superintendent Mallon agreed to have Mossop with me on this case.'

Boyle's eyes darted around. He passed his hand nervously across his eyes. He had to find a way out of this without loss of face. He turned to Mossop who was still seated on the filing cabinet, attempting to appear unconcerned as his two immediate superiors battled it out for his services for the day.

'It's your loss, Mossop. I'm givin' you the chance to do some real detective work o'yer own makin'. But if the chief says yer to carry the book for Swalla' I can't argue. I'm sorry, Son.'

He shook his head with feigned sympathy and then glared at Swallow. 'And who else, if ye don't mind, do ye intend to take off me roster today?'

'I'll need Swift or Feore. They led the search teams on house-to-house at Chapelizod Gate and around the area by the river. We have to collate what information we have after those inquiries.'

'Jesus Christ!' Boyle threw his hands towards the ceiling in a gesture of despair. 'Mossop *and* Swift or Feore? How am I expected to do this bloody job?'

He resumed the task of handing out the incident forms, shaking his head and muttering as if he had been the recipient of deeply tragic news.

He pointed a finger at Eddie Shanahan, another newly minted detective, who was sitting near Mossop. 'Shanahan, you'll do the assaults inquiry with Collins.'

Shanahan stood. He took the incident forms from Boyle's sweaty hands and distributed them to his colleagues. They only needed a few moments in which their eyes ran over the details.

The youthful Collins looked up from the forms. 'Sure, it's as plain as the nose on my face, Inspector. The Cussen and Moore gangs have started their war already.'

Shanahan concurred. 'That's how it looks to me too. Swann knows most of these fellows better than any of us. He should be doing this job… see if he can knock some sense into them before it hots up.'

'Don't even think of arguin' about it,' Boyle growled. 'I've tried to do me best here. Detective Sergeant Swalla' has his orders from higher authority. So you can best please me now be' gettin' on wid your duty.'

Shanahan shrugged his shoulders. He folded the incident forms and put them in his pocket.

'Now,' Boyle raised his voice, 'Every wan o' ye otherwise is on observation and inquiries for the Jubilee tomorrow and for Ces Downes's funeral today. I have a list of special posts that I'm givin' out now. I want every detail recorded. Every suspicious man, woman or child that moves in an' around the city is to be questioned and their movements noted.'

He distributed another set of sheets from one of the folders under his arm. He drew himself to his full height to deliver a parting oration to the shift.

'There's Fenians and Land Leaguers and God knows who else that wants to disrupt the celebrations tomorra'. And there's a lot o' smart lads that'll be out to tear down flags and decorations that're put up be people over their shops and offices. They're to be stopped. Restrain them. Use the baton if you have to. If they're arrested, let the uniforms take them to the Bridewell. As G-men, yez have to stay on the street.'

The G-men gave no indication of being inspired by Boyle's exhortations. It would be a long day in the heat of the city streets. Some of the group began to move towards the door, anxious to be out of the tension and the bad air of the detective office.

'Not so fast. Not so fast,' Boyle moved to block the exit. 'We'll present accoutrements an' firearms first, please.'

There was a collective groan. Regulations required the completion of the ceremony before each shift went on duty, but no inspector apart from Duck Boyle ever insisted on it.

Each man dug in his pockets and produced notebooks, baton and handcuffs and placed them on the trestle table. Then the heavy Webley Bulldog revolvers came out of the shoulder-holsters and were placed along side the 'accoutrements.'

Boyle walked along the table counting the notebooks, sets of hand-cuffs, the batons and the Bulldogs, telling each item off against the men scattered around the room with a pudgy finger. He then drew himself to his full, corpulent height and assumed a sorrowful expression. It was intended to indicate he was anything but satisfied with his unit's pre-paredness to confront and put down crime and disorder wherever they might find it across the city of Dublin.

FOURTEEN

Before his 11 o'clock briefing with the inquiry team on the Chapeli-zod Gate murders, Swallow equipped himself with a set of photographs from the scene and presented himself to the clerk at Mallon's office.

'He's expecting me to bring him up to date on the murders in the park,' he told the clerk, who had standing instructions not to have the Chief Superintendent disturbed while he read through the morning's divisional reports.

'He is, it seems,' the clerk acknowledged grudgingly.

He rose and knocked on the door connecting to Mallon's private office. On the call of 'enter' he stepped in. Swallow could hear muffled voices. The clerk came out and jerked a thumb over his shoulder.

'G'wan, Sergeant. He'll see you. He'll want to hear about what happened down at the Royal Hibernian Academy last night. He's just finished the report… And just to mark your own cards, there's somebody with him.'

Swallow was not surprised to learn that Mallon would want a first-hand account of the incident at the Academy. At the best of times, anything with a hint of politics was a matter of the gravest consequence to John Mallon. On the eve of the Queen's Jubilee and with a royal visit just a week away any possible threat to the safety of a senior Castle official would be very close to the top of his list of priorities.

He could give Mallon a full account of what had happened after Horan, O'Donnell and their friends had attacked the platform, but he hoped that his sharp-minded boss would not press him too hard on other details of what happened and why he was there. It was essential to keep Harriet out of the narrative.

Mallon sat behind his oak desk, the sash window behind his head wide open in the vain hope that some current of cool air might blow in from the Yard. Seated beside the Chief Superintendent was the Assistant Under-Secretary for Security, Howard Smith Berry.

Swallow tried to conceal his surprise but reckoned he was not wholly successful. It was rare for any of the grandees of the Upper Yard to descend to the buildings in the Lower Yard. It could indicate a catastrophe or it could be intended as a compliment. Swallow simply did not have sufficient experience to decide which this was.

Mallon gestured towards Swallow. 'Mr Smith Berry, may I introduce Detective Sergeant Swallow. You probably didn't have the opportunity of a formal introduction when last you met.'

Smith Berry stood, leaned across the desk and extended his hand. He smiled, much as a gentleman might smile at a helpful shop assistant or a particularly efficient waiter, Swallow thought.

'You did damned good work at the Royal Hibernian Academy last night, Swallow. It's noted. And I considered it appropriate that I should tell you so myself in the presence of the Chief Superintendent.'

Swallow thought he saw a slightly uncomfortable look in Mallon's eyes. The chief nodded, gesturing to a chair and indicating that Swallow should sit.

'I think you know, Sergeant, that we've done well to get through the week leading up to the Jubilee without any major incidents in the city,' Mallon said. 'There's been trouble in a few places around the country, but this business at the Academy could have been very serious, very serious indeed.'

He gestured to a selection of the morning's newspapers on the desk. Swallow strained to read the upside-down headlines.

SHOTS FIRED AT ACADEMY
OUTRAGE AGAINST ALDERMAN FITZPATRICK AND MR SMITH BERRY

With mild relief he read a line of type below.

POLICE FOIL AN ATTACK. A GUN IS SEIZED.

Then he saw another set of headlines on the opposite page.

POLICE MISTAKE IN MURDERS INQUIRY
THE DEAD 'MAN' IS A WOMAN
HOW A SHOCKING CASE IS MISHANDLED
TERRIBLE BLUNDER BY G DIVISION IN
PARK MURDERS

He cursed silently. He had hoped that the daily newspapers might have moved on, leaving the story to their counterparts that published on Sundays.

'This incident was potentially much more serious than the murders you're investigating, bad as they are,' Mallon said. 'As Mr Smith Berry says, you did well at the scene. He or Alderman Fitzpatrick might have been injured or worse if you hadn't moved in so quickly.'

'Thank you, Sir. But I wouldn't make too much of it.'

Mallon shot a reproving look at Swallow. 'When any of the so-called patriots gets near an officer of the Crown with a loaded gun, I have to make much of it. My contacts at Scotland Yard have a score of them under surveillance in London just now.'

'What I meant, Sir, was that I wouldn't make too much of my own part. I just did what any policeman should do when he encounters a threat to the peace. And, as Mr Smith Berry may have told you, I had some assistance from a young man, a journalist named Sweeney, working for the *Evening Telegraph*.'

Mallon raised an interrogative eyebrow. 'I have the official report. Mr Sweeney's presence is mentioned but only very briefly. Tell me what happened.'

'One of the gang was getting the better of me in the melee. Sweeney got stuck in and used his walking cane on him – to good effect.'

'An unusual case of press and police co-operation, I would think,' Smith Berry laughed. 'I know young Sweeney, of course. He was a few years behind me in Trinity but I knew him in the Officer Training Corps there. He's very close to Alderman Fitzpatrick. He supports his moderate political stance and he gives him good coverage in the *Evening Telegraph*.'

'We have two prisoners in custody for the attack,' Mallon said. 'I see the names here on the file – O'Donnell and Horan. Neither of them is familiar to me. Intelligence says they're linked to the Hibernian Brothers.'

'Yes, Chief. They're in the cells. I spent quite a while last night assisting with the interviews. I'd say they're a pair of amateurs. We didn't get much, but it's early days yet.'

'I'd like to stress the importance of what the Chief Superintendent has been saying,' Smith Berry interjected. 'Amateurs they may be, but a shot fired by an amateur can be just as deadly as a shot from an experienced agitator.'

Smith Berry brought his hand down on Mallon's desk for emphasis.

'Mr Balfour has made it absolutely clear that we mustn't have any signs of disaffection in the city during the royal visit. God knows it's bad enough to have the countryside in turmoil. There must be nothing to suggest that the capital city is other than safe and secure.'

Swallow reflected silently that the Smith Berrys and Fitzpatricks and the other *habitués* of the Upper Castle Yard, along with their hangers-on in Dublin society, would be on their toes. There would be the usual scramble for preferment and prominence. It was customary when the monarch or her representative paid a visit that there would be honours and sinecures, knighthoods even, and business deals, mainly government contracts, would be assured for the fortunate ones.

So far the murders at the Chapelizod Gate had hardly been mentioned, but he reckoned it was best to go with Smith Berry's agenda.

'I understand that, Sir.'

As if he sensed Swallow's thinking, Mallon picked up the Chapelizod Gate investigation file from the desk.

'I got your report from Mossop on Saturday evening. I hope there's been some progress. How in the name of God did you confuse a dead woman for a dead man? I'm sure Mr Smith Berry is as anxious as I am to get this business cleared up.'

'I have a set of the photographs here with me, Sir. So you can see for yourself how a mistake might have been made. We were following best detective procedure in not interfering with the body at the scene. Even the doctor didn't realise the mistake until he got to work at Marlborough Street.'

Smith Berry uttered just one word. 'Bizarre.'

Mallon took it calmly. 'As you can see, our friends in the press are doing well out of this, Sergeant,' he said after a moment. 'I'm not going to have an easy time explaining it to Commissioner Harrel. I already had to make excuses for the statements attributed to you in Saturday's editions.'

'I know, Chief,' Swallow said quietly.

'Let me see the photographs please,' Mallon extended a hand.

Swallow passed the photographs across the desk. Mallon studied them for a moment.

He allowed himself a weak grin.

'I wonder if the Commissioner will be able to tell the difference when I show him these.' He passed the photographs to Smith Berry.

'I take your point about not interfering with the body on the scene. And I can see from these photographs how the error might be made, Sergeant. It's just damned unfortunate.'

'There's a couple of other pieces of information that have come to light, Sir. They might be important.'

Mallon raised an eyebrow inquisitively.

'We found the return halves of two sailing tickets for the mail boat on the woman's body. It appears she and the child crossed from Holyhead on Wednesday last. And it seems likely that they travelled on the train from Chester and perhaps from Liverpool.'

Mallon inclined his head appreciatively. It was a lead, but it might also widen, rather than narrow, the scope of Swallow's inquiry. He sighed.

'So now, in addition to searching Ireland, all we have to do is search England and Wales as well? I take it you've notified the authorities across the water?'

'Yes, Sir. We're interviewing all the crew on the mail packets and the Railway Police are checking with the railway staff along the route.'

Mallon nodded.

'And there was something else?'

'We've found that the ammunition used in the killings was of a rather unusual type. It was .38 calibre, a low-propellant variety, perhaps the sort that might be used in target practice.'

Mallon raised a doubting eyebrow. It could be of value as evidence if the gun and the person who used it were ever located. But it was scarcely a breakthrough.

Mallon tapped one of the files that comprised his morning report on the desk. 'I want to revisit the affair at the Academy last evening. Tell me, Swallow, why were you there? You weren't rostered on protection duty.'

Swallow sensed danger again. He had hoped that the conversation would not veer towards his reasons for being at the exhibition. He opted for an answer that was not untrue, but neither was it the full truth.

'I had promised to meet my sister there, Chief. We both have an interest in painting.'

'Yes, I remember about your painting. You weren't actually on duty then?'

'No, Chief, I wasn't. That's why I didn't have my firearm with me.'

'Well, it's a very good thing that the detective sergeant was there,' Smith Berry said.

Mallon seemed doubtful. 'Anything else at the moment, Swallow?'

It was Mallon's standard question at the end of any interview with his officers.

'Not in connection with what we've been speaking of, Sir. But there's a report of a dead woman in the canal at Portobello. The inspector at Lad Lane seems to think there's foul play. Inspector Boyle has assigned me to attend as soon as I can.'

'Then you'd best get up there, Swallow. Don't linger on it any more than you have to. You can't afford to let the trail go cold on these killings. And with the Jubilee tomorrow we'll need every man we can spare on the streets to keep the city's wilder spirits in their place.'

He nodded towards the door indicating to Swallow to get moving.

FIFTEEN

Swallow was relieved that the topic of his sister had not gone further with Mallon. It would only be a matter of time before her name would come up in the investigation. Someone would make the connection to him. By then it might be too late for him to get her out of trouble.

He hurried to the post office on Dame Street. He scribbled a telegram to Harriet and addressed it to the training college.

MUST SEE YOU WHITES 8 P.M. THIS EVENING JOE

White's coffee shop was on Westmoreland Street, close by the terminus of the number 7 tram that Harriet could take from Blackrock. Swallow and his sister often met there. By 8 p.m., Swallow reckoned, she would be well finished with whatever programme of the day she had to follow at the college.

He retraced his steps to Exchange Court and made for the crime sergeants' room where the investigation team had assembled.

Stephen Doolan was already there, with half a dozen constables. As with the inquiries shift that had assembled earlier in the parade room, the men had sought to position themselves strategically by the open windows to gain a current of air. They supported themselves with their backsides on the window-sills, helmets upside down on their knees like flowerpots.

Detectives Tom Swift and Mick Feore were seated by the doorway, having commandeered two of the sergeants' chairs.

Doolan's left forehead sported a three-inch sticking plaster surmounting an area of black bruising. Seeing it catch Swallow's eye, Doolan pointed to it self-pityingly. 'Hurling yesterday… yeah… I know I should have more sense at my age.'

'Or stick to something safer, like cricket,' Swallow cracked.

Doolan grinned. 'I heard you were engaged in some fairly strenuous physical activity yourself, tackling a pair of Fenians at the Royal Hibernian Academy. Fair dues to you. Who are the two heroes you have in the cells?'

Swallow did not want any focus on the incident, at least until he could ensure that it did not implicate his sister.

'Two small fish,' he told Doolan. 'I think they got out of their depth.'

'Still, I hear they had a loaded *Reichsrevolver*,' Doolan nodded. 'That's serious, even for small fish, as you call them.'

Swallow sat at the duty sergeant's desk, giving him an elevation over the group. He indicated to Pat Mossop to sit beside him.

'Good morning again.' He raised his voice to still the hum of conversation.

'I'd like to be able to tell you that we've made a lot of progress over the past 24 hours, but unfortunately that isn't so. We've got a little more information about when the woman and child crossed from Holyhead, but we still haven't got any identification.'

A murmur of disappointment went around the room.

'They're going to be interred today at Glasnevin Cemetery. Since there's nobody to claim them they'll be buried in one of the public plots. We'll need a constable there to comply with regulations. Can you have one of your lads there, Stephen, preferably not in uniform?'

Doolan nodded to indicate that it would be done.

'We believe they crossed from Holyhead to Kingstown on Wednesday on a mail packet that would have docked around noon,' Swallow resumed. 'So they were here on Wednesday night and during Thursday. They had to stay somewhere and they had to eat somewhere. So the most promising line we can follow just now, I suggest, is to try to find those places.'

Doolan drew on his pipe and expelled a cloud of blue tobacco smoke across the room.

'Every man on beat across the divisions is checking with the boarding houses and the hotels. So far, there's nothing coming up. Maybe they stayed with relatives or friends in a private house somewhere?'

'That's possible,' Swallow said. 'If that's the case it will make tracing their movements a lot harder.'

'I wouldn't rule it out,' Doolan agreed. 'The beat men are talking to shopkeepers, cabmen, tradesmen, publicans. I'll ensure they start knocking on the doors of private dwellings too.'

It was difficult to be optimistic, Swallow acknowledged silently. The beat men could not check every house in the city. Up to twenty families might occupy a tenement building that was once the city dwelling of a rich merchant or professional man. In places like these nobody took much notice of comings and goings.

'What about missing persons in England?' Swift asked. 'Maybe there's a missing woman and child reported to one of the police forces across the water?'

'That's been done,' Swallow answered. 'We telegraphed all the police forces in England, Wales and Scotland yesterday and last night. There's nothing back so far, but a lot of folk are on the move because of the Jubilee. A lot of factories and businesses have given employees a couple of days off work, so someone mightn't be missed just yet.'

Mossop looked up from his murder book. 'Is there any progress in identifying the carriage marks on the grass?'

He checked the page in order to refresh his recollection. 'There was to be an inquiry by… Constable Culliton at Hutton's the coach-makers.'

'Culliton's over at the Coombe again this morning,' Doolan said. 'Their clerical staff only works a half day on Saturday and they're closed on Sunday. They said if he came back this morning they'd see what they could do for him.'

'Fair enough,' Swallow said. 'Stephen, I think your men should probably get out to the F Division at Kingstown and keep checking the smaller boarding-houses there around the harbour.'

He nodded to the two detectives. 'See what you can pick up from your own informants. There's been more than the usual crime tally over the past few days. You never know where there might be a connection.'

He gathered his papers and called over the hubbub as the policemen began to filter out of the room.

'There's another dead woman in the canal at Portobello. I'm going up there now. And tomorrow every available man is going to be on special duty for the Jubilee holiday. We'll regroup here again on Wednesday morning at 10 o'clock. If there are any significant developments in the meantime I'll deal with them along with Pat Mossop.'

It was hot and dry across the city, and indoors at Exchange Court it was also humid and airless. Even if the rest of the day was to be a grind of door-to-door inquiries, for the men working outdoors there was the prospect of occasional shade and perhaps some cooler air from the river or the bay.

'I've a car and driver in the Lower Yard, Boss,' Pat Mossop told Swallow as they came downstairs. 'We can be at Portobello and back in an hour with a bit of luck.'

Swallow had thought to walk the mile and a half. It would be quicker than the tram that would be running intermittently on its late-morning schedule, but in the gathering heat it would be draining. Mossop's offer of the car was welcome.

The area of the Castle within the walls was divided into a series of Courts and Yards of which far and away the most important was the Upper Yard.

Here the apartments of the great Officers of State were ranked side by side. The Chief Secretary for Ireland, the Lord of the Exchequer and the Chief Herald were to be found here. So too were the offices of the 'gentlemen ushers,' who attended the Viceroy when he resided in the Castle during the Dublin 'season.'

Lesser functionaries like the police, the Army Medical Office and the Office of Works were quartered in the Lower Yard. It also housed the Castle stables and the riding school.

The two great Yards were divided by a cross-block with a high archway. As they made their way to the waiting car, Swallow could see through the arch that the regimental band of the day was preparing for its performance in the Upper Yard. Scarlet tunics and gold braid were illuminated by flashes of sunlight reflected off their instruments.

They crossed to where the police side-car waited in the shade of the Bedford Tower. The driver reined his horse towards the Palace Street Gate, then they were out into the city traffic, moving along Dame Street.

'You were in with Chief Mallon earlier, Boss.'

Pat Mossop delivered the words as a statement but they were intended as a question.

'I was.'

Mossop pretended to be interested in brushing dust from his shoes as the car moved through the busy street. 'How'd it go?'

'It could've been worse. He has problems from on high. He's worried about what happened last night at the Hibernian Academy, I suppose in case it's part of a wider plan by the damned Fenians or who-ever else. And the newspaper stuff this morning didn't help. He had Smith Berry with him.'

Mossop laughed.

'Well, you're moving in very exalted circles then, aren't you, Boss? That's the cost of high rank, having to worry about that kind of thing. I'd be wary about that crowd if I were you.'

'You're right, Pat,' Swallow said. 'It's ironic. They're so worried about the bloody Jubilee and the royal visit, they hardly care that we mistook the dead woman for a man. The main thing worrying Mallon and Smith Berry about the case is the newspaper coverage and how it might reflect on them.'

A hundred yards from where the street rose to meet the Portobello Bridge, Swallow saw the knot of onlookers that invariably marked a Dublin mishap or incident. He caught the sun flashing on a police hel-met. He prayed silently that this would be little more than a tragic misadventure, but with his current run of luck he doubted it.

There was nautical chaos on both sides of the Portobello Lock. Up to a score of barges should have moved up and down the narrow waterway by this hour, but they were backed up, east and west. Swallow counted a dozen of them, moored and stationary in the water.

As they drew closer he saw another barge moored just outside the lock. Two constables stood alongside, their backs to the water, pre-serving the scene. To his dismay, beside the line of uniformed officers, Swallow saw a group of pressmen, among them Irving from the *Daily Sketch*.

Twenty yards away, the bargemen, some civilians and another group of three or four policemen formed a half-circle around something that lay covered by a police cape.

The pressmen surged forward as one towards Swallow. He halted and beckoned to the nearest constable, then he pointed to the advanc-ing reporters.

'If any one of those men causes an obstruction I want him arrested and taken to the Bridewell.'

Irving pointed an angry finger at Swallow and called to his colleagues.

'That's more fine work by the Dublin Metropolitan Police, lads. Pre-venting the press from doing their job when they can't do their own. Maybe this time Sergeant Swallow can tell us if it's a man or a woman that's been taken from the water.'

Swallow ignored the provocation and stepped forward to where the body lay. A constable raised the end of the cape a few inches to enable him to see the face.

Swallow did not have much doubt that he was looking at the result of foul play.

'Who found her?'

'It was the two bargemen over there, Sir.'

'Have we any identification for her?'

'No, Sir.'

'Go down to Harcourt Street to Doctor Lafeyre's house. Tell him Detective Sergeant Swallow wants him up here. When you've done that, go to Lad Lane station. Tell the sergeant in charge that I'm confirming a likely murder here and we want manpower. Get the sergeant to contact the Commissioner's office in the Castle and say I want the official photographer here too.'

'I will, Sir.'

Swallow turned to the other policeman.

'Go across to the hotel. Get me something for a screen, blankets or sheets, with a few poles. Broomsticks will do if you can't get anything better. We'll need a bit of privacy here.'

The constable strode away towards the hotel. Swallow beckoned to the two bargemen.

'Tell me what you saw.'

'It was me that spotted her, Sor. I'm the stopman. We were just turnin' in for lock and I went to light me pipe. I looked inta the water and saw somethin' dark. So we pulled the boat outa the lock and...'

The master interjected. 'Her clothes was caught be the tiller blade. I wint down in the water wid the gaff and pulled her in.'

'No idea where you picked her up? Could she have been under the barge before you started up?'

The master shrugged. The stopman shook his head.

'Did she come in easily?' Swallow asked. 'Was she heavy?'

'I think I know what you're gettin' at there, Sor,' the master said. 'I've hauled me share o' corpses outa this canal. She's not a slight little thing, but she came out fairly easy.'

Swallow saw the constable coming from the Grand Canal Hotel, followed by two porters. One had an armful of bedsheets and the other carried half a dozen rough stakes, each about the height of a man.

'Put them in a square around her. Leave a clearance of 6 or 7 feet for the doctor to work when he gets here,' he ordered the constable.

'I want you to wait until we get some more police,' he told the bargemen. 'We'll want to take statements from you both.'

The two bargemen looked despondent.

'And I need to examine the vessel myself.'

'Ah, Jaysus,' said the master. 'We done all we could. We've a load a' malt to get ta Shannon Harbour be tomorra' noon. Sure haven't we told ye what we know? Ye can't keep us here settin' around all day.'

Swallow eyes drilled into his coarse face.

'Be clear about this,' he said icily. 'I want full, detailed statements from you and your stopman. Meanwhile, I want to check your barge from bow to stern. If there's a hint of trouble from you, you'll be on your way to Mountjoy or Kilmainham or the Bridewell until I'm done.'

'It isn't meself, Sor,' the master said more respectfully, 'it's the comp'ny and the cargo.'

Swallow raised his voice.

'The company and your cargo can damned well wait. There's a woman lying dead there on the canal bank. Very likely she's been murdered. I don't give a curse for either the company or your bloody load of… whatever it is.'

'Malt, Sor, 'tis a load a' malt,' the man said apologetically and stepped back.

A brougham clattered across the cobbles of Charlemont Mall and drew to a halt by the grassy canal bank. Swallow recognised the driver as Scollan, Harry Lafeyre's man.

Lafeyre dropped smartly to the grass, hauling his bag from the carriage. Swallow led him through the makeshift screen of sheets and poles. The two men squatted beside the corpse, still covered with the constable's cape. The medical examiner reached across, lifted the cape and draped it on the nearest stake supporting the screen.

He surveyed the battered face and the gaping wound above the left temple.

'Jesus, Joe, you're stacking up a lot of work. It's beginning to look like an epidemic. What do you know about this one?'

'It's not a straightforward drowning. The bargemen found her down by the tiller blade and took her in with a gaff-hook. It seems the dress was caught by the blade and it ripped when they hauled on the gaff.'

The woman looked to be in her twenties. She was of average build. Swallow estimated her height at perhaps 5 feet and 3 or 4 inches. She had long, dark hair which now came down below her shoulders. Her sodden clothing was plain but of good-quality cotton, well finished. She wore a dark red dress, with buttons running to the neck, although the top three were missing. There were no shoes or stockings. There was no jewellery of any kind.

The right arm was flung forward of the head but the left hung by the side of the torso, hidden by the folds of the dress.

Swallow anticipated the medical examiner's anxiety to follow procedure. 'She's been moved about. You're not going to lose any evidence by taking a closer look here.'

Lafeyre lifted the sodden cloth and raised the arm, buttoned to the wrist. He turned the hand palm upward and examined it, then he repeated the examination with the other hand.

'Well at least this time I'd say we're right about the gender,' Lafeyre told him sardonically. 'You've got a second dead woman within 72 hours. It's harder for me to guess the time of death here because of immersion in the water. There's some rigor mortis so she's certainly dead for several hours.'

'Anything else you can tell me at this stage?' Swallow asked.

'Not much that you can't see for yourself. There's plenty of hard work done by those hands,' Lafeyre observed. He raised a quizzical eyebrow to Swallow. 'Why do you think she didn't drown?'

'Well you can see that damned great wound on the head. And the bargemen said she was fairly light to haul in. If she was buoyant then her lungs weren't full of canal water.'

Lafeyre knelt beside the body, placed his right hand over his left, palms downwards and pressed hard on the woman's breastbone three times.

'I'm inclined to agree. There's no great amount of excess fluid there. She might have been dead when she went in the water, but I won't be able to say definitely until we've got her to Marlborough Street for a full examination.'

He took a steel probe from his bag and folded back the flesh that had opened around the wound on the temple.

'Again, I don't want to say anything with certainty until after I've done a full examination, but I'd wager that's the cause of death. Hard to know what caused that much damage, but it was a hell of a blow with something. There was a lot of force behind it. Some of the other marks might be post mortem – damage from the tiller blade or the walls of the locks.'

He replaced the police cape over the body.

Swallow's apprehensions were confirmed. What he had hoped might be a simple drowning case was beginning to look anything but simple.

'I've a quiet day so I can do the post mortem this afternoon,' Lafeyre told Swallow. 'If you want to be there, could we say 4 o'clock?'

A DMP side-car arrived with the official photographer. Swallow briefed him as he set up his field camera on its awkward tripod. A horse-drawn ambulance of the Dublin Fire Brigade had also drawn up behind Lafeyre's brougham.

'First, I need pictures of the body and in particular of the wound on the head. Then get some general directional pictures showing the location and the barge and the lock.'

The camera man nodded and went about his task silently, starting with the corpse and closing in on the head wound. Swallow watched while he completed his task, then he called the uniformed sergeant.

'We need a search of the canal, both banks, from here right down to the Grand Canal Dock. We don't have identification so we need anything that might be in the reeds or on the banks – a bag, shoes, stockings, a hat...'

The sergeant nodded.

'Anything else?'

'Dr Lafeyre is fairly sure this is a case of foul play. Make contact with the A Division and tell them to get a message out to Detective Feore. He's with the search teams near Chapelizod now but I need him as Book Man on this. I'll want a full report on the search when you're done.'

Lafeyre gestured to the ambulance attendants. They stepped forward carrying a canvas stretcher.

'The photography seems to be completed here. Bring her down to the morgue at Marlborough Street. I'll be doing a post mortem in the afternoon.'

The ambulance men went about their task. A few moments later they emerged from behind the screen, one at either end of the stretcher. The constables formed a phalanx as the body was carried out.

The ambulance men halted beside their vehicle. The constable who had placed his cape over the body bent to retrieve it, leaving the corpse momentarily visible.

There was a scream from somewhere among the onlookers. A thin, young woman with a shawl drawn around her shoulders was staring with a look of horror at the body on the stretcher.

She screamed again.

'Oh Jesus… Oh Jesus… it's Sarah.'

SIXTEEN

Upwards of a score of funerals took place on the hot Monday morning at Mount Prospect Cemetery, Glasnevin, just north of the city. At one stage, five separate cortèges were drawn up on the Finglas Road awaiting their turn to be cleared through the gates of the necropolis by the sweating officials in their blue tunics and top hats.

The mortality rate had risen as the extraordinary heat of the previous week took its toll. Inevitably, in the poorer districts where primitive sanitation and overcrowding prevailed, the casualties tended to be the old and the very young. The other big city cemeteries serving Dublin and Kingstown, Mount Jerome and Dean's Grange, were to be busy all day as well.

Shortly after 11 o'clock, the hearse carrying the remains of Cecilia Downes passed through the village of Phibsborough and along the Finglas Road. The glass-panelled hearse was drawn by four jet-black, plumed horses. Men and women who stood by the roadside to watch the unusually fine funeral procession could see that the coffin inside was made of polished oak, set with solid brass handles.

A black phaeton, draped with mourning silks, followed immediately behind. Dublin funeral protocol required that the first carriage after the hearse should carry the chief mourners. That dubious distinction in this case belonged to Charlie Vanucchi and Vinny Cussen. The two criminals, incongruously dark-suited and top-hatted, sat grimly facing forward and as far apart as possible on the phaeton's padded leather seat.

Father Laurence from the Franciscan monastery at Merchants' Quay sat opposite the two men. At Ces Downes's instruction there had been no funeral Mass or church service. She had insisted that she would be brought directly from her house at Francis Street to Glasnevin.

Half a dozen clarences and broughams followed immediately behind the lead mourning car. The occupants were a mixed lot. Some of the men wore dark suits as propriety demanded, but elsewhere loud checks and coloured waistcoats stood out.

Many of the women were equally indecorous with bright dresses, summer parasols and floral hats. Near St Peter's Church at Phibsborough, passers-by saw one female mourner cheerfully wave a gin bottle through a brougham's curtained window.

Behind the closed carriages came a trailing procession of perhaps 40 side-cars, traps and Ringsend Cars. They stretched in a disorderly gaggle along the road back towards the city. Men and women and even a few children perched on the high seats or squeezed into the spaces between. Others clung to the sideboards or maintained a precarious grip on the baggage straps.

The pretence at solemnity receded further along the procession. A medley of drinking songs rose from two of the cars. Most of the passengers clutched bottles or jugs of drink. Clay pipes and cigars were passed around. At one point on the Finglas Road a group of women descended from the caravan to dance a jig in the dust, waving their skirts and whooping as a fiddler played away from the back of a Ringsend Car.

Two G-men watched from a vantage point opposite the main gate to the cemetery. There were slurred greetings and hoots from the mourners, but there was no disorder.

Technically the policemen might have tried to make arrests for public drunkenness. One officer had a vague idea that there was a specific offence of being under the influence in a burial ground or a place of worship. The officers agreed, however, that Ces Downes's funeral was not an occasion upon which to test their knowledge of the law on public order.

The pallbearers, fronted by Vinny Cussen and Charlie Vanucchi, carried Ces Downes's coffin to what the cemetery authorities described as a 'first-class grave,' being prominently located close to one of the main wide pathways.

At the graveside, after Ces Downes's coffin had been lowered into the ground, Father Laurence recited the prayers for the dead and led the attendance in a decade of the rosary. Three gravediggers moved forward and began to shovel the clay over the coffin. The mourners, led by Vanucchi and Cussen, started to move away towards the cemetery gates.

Half an hour after Ces Downes's mourners had left Glasnevin, another quite different kind of funeral party made its way along a side avenue to one of the paupers' plots at the northern end of the cemetery.

The cortège of the woman and the child whose bodies had been found at the Chapelizod Gate three days previously consisted of just two vehicles, each drawn by a single horse. The lead vehicle was a closed cart such as might be used by a merchant to deliver groceries or other goods. The second vehicle was a Dublin Metropolitan Police side-car with a driver and a solitary plain-clothes policeman seated beside him.

Two hours earlier, a jury of nine shopkeepers, tradesmen and publicans had returned a verdict of death as a result of gunshot on the unknown woman and child. The verdict enabled the coroner to release the bodies for burial.

The small cortège stopped at a point where four or five cemetery labourers lounged, smoking and talking, around a makeshift trestle. The driver of the closed cart dismounted and opened the doors at the back, then he beckoned the labourers to help him to carry down the two plain-box coffins that were inside.

One of the coffins was proportioned to take the body of an adult. The other was made for a child. The men laid them together on the trestle and then lifted them to the side of an open grave that had already accommodated six other burials during the morning.

They looped ropes around the coffins and lowered them into the ground on top of those put down earlier in the day. The plain-clothes policeman did not descend from the side-car. When the coffins had disappeared from sight and the ropes had been retrieved, he leaned down and thrust a sheet of paper and a pencil at the foreman labourer who signed it without a word.

The police driver wheeled his car and started back along the route by which he had come. The driver of the closed cart resumed his seat and followed.

Later in the morning, an old priest with an altar boy came to the open grave and sprinkled holy water onto the coffins. He prayed, as he did every morning, for the souls of the deceased, whose names he did not know and whose passing was not of significance to the world.

SEVENTEEN

Officers Martin Collins and Eddie Shanahan started their investigations into Sunday night's violence with the Mecklenburgh Street attack on Vinny Cussen's muscleman, Tommy 'Tiger' McKnight.

Had Detective Inspector 'Duck' Boyle not stood on his dignity and assigned the experienced Detective Tony Swann to the gangland attacks, things might have worked out differently. Had it been Swann who went to the Meath Hospital to take the statement from Tommy McKnight, lying in the casualty ward with multiple broken bones and a fractured skull, it is possible that a more circumspect course of police action might have followed. But since the inexperienced Shanahan and Collins were out of their territory and out of their depth, they did as good policemen should do. They acted on their initiative.

It was a serious mistake, if one easily made by novices.

At about the time that Swallow and Lafeyre were examining the woman's body at Portobello, Shanahan and Collins arrived at the Meath Hospital, untroubled in their certainty that even if they found him conscious, the victim would assure them that he had fallen down stairs or been kicked by a horse. But when they were led to his bedside by the heavy-set nurse in charge of the ward, they were greeted by the sight of McKnight, bloodied and bandaged, his split lips framing a jagged array of dental fragments.

'We've had to fill this fellow with laudanum.' The nurse's tone was unsympathetic. 'He was drunk, of course, when he got here. I don't know what happened to him but it seems there was a fight. He was in pain. Nobody in the place could get a moment's peace with him shouting and bawling all night.'

Suddenly, McKnight began to moan loudly. He tried to join his bruised hands together as in prayer, but he failed the test of coordination so that his arms fell crossways over his chest like an Egyptian mummy.

'Jesus, I'm in agony,' he muttered.

The nurse thrust her face aggressively up to the bandaged and bloodied head.

'Ah, give over your moaning and groaning. You're not too bad. If you'll do what you're told you'll be fine when the wounds heal up.'

Then, striking a fractionally softer tone, she added, 'I'll give you something to knock out the discomfort for a bit now. And there's two young gentlemen here to talk to you.'

He moaned again.

The nurse spooned a dose of laudanum into a cup and put it to his broken lips. He swallowed without resistance.

'That should keep him calm for a while,' she said flatly. 'Don't stay with him too long. I've got work to do.'

She left the two policemen at the bedside. It took a minute or two for the drug to take effect. McKnight gradually relaxed against the pillow. He smiled at Collins.

'Yer... very good to be here wid me... Father...' McKnight's eyes focused on Collins who, despite the heat of the day, was wearing a dark suit that might easily cause him to be mistaken for a clergyman.

Shanahan stifled his mirth. Collins was a Presbyterian without any knowledge of Roman Catholic confession. Collins saw the joke too, but glanced around furtively, sensing opportunity. An elderly patient in the next bed was asleep. The nurse was nowhere to be seen.

'Eh... Yes, my son,' Collins muttered quietly, '...tell me what crimes you have committed. But first tell me who inflicted these injuries on you.' He indicated to Shanahan to have his notebook and pencil ready.

'It was Charlie Vanucchi and his lads, Father,' the victim whispered urgently. 'There was a few o' them. But it was Vanucchi who did the damage to me.'

'And... ah... why were these men... I mean, are they known to you?'

'The Vanucchi crowd are tryin' to take over everythin', Father... with Ces Downes gone... We caught two o' them across in Rutland Street last night and we done them over. Then Vanucchi and the others... just landed on me in Mecklenburgh Street, an' me goin' home, mindin' me own business.'

'You're sure that's who it was?' Collins whispered. 'Charlie Vanucchi?'

'As sure as me own name, Father.'

Shanahan scribbled in his notebook.

'Eh... Father... I need yer blessin'.' McKnight's voice struggled to achieve a tone of urgency. 'I need th' abs... absolution...'

Collins waved his right hand up and down in a haphazard imitation of a blessing. 'I... ah... bless thee and forgive thee...'

McKnight cocked his head and grinned stupidly at Shanahan. Shanahan nodded enthusiastically and stuck the notepad in front of McKnight while thrusting a pencil in his hand.

'Sign there, like a good man,' he said softly.

'Whas' it for?' McKnight asked.

'Ah, it's just a form for the hospital.'

'I can't write... never learned how.'

'Well, just make an "X".'

McKnight scrawled two intersecting lines with Shanahan's pencil, then he uttered a deep, terrible groan. There was a great exhalation of breath and his head fell forward, the jaw dropping open onto his chest.

'Nurse!' Shanahan called. 'Nurse, come quickly. Something's happened.'

The heavy-set nurse came running. She raised McKnight's head and checked the pupils of the open eyes between thumb and forefinger. Then she took his pulse. She turned to the two G-men, shaking her head.

'He's dead. Oh dear God, I didn't expect this. It must have been heart failure... or a thrombosis. Wait here. I'll have to get the doctor.'

Had Collins and Shanahan, even at this stage, chosen to return to Exchange Court to take instructions or to seek advice, it is possible that the emerging debacle might have been avoided. But Shanahan believed he saw potential in the situation that had now presented itself. He drew Collins to one side.

'Listen, do you realise we've just solved a murder? McKnight is dead and he's given us a signed statement. What we have here is what's called a dying declaration. And it identifies Charlie Vanucchi as his killer.'

Collins was inclined to be doubtful, but he too saw the possibilities in what had just unfolded. This was possibly a situation that a clever policeman could turn to his career advantage.

'I don't know much about a dying declaration. How does it work?'

'I'm not a bloody lawyer,' Shanahan responded, 'but I know that it's admissible as evidence. You don't have to have the witness there in the box. Well, you can't, him being dead. But you can report what you heard him say and that's acceptable as evidence in court.'

He checked his pocket-watch. 'Ces Downes's funeral is well over. They'll all be back drinking now, pouring out their grief. It's only a question of finding where they are.'

Collins figured that what Shanahan said made sense. Charlie Vanucchi would be a big fish to land. He could almost certainly be picked up at one or other of his drinking haunts in the Liberties in the aftermath of the funeral. They would have him in the cells at Exchange Court and charged by early afternoon and, with luck, lodged in the Bridewell by 5 o'clock.

Shanahan and Collins, with a significant feat of crime detection to their credit, would have a lengthy evening ahead for reflection in some suitably cool public house. In the longer term there would be commendations for good police work. There might even be something coming their way from the Commissioner's reward fund. The possibilities were considerable.

'Let's start with Lawless's in the Coombe,' Shanahan suggested enthusiastically, making for the door.

They reckoned it the most likely location to find their suspect in the aftermath of the funeral. They were right.

What they did not think to reckon with was the presence, also in Lawless's, of upwards of twenty members of Charlie Vanucchi's gang who had decided to extend their grieving by alternating between two or three hostelries in the Coombe and Francis Street.

While the sense of mourning for Ces Downes was at least partly genuine, Charlie Vanucchi was also using the occasion to gather his loyalists for a show of force against his rival, Vinny Cussen. Vanucchi was planning to waste no time in establishing his credentials as the heir to Ces Downes's criminal network.

Nor did Collins and Shanahan reckon with the attendance in Lawless's also of up to a dozen of the Vanucchi faction's womenfolk, who had assembled partly in support of their men and partly to express their sense of loss at Ces's passing. Above all else they were present to benefit from the drink which was certain to flow on an occasion which combined the pain of bereavement with the exciting prospect of new business enterprises.

It took Shanahan and Collins little more than a quarter of an hour's brisk walking from the Meath Hospital to reach the Coombe. By the time they reached Lawless's they were perspiring in the day's heat, but the urgency of their mission was such that they did not hesitate or reconsider their proposed course of action.

They had pushed their way through the swing doors of the public house and were several paces into the saloon bar before they realised that something was seriously amiss. Instead of the early afternoon quiet, with a few regulars at the bar and, hopefully, their quarry at a table in the snug, the place was filled with a hubbub of conversation and a thick fog of tobacco smoke. Hoots of derision and angry curses fuelled by the abundance of alcohol began to rise from around the bar as the newcomers were recognised for what they were.

'Bobbies. What're they doin' here?'

'Bastards. No shaggin' manners. No respect for the dead.'

A young woman rose unsteadily from a table and stepped forward to spit on the sawdust floor in front of Collins.

'G'wan, get outta here, the pair o' yiz. Yer not wanted… and ye should know it.'

Shanahan took a step backwards towards the door, but Collins saw that half a dozen men behind them had moved to block any line of retreat. Whatever Collins lacked in an instinct for danger was partly compensated for with courage and nerve.

'Steady,' he told his colleague quietly, 'there's only one way out of this now.'

Slowly, he opened his jacket. He drew it back with his left hand, revealing the Webley Bulldog revolver. He brought his right hand across his chest until his fingers brushed the metal butt.

'We've no business with any of you here except Charlie Vanucchi,' he called loudly across the room.

There was a murmur of anger as Vanucchi rose from the wooden chair on which he had been seated by the back wall of the saloon. By now Shanahan had followed Collins's lead and the steel of his Webley jutted forward under the lapel of his coat.

'Right, Charlie,' Collins said in what he hoped was a tone of authority, 'we'll go outside for a chat.'

Charlie Vanucchi roared with laughter.

'We will in my arse, Son. I'm here with friends on this very solemn and sad afternoon. We've just buried our dear friend and benefactor, Ces Downes, as you well know. So just fuck off outta' here with yer mate while you have the use o' yer fuckin' legs.'

Collins's right hand fastened on his gun. He moved forward.

The young policeman had taken just one step when the pint bottle hit his head, hurled from somewhere to his left. He staggered momentarily, trying to recover his balance when a heavy, wooden chair slammed into his back, propelling him forward. As he fell, a woman's leg shot out to trip him, bringing him violently down on the sawdust floor.

Now Shanahan's revolver was out.

In the corner of his eye he saw a youth lunging forward from the bar, a bottle raised in his right hand. He swung the gun backward and brought it hard across the young man's face. There was a sharp crack as the weapon connected with his cheek-bone.

Somebody kicked fiercely from behind at Shanahan's leg. He swung again, bringing the heavy revolver down hard on a shin-bone. A woman's face appeared before him, her hands reaching for his throat. He punched her squarely between the eyes and she fell, cursing. The room was in a roaring fury.

Shanahan saw Collins try to rise to his feet. Half a dozen men piled onto him, bringing him down again amid flying fists and boots. In spite of the blows raining in on him, Collins kept his grip on his revolver. Then Shanahan saw a man reach for the gun through the tangle of arms and legs.

Shanahan raised his own Webley towards the ceiling and fired twice.

The reports were like artillery rounds in the confined space. The concussion hit every eardrum across the room. Two clouds of white cordite swirled out over the heads of the crowd as plaster and laths began to shower from the ceiling where the slugs had penetrated. As the echoes of the shots died down there was an eerie silence.

Collins rose from the melee on the floor, his Webley still in his hand. He pushed his way to where Shanahan stood, wielding his gun across the room in an arc.

'Hands in the air... hands in the air... every bloody one of you! I swear I'll fuckin' plug the first one that makes another move!'

The two G-men began to step backwards towards the door. Collins waved the weapon to clear away four or five members of the gang who had moved to block the exit just moments before. The men moved away sullenly, their hands high.

As Shanahan and Collins reached the door it swung inwards from the street, propelled by the shoulders of two constables with drawn batons. Two more followed, and then two more. Within a few moments more than a dozen uniformed policemen had deployed across the room.

A burly sergeant who had come through the door with surprising velocity surveyed the shambles of the saloon. He took in the sprawled bodies on the floor, perhaps twenty men and women with their hands in the air, the two G-men with revolvers in hand and the air thick with gunsmoke and plaster dust.

He looked at Shanahan and Collins, shaking his head slowly.

'Ye can be damned thankful ye were spotted comin' in here by a beat man. He recognised ye and knew ye'd be in trouble on ycr own. We've been countin' the numbers of these gougers here during the day. Ye must be mad, just the two o' yez comin' in here on yer own. Sure there's an army of them. What do ye want to do now?

'We're… taking the prisoner… we came for,' Collins gasped, 'Charlie Vanucchi. He's to be charged.'

The sergeant gestured to a constable beside him. 'Get Vanucchi, I see him there at the back.'

A distinct gurgling sound, like milk being poured from a pail, could be heard across the saloon. A faintly amber liquid was falling in a steady trickle from one of the two gaping holes blown in the ceiling by Shanahan's warning shots. It splashed noisily onto a tabletop where three of the Vanucchi gang's womenfolk were sitting, half-empty glasses of port wine in front of them.

The trickle eddied and twisted as it fell from the shattered ceiling and momentarily splashed on the face of one of the women. She gave a little shriek and her hands flew upward to wipe it away. Suddenly, she was licking her fingers, then she was holding her two hands out, palms cupped to catch the fluid that gurgled from the shattered cases of liquor in the storeroom above. She squealed delightedly.

'Jaysus girls, we're blessed. It's whiskey!'

EIGHTEEN

Sometimes the laws of chance worked in a policeman's favour. It was not a frequent occurrence. Like a comet blazing through the solar system, it was a rare but verifiable phenomenon. Swallow had experienced it himself. A casual encounter or a scrap of unexpected information on occasion had saved him hours, even days, of shovel-work, knocking on doors and making inquiries in shops and public houses.

It had to be pure luck that the gaunt young girl in the circle of onlookers by the canal bank had recognised the dead woman's face in the moment that the constable's cape had been taken away.

'It's Sarah...' She repeated the name as if not believing what she was looking at. 'Jesus... it's Sarah.'

For a moment she appeared to go faint. Two women onlookers moved to support her. Swallow called to a constable to bring her to the side-car and make her comfortable on its bench seat. He reckoned she might be 17 or 18 years of age.

'I'm Detective Sergeant Swallow from G Division,' he said quietly. 'Will you tell me your name?'

The girl was trembling in spite of the day's warmth.

'It's Hetty... Hetty Connors, Sir.'

'Do you know that poor woman?'

She looked at him quizzically for a moment. 'She's Sarah, Sir. I know her from where I used to work.'

'What's her other name?'

She hesitated. 'I don't know, Sir. We just called her Sarah. She is... was... the housemaid.'

'Were you a friend of hers?'

'I used to work with her before I got a position at the hospital – Sir Patrick Dunn's, that is. Sometimes when I have me time off I like to come up here for a walk and she did the same. I'd meet her, sittin' be the water, like. We'd always talk for a bit.'

'When did you see her last? Have you any idea why this might have happened?'

'I suppose a few days ago. I took an evenin' walk, like I do, when the weather is fine. She was just there on the little wall by the canal. That's the last I saw of her.'

'Who was your employer, Hetty, before you went to the hospital?'

'It was Mr Fitzpatrick, Sir, down at Merrion Square, number 106.'

'And that's where she… Sarah… works, is it?'

'It is, Sir.'

More than twenty years of police work had also taught Swallow not to underestimate the possibility – or the power – of coincidence. 'Do you mean Alderman Fitzpatrick? Thomas Fitzpatrick?'

'Yes, Sir. He's very important.'

That might be understating it, he thought. It was not information that he welcomed. A violent death – even of a servant – linked to the household of a man in the public eye, a senior member of the City Corporation and protégé of the administration would be publicised and then scrutinised at the highest levels.

At that moment Swallow was relieved to see the bulky figure of Detective Mick Feore climbing down from a DMP car that had drawn in across the street. Feore would probably never make quite as good a Book Man as Pat Mossop, but just at this moment Swallow would settle for anyone who could write fast, accurately and legibly, keeping track of scraps of information and logging their sources.

Feore was a farmer's son from Galway. He had once been a member of a religious order of teaching brothers. At an early stage of working together, Swallow noticed that he picked up the techniques of crime investigation more quickly than many of the others who came into G Division, and reasoned that it was because of his educational training. His classroom experience stood him in good stead when he abandoned the religious life and opted for a policing job. His English was accurate and precise. His writing hand was clear and steady.

Swallow beckoned to the big detective.

'I'm sorry to pull you in at short notice but I need a Book Man here. They've taken a woman over there from the canal and she's gone to the morgue. I think she's had her skull beaten in although we can't be 100 percent certain until Dr Lafeyre has finished his examination.'

He ran Feore through what he had learned from the bargemen, then he recounted the details that Hetty Connors had given him. Feore's pencil flew over the pages of his notebook, filling them with Swallow's rapid-fire narrative. He gave out a little whistle when Swallow told him where the dead woman worked. Feore understood the implications. Any investigation that would bring G Division into contact with the influential and well-connected was always problematic.

The uniformed sergeant had formed two lines of constables to start searching the canal banks. Ultimately they would cover all of the ground stretching back to the Grand Canal Dock.

Swallow stepped onto the moored barge and walked to the stern from where the stopman had spotted the dead woman in the water. There was a clear line of sight from the deck across the channel, but the body would not have been visible to anyone on the canal bank. That was consistent with the bargemen's version of the find.

He told a constable to remain on duty until the photographic technician completed his job. The bargemen's details and statements were to be taken and they could continue on their way when the police work was finished.

There was little more that he could do at the scene. There were no witnesses of significance. A woman who might have been a cook had emerged from a nearby house and taken the distressed Hetty Connors to her kitchen to comfort her with some tea. The body of the dead girl was on its way to Harry Lafeyre's morgue.

'Somebody's going to have to go down to Merrion Square and tell Alderman Fitzpatrick what's happened,' Feore ventured.

'Well, that'll be you and me, Mick.' Swallow responded without enthusiasm. 'I suppose we'd best make a start.'

It would be perhaps a 15-minute walk.

His sense of foreboding was rising. Anything touching on the Fitzpatrick household would have the entire chain of authority rattling and shaking, from the Security Secretary's office down. He silently cursed his luck. Sometimes months could pass by without landing a murder inquiry, and when they did occur they were often straightforward, although inevitably demanding of time and effort. There were family feuds, lovers' quarrels, acts of violence fuelled by alcohol. Now it looked as if he had not one but three murders to deal with in almost as many days. And so far they were proving to be anything but straightforward.

The doubts that had worried him on Sunday afternoon when he talked to Maria were asserting themselves even more strongly. He already had two unsolved, brutal murders on his hands. How was he to cope with another one that was already throwing up problems?

He crossed the Portobello Bridge with Feore, glancing down at the black, churning water in the lock below. They followed the towpath to Huband Bridge, then they turned into Upper Mount Street and past St Stephen's – the 'Pepper Canister' – Church. An ancient dog sat in the shade beside the steps, panting in the heat. Swallow saw that someone had mercifully put out an enamel bowl of water for the animal.

At Merrion Square the gardens were patterned with yellow and green. The sunlight reflected off glossy beech and chestnut and sparkled on scrubbed granite steps and brass door-knockers.

G Division's line of work rarely led its members to Merrion Square or anywhere within the city's exquisite Georgian quarter. This was an enclave of the wealthy and the privileged. Many of the four-storey houses were the property of titled landowners from around the country who kept them for use during the Dublin 'season.' Then there were the homes of the judges, the successful lawyers, the senior Castle officials, the prominent surgeons as well as the families that had grown wealthy on industry and trade.

Police business was almost invariably centred on the less salubrious districts. It was generally transacted in streets where the names of the inhabitants did not figure on the Lord Lieutenant's invitations lists. Privilege in such places might be defined as a communal water pump and an outdoor toilet.

Swallow could see children's nurses minding their charges in the gardens of the great Georgian square. The faint sound of a dining gong, deep in one of the tall mansions, chimed through an open window. Someone was about to sit to lunch. Swallow surmised that it was likely to be a good one.

He realised he had not eaten since early morning. The sun and heat had suppressed his appetite. He could be easily persuaded to a glass of stout or a cool bottle of ale, he reflected, but it was not an immediate prospect.

Things went wrong almost from the moment Swallow and Feore arrived at Number 106 Merrion Square. They climbed the high granite steps to the main door. Feore tugged on the stiff bell-pull. He had pulled three times before the door was opened by a frail-looking butler in morning dress.

He squinted at the detectives. 'Yes? Wha' is your business please?'

Swallow was good on accents. After one sentence he could place this one somewhere in the Scottish lowlands, perhaps Aberdeen or Dundee. The man's shoes were in need of polishing, and two loose buttons dangled on his vest. He was not young, perhaps 60 years of age, and had shaved none-too-well. It was not what Swallow had expected in the house of an influential Alderman.

It was also in contrast to what Swallow could see of the contents of the well-proportioned hallway. Silver candle-holders glistened from a polished side-table. Two matching sets of what looked like fine Dutch interiors adorned the walls. A magnificent, crystal glass chandelier hung from the plasterwork rose in the centre of the ceiling.

He showed his warrant card. 'I'm making inquiries about a member of your staff who may be missing from this household. I need to speak to someone in authority please.'

The butler drew the door half closed behind him as if to deny the detectives any sight of the interior.

'If it's a matter concernin' the staff, Constable,' he nodded towards the railings underneath, 'ye'll have to go below.'

He moved back into the hall and made to shut the door.

Swallow's anger at being ordered to the tradesmen's entrance was instinctive. He shot his left foot forward, blocking the door. He stepped across the threshold, pushing against the man and momentarily knocking him off balance. He heard Feore draw a deep breath as he stepped in behind him.

'I'm not a constable,' Swallow said in the cold voice that he could summon to mask anger. 'I'm Detective Sergeant Swallow of the G Division. I'm investigating a violent death, probably a case of murder. Now, get me your master or whoever is in charge of the house.'

The older man recovered his balance. 'How dare you force your way in here, I told ye to go downstairs!'

He raised his arm as if he would attempt to sweep the two policemen back over the threshold. Swallow flexed himself, but he knew that he had stepped over the law in pushing his way past the door.

'Easy,' he said. 'You could go to jail for assaulting a policeman.'

A man's voice came from the hallway.

'What's going on here, McDonald?'

Thomas Fitzpatrick emerged from a room to the right. He held a sheaf of papers in one hand and a pair of spectacles in the other. He fixed the two detectives with a glare. Then, almost immediately, he recognised Swallow.

'You're the G-man from last night at Academy,' he announced. 'You have a couple of the troublemakers locked up in the Castle, I believe. That was good work.'

He seemed to relax. 'I think this is probably in order, McDonald,' he told the butler, gesturing to him to step aside. He turned back to Swallow. 'I'm afraid I didn't catch your name last evening but I'm sure I owe you my thanks. What is it that I can do for you?'

Swallow showed his warrant card.

'I'm Detective Sergeant Swallow, Mr Fitzpatrick. This is Detective Officer Feore. And you're correct in what you say. I was at the Royal Hibernian Academy last evening. We have two men in custody, but I'm afraid this call is about other business. We're investigating the death of a young woman whose body was found in the Grand Canal this morning. I have reason to believe she may have been a servant in this house.'

Fitzpatrick drew back in surprise. 'Found in the canal? Good God, I've heard nothing about this. Why do you believe that this… young woman… may have anything to do with this house?'

'We believe she was called Sarah, Sir. Do you have a servant by that name employed here?'

Swallow thought he saw Fitzpatrick stiffen a little at the question.

'There's a housemaid here called Sarah, yes. A rather slow-witted girl. But how do you know it's the same person?' he asked testily. 'Don't you think you should be sure of your facts before you start calling at people's private houses? And more so, I'd suggest, at the house of an Alderman.'

Swallow's irritation began to stir again at Fitzpatrick's crude invocation of his rank.

'I'm sorry if I haven't made myself clear, Alderman Fitzpatrick. We're investigating what appears to be a case of murder. As I've said, the victim may have been a member of your household staff.'

Fitzpatrick grimaced. 'You're talking about murder? That would be dreadful… a very serious matter. But if there's some connection to my staff it would be best to have your superiors communicate with my solicitors. Mr Smith Berry at Dublin Castle knows who they are.'

Swallow saw a smirk flicker across McDonald's face.

He drew his notebook from his inner pocket. Slowly and officiously he poised his pencil over the open page.

'Mr Fitzpatrick, I'm sure my superiors know who your solicitors are. But this isn't a matter for solicitors. It's police business, a criminal inquiry. There's a general requirement at law for a citizen to assist a police officer investigating any serious crime. I'd have thought that a gentleman of your position would particularly want to help the police.'

He paused for effect.

'So I am now noting the date and time of my visit in connection with my inquiries and I'm noting your response. I may be obliged to seek a warrant from a magistrate's court, to enable me to search this house or parts of it. I will also want to question members of this household, including yourself, about these matters. I'm confident that I can have that warrant this afternoon.'

For a long moment there was silence in the hall. The shout of a young child at play came faintly from the square.

Thomas Fitzpatrick shrugged. 'That would be a waste of effort and of everyone's time, Mr Swallow.' He turned to the butler. 'McDonald, tell the sergeant what you said to me earlier about the housemaid not being available for work this morning.'

If there was a smirk it had now vanished. 'I'm sorry, Sir,' McDonald said hesitatingly. 'Like I told you, all I know is that she's no' been at work. She's no' in her quarters. None of the other servants have seen her. She's gone.'

Fitzpatrick turned his eyes towards the ceiling as if weary. 'Well that may be the very point of what Sergeant Swallow and his colleague have come here for. You say she's gone. They say they may have found her in the damned canal. Is there anything more you can tell the officers?'

McDonald glowered at Swallow and Feore.

'It's Sarah, the housemaid. She left here last night and didn't come back. She a bit slow, as Mr Fitzpatrick has told you. But she can read the clock. She was due for cleanin' the dining room and the staircases this mornin'. I had to get one of the others to do her work.'

Swallow felt himself relax a little as the challenge to his authority appeared to ebb. He flicked the notebook open. 'Now we're getting somewhere, it seems. First, I'll have your name.'

'James McDonald.'

Swallow repeated the name. He wrote it down slowly while seeking to give the impression that he was reflecting on some dubious connection that had come to mind.

'What's her full name – Sarah's?'

McDonald hesitated. 'Tell the officer what he needs to know,' Fitzpatrick said.

'Hannin. Sarah Hannin.'

'And her age?'

'I think she'd be 24 – perhaps 25 years.'

'Native of… where?

'I don't know. These girls come from anywhere. You're no' told. She was a country girl. She wasn't one for talking much.'

'Have you any knowledge of her family, next of kin? Is there anybody who will need to be notified?'

'No. I don't think she had any family. And as I told you, I don't know where she came from.'

'She had accommodation in the house?'

'She slept in the servants' rooms at the top. She shared a bedroom wi' the day maid, Joan.'

'Who saw her last and when?'

'I don't know. I saw her myself in the kitchen last night after supper. She was plannin' to go to visit someone.'

'Do you know who she planned to visit or where?'

'No, of course not, it's no' my business to keep track of the staff when they're on their time off.'

Feore interjected. 'Would it be usual to have servants – female servants in particular – still out of the house after 9 o'clock?'

'It's no' dark these evenin's until after 10.'

'Can you describe what she was wearing?'

'A dress and a bonnet of some sort… I can't remember.'

'What colour was the dress? Would you recognise it if you saw it again?'

'It was red, I think. I don't know tha' I could say wi' certainty.'

'Is there anything else you can tell me about her? Had she any friends among the servants who might know where she was going? Was she keeping company with a man? Have you any reason to believe she might have been in danger?'

Fitzpatrick stepped forward.

'Mr Swallow, it's a busy household here. If this young woman has had a mishap then that's very, very regrettable but it doesn't have anything to do with this house. I won't have my staff interrogated by you or by anyone else. Mr McDonald has told you that this girl is gone missing without permission. It's already caused enough disruption. Now, I insist that you leave.'

Swallow had to make a strategic decision.

He had an identity for the dead woman, but he needed to establish her movements from Sunday evening until she met her death. If she left the Fitzpatrick house, where did she go? Whom did she meet?

The next steps in an investigation would be to question the rest of the servants and anyone else who had contact with her. He would need to see her quarters and to examine her effects. If she had any papers he would have to scrutinise them to see if any family or relations might be traced. There would probably have to be a search of the house. On the basis of Harry Lafeyre's preliminary report there had to be a murder weapon somewhere.

But if he pressed these points now he knew with certainty that he would be obstructed. A tactical retreat might be best. He had made some progress in a difficult situation. Better to allow things to cool before pressing on. He closed the notebook.

'I'll require someone to come to the City Morgue at Marlborough Street to formally identify the body.'

'I can't spare Mr McDonald until later this afternoon, but I'll release him for an hour. I wouldn't want it suggested that I didn't co-operate fully with the authorities,' Fitzpatrick said.

'What about burial arrangements?' Feore asked. 'If the body is formally identified as that of Miss Hannin we'll have to try to find some family contact, even if it's remote, in order to arrange things.'

'As Mr McDonald has said, we don't have any knowledge of the girl's family. But if there are expenses to be incurred in her burial, I'll be willing to meet those, within reason, of course, since she was my employee.'

Swallow thought it prudent to strike what he hoped would be a conciliatory tone.

'It's rare enough to find that there's no family at all, even distant cousins. So in the circumstances that's a kind gesture, Sir. The Coroner will probably make those arrangements in the absence of any next of kin. I believe that if there are any costs they will be very moderate.'

'Be at the Morgue at Marlborough Street at 4 o'clock,' he told McDonald. 'Tell the attendant that you're to meet Detective Sergeant Swallow.'

He turned towards the door. 'Thank you for your co-operation, Mr Fitzpatrick,' he nodded. 'And I'm glad that you didn't come to any harm last evening at the Academy.'

Fitzpatrick did not reply. He turned on his heel and walked back into the room from which he had emerged.

The two detectives stepped to the front door. McDonald closed it quickly behind them. They stood in the half shade of the Georgian doorcase for a moment.

'An unlikely bloody story,' Feore said quietly. 'Housemaids don't get taken into service in Merrion Square houses without references from someone. These are plum jobs. Servants don't just walk in here off the street. You can be sure they know where she came from. There's a phrase in Latin, "*scio nihil*" – I know nothing. It was always meant iron ically, of course.'

Swallow glared at him. Feore had a tendency to let the schoolteacher in him break through at intervals.

'You'd best go back to Exchange Court and make a start on the paperwork,' he told Feore. 'Send a short report over to Chief Mallon and meet me down at the morgue at 4 o'clock.'

They stepped out into the hot sun of the day.

'You can't beat a classical education,' he added sarcastically. 'A few words of Latin make a nice touch when you're being put in your place by your betters.'

NINETEEN

Swallow needed food and something to cool his thirst. He had not eaten since his early breakfast at Maria Walsh's. He flanked the railings of Merrion Square, passing the Royal Dublin Society's premises at Leinster House and the pillared facade of Francis Fowke's National Gallery.

In less pressured circumstances he would sometimes take an hour to wander in the Gallery. He would marvel at the ability of John Constable or Franz Hals to capture a rural scene or an individual's mood, contrasting it with his own poor efforts to represent sunshine or rain on Dublin Bay. Most of all he liked the recent landscapes by Osborne, with shades of blue and green and dapples of white.

But that was not for today. In Fanning's public house on Lincoln Place he found an empty snug and ordered bread, cheese and a glass of light ale.

He sifted his thoughts in the quiet of the snug as the barmaid cut into a yellowed cheddar and carved slices of bread from a crusted batchloaf beside it.

He knew that he had been wrongfooted at the Fitzpatrick house. He was unsure what he should have expected. Policemen rarely get a warm welcome on official business, but he had not anticipated open hostility. Dublin's privileged classes might hold their police force in poor esteem, contempt even, but they generally lent their co-operation in the course of inquiries – if only to serve their own interests.

Perhaps his hostile reception at Merrion Square was the result of a misunderstanding. But he was puzzled by Fitzpatrick's lack of reaction when he was told that a body in the Marlborough Street morgue was probably a member of his household staff. There seemed to be little surprise – and no concern. Fitzpatrick had been swift to call in his rank as an Alderman in order to bring the G-men's questioning to a close. Yet when Swallow threatened a warrant and a search, he gave ground, agreeing to send the butler to Marlborough Street to identify the body.

He reasoned that Fitzpatrick understood the inevitability of the detectives taking further steps to advance their inquiries. He would know enough of official procedure to realise that they would want to examine the dead girl's belongings, to question other members of the staff and conduct a search. Even an Alderman could not demand that a murder investigation be halted because of domestic inconvenience. Swallow had the sense that he was seeing only fragments of an emerging picture, and that it boded nothing but trouble.

He finished his bread and cheese. He lingered over his ale for a few minutes and then set out across the river to the City Morgue.

The shortest walking route was through Trinity College. Lawns and cobbles shone green and black in the sunshine. There was a time when he would have found it difficult to be back in a place devoted to books and learning, but there were no longer any unmanageable pangs of regret for what might have been.

The Liffey tide was low as he crossed Carlisle Bridge, resulting in sulphurous vapours – and worse – floating upwards from the riverbed. But a faint breeze stirred from the direction of the bay offering some relief from the heat.

It was his second visit to the Morgue in as many days on murder inquiries. And that was unusual.

Lafeyre was already in the examination room on the first floor. It ran the length of the building with long windows set high in the wall in the manner of school classrooms everywhere. The pine flooring still showed staining from the ink-spillages of generations of scholars long gone.

The dead woman from the canal lay on the steel table nearest to Lafeyre. The tailor's scissors in his right hand indicated that he had just finished cutting away her clothing. Now dress, petticoat and cotton underwear lay in a sodden heap to one side of the table.

'I'm just about to start.' He laid the scissors on the tray behind him and took up a medium-weight scalpel. 'Have you made any progress with your identification?'

Swallow told him what had happened at the Fitzpatrick house.

'In the end, Fitzpatrick agreed to send this fellow McDonald, the butler, down to make a formal identification,' he added. 'I told him to be here at 4 o'clock.'

Lafeyre grimaced. 'You've drawn the short straw for yourself, haven't you? The dogs in the street know that Fitzpatrick is viewed as a protected species by the Castle. The City Corporation won't give an official welcome to the Queen's grandson so he's being put up to make some sort of address instead. You're not in the healthiest position for a G-man.'

He might have added, a G-man who's in enough trouble already, Swallow thought darkly.

Lafeyre gestured to the body on the steel table. 'I won't prejudge anything until I've completed the post mortem. But as I said up at Portobello this morning, what I've seen so far looks like foul play to me – and brutal at that. Three of these in one week is more than we usually bargain for.'

He laid the scalpel aside.

'I'll wait a few minutes to see if this McDonald arrives. Better not to give him any excuse if you feel he might hesitate over a positive identification.'

Swallow nodded in agreement. Lafeyre was a first-rate examiner, but he still thought like the practical policeman he had been when he served in Africa. He understood how evidence had to be secured and put together in order to have it admitted in a criminal court.

'By the way,' Lafeyre said cheerily, 'I have tickets for the Queen's Royal Theatre on Friday evening. It's a new comic opera called *La Fille de Madame Angot*. Would you and Maria like to join Lily and myself? We could have dinner together later?'

Swallow was not a theatre enthusiast. It rarely fitted in with his work schedule, and he reckoned that he saw enough tragedy in real life without spending his evenings watching more of it on the stage. But a little light opera might be enjoyable. And it was always good to see how Maria and her younger sister relaxed and enjoyed each other's company.

'That would be a good idea,' he heard himself say, even as his mind ran forward to a week which looked increasingly certain to be dominated by three problematic murder investigations.

'Maria would love it. I'll let her know so she can have the two barmen in to look after the business on the night.'

Mick Feore came through the door, perspiring from the heat of the day. He carried a new murder book, freshly drawn from the stationery stores at Exchange Court. He nodded politely to Lafeyre.

'The short report is done and gone to Chief Mallon, Sir,' he told Swallow.

'And I've got everything else started here in the book.'

Swallow nodded with satisfaction. The big detective's bulk might give the impression of a man who would be slow in his movements, but by God he could write fast.

Lafeyre's assistant, Scollan, appeared at the door of the examination room. James McDonald was standing behind him.

'Witness here to do the identification, Docthor,' Scollan croaked. 'Sent in be Sergeant Swalla'.'

'Come this way please,' Swallow waved McDonald towards the table.

Mick Feore formally noted McDonald's attendance in his murder book. Swallow countersigned the entry.

He turned to McDonald.

'Mr McDonald, look at the remains on the table beside Doctor Lafeyre please and tell us if you can identify this woman.'

Swallow thought he looked uneasy and nervous. His face was filmy from the day's heat. Beads of perspiration were suspended on the untidy ends of his grey hair. He had changed from his morning suit to a heavy tweed jacket and dark flannel trousers. Swallow tried to think how uncomfortable it had to be in the heat of the day. He was surprised to find himself feeling a twinge of pity for the man.

McDonald stared unblinking for a long moment at the dead woman.

'Tha's her all right. Wha' in the name o' God happened to her?'

'That's who, Mr McDonald, please?' Swallow asked. 'If you know her, state her name so that Detective Officer Feore can write it down.'

'It's Sarah Hannin. She's... she was... a housemaid at my master's house, Mr Thomas Fitzpatrick, Number 106, Merrion Square.'

He turned to Lafeyre. 'You know that Mr Fitzpatrick is an Alderman of the City Corporation,' he said solemnly. Swallow knew that he was delivering a message to the medical examiner.

'You're sure it's her body?' Swallow asked.

McDonald's face had lost its colour, accentuating the sheen of perspiration. He swallowed nervously and rubbed the palms of his hands across the sleeves of his tweed jacket. He seemed to be genuinely affected by the sight of the dead woman.

'Of course I'm sure. I supervised the girl at work for wha'… more than a year maybe. Do you know wha' happened to her?'

'She was found in the Grand Canal at Portobello Bridge this morning by a barge crew,' Feore said. 'Have you any idea how she might have got there or what happened to her?'

McDonald stepped closer to the examination table and craned his neck forward. He focused on the gaping wound on the dead woman's forehead. It seemed for a moment that he would not answer Feore's question.

Then he retorted urgently.

'I told you… I told you earlier at the house. She went out last night and didn't come back. I can't be accountable when a housemaid gets into trouble like this.'

He stepped back from the table and pulled in agitation at the sleeves of his jacket. 'Now… can I go back to work please?'

'Are you sure she doesn't have any family? Or did she have particular friends? Is there a grandfather or a grandmother, any cousins to be notified?' Swallow asked. 'Isn't there someone who can tell us about why this might have happened?'

'I've told you already. She just worked at the house. I don't know where she came from or anythin' about her.'

'What kind of person was she? Surely you got to know her enough to make some judgment of her character?'

'She gave no trouble. She did her work well and she got on well wi' the other servants, if that's what you mean.'

'Did she have a man-friend? Was she keeping company with anyone?'

'I don't know.'

'How long did she work at Fitzpatrick's?'

'Like I said, she might have been there a year, maybe longer. I don't know.'

For all the appearances of stress, the man was stonewalling. Whatever he might know about Sarah Hannin he was not going to pass it on to the G-men. Swallow had perhaps one minor tactical advantage. He played it.

'I think, Mr McDonald,' he said slowly, 'that you know a servant by the name of Hetty Connors, a former employee at Alderman Fitzpatrick's.'

McDonald blinked as if trying to concentrate. 'Yes, there was a kitchen maid by the name. She was insubordinate and lazy. I go' rid o' her. What's she go' to do wi' this?'

'Well,' Swallow said, 'To the best of my knowledge Hetty Connors was a friend of Sarah Hannin's. They kept contact after she had left her employment at Alderman Fitzpatrick's. I find it odd that you didn't mention her in connection with Miss Hannin even though I've asked you several times if she had any particular friends.'

McDonald threw his hands upwards.

'I didn't know they stayed in contact wi' each other. If you tell me that they did, then you know more than I do. I'm sure that the servants have many friendships among themselves. I don' necessarily know about it, or care.'

'Surely Sarah Hannin would have had to provide you with references before she was taken into employment?' Feore interjected, looking up from the murder book. 'Somebody must have recommended her, testified as to her character, that sort of thing? Where did she work before?'

'I don't know,' McDonald said. 'Tha' sort of business would be dealt with by Mr Fitzpatrick.'

'It seems as if what you don't know is a great deal more than anything you do know,' Swallow snapped, his earlier sympathy for McDonald starting to yield to frustration.

McDonald picked up his angry tone and glared. 'I've come here an' I've done me duty in accordance wi' me employer's instructions.'

The Lowlands accent thickened. 'I'm no' here by me own choice. Now I've done wha' is required of me and I'm goin' back to work.'

Swallow silently fumed. He had no authority to hold McDonald. He made a show of striding to the door of the examination room and flinging it open.

'Right then, *Mister* McDonald,' he growled, sarcastically. 'You can be assured that I'm coming back to that house. And by the time I'm done there I'll know more about you than you do yourself.'

It was as if the butler decided it was time to put on his own show of force. The perspiration had dried. The nervous plucking at his sleeves had stopped. He brought his face a foot from Swallow's.

'Don't you threaten me, Swallow. You think you're a little God, wi' your wee cardboard badge and your han'cuffs. Maybe you're a good match for the beggars and thieves of the city, but Mr Fitzpatrick is a very powerful man.'

He stepped out into the corridor. Swallow shrugged.

'I just wanted to frighten him a little. I started off feeling sorry for him, but that old bastard knows a lot more than he's telling us, I'm sure of it.'

'I'd say you're right,' Lafeyre said. 'But he doesn't seem to frighten easily. I've a post mortem to get on with. Are you sure you want to be here? I'm sure that Detective Feore can take a full note for you.'

'I'd rather stay. Three sets of eyes are better than two.'

Feore took a seat on a high stool at the head of the table and poised his pencil to write. Lafeyre clad himself in a green surgical gown and heavy rubber apron. Then he got to work.

'The body is that of a female somewhere in her mid-to-late twenties. Height is 5 feet 4 inches. Weight is 7 stone, 2 pounds and 4 ounces. There are no visible abnormalities.'

Feore's pencil began to work vigorously across the page.

'She appears adequately nourished. The teeth are strong and healthy. The limbs are well formed. The hair colour is fair and appears to be her natural colour. The eyes are light blue.'

He half rolled the body to its left side in order to allow Feore and Swallow to see the back and underside.

'There are some marks on the back of the body and on both legs but it is likely that most of these were made post mortem, possibly by the body being dragged by the barge. There are abrasions, with some skin torn away – from the right lower leg, from the left shoulder-blade and from the face, around the chin and neck.'

Lafeyre reached for a steel spatula and depressed the skin around the wound on the forehead.

'There is a bruise across the right cheekbone, extending to the eye socket, measuring approximately 3.5 inches by 3. It could be a blow from a fist or possibly a boot. However, the skin is unbroken so I am inclined to think it more likely to have been the former. The blow would not have been fatal although it would possibly have stunned.

'Very much more seriously, there is a large and deep wound on the left, frontal area of the cranium. It measures approximately 2 inches across and 1.5 inches down. Bone and cerebral matter are visible through this. Small splinters of bone from the skull are splayed at the edges of the wound. This is a most serious injury and, even from an external examination, I can say that it would potentially be fatal.'

He turned to Scollan. 'The sectioning saw, please.'

Scollan sectioned the forward skull, cutting through the cranium above the eyes and taking a perfect wedge of bone. He placed it in a steel kidney dish beside the examination table. Underneath, the dead woman's brain was a whitish grey.

The section under the wound was visibly different. There, a dull red, almost black inundation of the cerebral matter was apparent. Dark blood flooded the forward section of the brain.

Lafeyre resumed his narrative.

'The left frontal lobe of the brain has sustained a severe trauma. There is extensive bleeding from a wound which appears to have been caused by an impact of very considerable force. The bone has been shattered and the brain matter to a depth of a quarter inch has been compressed and broken. There would have been an immediate loss of consciousness with such a blow and death would have followed within a very short time.'

The weight of the heavy surgical apron and his exertions with the corpse were causing Lafeyre to perspire. He passed the back of his sleeve across his forehead.

'A blow was delivered with very great force. I would speculate that it was caused by a heavy, blunt-edged instrument such as a club or a bar.'

After that, it was a slow, painstaking process. Lafeyre opened the chest with the scalpel and brace, splitting the sternum and probing the lungs. There was a small amount of water, confirming Swallow's intuition and Lafeyre's own initial judgment that Sarah Hannin had not drowned and was dead before she entered the canal.

The stomach revealed little. The dead woman had eaten some bread and cereals a few hours before she died. Sectioning of the womb confirmed that she was not pregnant, but Lafeyre reckoned from his examination that she was sexually active.

'Maybe Mr McDonald doesn't know anything about it or maybe he does and won't say, but it seems that Miss Hannin wasn't entirely a stranger to male company,' he told Mossop.

Lafeyre signalled to his assistant that he was finished and to clean up. He turned to Swallow.

'She was killed with a massive blow to the head and then dropped in the canal. The water influences the processes of rigor mortis and I can't be sure but I'd say she was killed last night, Sunday, or in the early hours of this morning.'

Swallow grimaced. 'You can see that I'm just overjoyed with all that information, Harry. Sure, it'll be a cinch clearing this one.'

Lafeyre grinned as he peeled off his green sterile overalls and the heavy apron.

'Come on. Let me show you something that might amount to a bit of good news. Come up to the office while Mick tidies up his notes.'

He led Swallow to the first floor. The medical examiner's office was a large, rectangular room, not unlike his room in the Lower Yard of the Castle. Mahogany bookshelves lined one wall and a range of glass cases displaying a variety of specimens lined the other. A leather-topped desk stood against a corner. Beside it, a small table was topped by a bulky object hidden under a black, baize cloth.

'Have a look at this,' Lafeyre said. He lifted the covering.

Something approximately human sat on the tabletop. It had the shape and contours of a human head, but it was without eyes or ears. The skin was represented by white and pink plaster of Paris. It was a travesty of the human aspect, and yet it had a form and a shape that were distinctive.

Lafeyre extended a hand in a mock gesture of formality.

'Allow me to introduce someone. I'm only getting to know her myself by following Professor Hiss's methods of reconstruction. Say hello to "Chapelizod Gate Woman".'

TWENTY

The peak of the day's heat had passed by the time he left the morgue with Feore, but the city air was humid and cloying. They walked along Abbey Street and turned for Sackville Street. The flower-sellers at the Nelson Pillar had congregated on the northern side of the plinth in order to gain the shade. Every shop along Sackville Street had its blinds and canopies extended to the full.

Cab-drivers had shed their jackets as had most of the men waiting to board the trams that would take them home after their day's work. Here and there in the waiting lines, a lady's parasol splashed colour among the dark suits and white shirts.

The evening newspapers had latched on to the latest violent death with enthusiasm. The poster boards screamed the story.

'ANOTHER WOMAN BRUTALLY MURDERED
IN DUBLIN'
'MYSTERY OF WOMAN'S BODY IN THE GRAND CANAL'
'MURDERER STRIKES AGAIN – POLICE BAFFLED'

The clock on the Imperial Hotel showed a quarter to six. Swallow knew it would be too late to secure a warrant to search the dead woman's accommodation and to conduct inquiries among those who had known her at the Fitzpatrick house. It would be morning before he could expect any request to be processed. Since all of the public records offices were now closed, and would not reopen until the day after tomorrow, he was equally unlikely to make any progress on establishing the background or next of kin of the dead Sarah Hannin.

The two G-men turned from Sackville Street along the north quays and crossed the river at Essex Bridge. The faint stirring of the air that Swallow had sensed earlier in the day had abated. There was no hint of a breeze from the bay. He looked westward along the river's course and saw the same perfect blue sky that had extended over the city for six days.

The first signal that something was out of order at Exchange Court was the sight of a grim-looking Tony Swann, flanked by two uniformed constables, guarding the front door. Swann crooked a Remington shotgun in his left arm, his right hand resting on the trigger-guard.

Swallow reached the step.

'Jesus, are we under siege?'

'Damned if I know. Boyle told me to take position here. You haven't heard about Tommy McKnight and Charlie Vanucchi?'

'I've been on a murder inquiry all day. What's happened?'

The G-man jerked his head towards the door.

'McKnight died of his injuries in the Meath Hospital a couple of hours ago. Shanahan and Collins were with him. The man seemed to be all right. The nurse attending him had just told him that he'd be fine, then he turned over in his bed and died. But they got a dying declaration from him naming Vanucchi for the assault. So Shanahan and Collins arrested Vanucchi in Lawless's public house. There was a riot up there. The two boys had to open fire.'

'Jesus. Did they hit anyone?'

'Not as far as I know. But there's blood and damage. And tempers are up.'

Swallow was taken aback. Dublin policemen, even G-men, were rarely obliged to have recourse to their guns. When they did it was usually in encounters with the politicals – Fenians, Invincibles and the like.

He pushed the door and stepped into the public office. Half a dozen detectives milled around behind the counter. The buzz of the conversation was high and the air was thick with tobacco smoke. Between the bad air, the heat and the smoke, it was suffocating.

'Where's Inspector Boyle?' he asked the duty officer.

'He's upstairs, Sergeant, in the inspector's office with Shanahan and Collins and the prisoner.'

Swallow took the stairs quickly and followed the narrow corridor to the small office at the rear of the building.

The cramped office was barely capable of accommodating the four men inside. Charlie Vanucchi sat on a boxwood chair beside the wall.

He leaned forward, head bowed. His handcuffed wrists were thrust forward between his knees.

Duck Boyle was standing in front of the prisoner, a sheaf of papers in one hand, a stubby pencil in the other. Collins sat with his back against a window-ledge. His colleague, Eddie Shanahan, stood by the mantel shelf, packing the bowl of his pipe with tobacco.

Boyle swung around as Swallow entered the room. The inspector's face glowed with excitement. 'Very nice of ye to join us, Mr Swalla'. Needless to say, ye were elsewhere when these officers under my direction apprehended a murderer this afternoon.'

He waved the papers in his hand. 'Here's a signed statement by Thomas McKnight, identifyin' the man who assaulted him. A few minutes after signin' it, McKnight died of his injuries. He named Charlie Vanucchi.'

At the mention of his name, Vanucchi lifted his head slightly and appeared to attempt to speak. Boyle's right hand swung sharply and cracked across the prisoner's left cheek. Swallow saw that he was already bleeding from a cut on his lower lip.

'Shut yer face, ye Eye-talian bastard,' Boyle hissed. 'Ye'll speak only to answer my questions.'

Vanucchi hung his head again.

'Now, Vanucchi,' Boyle hissed, 'I'm givin' ye wan last chance. I want you to make a statement and sign it, admittin' that you assaulted McKnight.'

The prisoner raised his head and looked beseechingly at Swallow.

'I'm tryin' to tell this man, I don't know what he's talkin' about. I was just havin' a quiet drink with me friends after the funeral when these two eejits walked in,' he nodded towards Collins and Shanahan.

'They started throwin' their weight around. There was a fight broke out and they took out their feckin' guns. There was a lotta panic and shoutin'. But it wasn't me that caused it. These fellas tell me that Tommy McKnight says I done him over, but it's not true. I never touched him.'

Shanahan strode across the room. He stood aggressively in front of Vanucchi and bunched his fist an inch or two away from the prisoner's face.

'Don't tell me I'm a liar, Vanucchi. I was with Constable Collins when McKnight made the statement. I'll swear with him. You'll go away for a hell of a long time if you don't come clean now with us and with Inspector Boyle.'

'I've nothin' to say,' Vanucchi muttered.

Boyle threw his papers and pencil to the tabletop and grabbed Vanucchi by the collar, attempting to lift him from the chair.

'Ye'd bleddy well better have somethin' to say, Vanucchi!' he shouted. 'Ye'd bleddy well better tell us or I'll lave every bone sore in yer dirty body.'

Vanucchi shouted back.

'Go on then! Yer a great fuckin' man, aren't ye? Hit me when I'm chained up and wid yer hard men all aroun' ye. But some fuckin' night, I'll meet ye down a dark street, Misther Boyle, when ye won't have yer hard men and I won't be wearin' these.'

He raised his manacled fists defiantly in front of Boyle's face.

Boyle looked for a moment as if he was about to hit the prisoner again, but he released his grip and stood back. He threw himself into the chair opposite Vanucchi.

'Well, Swalla' what do ye make o' that?'

Swallow could have answered that of all the methods of interrogating Charlie Vanucchi, the one chosen by Boyle was probably the least likely to achieve the desired result. Anything that the flabby Boyle could physically inflict on Vanucchi would be a trifle by comparison with what the criminal strongman would absorb in an average Saturday night brawl. Instead, Swallow adopted a patient tone, preceded by the dose of flattery he knew was expected.

'A great catch, Inspector, and damned well done by Shanahan and Collins. You should get great credit for this.'

He saw a smirk cross Boyle's face. 'Well, if Mr Vanucchi here doesn't want to make a voluntary statement, that's his problem,' Boyle declared. 'We'll be bringin' him before the court charged with murder on foot of Tommy McKnight's dyin' declaration.'

The smirk extended. 'I expect you wouldn't know about the effect of a dyin' declaration, Swallow, do ye?'

He paused, savouring the opportunity to demonstrate his knowledge.

'I mean, seein' as how your education was to be in matters medical rather than legal. Well, let me tell you about it.'

He reached for a textbook on the table beside him, and ostentatiously opened a dog-eared page.

'*Nemo moriturus praesumitur mentire* – a man will not meet his maker with a lie in his mouth,' he intoned ponderously, articulating each of the Latin syllables slowly.

'No one at the point of death is presumed to lie. That's what the law says. So McKnight's dying declaration will be accepted as the truth when we bring Vanucchi to court… and if I have me way, on to the gallows.'

He turned to Vanucchi and spat the last words at him.

Swallow nodded thoughtfully as if reflecting on the solemnity of Boyle's legal declamation.

'There's only one possible snag in the line you're following, Inspector,' he said. 'The Criminal Procedure Act, if I understand it correctly, says that a dying declaration is only valid if the declarant is absolutely certain that he's facing death.'

He saw Boyle's eyes narrow, irritated by the possibility of contradiction.

'So what's yer point, Sergeant?'

'That's what makes a dying declaration so important,' Swallow continued. 'The declarant has to be sure and certain that his life is at an end. But from what I've been told, McKnight didn't know he was dying. As I heard it, the nurse told him he would be all right. It's far more likely that he simply wanted to finger Charlie Vanucchi, to have us remove him from the scene for a while.'

He turned apologetically to Collins and Shanahan.

'I'm sorry, lads. You did your best. But this so-called dying declaration isn't worth a toss. You've no evidence against Vanucchi that you can bring into a courtroom without being thrown out on your backsides. My advice is to turn him loose.'

Boyle's mouth dropped open. Collins turned red with embarrassment. Shanahan looked as if he had been struck in the face. The mood in the room changed instantly from elation to despondency.

Except for Charlie Vanucchi, who was grinning from ear to ear.

'Jesus, there y'are now, listen to Mister Swalla,' he whooped. 'That man has more brains than the whole feckin' lot of yiz put together. Yiz had better let me out outta here now before I send for a counsel and have yiz all sued for kidnappin' me and assault… for a start.'

Boyle stood rooted to the floor for perhaps a quarter of a minute. Then he went behind Vanucchi and opened his handcuffs.

When he found his voice it was strangled with rage. 'Sergeant Swallow. Would you please see Mr Vanucchi safely off the premises?'

Swallow gestured to Charlie Vanucchi to stand. He walked him across the room, through the door and down the stairs to the front entrance of the detective office. They stopped inside the threshold.

'Mr Swalla', I owe ye for this,' Vanucchi said. 'And Charlie Vanucchi doesn't forget a debt to a friend. I promise ye. Ye won't regret doin' the right thing for me today.'

Swallow pushed him violently through the open door of the waiting room. He kicked the door shut behind him, at the same moment seizing Vanucchi by the lapels of his jacket and lifting him against the wall.

'For your own sake you'd better make sure that I won't regret it, Charlie. I've gone out on a limb here for you in a way that no other G-man would have. Those fellows were planning to put you out of circulation for a very long time. You know that, don't you? All I had to do was to say nothing.'

Vanucchi nodded, his eyes goggling.

'I'm taking a calculated gamble that you're the man of the future after Ces Downes's death,' Swallow hissed. 'I'll be counting on you to tell me everything that's happening around this city. So don't ever forget the debt you owe to Joe Swallow. It's a big one.'

'All right, all right, Mr Swalla'.' Vanucchi raised his hands in a gesture of conciliation. 'What do ye need to know?'

'I need to know what these murders in the park are about, the woman and the child. I'm bloody sure some of your people can take a damned good guess at the answers.'

Vanucchi shook his head.

'Like I told ye on Saturday night, none of my lads would be involved in anythin' like that. But I know Vinny Cussen had men out watchin' the streets and the trams for some woman last week. Mebbe there's some connection there.'

'What woman, Charlie?' Swallow shook Vanucchi by the lapels again. 'Vinny must have given them a name, a description, something?'

Vanucchi's eyes were pleading. 'I swear I don't know any more, Mr Swalla', I swear it. If I did, wouldn't it be in me own best interests to tell you?'

That actually made sense, Swallow acknowledged silently.

He pulled the door open, and releasing his grip on Vanucchi's lapels he propelled him out into Exchange Court.

TWENTY-ONE

When Swallow returned to the inspector's room, Boyle seemed to have recovered his composure.

'So, Swalla', tell us what you've been doin' to justify yer existence. What's the story on the drownin' up be the Portobello lock?'

'It's not a drowning,' Swallow said. 'I've been down at the morgue with Dr Lafeyre for the post mortem. The woman's head was battered in. She was dead before she entered the water. I've had to call Mick Feore off the Chapelizod Gate inquiry and get him to do Book Man on this.'

Boyle groaned.

'Jesus Christ, three murders in two bloody days. And you haven't a touch of a clue or a decent line of inquiry on the first two yet. You'll be lookin' at bein' reverted to uniform, Swalla,' d'ye know that?'

'I've made some progress on this case,' Swallow replied. 'I have her identified. She was a housemaid called Sarah Hannin. I'm going to have to get a warrant to search the house where she worked and to question the people who knew her there.'

'Well you won't get it this evenin', Swalla,' Boyle snorted. 'Chief Superintendent Mallon's gone to an official reception at the Chief Secretary's lodge in honour o' the Queen's Jubilee.'

He paused as if to emphasise the solemnity of mentioning the monarch.

'I'm not goin' to have him bothered at this hour. Even if he cleared it tonight ye'd have to find a magistrate or a Justice of the Peace to countersign it, and with the Jubilee holiday tomorrow you wan't get any of those gentlemen waitin' about. You'll have to leave it until tomorrow or even the day after.'

Swallow fought down his frustration.

Boyle would learn from the newspapers, if nowhere else, that the dead woman worked at the home of Alderman Thomas Fitzpatrick, but he was in no hurry to tell him. If the inspector knew of a connection to any figure of influence he would insist on taking charge of the inquiry himself. Given Boyle's near total lack of investigative skills, any likelihood of solving the crime would recede.

'I'm planning two conferences for Wednesday, Inspector. We'll meet to review the Chapelizod Gate case and we'll have to put a second team to work on this death,' he said. 'I'll make out the paperwork on the warrant this evening. Will you move it to the Chief Superintendent's office as soon as you can?'

'I will,' Boyle answered, affecting an air of preoccupation. 'But I'm a busy man. Tomorrow will be a day out of the ordinary with all the celebrations around the city. I say again, I think it'll be the day after tomorrow before you get any progress.'

Resigned to a delay, Swallow decided to write up a preliminary report. He hammered out three copies on the typewriter, passing one to Mick Feore for the murder book. The second copy would go to the night sergeant in the detective office and, in turn, to Chief Superintendent Mallon in the morning. The third copy was his.

Mick Feore had already received a briefing from the search parties along the canal. The parties had collected an assortment of detritus, hardly any of which, Swallow suspected, would prove to be relevant. The trawl had yielded a dozen assorted buttons and hooks, a rusty knife, some fragments of newspapers and half a dozen assorted shoes and boots in various stages of decomposition.

Swallow reminded himself that he had a rendezvous with Harriet for White's coffee shop at 8 o'clock

'Sorry it's late. Put it in the book and go home and get some rest,' he told Feore, handing him the report.

'We'll meet in the morning and we'll celebrate the Jubilee,' he quipped.

He walked from Exchange Court to Westmoreland Street. The streets seemed quieter than usual for the hour of the evening.

Swallow reckoned that many of the office-workers and business people who might normally linger in town had opted to make for the coastal suburbs or the municipal parks in order to catch the evening sunshine. Some businesses had allowed their employees to finish work early, adding some free time to the Jubilee holiday of the following day.

White's was rich with the aroma of coffee beans. Sharp Arabicas contested with milder Ethiopian blends. The scent of the robust varieties from Brazil and Ceylon dominated. White's offered teas and chocolate too. The chocolate was served steaming hot in winter and chilled in the summer. Swallow could smell its sweetness, mingling with the coffee, on the evening air.

He took a booth with a view on to the street and ordered a pot of Chinese tea from the waitress.

Harriet was on time. She saw Swallow as she stepped in from the street and made straight for his table. A sharp observer would readily pick them out as brother and sister. They had the same dark brown hair, although his temples were now showing grey. They had the same dark eyes under prominent eyebrows and the same pale complexion. They had the Swallow family nose, with slightly flared nostrils.

She looked strained. Her normally ready smile was missing. That might be a good sign, he thought. Perhaps in the aftermath of the incident at the Academy she had begun to recognise that she was moving into perilous waters. Ordinarily he would have words of solicitude and comfort for his younger sister in any distress, but he knew he had to stifle them on this occasion. The business in hand could hardly be more serious.

She ordered a Brazil coffee from the waitress. 'You said you wanted to see me. Is it important?'

She was testing him. The question was a challenge. When her coffee came to the table, she sipped it looking over his shoulder through the window, pretending to be interested in what was happening in the street outside.

Swallow was patient at first. 'You know you could be in very serious trouble?'

'Really? Why would that be?'

He sighed. 'I don't have to spell it out. It's because you were part of − or at least were in the company of − a gang that came armed with a deadly weapon to attack a senior official from the Castle along with a leading member of the City Corporation. You're lucky not to be in Kilmainham Jail this evening. You're getting into something that's a great deal more dangerous than you seem to understand. Is that clear enough?'

She shrugged her shoulders. 'Maybe you're the one who doesn't understand what's going on, Joe.'

She clattered her coffee cup on its saucer and glared at him across the table.

'Our country is being subjected to England's will. We're expected to give loyalty to a foreign Queen while her agents drive our people from their farms to starve in the fields or take the emigration ships to America. All over the country this summer there are people being turned out of their houses while your colleagues in the Royal Irish Constabulary stand guard for the eviction agents.'

She waved towards the window.

'What do you see? You see flags and emblems to celebrate half a century of this Queen's rule. Well, it might have been a good half century in England, but for this country it's been famine, starvation and disease. It's been half a century of evictions and clearances and of emigration for those lucky enough to get out. What has Ireland got to celebrate?'

She spread her hands across the table for emphasis.

'We have to break the connection with England and we have to protest against opportunist politicians who try to fool the Irish people. That's why we were at the Academy. It's well known that Thomas Fitzpatrick is being put up as a puppet to make a show of welcome for this Queen's grandson. We can't be silent.'

Swallow seized on her word.

'"We"? Do you realise who the hell "we" actually are? The people you were with – the so-called "Hibernian Brothers"? Do you know that most of them are on file at G Division in the Castle as people who are violent and dangerous? Do you know the penalties for possession of a firearm with intent to endanger life? Do you realise that a court of law would see you and your friends as being just as guilty as the man with the gun in his pocket?'

She was silent for a moment. 'That's absurd.'

'That's the law.'

He saw her hesitate. 'I didn't know he brought that Prussian revolver with him,' she said quietly.

'"That Prussian revolver"?' Jesus, Harriet, what do you know about revolvers, Prussian or any other kind? What would you know about the difference between a Prussian revolver and... and... that teapot?'

'I know enough,' she said quietly.

She was more deeply involved than he had imagined. There were perhaps half a dozen clandestine organisations around the city, some on the fringes of the Land League and the Plan of Campaign, others with their own schemes to overthrow the British Empire's rule in Ireland. Their memberships varied from a handful of people to hundreds, in some cases.

The Invincibles who had murdered Cavendish and Burke were only one of a number of self-appointed avengers of Ireland's ancient wrongs. There was an unknowable proliferation of splinter groups.

Membership often overlapped between the various groups, making it difficult for G Division to achieve accurate estimates of numbers. It was said that the full complement of some of the minor groups could be carried on a bicycle. The active numbers of the mainstream Irish Republican Brotherhood – the Fenians – on the other hand, were to be reckoned in many hundreds, including quite a few with military experience in America.

'You know I can only protect you to a certain extent,' he said after a pause. 'If you don't get out of whatever it is you're involved in, you'll end up spending a very long time in prison when you should be doing what you set out to do, learning how to be a teacher and building a life for yourself.'

She drained her coffee cup and looked around for the waitress.

'You know I'm not a person who would support unnecessary violence, Joe.'

She looked him earnestly. 'But men like Fitzpatrick have to be confronted. He's making himself rich by exporting Irish farmers' cattle and produce to Britain for her armies. He pretends to be an Irish nationalist, but in reality he's protected by Dublin Castle.'

The waitress came to the table. Harriet ordered a second Brazil coffee.

Swallow's impatience was rising.

'Christ, Harriet. Who's filling your head with this… this… bullshit? It may be true, Fitzpatrick may be an opportunist. Maybe the authorities are using him to put up a front of loyalty to this bloody Prince Albert. But you don't have to get yourself into this kind of trouble to show your patriotic mettle.'

His teacup was empty.

'All right, maybe Fitzpatrick is making money too, selling cattle to the army. What about it? Leave it to the politicians, to Parnell and

Davitt and Healy and all the others. They seem to me to be doing a fairly good job in throwing bricks. It doesn't concern people like you. For God's sake, women aren't supposed to be involved in politics. They're not even supposed to vote.'

Her face was scarlet with anger.

'Well it should concern people like me – and you,' she shot back. 'I've held back from saying anything about your job as a policeman or what you do in the G Division. But I don't imagine you can be very proud of it. You're telling me I can be a teacher. That's fine. But if I say to you that you might have been a doctor and that you could have worked saving lives you'd not like to be reminded of that, I think. You're a good man, Joe, but you're supporting a system that's rotten and that keeps your own people in subjection and ignorance and poverty.'

She paused in her onslaught as the waitress put the fresh coffee on the table. As soon as the girl moved away she started again.

'And as for women, let me tell you that the women of Ireland are going to make changes. I'm going to be one of those women that stand up for Ireland and for themselves. And if you say women shouldn't be in politics, then what about this damned Queen you're working for? What could be more political than presiding over the British Empire?'

Swallow was relieved to see the waitress coming back.

'Would you like another pot of tea, Sir? That one must have gone cold by now.'

He nodded to the girl. 'Yes, thank you.'

Harriet added milk to her coffee. Swallow knew he had to avoid getting angry. However much it might inflame him, and whatever she had to say, this conversation was not about him or what Harriet thought of him. It was not about the job he did now or about the doctor that he might have been. The conversation was not about the life of Detective Sergeant Joe Swallow. It was not about the British Empire or Ireland's wrongs. It was about his sister, about her life, about saving her from the pit of disaster towards which she was headed and which she did not even see in front of her.

His instincts told him there was more to Harriet's attitude than some awakening of political awareness. There was a great deal of passion and an insufficiency of logic in her tirade. He followed a hunch.

'Did O'Donnell get you into this?'

'James?'

'I'm not aware of any other O'Donnell that you know.'

She lowered her eyes and sipped at her coffee. He could see that her rage was passing. He guessed that in spite of their tense exchanges she wanted to talk about James O'Donnell.

'He's highly intelligent and he's very well read. People look to him as a thinker and a leader. I think if you talked to him you'd be impressed by his arguments.'

He knew he was on the right track. 'How long have you known him?'

'I've known him for about six months or so.'

'So where did you meet him?'

'There was a public meeting in Kingstown. We all went down there from the college. He was on the platform along with Mr Davitt and Mr Parnell. He didn't actually deliver an address. He introduced other speakers. Later, one of the lecturers from the Royal College introduced us.'

Harriet looked past him again, appearing to focus on the street beyond the window. Swallow sat back from the table. He knew that she was waiting for his reaction. For all their differences, he knew that her older brother's opinion was important to her. It had always been so since her childhood.

'Do you... have feelings for him?' he asked, when the silence had run its course.

'Yes, I do,' she said quietly.

In his mind's eye, he saw O'Donnell from the evening before, leering at him, half-drunkenly.

There was nothing to be gained from pulling his punches. It was best to be frank with his young sister, although he knew that her initial reaction, at any rate, would be defensive.

'I think you could do a lot better than Mr O'Donnell,' he said.

'It isn't any of your business,' she snapped. 'This is a personal matter and it's my choice. I don't need your approval and I don't need to have you telling me who I should see or what I should do with my life. I'm an independent woman and I'll make my own decisions. I wouldn't dream of making that sort of comment to you. You have some rather odd arrangements in your own personal life.'

He resisted the urge to take up the implicit challenge over his relationship with Maria.

'He's a troublemaker, and he's dangerous. He's dangerous, among other reasons, because he doesn't seem to understand that he's playing with fire. He wasn't sober last evening at the Academy. You must have seen that yourself, Harriet.'

'You're not exactly a model yourself in that respect,' she shot back. 'I was only a young girl but I saw the sorrow you caused your father and mother when they were trying to set you up in the world. Who are you to accuse someone of having a drink too many?'

'Well let me tell you that if I was going out on a mission to save Ireland, or whatever he thought he was doing, and if I had a loaded gun in my pocket, I'd make damned sure I was fully sober.'

'The gun wasn't in James's pocket. I told you we didn't know that Horan had it with him.'

'And I've told you that won't make a ha'penny worth of difference in court.'

He lowered his voice for emphasis.

'Look, I'm not concerned with your private business. I've told you what I think of Mr O'Donnell and there's no point in my repeating myself on that. But let me explain what's going to happen now so that you understand fully.

'Your friends are in the cells at Exchange Court. They're facing charges of assault with a deadly weapon and possession of a firearm with intent to endanger life. If convicted, and they will be, they'll face anything up to 20 years apiece in prison.

'They're going to be questioned, many times over, by some of the political fellows from the G Division. It won't be very gentle and inevitably one or more of them is going to start giving information in the hope of getting a reduced sentence or having some of the charges dropped. Believe me, I've seen this happen a hundred times. The G-men will want names. They'll want to know their associates and supporters, their contacts and their sympathisers.'

He paused as the waitress placed a fresh pot of Chinese tea on the table.

'Your name will come out. And then you'll be brought in. Maybe you'll be charged and go to prison too, maybe you won't. But what I can tell you is that one way or another you'll be marked for the future. You'll be blacklisted. You won't get a teaching post anywhere. Your training and your qualification will be wasted. You might as well pack up and go to America and get a job as a governess. That's if you're lucky.'

She stared into her coffee. Her lower lip quivered. She spoke after a few moments.

'Look, let's leave our differences aside for the present. I know that you're trying to help me. What can you do then? Can you help James? Can you help us?'

He stared out the window. Queues of Dubliners were waiting for their trams. The sun had begun to drop away behind the high buildings on the western side of the street. A steam tram swung over to its stopping point, the driver yanking the bell as it approached the crowded pavement.

It all seemed so pleasant, he thought, these people going about their ordinary lives in the late evening sunshine. But there was nothing pleasant or ordinary about the situation he found himself in with his younger sister. Just 24 hours ago he would have said that she had the world at her feet. Now, from what he could see, her life was heading towards disaster.

'I don't know,' he said eventually. 'I'll have to make some inquiries as discreetly as I can. I do know the high-up powers are taking what happened very seriously.'

He gestured to the waitress for the bill.

'What I'd suggest is that you go back to the training college. Talk to nobody about what happened last evening at the Academy. If you're asked by anyone about it, just say you went there to meet me.'

He put a handful of coins on the table where the waitress had written out the bill.

'If you have any papers, documents or anything that could connect you to these Hibernian Brothers, get rid of them. Burn them. And I needn't add, if there is anything like another gun or ammunition around, get rid of them too. Don't just hide them somewhere and think they'll be safe. They will be found, I can promise you.

'It's absolutely essential that you avoid all contact with anybody in this organisation. Just keep to yourself. If you're visited by any police or detectives, tell them that your brother works in the G Division and get a message to me as quickly as possible. Whatever you do, don't answer any questions beyond giving your name, your age and your address.'

He softened his tone. 'Is all that clear? If so, I'll see what I can do.'

She nodded, but when she looked at him across the table he could still see the defiance and obstinacy in her eyes.

Outside, the dipping sun had started to cast shadows across Westmoreland Street. He walked Harriet to her stop and waited with her until the next tram came up.

She kissed him quickly on the cheek as she boarded. He stood watching until the vehicle clanked its way past Trinity College and out of sight.

It was pointless, he told himself, trying to argue a woman like Harriet Swallow out of love or out of her patriotic ideals. He reckoned he should be able to fix the immediate issues arising out of Sunday evening at the Academy, but once he had done that, he told himself, he would deal ruthlessly with the sodding little shit called James O'Donnell.

Tuesday June 21st, 1887

TWENTY-TWO

The public holiday marking the Golden Jubilee of Queen Victoria's ascent to the throne started across Dublin with a morning that was perfect for a celebration.

The sun shone in a crystal-blue sky. It would be oppressively hot later in the day, but in the hours before that, the air would be sufficiently fresh for citizens to get full enjoyment from the various entertainments and spectacles that had been arranged.

Dublin's celebrations would not be on the impressive scale planned for London. The imperial capital was thronged with visitors from all over the globe. At Westminster Abbey, forty crowned heads and leaders from Europe and the Empire would join in a thanksgiving service to mark the half-century of Victoria's rule. On the previous evening they had dined at a celebration banquet at Buckingham Palace. All over Great Britain, celebrations, services and street parties were being planned to take place in the midsummer sunshine.

In the main cities, and particularly in the London area, detectives from Scotland Yard's Special Irish Branch shadowed the movements of Irish nationalist activists. One informant report after another had brought intelligence of a 'Jubilee plot' to bomb or shoot the Queen or other members of the royal family.

It was known that explosives had been shipped into England through the port of Liverpool. Key Irish suspects were on the move. The telegraph wires and the telephone lines between the various police offices across the United Kingdom and between Scotland Yard and the Home Office in London were busy.

At the Dublin locations where Victoria's loyal Irish subjects would gather to mark the anniversary, the celebrations would be suitably fervent. Virtually all business and public offices had declared the day a holiday. At the Ball's Bridge grounds in Dublin's southern suburbs, a great athletic tournament with generous cash prizes had been arranged. In the wealthier districts, householders had organised children's parties. The principal streets in the city centre were decorated with floral wreaths, Union flags and bunting.

There were religious services at the city's two cathedrals, Christ Church and St Patrick's. A special hymn, *The Queen Shall Rejoice in Thy Strength*, had been composed by the Professor of Music at Trinity College, Sir Robert Stewart. Bands played in the city parks, and there were military parades. Later, each barracks would put on a celebratory banquet for the soldiers, their families and guests. At the Officers' Mess of the Royal Irish Constabulary at the Phoenix Park Depot, the evening would be marked by a full-dress ball and fireworks.

The detectives of the G Division of the Dublin Metropolitan Police were afforded little opportunity for celebration, however. From earliest light, every available man was assigned to special duties, shadowing people who might be likely to cause an incident or watching at locations where any unbecoming display of disloyalty might be likely to occur.

Detectives patrolled behind the choir-stalls in the cathedrals and along the principal streets where the bunting and decorations were at their most profuse. They mixed with the sightseers who gathered to hear the bands in St Stephen's Green, at the Forty Acres in the Phoenix Park and on the East Pier at Kingstown.

Swallow was assigned to supervise a team of ten G-men tasked with patrolling a stretch of central Dublin from the general post office in Sackville Street to St Stephen's Green.

It was considered a sensitive area, in which incidents might be likely to occur. A special eye was to be kept on the Westmoreland Street offices of the Dublin Port and Dock Company. The directors had arranged to put up a particularly impressive, large-scale portrait of the Queen, surmounted by a crown and the initials 'V.R.' The display would be illuminated at dusk with coloured gas jets. Intelligence reports indicated that it had been identified as a primary target for destruction by one of the militant nationalist splinter groups.

The morning was uneventful with good-humoured crowds moving through the city centre. Shortly after 1 o'clock, with everything apparently under control in the streets under his supervision, Swallow decided to check back at Exchange Court. He wanted to see if anything further had come in from the search parties that had scoured the canal banks where the body of Sarah Hannin had been found. Or perhaps there might be some results from the inquiries on the mail packets and the railways in connection with the Chapelizod Gate murders.

And he had to advance matters in regard to James O'Donnell and John Horan.

As the arresting officer, it would fall to him to charge both men with whatever offences might seem appropriate. There was scope for imagination there: conspiracy to cause an affray; assault on the Security Secretary and on Mr Thomas Fitzpatrick; unlawful possession of a firearm with intent to endanger life. It would not be long, he knew, before one or other of the prisoners would start talking to his G-Division colleagues. Harriet would be identified as a member of the group that had organised the protest and attack. Once that connection had been established it might be too late to save his younger sister from the rigours of the law.

An earlier slight drop in the morning temperatures had reversed. Any stirring of the breeze had abated. He turned into Fleet Street towards Temple Bar to make for the Castle. At the junction of Crow Street, he saw the figure of a young woman who instantly seemed familiar.

It took Swallow a moment to name her. It was the girl – the former kitchen-maid at the Fitzpatrick household – who had identified Sarah Hannin's body by the canal.

Hetty, Hetty Connors.

He stopped, watching as she crossed the cobbled Crow Street, head down, her shawl drawn tightly across her narrow shoulders. Swallow stepped behind her. The slight figure scurried along Crow Street and he saw her turn into the door of Naughton's public house. Swallow knew Naughton's well. It was a rough place, frequented by alcoholics, beggars, petty street-criminals and prostitutes. He followed the girl across the street and entered the public bar.

A wave of bad air, smoke and the reek of body odours hit his senses as he entered. The bar was not crowded, but the dozen or so patrons who stood against the counter knew what he was. Each contrived to look elsewhere, at the ceiling, at the filthy mirror behind the bar, through the no-less filthy window that gave out onto a laneway at the back. Swallow knew most of the faces, but there were no signs of recognition. Few of Naughton's clientele were interested in the Jubilee celebrations in the streets outside, it seemed. They turned to their drinks and resumed their muttered conversations. Hetty Connors was nowhere to be seen.

Two wooden-walled snugs were located at either end of the bar. Swallow knew that she must be in one or the other.

He found Hetty on the banquette seat in the first snug, about to raise a glass of clear spirits to her lips. Her other hand clutched a small, embroidered bag. She started when Swallow pushed the door. Her eyes were red rimmed. The round, pock-marked face reminded him of the dull features that the Dutch masters often gave to household servants in the paintings that he sometimes saw at the National Gallery.

'I suppose you've been out celebrating the Jubilee, Hetty,' he said amiably. 'But I'd like to talk to you for a few minutes.'

She looked at him angrily and grasped the embroidered bag tightly to herself.

'I… I was just goin'… I have to… to… be back at the hospital,' she stammered.

Swallow drew a battered, wooden chair and sat opposite her, pushing the door of the snug shut behind him. 'Just relax and enjoy your drink, Hetty. I won't be any harm to you. Do you remember me from yesterday morning?'

The girl continued to stare angrily at him in silence for a moment, then she gave a silent nod.

'Good. Well, I need a little help, a little information about Sarah Hannin, and I thought you might be able to help me.'

She drained her glass.

'I'm not sayin' nothin' to you… nothing. I don't want to talk to you. Let me go to me work now.'

She rose to leave. Swallow gestured to her to stay where she was. She took her seat again slowly. Her eyes filled with tears. Swallow estimated that she was both frightened and defiant.

'Please, Mister, I don't want to get into trouble. I can't tell you anythin'. Let me go now please.'

He lifted her empty glass and sniffed. It was a rough, almost raw gin, imported from England and probably mixed with illegal spirit – poteen.

'I'll get you another one of these, Hetty. All I want to do is talk to you for a few minutes. Nobody needs to know.' He rose and checked that the door of the snug was shut, then he went to the hatch. He rapped hard on the counter and indicated a refill to the barman.

'And a Tullamore for myself,' he added hopefully, recognising that in these premises ordering any branded spirit was a pointless exercise. Virtually everything crossing the counter was a cheap English import or bootleg whiskey from the Wicklow hills or the midlands.

She took the drink that Swallow had bought and gulped half of it down. She ran her hand through her greasy, dark hair, finding just enough courage in the gin to leer faintly in his face.

'Right, thanks for the drink. Now, I'm goin' back to me work, you've no right to keep me here.'

At that moment the snug door opened behind Swallow. He turned to see a heavily built man of perhaps 30 years with a thin, black moustache. He wore a dark jacket, a brocaded waistcoat and a bowler hat. His eyes ran from Hetty to Swallow, then they swivelled back to Hetty. Without a word, he stepped backward through the door of the snug and fled.

Swallow knew him. It took a moment to bring the man's name out of memory. Tony Hopkins was a small-time robber, and he was a fence; a receiver of stolen property. Whatever servants and pickpockets could steal, Tony Hopkins could sell on at a profit. Swallow knew he had come to meet Hetty in the snug. He had recognised the G-man and taken off.

'So you're working for Tony Hopkins?' Swallow looked disapprovingly at Hetty Connors. 'You're not just an amateur, are you?'

'It isn't that,' she said with a hint of coyness. 'Tony an' me… we're sweet on each other, as you might say.'

Swallow groaned silently to himself. There was no point, he knew, in telling Hetty Connors that nothing but grief would lie ahead in any relationship with the likes of Tony Hopkins.

The girl had shrunk back into the wooden banquette, the almost-empty glass clutched in one hand. Swallow reached across the table and wrenched the bag from the other. He opened the cord at its neck and emptied the contents onto the table.

Four pennies, a large, iron key, a gapped, whalebone comb and a small, gold-topped, propelling lead pencil, fashioned from tortoiseshell.

Swallow put his notebook onto the table and opened it at a blank page. He took the top from the tortoiseshell pencil and handed the pencil to the girl.

'Write your name there, Hetty.'

She sat silently, staring at the floor.

'Just your name, Hetty. Go ahead.'

'No, why should I?'

'Because I'm a policeman and I'm ordering you to do it. If you don't, I'll arrest you for obstruction and land you in jail.'

'I can't. You know I can't.'

Swallow snapped the cover back on the pencil.

'I didn't think you had much use for a gold pencil yourself. You can't write. You're a thief, Hetty. How long have you been at it then, sneaking valuables from patients in the hospital? It could be a pencil tonight, maybe a bit of money another time? How much would you get from your fancy-man there with the fine moustache for that pencil? Half a crown maybe?'

The girl began to tremble. She reached for the glass and finished the remainder of her drink. It seemed as if she wanted to say something but no sound came out.

Swallow thrust his right hand to the back of his belt and found his handcuffs. He clanked the steel manacles on the tabletop in front of Hetty Connors, then he got to his feet.

'Right, we'll go across now to the hospital and we'll see who you lifted this from. Then we'll see what else is missing over the last few weeks or months. I imagine they'll remember that a lot of things have gone missing. Then it'll be the Bridewell for you tonight, court tomorrow and the women's prison for a couple of years.'

Hetty burst into tears. They flooded down her scarred face as she buried her head in her hands.

'Don't do that, I'll put it back…' she blubbed. 'I swear it was th'only time I done anythin' like it. I'll tell you anythin' I can about Sarah and wha' happened to her. Just let me off this once. An' I swear it'll never happen again.'

It was an absolute lie, Swallow knew. God alone knew how much the girl had purloined at the hospital. Clearly her *modus operandi* was to meet her fence in the public house, hand over whatever she had collected and then get whatever few shillings he would offer. But it was a small matter compared to the business of murder.

'Well, you'd best start talking then, Hetty. You can start by telling me about who might have killed her and why.'

'I swear I don't know.' She rubbed her eyes, reddening the rims even more. 'All I know is that when we worked together at Fitzpatrick's she was a strange one, always holdin' herself out t' be better 'n the rest of us. She always was goin' on about how she'd come into her own, wha'ever that meant. But I liked her... we stayed friends.'

'How did you get to work at Fitzpatrick's, Hetty? It must have been hard enough to get to work in a fine house like that?'

She shrugged. 'They're not that particular about workin' in the kitchen. It was Sarah got me the start.'

She giggled. 'In truth, it was Sarah writ me a reference for Mr McDonald, sayin' I'd been workin' in a house in Meath. She wasn't a girl who was too bright... too smart like... but she was educated to read an' write ye know.'

Swallow rose, went to the hatch and rapped again for service. The barman silently poured the order a second time. Swallow put a florin on the filthy counter and waited for his change. When the gin and the whiskey came up he passed the girl her glass and sat down again.

'Tell me about her, Hetty. Had she a man-friend? What did you know about her?'

Hetty gulped from her glass. The third gin was beginning to show its effects. Her head lolled a little sideways and she began to giggle quietly.

'What? A man-friend with Sarah? Aw... I don' know... I don' think so. She used to be jealous of me because I had Tony. I'd ask her had she any wan special but she wouldn't tell me anythin' like tha'. But who was she anyway? Sure, no more 'n the rest of us. Wasn't she raised a bastard child in an orphanage?'

She waved her glass unsteadily in Swallow's face.

'Raised a bastard and not too smart... but always pretendin' she was somethin' better,' she repeated. 'But sure, who'd blame her? Not me, I wouldn't.'

Swallow sensed that he was getting somewhere.

'Do you know where she was raised, Hetty?'

'Oh, some place in the arse end of the bog. Queen's County, she used to call it, no less, when she was bein' all hoity-toity wi' me and th' other servants in the kitchen.'

'Can you remember the name of the place?'

'Somethin' like "Green House," or "Green..." green somethin'... tha's all I know.'

It meant nothing to Swallow. 'When did you last see Sarah alive?'

She hesitated. 'It was one o' them fine evenin's. We'd just meet an' talk, you know, up by the canal. Sometimes one of us would have a bit o' bread and we'd feed the birds there by the water.'

'You didn't see her on Sunday?'

'No. Defni'ly not Sunday, I was workin' at the hospital.'

Swallow changed tack.

'What do you know about Mr McDonald, the butler at Fitzpatrick's, Hetty?'

'*Misther* McDonald? Tha's... an ould bastard is... McDonald...' Her voice trailed. The three poisonous gins had all but reduced her to incoherence.

'You didn't get on well with him, I think.'

She looked past Swallow towards the filthy windows of the public house as if trying to recall something important.

'I'll tell you wan thing about... Mister McDonald – he's not Mister *McDonald* at all. His name is... McDaniel. Sarah told me she was cleanin' his room one day an' she found his army pay-book with his real name on it. He caught her lookin' at it. The language and the curses outta him were all over the house.'

'Do you know anything more about him? Where's he from? How long has he been working there?'

'All I know is he's a right oul' bastard... to me and to the rest of the staff. He thinks he's still... still in the bloody army.'

'He was a soldier?'

'In one o' them Scottish regiments... or somethin'... bastards. I've heard some of the other servants say so.'

Swallow jotted the details in his book. He stood up. He handed the gold-topped pencil to the girl.

'Okay, Hetty. You go home now. I don't think you're in much fit state to go to work. But when you next go to the hospital, this pencil goes right back to where you took it from. If you touch one more piece of property there I'll have you in Kilmainham, like I said. You understand that?'

She nodded, and got to her feet uncertainly. She moved past him to the door. Without a word, she exited the snug on unsteady feet. Swallow sat quietly and finished the rest of his drink.

He drained what had been passed to him for Tullamore and left the public house. There was still no breeze, and the air that came up from the river into the narrow lanes and streets of Temple Bar was heavy. He started back towards the Castle.

He checked at the telegraph office, but no messages had been sent through from England. Perhaps, he thought, it was unreasonably optimistic to expect anything given that it was a holiday.

He walked down to Delaney's public house in Parliament Street and ordered cold herring and potato and a glass of ale. The G-men had the city under control, and he reckoned he was under no time pressure to return to his squad on Sackville Street.

When he finished his food he bought a quarter bottle of cheap Tipperary Colleen whiskey from the barman and put it inside his coat pocket. He decided it was time to visit James O'Donnell.

TWENTY-THREE

Swallow signed himself into the cells area in the Lower Yard, scarcely disturbing the G-man dozing at the entrance. He dropped his revolver into a drawer on the duty officer's desk and checked the custody book to see where he would find Horan and O'Donnell.

Horan's cell was next to the entrance. Through the Judas hole he could see that the prisoner was asleep on his bunk. O'Donnell's cell was at the other end of the building. That way no communication would be possible between the two suspects.

When he peered into the second cell, Swallow could see that O'Donnell was sitting upright on his bunk, his head in his hands, staring at the stone-flagged floor.

He opened the cell door and stepped inside.

A gas mantle projected a thin pool of light onto the floor. In spite of the heat of the June days, the place was freezing. The brick walls of the cell, set hard on the rock foundations of the Castle, glistened with damp. An enamel plate and an upturned mug at the end of the bunk indicated that the prisoner had been given something that passed for a meal.

O'Donnell looked up. Swallow was used to seeing the effects of incarceration on people who had been accustomed to their freedom. Anger and defiance gave way to anxiety and agitation, then came withdrawal and depression. Reflexes began to slow, and the capacity to measure time diminished. Isolation, cold and hunger accelerated the processes.

But he had rarely seen so rapid a deterioration. In less than 48 hours, James O'Donnell had changed from a seemingly confident, healthy-looking young man, albeit under the influence of alcohol, to a huddled, shivering wreck. His hands gripped the edge of his bunk. The knuckles gleamed white against the grey blanket. His knees were trembling. Despite the cold, O'Donnell seemed to be perspiring. His forehead and cheeks were damp. There were traces of either dry vomit or food at the corners of his mouth.

'Good evening, Mr O'Donnell,' Swallow said formally, trying not to display his surprise at what he saw.

He recognised the condition from his own drinking days. O'Donnell was showing classic symptoms of alcohol withdrawal; *delirium tremens*, the 'DTs.'

He took the Tipperary Colleen from his pocket, thumbed the cork and offered the bottle to O'Donnell.

'Here,' he said gruffly, 'get some of that inside you. You'll feel better.'

Without looking at Swallow, O'Donnell put the whiskey to his lips and took two fast mouthfuls, then a third. He handed the bottle back, giving out a deep exhalation that set off a shudder along his whole body.

He raised a hand slowly, recognising Swallow. 'It's you,' he muttered. 'Can you get me out of... this bloody place.'

Swallow looked around the cell, feigning surprise.

'Oh, I don't know, Mr O'Donnell. It's nice and cool in here after the heat outside and all the noise and fuss over the Jubilee. It's quiet and private. And it's better than Kilmainham where they'd have you wearing your fingers out stitching door mats. I'd relax and make the most of it, if I were you.'

O'Donnell put his head in hands again. Swallow could see that the whiskey was being absorbed into his bloodstream. The trembling in his knees had stopped, and the running perspiration was drying.

'You can't afford to mock me, Swallow. If I'm to be charged you know that your sister is going to come into the frame. Are you willing to see her in prison too?'

Swallow attempted to sound unconcerned.

'My sister has to look after herself. She should have thought about the implications of getting involved with people like yourself and Horan. In any event, she's only a support player. Whereas you and Horan are what might be called principal actors.'

O'Donnell raised his head again.

'I didn't even know he had the bloody gun with him. He wasn't going to use it. If that was the plan, Fitzpatrick and maybe Smith Berry wouldn't be alive now.'

'I promise you that a court will take a different view,' Swallow said. 'You were acting in common design. That's called a conspiracy. It can sometimes be a bit difficult to prove, but Mr Balfour's Crimes Act makes it a lot easier where a policeman gives evidence of association between accused persons. You could be facing 15 to 20 years in Maryborough convict prison.'

O'Donnell was silent. The only sound in the cell was the hissing of the gas mantle.

'And I suppose there'll be a policeman who's willing to give that evidence,' he said bitterly, after an interval.

'I suppose so,' Swallow answered.

'Christ,' O'Donnell said angrily, 'how did this country produce creatures like you? Have you any principles? Have you any sense of patriotism?'

Swallow raised his voice.

'You've got nothing to teach me about principles, O'Donnell. I've put a lot of your type through my hands. You think any crime is justified if you label it as patriotism. And you'll all sell each other out when you have to. As to patriotism, my grandfather was out with a pike against General Lake and General Cornwallis, fighting for Irishmen's rights in 1798. I wonder where your own antecedents were?'

For a moment it looked as if O'Donnell wanted to continue the argument. Then he waved a hand dismissively.

'Forget the history for a while. What would I have to do to get out of this?'

'I'm not sure there's actually anything *you* can do, Mr O'Donnell.' Swallow paused for effect. 'It might be a question of what a friendly G-man might be able to do.'

He handed the whiskey bottle to O'Donnell again. 'Here, have another shot.'

O'Donnell took two more mouthfuls. He wiped his lips and handed the now half-empty bottle back to Swallow.

'And in return for… doing whatever it is… what would this friendly G-man want of me?'

'Oh, that's something we'd need to think about, Mr O'Donnell. I don't imagine you're sufficiently important to make yourself a valuable informant. You haven't much to trade, I'd say.'

'I can get some money. Not a lot. But I could get it.'

Swallow laughed. 'Ah, police pay isn't that bad, Mr O'Donnell, that I'd need your money. At least it's not bad when you're a sergeant in G Division. My 30 pieces of silver that you mentioned the other night at the Academy is actually more like 40 – a week that is. It doesn't put me in the Thomas Fitzpatrick class but it's enough for me to get by.'

'Fitzpatrick?' O'Donnell grimaced. 'Now if the damned police were doing the job they're supposed to be, he's the fellow who should be here in this bloody cell instead of me.'

Swallow decided to be deliberately provocative.

'Alderman Fitzpatrick is a citizen in good standing. He gives good employment to a lot of people in this city. And isn't he a believer in Irish freedom, a patriot like yourself, Mr O'Donnell?'

O'Donnell shivered but managed a mirthless grin.

'It shows how much you don't know, Mr Swallow, doesn't it? He's a fraud and a charlatan. We've had people gathering stuff on him for years. I'm not given to violence, but if Horan had shot him it would have been a public service.'

'Be careful, Mr O'Donnell. You're in danger of walking yourself even deeper into trouble.'

Another convulsion, but a lesser one this time, ran down O'Donnell's body. Fresh beads of perspiration appeared on his face and trickled down his neck to the already-sodden shirt. When the tremor passed he focused his gaze on Swallow again.

'It would be a pity to leave the rest of that Tipperary Colleen in the bottle, Sergeant. I'm sure you wouldn't want to be found on duty carrying hard liquor, and cheap liquor at that.'

Swallow handed the bottle to him. 'Finish it off, Mr O'Donnell. You're right. It isn't to my taste.'

O'Donnell put the bottle to his mouth and emptied what was left of the Tipperary Colleen. He threw the bottle onto the bunk beside him. Swallow retrieved it and put it in his pocket. A prisoner could do a great deal of damage to himself or somebody else with a broken bottle. Swallow had seen more than one suicide in the cells effected that way.

'I'm not afraid to say it, Swallow, even if you find it disturbing to your view of things,' O'Donnell said, newly coherent with the alcohol running in his system. 'Fitzpatrick is going to be put up as the welcoming face of Dublin when this idiot of a prince comes to town next week. We haven't any shame left.'

'What do you mean when you say you've had people 'gathering stuff' on Fitzpatrick?'

O'Donnell sensed something more than casual interest in the question.

'Ah, so you're curious?' He gave a weak laugh, his face becoming suddenly animated. 'You're looking for information about the man whose interests you and your colleagues are supposed to be protecting.'

Swallow considered for a moment telling him about the dead Sarah Hannin who had worked at Fitzpatrick's house, but decided against it. It would probably only play into O'Donnell's sense of self-justification.

'That's the right word. I'm curious. You and I have more important matters to consider, Mr O'Donnell. As I said, my sister has to look after herself. At the same time, I want her to be able to continue with her career. Our family has invested a lot in her education. So it might be that we can come to an understanding that might be mutually beneficial.'

'So… what are you saying to me?'

'I'm saying that whether you can avoid a long jail sentence depends on my report. I can tie you in directly with Horan and the gun, or I can say that you were just someone who was in the wrong place at the wrong time. In that case, I'd expect that you'll go free.'

'And in return for that, what do you expect?'

'I need two things. There has to be no mention of Harriet's name in any account of what happened at the Academy. She isn't to be mentioned in any conversations about this Hibernian Brothers outfit you're involved in. You don't know her. You haven't ever talked to her. And you're never to go near her again. As far as you're concerned, she doesn't exist. Is that clear?'

'And what's the other thing?'

'You and I will keep closely in touch once you're released. You'll tell me what's going on in your organisation, who has joined, who has left, what you're planning to do, what money you have, what weapons and so on. You'll have a code name and nobody but you and I will ever know that we're in contact.'

He paused. 'And, of course, if the information you give me is accurate and useful, you'll be decently paid for it.'

O'Donnell ran his fingers through his thin hair and smiled. Swallow saw a flicker of interest in his eye at the mention of money. He knew that O'Donnell would dissemble for a moment. And so he did, just for a moment.

'You're asking a lot, Mr Swallow. You want me to give up a beautiful, intelligent young woman who has strong feelings for me, and you want me to become a police spy?'

'Take it or leave it, O'Donnell. You won't have much opportunity for romance doing 20 years in Maryborough Prison.'

O'Donnell kneaded his eyelids with his fingers.

'I think you don't leave me any damned choice, Mr Swallow. What do I do?'

'When I come back to take a statement from you, your evidence will be that you went along to the Royal Hibernian Academy on your own because you're interested in Stella Purcell's paintings. You don't know this fellow Horan other than to see him around the city. You don't ever mention the name of Harriet Swallow. Your story is that you were just arrested in the melee. I'll confirm that from what I saw this is accurate. Unless my superiors take a different view, you may not even go to trial.'

O'Donnell's eyes flickered. 'You'd write that… that sort of report?'

'On the conditions I've just set out. And if you break any of them, or even bend them, or if you breathe a word of it to anyone, myself and a few G-men will take you out to the Wicklow Mountains where I'll put a bullet through your skull and drop you in a bog-hole. And I'll enjoy doing it.'

O'Donnell grimaced. 'I believe you would, Mr Swallow. And I believe you when you say you'd enjoy it. So what do we do about Horan then?'

'What about him?'

'What happens to him?'

'It's open and shut. He had the gun. He fired it. He won't see daylight for a while.'

'Jesus. I'm telling you he didn't intend to use it.'

'He'll still be put away for a long stretch. That is unless I decide to make it easy for him too.'

'Can you do that?'

'I can testify that the gun went off accidentally. Maybe it did. We can probably get his charge down to unlawful possession. I can't promise anything, but with luck he'd get a year, maybe six months. But I'd have to be certain that you can deliver silence from him about my sister as well.'

Swallow moved to the door. 'Think about it, Mr O'Donnell. It's the best offer you're going to get. It's not very pleasant here, but Maryborough Convict Prison is bloody freezing in the winter. And the rocks in the breaking-yard there are damned big ones, I'm told.'

Wednesday June 22nd, 1887

TWENTY-FOUR

Swallow slept soundly in the big double bedroom over Grant's public house after the city had fallen quiet. He had resumed patrolling the area from Sackville Street to St Stephen's Green with his posse of G-men until midnight.

By then the fireworks had long finished. The gas-lit illuminations on the buildings had been darkened. The drunks in the streets were good-humoured and happy. They sang *God Save the Queen*, *Hail Glorious St Patrick* and a variety of suggestive parodies from the music halls.

One tipsy reveller recognised a G-man and offered him a celebratory swig from a bottle of something that smelled strong and peaty on the warm air. Swallow discreetly turned away and pretended to be interested in the viewing platform at the top of the Nelson Pillar.

He rose early and made his way to Exchange Court. With the security demands of the Jubilee celebrations out of the way he could get on with securing a warrant to search the Fitzpatrick house and to question the members of the household.

Any expectation of abatement in the uncommon heat that had baked the city for ten days was dashed when the sun rose again in a clear, blue sky. It was to be another day of prolonged sunshine with the city dry and airless. The layers of dirt that had gathered in the streets, in the yards and courts, were being slowly baked to solidity. In the Phoenix Park, butts of water were put out for the deer. In St Stephen's Green, the parched grass was showing shades of brown and yellow. The keepers made efforts at irrigation with buckets and watering cans.

Pat Mossop and Mick Feore, Swallow's two Book Men, had made an early start. Mossop had cleared a wall space in the Crime Sergeants' office and was hanging sheets of drawing paper with inquiry results set out in blue and red ink. Mick Feore stood beside him, drinking tea from a tin mug.

The two Book Men were in their shirtsleeves. Mossop held a sheet of flimsy paper in one hand and a bottle of adhesive gum in the other. He dabbed the back of the flimsy with gum and banged it onto the wall with a satisfied grunt.

He saw Swallow come through the door just before 9 o'clock. It would be a busy morning with two separate crime case conferences.

'There's a bit of good news on the Chapelizod Gate, Boss,' Mossop said, making a fair attempt at cheerfulness. He reached across the desk to hand Swallow a report pad.

'We got something in from England this morning. A transport policeman at Chester Railway Station says that he had a complaint last Wednesday morning – that's a week ago today – about a man who had entered the ladies' waiting room with a young boy.

'When he questioned the man he apologised and said he'd made a mistake. He said that he and his son were going to catch the Holyhead train in order to connect with the mail packet to Ireland.'

Swallow scanned the ruled pad.

The man kept his head down during his conversation with the railway policeman. The man and boy were neatly dressed and well presented. The man's accent was definitely English; probably Liverpudlian. The officer demanded his name and address and his destination in Ireland. He warned him that a further incident would result in a prosecution. The policeman also noted that the man had somewhat prominent eyes.

He had given the name of Edward Jones, Gordon Street, Wavertree, Liverpool. The Railway Police office had checked with Liverpool City Police. Gordon Street was real enough, but nobody there knew of an Edward Jones.

The man's forward destination in Dublin was given as St Brigid's, Abbey Street. Almost certainly false again, Swallow reckoned.

Swallow knew St Mary's Abbey, close by the intersection of Capel Street and Abbey Street. It was a court or yard, built around the remains of an ancient abbey, originally Benedictine and later Cistercian, now given over to warehouses and with a Jewish synagogue nearby. But St Brigid's, Abbey Street was a fiction, at least to the best of his knowledge.

'It's a help,' he said unenthusiastically. He handed the message pad back to Mossop.

Mossop looked tired. He had been on duty for 14 hours during the previous day's Jubilee celebrations. His normally well-waxed moustache drooped down the sides of his mouth making him look rather forlorn. His spare frame seemed to droop in its loosely fitting suit.

Swallow queried Mick Feore, who had returned to his own desk. 'Have we any developments on the Hannin case?'

'A cab-man handed in a woman's bag he said he found down by the canal at Baggot Street Bridge on Monday afternoon. He says he stopped to draw water for his horse. He spotted it in the grass by the towpath. Our search parties hadn't got to that point on the canal by then.'

'So where is it now?'

'He handed it in at College Street. They're sending it over shortly.'

'Baggot Street Bridge,' Swallow noted. 'If it's Sarah Hannin's bag I suppose that could indicate the point at which she went into the water.'

Pat Mossop looked up from his desk. 'I know that place from my time in the E District. There's a spot under the bridge that isn't easily visible from the street. It's a place where sweethearts can meet discreetly. But it's also a place where mischief could be done without being noticed. We always had to check it out on our beat, night or day.'

'Is there anything else?' Swallow asked Feore.

Feore tapped at the pages of the book on the desk. 'They have a few statements from people who think they might have seen the girl but there's nothing here that jumps out as being useful.'

When Mossop and Feore had departed to the police mess-hall in the Lower Yard for breakfast, Swallow spent an hour going through the paperwork on the three murder cases.

It was a depressing exercise. Other than the identification of Sarah Hannin, there was no real progress anywhere. It had almost invariably been Swallow's experience in serious crime investigation that motive emerged fairly quickly. Witnesses, even reluctant ones, could usually be pinpointed at an early stage. Similarly, the identification of victims rarely took more than a day or two when families or workmates came forward.

Six days into the investigation he still had no idea who the Chapelizod Gate victims might be. There was no clear way forward with the case. The reported sighting at Chester railway station and the questioning of the mail-packet crew might lead somewhere in time. Equally, it might be a blind alley.

And the immediate requirement in the Sarah Hannin case was to secure access to the house and the other servants.

Sarah had left Fitzpatrick's on Sunday evening. At some point after she had encountered some person or persons who took her life and placed or dumped her body in the canal. Was that meeting by arrangement? And if so, with whom was it? Or was it a chance encounter that ended in violence?

The chances were that some of the other servants were aware of her plans or who she was likely to meet. One or other of them could very likely throw some light on who might have done her violence and why.

The crime conference was scheduled to start at 10 o'clock. Stephen Doolan had allocated a junior sergeant from Kevin Street and half a dozen uniformed constables to attend.

As Swallow could have predicted, Feore had done a good job on setting up the briefing. The photographic prints from the scene at Portobello Lock were neatly displayed on the wall. Beside them, a sheet of white board set out the essential points that had been gleaned from the investigations to date.

Feore and Mossop returned from their breakfast. 'We're ready to go, Sergeant,' Feore said.

Swallow took his place at the desk, and gave his short account of Monday's events and the recovery of Sarah Hannin's body at Portobello. Then Feore took the group through Harry Lafeyre's post-mortem report.

Swallow resumed his narrative from the moment that the dead girl had been identified by Hetty Connors.

'After the identification I visited the home of Sarah Hannin's employer with Detective Mossop. She worked as a housemaid at the home of Alderman Thomas Fitzpatrick at Number 106 Merrion Square. They didn't give us a great reception. There's an unhelpful butler at the house who goes by the name of McDonald. He's Scottish, I think. He's maybe 60 years of age, I'd guess. I had a confidential whisper giving me reason to believe his real name is McDaniel. I'd like inquiries to be made in the area if anything is known about him.'

He saw no advantage in identifying Hetty Connors as the source of his information about the butler's alias.

'We know very little about the victim apart from her name, or at least the name she worked under at Fitzpatrick's. This butler and Mr Fitzpatrick himself say they don't know of any family or relatives. They say they don't even know where she was from. We know from Dr Lafeyre that she was sexually experienced so there must be a male somewhere with whom she was intimate. But McDonald says they don't know anything about a gentleman friend either.'

'I'm seeking a search warrant for the Fitzpatrick house,' Swallow told the group. 'She was killed some time before she was put into the water, so the murder site may be within the house. At the very least, we need to examine her quarters and her personal effects. I'd ask you to assemble back here at 2 o'clock. I should have the warrant by then and we can proceed to execute it.'

There was bravado in this, he told himself silently. Fitzpatrick had made it clear he wanted nobody poking around in his house or questioning his servants. And he probably had enough clout with the powers in the Upper Yard to get his way. It might require a more unorthodox approach to find out about Sarah Hannin's life and why it had been ended so violently.

He stood from the desk. 'Are there any questions?'

The young sergeant from Kevin Street drew a folded morning newspaper from inside his tunic and placed it on the desk in front of him.

'Not so much a question as an observation. This sort of stuff doesn't help to keep the lads' spirits up, does it?'

He tapped the open page with his finger and turned the newspaper for Swallow to read.

It was the main news page of the *Daily Sketch*. Much of the space was devoted to the Jubilee events of the previous day, but the editors had not forgotten about Dublin's three gruesome murders. Crime always sold newspapers, Swallow reflected ruefully.

He read the descending headlines:

'YET ANOTHER DUBLIN MURDER'
'POLICE HAVE NO CLUES'
'EMPLOYEE OF ALDERMAN FITZPATRICK'
'SERGEANT SWALLOW THREATENS THE PRESS'

Swallow's heart sank as he read the report. He recognised Irving's racy, sensational prose describing the scene on the canal bank, the identification of the dead woman and his warning to the reporters to stay back from the scene.

'Well, you'll all be famous by the end of this. Nothing like a bit of publicity to make you feel appreciated,' he grimaced.

The sergeant nodded. 'Ah sure, it's only a rag,' he said unconvincingly.

When the uniformed officers had left, Feore set about updating the murder book. Swallow gave him his instructions.

'Contact the office of the Army Paymaster in London to see if we can get a trace on McDonald or McDaniel. See if they can find any details of an old soldier, maybe a deserter. He might have continued to use his first name, James. People often do, even when they adopt a different surname. He'd be perhaps 60 years of age, so his date of birth would be in the '20s with enlistment maybe in the late '30s or '40s. His discharge could be 20 years ago, maybe longer. And they could start with the Scottish regiments.'

Feore noted the details.

'I'll get a telegram off. Their records are good. And they're usually fast on this kind of thing, especially if the fellow is in receipt of a pension. You mentioned that you got a whisper. Is that why we're interested in him?'

'I got a confidential word that he may be living under an alias. There might be nothing to it, but it's worth checking.'

Feore nodded. 'It wouldn't surprise me if he's got a record behind him. He's a shady old bastard. I didn't like him from the moment I saw him. The bad ones have a way of letting a bobby know they think he's just a bit of dog shit.'

Mick Feore sometimes had a way with words, Swallow reflected. It had to be the teacher in him.

The second crime conference of the morning – for the Chapelizod Gate murders – was set for 11 o'clock. Swallow had time to spare before that, and he had a useful purpose in mind for it.

He walked down to the Lower Castle Yard, making for a grey-bricked building similar to the detective office at Exchange Court. His destination was the Board of Educational Charities. Among many other functions it supervised the operation of more than 200 orphanages, endowed schools and institutions of care which were spread across Ireland.

The chief clerk was a Welshman called Rankin. Swallow knew him from encounters in various public houses around the Castle and he had rendered him more than one policing favour. If a man working in one Castle office could do a good turn for someone working in another, why not?

In particular, Mr Rankin had reason to be grateful for the inexplicable loss somewhere in the system of one particular police file. Had it been progressed to a conclusion, it could have led to a conviction for attempting to perform a lewd act in a public place, to wit, the precincts of a brothel in Bull Alley.

The chief clerk greeted him by name. 'Well, Sergeant Swallow, this is an unexpected pleasure. Come in, take a seat.'

He gestured Swallow to a chair beside his desk. 'What can we do for the G Division this morning?'

'A little information, Mr Rankin,' Swallow echoed the Welshman's mock formality. 'I'm trying to find about an institution in which you might have an interest.'

'Quite a few of those,' Rankin grinned, showing dark, stained teeth through his beard.

'This one is in Queen's County. It's called Green something-or-other. Green House, or something like that.'

Rankin scratched an expansive stomach and nodded. 'Only institution there with a name anything like that is Greenhills House. Would that be it?'

'It could be. Tell me about it.'

Rankin looked thoughtfully at the ceiling.

'It's a few miles outside Maryborough. Greenhills is a small institution by our standards... maybe 20 or 25 female children. It's been endowed through the estate of a Roman Catholic lady now deceased... provides accommodation and training for young girls of respectable families come on hard times. Some will be adopted. Mostly they're prepared for domestic service... housemaids, ladies' maids, governesses, that sort of thing. Quite well run, when last I heard about it. Although their endowment is running down and they'll need a new benefactor if they want to carry on. Why do you ask? Is there some problem there?'

Swallow shook his head. 'No, I'm just trying to put some details together about someone.'

'It's nothing to do with that damned business at the Chapelizod Gate, I hope. A dreadful, shocking affair that.'

'No, not at all, I assure you,' Swallow told him, not wholly untruthfully.

Rankin crossed the room to the set of filing cabinets that lined the wall. He opened a drawer in one of the cabinets and lifted out a dark green file.

'Greenhills House. Latest report is 1885 – two years. That's acceptable. Although one of our inspectors should be through there again soon, I'd imagine. Unusually, this place isn't in the hands of one of the Roman Catholic religious orders. The guardian is an individual named Pomeroy – Richard Pomeroy. 22 inmates at last count. No infectious or notifiable diseases. No complaints. No disruptions or absconding.'

He looked up from the file. 'It all seems a well-run operation. It would be a pity if it doesn't find a new benefactor to fund it.'

'Would you have files on past inmates, children who were accommodated there?'

'No, they wouldn't be here. Those files remain with the individual institutions. We just deal here with overall numbers. But the files are confidential in any event. We can't have people trying to unpick arrangements that have been made for their own good. You couldn't run a system like this if you didn't lock down all the information.'

Although the registration of births, deaths and marriages had been compulsory in Ireland for more than 20 years, the bureaucratic arrangements for dealing with illegitimate children were designed by the authorities to be inflexible and impenetrable. Swallow nodded his understanding.

'Is there anything else I can do for you, Sergeant?'

'I don't think so, Mr Rankin.'

Rankin walked back to the filing cabinet and replaced the file.

In the moment that his back was turned, Swallow reached across the Chief Clerk's desk and slipped three sheets of the Board of Educational Charities' headed notepaper into his own file.

He thanked Rankin and retraced his steps across the Lower Yard of the Castle to the detective office.

TWENTY-FIVE

Inspector Duck Boyle was late. There were puffy bags under his red, watery eyes. Swallow guessed that after he had finished his tour of duty the previous night he had perhaps entered a little too enthusiastically into the spirit of the Jubilee celebrations. He glared at Swallow.

'I've been thinkin' about that business with Charlie Vanucchi yesterday. You've a funny way of lookin' at things, Swalla'. Yer colleagues put their skins at risk. We arrest a murderer. We have th'opportunity to put one of the city's leadin' gangsters behind bars – and you're arguin' we have no case.'

'The dying declaration was useless, Inspector,' Swallow said. 'We'd have been thrown out of court. You should be grateful that I saved you the embarrassment.'

Boyle waved a pudgy finger.

'You could have kept your mouth shut. There wasn't no need for anyone to know that the damned nurse told McKnight he'd be all right. If Mcknight thought he was goin' to die then the declaration would have been valid. A damned bad day's work you did.'

Swallow shrugged. There was no point in arguing. Boyle was impenetrable. If Vanucchi had been charged and brought to trial, the nurse's evidence given in court would have immediately undermined the case.

'I don't agree, Inspector,' he said simply.

'Let me hear no more o' this nonsense, Swalla'. Get on and do yer own job. There's no signs o' spectacular success in that department, I gather. And in future let me get on wid mine.'

Exchange Court was facing into a busy day. Many of the criminals and hangers on who had congregated around the Liberties for Ces

Downes's funeral had not yet dispersed back to their usual haunts. The Vanucchi and Cussen factions were still ensconced in various dives and public houses around the city. The threat of further violence between them had not abated. The G Division would have to keep a careful eye on them for a while yet.

It would be another day of long hours on the job for the men on Boyle's duty roster. In twos and threes, he told off the morning detail and then turned to Swallow.

'Now Swalla,' how do you intend to justify yer existence for the day?'

Swallow put his sheaf of documents on Boyle's desk.

'I've got to run the conference on the Chapelizod Gate murders,' he said. 'We've already had a meeting earlier on the Sarah Hannin case and I need the warrant. You'll recall I did the paperwork on Monday, so if you'll countersign it I can send it to the Chief Superintendent for endorsement.'

Boyle grinned.

'Well, yer a very smart fellow, Swalla', but ye think I came down in the last shower a' rain, I suppose.'

He tapped Swallow's papers.

'Ye think I don't know whose house this is, Swalla'? Ye think I'm a fool that'd let the paperwork past me desk widdout checkin' the details?'

He pushed the file across the table.

'Take that away outta here, Swalla'. If you think I'm goin' to ask the chief super for a warrant to let you tear into Alderman Fitzpatrick's house, you must be even thicker than I thought ye were. Yer makin' no progress on three murders! It's not just one, but three murders! An' yer best idea is to charge into Mr Fitzpatrick's house wid a warrant.'

He pointed to the door.

'You should a' been out on the street, me man, and doin' some old-fashioned detective work. You should a' been findin' out who this woman was involved wid. That's where th'answer lies. It usually does. And you should be doin' yer job widdout tryin' to make yerself notorious.'

Swallow could hold back no longer. His exasperation boiled over.

'You're a coward and a fool, Boyle. You know damned well that if it was anyone else's house we'd have been in there on Monday like a cavalry charge. But you're so bloody frightened of annoying the nobs in the Upper Yard that you're willing to jeopardise a murder investigation. It's not a bloody housebreaking, you know. There's a woman lying dead down there in the morgue.'

Boyle's face turned a shade of scarlet, his eyes bulging. He shouted back angrily.

'Don't you dare speak to your superior in that tone, Swalla'! An' don't try to lecture me on crime investigation. You're livin' on an outdated reputation. Ye haven't made wan inch a' progress on the Chapelizod Gate murders. For the love o' Jesus, you haven't even established who the poor creatures were. Now, I'm tellin' ye once again, I'm not forwardin' the warrant application to Chief Mallon.'

The room had fallen silent. Feore and Mossop stood open-mouthed by the door.

Swallow had regained his composure.

'Very well, Inspector,' he said icily. 'You won't progress the application for the warrant. Just tell me one thing. Who told you the house belongs to Thomas Fitzpatrick and to keep our hands off? Because I know too bloody well that you didn't find it out on your own. You can hardly read your own bloody pocket-watch.'

Boyle leaped to his feet. He waved a fist in Swallow's face.

'Ye can count yerself lucky, Swalla', that I'm not a violent man. Ye'd be lucky not to be lyin' stretched on the floor there and facin' a disciplinary charge when ye kem 'round. Now, let me tell ye somethin' else, Mr Swalla'.'

He drew a sheet from his file.

'This is a letter signed be the Commissioner an hour ago. You're to be taken off the investigation into the death of this Hannin woman. There was a serious complaint about yer manners and yer methods – intrudin' and threatenin' at Alderman Fitzpatrick's house on Monday. You're taken off the case, Swalla – yerself and Feore. This investigation is to be handled by special detectives workin' out of the office of the Under-Secretary, Mr Smith Berry, in liaison wid meself.'

He turned on his heel and strode from the room, slamming the heavy door behind him.

Swallow gathered the papers he had laid out on the desk and replaced them in his own file.

That Boyle was acting under instructions was certain. He might have gleaned his information about Sarah Hannin's place of employment from the morning newspapers, except that he had never seen Boyle read a newspaper before. The word had come from somewhere on high that the Fitzpatrick house was to be left alone.

Swallow had encountered some of Smith Berry's men. He had no high opinion of their crime-solving capacities. The majority were English or Scottish, usually with a background in Scotland Yard's Special Irish Branch. They specialised in surveillance and political work. They lacked what policemen referred to as 'local knowledge.' The likelihood of their making any significant progress on the Sarah Hannin murder would be negligible, he reckoned. Moreover, it was clear that there were things the authorities did not want brought to light in a regular police investigation.

One half of his brain told him to walk away from it and to leave it to them. The other half boiled with resentment at being treated as a passive instrument of the Upper Yard's agenda.

As his anger cooled the sense of resentment grew. Then it turned to a cold determination. He went back to his desk and took one of the sheets of headed notepaper that he had purloined earlier from Rankin's desk at the Board of Educational Charities.

He slipped it into the Remington and typed three short paragraphs. He sealed the letter in an official envelope with the Crown's symbol of the Lion and the Unicorn. He addressed it to 'Mr Richard Pomeroy, Guardian, Greenhills House, near Maryborough, Queen's County,' then he put it in the outgoing mail tray.

TWENTY-SIX

The mood was marginally less gloomy than two days previously when the team assembled at 11 o'clock for the crime conference on the Chapelizod Gate murders.

Pat Mossop had circulated the news of the possible sighting of the woman and boy at Chester railway station. If the railway policeman's identification was correct, it reinforced the supposition that they had crossed from Wales on Wednesday and spent one or two nights in Dublin before meeting their fate.

The Dublin address given by the woman, though, was evidently a fiction. Mossop had checked the street directories and made inquiries with the Station Sergeants at the Bridewell and Store Street stations. By definition these were veteran officers who knew every inch of their districts. There was no house or building, no church or memorial anywhere near Abbey Street named for St Brigid.

Stephen Doolan's men had checked all the guest-houses, lodgings and doss-houses in the A Division, from St Stephen's Green to the river, and as far out as the villages of Kilmainham and Inchicore, for any sightings of a missing man and child – or a woman and child. Policemen in the other divisions had been making the same checks as they went about their beats.

Nothing had turned up. But there was progress of sorts on two other items.

Constable Culliton, who had taken the casts of the wheel-marks left on the grass by the Chapelizod Gate, had been back to Hutton's, the carriage-makers in The Coombe.

'They're certain on the wheel width,' he told the conference. 'It's unusual – 6 foot 7 inches exactly from outer rim to outer rim. Hutton's say that's the axle width of one of their clarence cars. It's a special, a big car – a sort of a double brougham. They say they made about 50 of them over the past 20 years or so.'

Stephen Doolan nodded thoughtfully. 'We could manage a check on 50 cars if we had the names of owners – and if we had a fair bit of time. It might be possible to place the vehicle on the night of the killing. Do Hutton's keep records of owners?'

Culliton looked doubtful.

'They might have some. I checked that. But they say it would be a lot of work to go through them all, so they're not keen. And anyway, these cars are often sold on to new owners. Hutton's wouldn't necessarily know who has them now if they've changed hands.'

Doolan snorted. 'I'll get over there this morning. They'll be a bit speedier with their paperwork by the time I'm finished with 'em.'

He opened his notebook.

'We got the clothing that the woman was wearing across to one of the Jewish tailors in Capel Street. They know their stuff those fellows. He confirmed that it's English cloth. But as he makes the point, where would you get any Irish cloth nowadays outside of an exhibition or maybe in Connemara or some blasted bog?

'He picked them right down to the seams and found everything in order. No broken threads or tears, no rents. No hidden pockets. And there's no damage to the clothing that might suggest the wearer was in a struggle or anything.'

Swallow nodded. 'It's worth putting in some time tracing these clarence cars.' In his heart he believed it would probably be a waste of effort.

There was one other possible line of inquiry that might be worth airing.

'I got a word that Vinny Cussen had men out last week watching the streets and the trams for a particular woman,' he said. 'I don't know why, or who they were looking for. It might be nothing of significance, but keep your ears open, especially if you run across any of his footsoldiers.'

'Could we not just take Cussen in and… persuade him to tell us a little more?' Doolan ventured.

'Maybe it'll come to that, Stephen,' Swallow said. 'But I'd prefer to have more hard information to work with before we do anything like that.'

There were nods and murmurs around the room.

'Do we have anything else?' Swallow asked. 'No report of a missing boy anywhere in the city?'

'Nothing,' Doolan said. 'There was a young lad gone missing about a month ago out on the Bull Island. The RIC think he got taken out to sea by a fast tide while he was collecting cockles. There hasn't been any sign of a body, but the tides could have taken him out of the bay. There's no other missing persons reports that might fit.'

Pat Mossop pointed to some sheets of paper inserted in his book.

'I've got the description of the victims written up, Boss. They're ready to go out to all the English forces when you've read it.'

Swallow had still not told the team about Harry Lafeyre's attempt at a facial reconstruction using Professor Hiss's methods. He preferred to see the results for himself first.

'Maybe we'll just wait a while on that,' he said. 'It's early days and there are telegraph costs involved. Mr Mallon would have to approve.'

There was little more that could be done. Doolan would revisit Hutton's the coach-makers, and hopefully that would accelerate the process of identifying the owners of the clarence cars they had made and supplied over the years. In the meantime, the house-to-house inquiries would go on, even though every policeman knew that with each passing day the likelihood of any positive result would diminish.

When the uniformed officers had left, Swallow sat with Pat Mossop in the crime sergeants' office, sifting yet again through the pages of generally useless information that had been accumulated in the murder book.

Shortly before noon, a constable from the B-Division station at College Street came to the public office at Exchange Court with a small, brown, cardboard box. It was tied with string, closed with a wax police seal and addressed to Detective Sergeant Swallow. Swallow guessed it contained the lady's bag, which had been found by the cab driver at Baggot Street Bridge.

Strictly speaking, it was no longer his business. The Sarah Hannin murder inquiry was now under the authority of the Assistant Under-Secretary for Security and his team of out-of-town agents in the Upper Castle Yard. But the word had obviously not reached College Street that Swallow was off the case, and so the evidence had been forwarded to him.

If he were to follow procedure he should simply forward the package to the Security Secretary's office, but Swallow was not in a mood to respect procedure. He opened the box and took out the small, black, velvet bag. The metal clasp was already showing corrosion from the elements. It was a factory-made accessory such as might be bought inexpensively in a 'monster store.' But it was relatively new, with no wear apparent, beyond the slight corrosion on the clasp.

Sarah Hannin had bought it recently, Swallow thought. Indifferent quality notwithstanding, it would have been a costly item on a house-maid's meagre wage. Or perhaps it was given to her? Or maybe it was stolen? After all, Sarah Hannin's friend, Hetty Connors, was a thief.

He upturned the bag and tugged at the lining, turning it inside out. It was empty.

He saw a small, white label stitched into the seam. He took it between thumb and forefinger to read it.

'WATKINS OF LIVERPOOL'

Swallow felt a mild frisson of excitement. Was there a slim connection here? It was likely that the victims at Chapelizod Gate had come from Liverpool. And here was a lady's bag from a Liverpool shop. Was it just coincidence that Liverpool seemed to be coming up in both cases? New possibilities began to form in his head. Until now there had been no evidential reasons to suspect a possible connection between the murders at Chapelizod Gate and the death of Sarah Hannin. But were there not some similarities?

Both women victims, killed within days of each other, were of much the same age. Both were killed, in all probability, during the hours of darkness. Neither of them had any evidence of identification. Sarah Hannin had been identified, it seemed, by the simple coincidence of her body being recognised as it was taken from the water. Was it possible that both could be linked, however tenuously, to Liverpool?

If so, it would probably not be good news, Swallow reckoned. It was bad enough to be at a full stop on three deaths. But what if they were to be connected? Failure would be the ultimate challenge and humiliation – a series of related murders but without any significant prospect of solving them.

He replaced the bag in the box and re-tied the string, then he went downstairs to the parade room and placed the package in his personal locker. If the investigation by Smith Berry's men ever got to the point at which they would come looking for the bag, which he greatly doubted, he would be able to produce it.

He realised that he felt cut off and adrift as never before in a serious crime investigation.

In the ordinary course of events, a new breakthrough or a sudden insight would have had him making straight for the inspector's office or even to John Mallon himself. He would want to tap into the wisdom and knowledge of other experienced detectives. He would have asked for a photographic technician to take pictures of the bag, and especially of the label with its 'WATKINS OF LIVERPOOL' stamp.

Now, though, the normal operating rules were suspended. There was no one in the chain of command to whom he could turn. For whatever reason, it was clear that G Division was not going to be allowed to continue its investigation into the death of Sarah Hannin. If he spoke to Boyle or any of his colleagues about the possibility of some connection between the three deaths he might find himself taken off the Chapelizod Gate murders as well.

One person he could talk to in confidence was Harry Lafeyre.

He glanced at the wall-clock. Lafeyre would be at the City Morgue until 1 o'clock, at which time, Swallow knew, he generally went to his house at Harcourt Street to have lunch and later to see his private patients.

He left the detective office and hailed a cab outside the Cork Hill gate. He gave the driver the address of the Morgue at Marlborough Street and settled back into the stiff upholstery for the short drive across the river. He was glad of the current of cooler air that came through the cab windows as it moved through the heat of the city.

As he dismounted at Marlborough Street, Swallow saw Lily Grant taking leave of Lafeyre outside the building. He made an effort to sound light-hearted.

'What are you doing here, Miss Grant?' he asked in a half-reproving, half-mocking tone. 'Aren't you supposed to be encouraging artistic appreciation among the younger generation at Alexandra College and not keeping this industrious public official from his important work?'

Lafeyre grinned. 'Well, this isn't a visit from my fiancée in any romantic sense. Lily is here helping me with what you rightly call my important work.'

Swallow raised an eyebrow interrogatively.

'I'll explain.' Lafeyre pushed the door inwards. 'Come up to the office. Can you stay a few extra minutes, Lily, to explain what we've been doing?'

'Of course,' Lily said. 'I don't have to be at Alexandra until 2 o'clock. You'll want to see this, Joe.'

They climbed the stairs to Lafeyre's office.

'Yesterday I introduced you to a version of "Chapelizod Gate Woman," but it wasn't anything like what we have now,' he told Swallow as he opened the door.

'I spent four hours last night working on the plaster reconstruction, but the fact is I'm only a doctor. I really needed an artist – someone who could make the leap of imagination from the sinews and muscles that I could put in place to composing a set of features that would fit. So I sent for the assistance of the best art teacher in Dublin: Miss Grant of Alexandra College.'

He bowed mockingly and extended a hand towards the tabletop. 'Now, let me introduce you to the new, improved version of "Chapelizod Gate Woman."'

Swallow recognised the same contours of the clay head from the previous day, but now he was looking at something utterly different. The features had come alive under Lily's hand. Swallow was looking not at an assemblage of plaster and hair but at a recognisable individual.

When Swallow first saw the body in the copse of trees by the Chapelizod Gate on the previous Friday morning the face had been a travesty. Now he was looking at the features of a woman in her late twenties. The facial structure was thin and angular. The nose was somewhat flat, but the features were handsomely symmetrical. The eyes were prominent, bulging as if the woman had just seen something that had frightened her. They were blue-green, set in a complexion that Lily had painted in sallow flesh-tones.

A dark wig mimicked the hair that Swallow had seen above the ravaged face. The lips were firm rather than full. The forehead, where the circular bullet wound had been, was smooth and high, showing a little furrowing between the brows.

'It's very realistic. But how do you know it's true to life?'

'Harry's quite sure he reconstructed the bone and muscle structure along the lines set out by Professor Hiss,' Lily said, 'so we know that the shape and the contours of the features are accurate. After that, I'm responsible for a bit of artistic licence, I suppose. I've made a guess about the skin tone. The eye colour is a bit of a guess too because the irises were completely destroyed. Insofar as Harry could make out, using the microscope on the fragments of tissue that were left, it seems they might have been green or blue. And as you know, there were some cysts around the sockets that would have made the eyes rather prominent.'

Swallow felt a surge of optimism.

'We'll get this to all police stations and post offices. The newspapers can get etchings done from a photograph and they can print those. If the method is really as accurate as you say, Harry, this might get us somewhere.'

Lily interjected. 'I really have to go now. I'll have to catch a tram in Sackville Street if I'm going to be on time.'

She kissed each of them in turn on the cheek.

'Joe, we're seeing you and Maria for the theatre on Friday evening, isn't that right? I'm looking forward to it.'

When she had gone, Swallow told Lafeyre of the morning's developments. He recounted Boyle's refusal to process the warrant and the transfer of the Sarah Hannin investigation to Smith Berry's department.

Lafeyre shrugged.

'That's how it is sometimes, I'm afraid. These fellows in the Upper Yard have their own plans and priorities. The death of a housemaid isn't going to weigh very heavily with them if it's a question of keeping the pressure off one of their protégés at a time like this.'

Swallow told him about the finding of the dead girl's bag with the 'Watkins of Liverpool' label on the lining.

'It's possible that there's some connection. When you look at the two cases, there *are* similarities.'

Lafeyre nodded. 'I agree. It's a theory worth exploring. But if it's correct then you're dealing with a multiple killer.'

'There's something else,' Swallow added. 'You recall McDonald, the butler from Fitzpatrick's who came in here on Monday afternoon to identify Sarah Hannin?'

'Of course. I thought I'd have to referee a boxing match between you in the examination room.'

'There's more to him than meets the eye, and I feel it isn't anything good. He and I got off to a bad start. But I'm sure he was put out by Fitzpatrick to block us.'

Lafeyre shook his head in disagreement. 'I'm not hearing much of the cool, detached crime detective here. You just don't like having your authority challenged.'

'Maybe that's true. But I ran into Hetty Connors yesterday in Naughton's of Crow Street. She's the kitchen worker from Sir Patrick Dun's who called out Sarah Hannin's name when they took her from the water. She used to work in Fitzpatrick's. She told me that McDonald operates under an alias. His real name is McDaniel, she says, and she thinks he has a military background.'

'Is that significant?'

'It could be. Old soldiers don't change their names without a damned good reason. They draw their pension under their enlisted name, as you know. If you change your name, how do you get your money? Pat Mossop is trying to check him out with the Pay Master's office.'

'Assuming, of course, that this Hetty Connors is telling the truth,' Lafeyre said.

'I think she is,' Swallow said. 'I caught her out thieving. She's stealing from all around her at the hospital I'd guess, and passing on whatever she collects to a known receiver called Tony Hopkins. But I got her red-handed and I put the fear of God into her.'

'So what can you do?' Lafeyre asked.

'I'm not entirely sure yet,' Swallow answered, 'but I'll find a way of putting the thumbscrews on Mr McDonald, or Mr McDaniel, or whatever he calls himself.'

Lafeyre withdrew behind his desk and swivelled in his chair, his hands thrust deep in his pockets.

'Well, I've no doubt you'll do that. But let's look at the political canvas around this. It's clear that the authorities don't want any focus on Fitzpatrick. Maybe it's at his insistence. I can think of some reasons why one wouldn't want one's household raided if one were about to lead a royal welcoming party.'

'There's one other possiblity,' Swallow said tentatively. 'I think I can probably trace Sarah Hannin's background to the orphanage where she was raised.'

Lafeyre was doubtful. 'How do you intend to do that?'

'When I talked to Hetty Connors she told me that Sarah came to work at Fitzpatrick's from an institution in Queen's County. I believe it's a place called Greenhills House.'

Lafeyre nodded. 'I know it. That's my part of the country. Greenhills is maybe 6 or 7 miles from Maryborough. It's a home for orphaned or abandoned girls. Roman Catholic, I'm sure. My father used to act as the attending doctor there from time to time when the regular man wasn't available.'

'Well then, maybe you'd like a day out in the country,' Swallow laughed dryly. 'They're expecting a visit from the Board of Educational Guardians any day now. And they're on the lookout for someone who might be able to help with an endowment. It seems they're running low on funds.'

He grinned. 'Do you think I'll pass for an inspector of orphanages? You could be my assistant.'

Lafeyre shook his head in disbelief. 'You can't be serious, Swallow. What have you done?'

'I happened to get my hands on a couple of sheets of Board of Educational Guardians' notepaper. So I sent off a notification of an inspector's visit to the guardian, a Mr Pomeroy, I believe. I'd say it should have arrived today.'

Lafeyre rose from the chair. 'What exactly are you proposing?'

'I thought I might take a day's leave on Saturday and travel down by train. I can hire a car at Maryborough to get me out to this Greenhills place. I'd like to have a look through the files and see what we can find out about Sarah Hannin.'

'But you're off the case.'

'I'm off one murder inquiry, but I'm still the investigating officer on the Chapelizod Gate deaths. There may be a connection.'

'You're splitting hairs. What you're proposing is completely irregular. There'll be hell to pay if it's discovered that you've gained access to confidential orphanage files by subterfuge. You'd be sacked and you'd deserve it.'

'First, nobody will ever know. Second, I'm at the point where I don't really worry too much about being sacked. Third, it's a very small deception to write a note introducing oneself as an education inspector. Sure, you could come with me and we might have a day out in the country.' He grinned. 'Fresh air, scenery and all that.'

'I can't,' Lafeyre's tone was exasperated, 'I've arranged to take Lily out on Saturday. We were planning to catch the train to Bray to walk the promenade. We're going to have lunch at one of the hotels by the sea.'

'Well, just think of it as a change of venue. Bring her along. Instead of the seaside why not have your day out in the country? I'll try to persuade Maria to come too. We'll make an outing of it. In fact having two ladies with us could be very helpful. We can represent them as possible benefactresses looking for a suitable place to make an endowment.'

Lafeyre shook his head in disbelief. 'I don't know. I'll have to talk to Lily. This is madness.'

He turned back to the files on his desk. 'Let's try to advance things one at a time. I've had Scollan arrange to have the photographic technician come down here to take pictures of "Chapelizod Gate Woman." I think the results are very good. There are three copies here for you.'

He handed a set of prints and a large envelope across the table to Swallow. Swallow glanced at the photographs. The images were crystal clear.

'I'll agree they're very good,' he said. 'I'll see if we can get some results by publicising these.'

He slid the prints into the envelope. 'I'd like you to have a think about coming with me on Saturday,' he said in a gloomy tone. 'I haven't had a lot of luck with these cases so far. I have to take any chance I can see.'

He walked back to the Lower Yard and exited the Castle through the Ship Street gate. His destination was the Dublin Metropolitan Police print shop.

Its staff of two printer-constables laboured daily in a Ship Street basement to produce the official forms and stationery that the force required for its bureaucracy. They also printed notices proclaiming rewards or posting descriptions of stolen property or missing persons. One of their principal tasks was to produce the official *Hue and Cry*, the weekly newssheet which contained such information.

Swallow requisitioned a sheet of plain paper and set out a notice in strong, clear capital letters.

DO YOU KNOW THIS WOMAN?
SHE WAS MURDERED IN THE PHOENIX PARK ON
JUNE 16th or 17th LAST AS WAS A YOUNG BOY OF
8-10 YEARS.
IF YOU CAN IDENTIFY HER OR IF YOU KNOW
ANYTHING ABOUT HER, CONTACT THE DETECTIVE
OFFICE, EXCHANGE COURT, DUBLIN CASTLE.
(Please ask for D/Sergeant Swallow or leave a message)

He drew a large square over the text and handed the sheet and one of the prints to the printer-constable.

'I need a few of these urgently. Then I'll need 100 more run off for later.'

The constable-printer peered at the photograph in puzzlement. 'That's an interesting one. Who is she?'

'It's the woman found murdered last Friday with the child at the Chapelizod Gate. But it's not who *is* she; it's who *was* she. It's a plaster and paint reconstruction put together by Dr Lafeyre and an art teacher from Alexandra College. It's an experimental technique from Germany.'

The man held the paper towards the light.

'This is a new one on me. I suppose anything is worth a try in a case like that, with a woman and child involved. I'll have a few prints for you in an hour. The full print run should be ready by tomorrow morning.'

A couple of minutes later Swallow was at Princes' Street where the offices of the *Evening Telegraph* were located. He went into a public office facing the street and walked up to the high, mahogany counter, passing a noisy line of people queuing to place advertisements.

He showed his warrant card to a thin, young man in a starched collar on a high stool behind the counter.

'Detective Sergeant Swallow, G Division. I want to see Simon Sweeney from the reporters' office please.'

The young man slid down from his stool to open a hinged section of the mahogany counter for Swallow. 'Do you know where to go?'

He did. Notwithstanding the current campaign of abuse by Irving at the *Daily Sketch*, Swallow's relationship with the press had by and large been a fruitful one. Until the unsolved murder a year ago of Elizabeth Logan, the prostitute found on Sandymount Strand, there had been general adulation among the journalists for the exploits and successes of Detective Sergeant Swallow.

He climbed a wide staircase to the reporters' room where a score of pressmen were banging out a noisy cacophony on their typewriters. It put Swallow in mind of a mad orchestra. There was a pall of tobacco smoke everywhere with men shouting between desks. Sweeney looked up from his typewriter as Swallow entered.

'Ah, here's the brave gendarme and devotee of the arts. To what do we owe the honour at this particular time, Sergeant? Are you here to give me a medal for my good work at the Academy on Sunday evening?'

Swallow drew a chair from beside Sweeney's desk and dropped one of the photographs in front of the reporter.

'No, I'm afraid I haven't got a medal for you, Mr Sweeney, although I was very thankful for your intervention. And I've told Chief Mallon and the Assistant Under-Secretary for Security so.'

He tapped the photograph with his forefinger. 'Now, Mr Sweeney, you're the man who's supposed to know everything. Who's that, do you think?'

Sweeney took the photograph and laid it on the desk beside him. 'Jesus Christ,' he said softly.

For a moment, Swallow could see that he had shocked the reporter. He leaned forward so it seemed that his head might fall onto the keys of his typewriter, then he straightened again. He reached into his pocket and dabbed his face with a handkerchief.

'I'm sorry, Sergeant. I… don't have a very strong stomach. This is rather grotesque. But it's graphic. Who or what is it supposed to be?'

'I'm sorry if it has upset you, Mr Sweeney. But it's something I need your help on.'

Sweeney nodded slowly. 'If I can help, I will, of course.'

'Well, it might help you too, Mr Sweeney, and your newspaper.' Swallow smiled. 'I'm giving you the opportunity to participate in a new chapter in the history of criminal investigation techniques.'

'I appreciate that, Sergeant,' the reporter grunted. 'It's just that I'm not accustomed to being confronted with this sort of image. It's life-like, of course, and yet it's… unnatural.'

Swallow tapped the picture with his index finger.

'This is a reconstructed feature image of the woman we found murdered with the child in the Phoenix Park. Dr Lafeyre, assisted by a gifted young art teacher, who happens to be his fiancée, reconstructed the features. He's used the techniques of the celebrated German scientist, Dr Hiss. What you're looking at here is plaster of Paris, dye, glass and paint, applied to a formula that follows the contours of muscle and bone structure. Final honours for the presentation rest with the photographic section of the Dublin Metropolitan Police.'

Sweeney had recovered his composure. He whistled silently.

'Jesus, that's impressive, Swallow. I'd swear she was real.'

'She was. She was – or is – "Chapelizod Gate Woman." Now you and your newspaper will have the chance to be the first newspaper in Ireland, maybe in Britain too, to print the results of this extraordinary technique. And maybe I'll get an identification as well.'

'We'll have to get one of our art people to make an etching from the photograph. It won't be quite as good as the photographic likeness, but they can capture all the important detail,' Sweeney said.

'I'll get it on the main news page of the late editions this afternoon for you. You'll need to give me details of this technique and a briefing on the latest developments in the investigation. We'll need to talk to Dr Lafeyre. That's an important angle, you know. I think we can have a headline, '*Dublin Medical Examiner at the forefront of New Scientific Method,*' or something like that.'

'Speed's vital on this, Mr Sweeney. I'm almost a week on this case and I'm not making great progress.'

Sweeney glanced at the clock.

'It's time enough. I'll drop what I'm on here and I'll talk to the editor right away. We can have it in the later editions of the *Telegraph* this evening. But it's important that we have it exclusively, you understand. You won't bring copies to any other newspaper until tomorrow?'

'You've got a big readership and that's what I need. The other newspapers won't get copies until tomorrow. It'll be going to all DMP and RIC stations in the morning also, and I'll be getting it posted in as many public buildings as possible – railway stations, post offices, the mailboat pier and so on.'

'Good. Let me go and tell the editor. We'll do our interview over a couple of drinks in Dwyer's across the road. You go ahead and I'll join you in a few minutes. Mine's a Powers whiskey. You put it up along with whatever you're having yourself, and tell the barman the *Telegraph* is paying.'

Swallow went down the same wide stairs that he had ascended to reach the reporters' room. He went through the counter area where the skinny youth with the starched collar lifted the hinged barrier to allow him to exit into the busy public office.

As he crossed the office floor he saw a man out of the corner of his eye closing the newspaper file he had been pretending to read. Swallow reckoned that he was moving just a fraction too swiftly as he abandoned his reading, jammed his Derby hat forward on his head and made to follow him out of the door into Prince's Street.

Swallow stepped out of the newspaper office and walked the 50 yards, not to Dwyer's but to another public house that stood two doors away. He turned in the doorway to the public bar and stepped into the shadow. 20 seconds later the man came past him into the bar. Now Swallow was following him.

The man was about 25 years or so, well-dressed, clean-shaven, carrying a small, leather case from which some papers protruded rather obviously, perhaps to give impression of being a clerk or perhaps a commercial representative. But Swallow knew from the methodical way his eyes searched the bar that he was a policeman or agent of some kind. Now the man stood, puzzled, looking up and down the bar for his quarry. Swallow coughed loudly. The man swung around, a mixture of irritation and puzzlement on his face.

Swallow grinned and tipped his hat. 'Now, my friend, why don't you relax and have yourself a drink. Enjoy it. I'll be next door in Dwyer's if you need me.'

The man muttered something about being in the wrong house and made for the door.

A few minutes later, Sweeney arrived in the bar. Swallow had ordered the drinks as Sweeney had told him, a Powers for the journalist and Swallow's customary Tullamore. They sat on two high stools. Sweeney put his notebook on the counter and started to probe him about the technique involved in Lafeyre's reconstruction of the dead woman's features. When Sweeney had filled several pages with notes he called for two more drinks.

'How is the investigation going in general? Have you any hope of progress apart from Dr Lafeyre's reconstruction?'

Swallow's instinct was to be cautious, but he needed Sweeney's co-operation. 'We're working away on a few lines of inquiry. Like I said on the morning the bodies were found, these things can move very slowly, especially when there are problems of identification.'

He decided to throw some bait at the reporter. 'One thing we do know is where the woman and the boy came from. We're building a fair bit of information around that.'

Sweeney seemed puzzled. 'What do you mean? Did they come from outside Dublin, outside Ireland?'

'I can't go any further,' Swallow said. 'We're piecing this whole thing together slowly but surely. You can't quote me directly on that, of course, but it might help you in getting the right tone for your news report. Let's call it background information.'

Sweeney added two lines to his notes. 'What's the story on the other case then, Alderman Fitzpatrick's servant that was taken from the canal?'

'I'm not very much involved in it at this stage,' Swallow said truth-fully. 'I attended at the scene, as you know, but the investigation has been assigned elsewhere.'

Sweeney smiled. 'I wouldn't be altogether surprised at that, Sergeant Swallow. Alderman Fitzpatrick is supposed to be holding some very sensitive political ground on behalf of the Castle authorities just now. They won't want anyone poking into his affairs.'

Swallow sipped the last of his Tullamore. 'I wouldn't know anything about that, Mr Sweeney,' he lied. 'Thankfully, mere detective sergeants don't have to concern themselves with such things.'

When he had finished his drink, Swallow crossed the river by the Ha'penny Bridge and returned to the Castle. His shadow had not had the nerve to follow him into Dwyer's, but Swallow knew as soon as he emerged into the sunlight that he had picked up the tail again. The man had removed his hat and detached the collar of his shirt in an effort to alter his appearance, but Swallow had no doubt that it was the same individual who now followed him across the river and through the narrow streets of Temple Bar into Dame Street.

As he entered the detective office he looked behind. The man was in the doorway of the pet shop that stood at the corner of Exchange Court. Swallow was tempted to stroll over and inquire if he was interested in buying a parrot or perhaps a pet monkey.

TWENTY-SEVEN

It was time to conclude his business with James O'Donnell, Swallow decided. He would be well softened after more than three days in the Exchange Court cells.

The prisoner was asleep on his bunk when Swallow swung the door open. The cell stank as always of dampness and gas.

'My apologies for interrupting your nap, Mr O Donnell,' Swallow called cheerfully. 'And I'm sorry it's taken me a while to get back for our chat like I said I would.'

O'Donnell turned to look at his visitor. He pushed the grey blanket under which he had been lying down to his chest. 'You again,' he croaked, rising slowly into a half-sitting position.

'It is, indeed, Mr O'Donnell. And I have some very good news for you. I've completed my inquiries into the incident that led to your arrest. I've stated in my report that you got caught up in the melee, nothing more.'

O'Donnell looked wretched. His hair was wild and his three-day growth of beard made him look gaunt. The half-presentable suit he had been wearing when he was arrested was creased and shapeless. His eyes were alert, though, staring at Swallow out of the pallid, grey face.

'I don't suppose you happened to bring any more of that whiskey with you?' O'Donnell's voice was stronger than might have been expected from his appearance.

'I'm afraid not, Mr O'Donnell. But we came to an arrangement,' Swallow said tersely, 'and now I'm going to honour my part of it. I'm going to bring you upstairs to where you'll sign for your belongings. For the sake of appearances, I'm going to ask you to sign an undertaking to be of good behaviour. Then you'll be free to go.'

He gestured towards the open cell door.

'Remember your side of the bargain. You'll keep Harriet out of all this. You'll not trouble her again. And you and I will keep in touch so that you can give me any information I might need about the activities of the Hibernian Brothers and any other lunatic gang you get involved with. And I warn you, O'Donnell, if you welch on any single aspect of the arrangement that we've made, I'll shoot you like I said.'

O'Donnell nodded wearily.

'And I'm giving you a code name so you can leave messages for me,' Swallow said. 'I'm calling you "Mr Brown," without an "e." The same colour as shit, in case you forget it.'

The vulgar jibe did not even appear to register with O'Donnell.

'What about Horan?' he asked.

'I told you I'd do what I could for him. I'll give evidence that the gun went off accidentally, and with any luck he'll be convicted of simple unauthorised possession. He'll get a stretch in prison, maybe a few months. You'll have to ensure that he keeps his mouth shut about Harriet too. And he'll need to consider himself lucky that he's in on the deal.'

O'Donnell attempted a grin. He nodded. 'I'll deliver on Horan.'

Swallow pulled the cell door open. O'Donnell levered himself up from the bunk and stepped uncertainly into the corridor. Swallow led him up the stairway to the duty desk. After the gloom of the basement cells, the day room was bright, and Swallow saw that it hurt O'Donnell's eyes.

He checked him through the discharge procedures. O'Donnell signed his undertaking to be of good behaviour. The duty officer restored his possessions: a cotton handkerchief, a comb, a half-metal pen with a broken nib, a pipe and a tobacco pouch, a small leather wallet with a sixpence, a handful of pennies and a few half pennies.

Swallow brought him to the steps of the detective office. O'Donnell looked around him in the bright sunlight, checking up and down the narrow court before stepping out. He walked, a little unsteadily at first but then with a firm step, towards Dame Street. At the end of the street, a paperboy waved copies of the *Evening Telegraph*.

The boy was shouting.

'SEE THE DEAD WOMAN FROM THE
PHOENIX PARK...'
'THE PICTURE OF THE MURDER VICTIM...'

Swallow could see that the boy had opened the newspaper to display the main inside news page. There, across two columns, was the improvised face of 'Chapelizod Gate Woman.'

He saw O'Donnell stop to look, then he fumbled in his pocket for a penny and snatched the newspaper from the boy's hand. He started to run back to the door of the detective office. Swallow waited until he reached the steps.

'By God, you're in a hurry O'Donnell. What is it?'

O'Donnell jabbed at the open page. 'There's something here you'll want to know about.' He glanced nervously up and down the street.

'Could we... go inside... Mr Swallow? You'd never know who's watching.'

Swallow chuckled silently. It had not taken long for James O'Donnell to adopt the cautious, ever-watchful ways of the informer.

He led him up the stairs to the crime sergeants' office. 'Sit down. You seem shocked. D'you want a drink of water?'

'I wouldn't say no, Mr Swallow.' O'Donnell allowed himself a nervous laugh. 'A drop of brandy or even some of that Tipperary Colleen would be nicer.'

'Not the right place and not the right time for brandy, James, not even for the Tipperary Colleen,' Swallow replied. 'Now, what has you so excited?'

He poured a glass of tepid water from a jug on the desk. 'You're like a cat with pepper in its milk. Have you something interesting to tell me?'

'You'll be the judge of that, Mr Swallow,' O'Donnell replied, spreading the newspaper out on the desk. 'I think you'll be interested... maybe more than interested. I need a few bob for a couple of drinks. You might give me, say, a pound?'

Lafeyre's "Chapelizod Gate Woman" stared from the etching on the sheet of newsprint. He placed it on the table, facing towards Swallow.

'You're supposed to be investigating these killings by the Chapelizod Gate, aren't you? And here's one of your victims, the woman.' He smoothed the paper with trembling fingers.

Swallow read the headlines and the report.

**'SEE THE DEAD WOMAN FROM THE
PHOENIX PARK...'
'ONLY IN THE *EVENING TELEGRAPH*...'**

'SEE THE DEAD WOMAN FROM THE CHAPELIZOD GATE...'

The degeneration of the photographic image in the etching process had, if anything, served to give it an added degree of authenticity. Swallow was looking at what might have been the picture of a living woman. Only the glassy stare of the artificial eyes implanted by Lily Grant would suggest anything otherwise.

Simon Sweeney's report was printed underneath.

FACE OF PARK VICTIM REVEALED
Dr Lafeyre Uses New Method

The Dublin City Medical Examiner, Dr Henry Lafeyre, has used a new scientific method from Germany to reconstruct the features of the woman who was found murdered along with a young boy of 8-10 years near the Chapelizod Gate on Friday morning.

The results are shown above, exclusively in this special edition of the Evening Telegraph. *Readers will agree that this is a remarkabl development and Dr Lafeyre is to be congratulated on it success.*

Detectives of the G Division, under Sergeant Swallow, are continuing their inquiries and are hopeful that the publication of Dr Lafeyre's reconstructed image may lead to the early identification of the woman and child.

Dr Lafeyre is at the forefront of medical jurisprudence in the United Kingdom and has studied under the renowned Prof Taylor at the University of Edinburgh.

He was assisted in the reconstruction by Miss Lily Grant, to whom he is engaged to be married. Miss Grant is a gifted teacher of art at Miss Jellicoe's Alexandra College.

'Now, Mr Swallow,' he said, taking a gulp of the water, 'it says you're looking for information about this woman and her child. It says you're "hopeful." I know enough about police language to know that means you're stuck. You haven't a bloody clue about this, have you? Well I can tell you where that woman went the night before herself and the child were murdered.'

'Go on,' Swallow said doubtfully.

'I saw her. I'm trying to tell you that I saw her. I'd swear it's the same woman, big eyes, sort of bulging almost, high forehead... a bit strange looking.'

Swallow raised a hand. 'Easy, will you start at the beginning please?'

'I told you that the Brothers had been watching that bastard Fitz-patrick for a long time. We put a lot of time and a lot of effort into watching his comings and goings. We wanted to see who his cronies were and who he was in contact with. Do you recall that, Mr Swallow?'

'That's what you told me,' Swallow said.

'We had someone for a while working in the house, but she got let go from the staff there, so we had to find other ways of gathering information.'

He slurped another mouthful of water.

'One of our fellows got a job as a gardener and handyman in Merrion Square, just across from Fitzpatrick's house. That way we got good descriptions of visitors, sometimes names too. Last week he was sick for a couple of days and I told the foreman I was his brother. I said he was afraid of being let go and that I'd do the job for him.'

Swallow tried not to look surprised. He was impressed by the extent to which the Brothers had organised their espionage. It would have done justice to the G Division, he thought quietly.

'And what do you think I saw, Mr Swallow, last Wednesday evening as I was locking up the gates of the square?'

O'Donnell drew breath sharply. 'I saw the same woman that's there in the newspaper, along with her child, going into the house through the basement doorway, just after… maybe about 7 o'clock in the evening.'

'You're sure of the date? It was Wednesday evening of last week?'

'I'm sure. I worked in the gardens Tuesday and Wednesday.'

He tapped the newspaper with his finger. 'This Doctor… Lafeyre… he knows his business I can tell you, because this is a very good… very accurate… picture of the person I saw. And you couldn't mistake the eyes.'

Swallow's brain raced to make sense of O'Donnell's information. If it was accurate, some link between the murders was much more likely.

'Are you sure about this?' he asked, deliberately striking a sceptical tone. 'It could have been any woman and a boy. It could have been anybody visiting a relative or a friend in the servants' quarters.'

O'Donnell looked offended. 'Well, it might have been. But I can only tell you what I saw.'

'How was she dressed?'

'I recall that it was a sort of dark blue… it was a dark dress with a blue and white hat. The boy was wearing a sort of brown corduroy jacket and trousers.'

That tallied, Swallow realised, with the clothing found on the dead boy.

'This could be important,' he conceded. 'Can you say how the woman and child arrived at the house? How long did they stay there?'

O'Donnell shrugged. 'I don't know.'

Swallow felt a surge of frustration.

'Jesus, O'Donnell! I've done a hell of a lot for you and your friend Horan. If it wasn't for me you'd still be in the cells downstairs. I've told you this could be important. I need to know everything you can recall about it.'

O'Donnell leaned conspiratorially across the table.

'If I knew more I'd tell you more. I can only tell you I saw the woman and child walking along the square… and going down the steps into the basement. Then I closed the gates of the gardens and finished up. I've no idea how long they stayed. Now, am I going to get that money you mentioned?'

He looked hopefully at Swallow. 'I'd say that what I told you is worth a fiver.'

'You're aware that a servant at the Fitzpatrick house, a girl called Sarah Hannin, was murdered and taken from the canal on Monday last?' Swallow asked.

O'Donnell shook his head. 'It's the first I heard of that. You'll recall that I was out of circulation, so to speak, from Sunday. Is there some connection? Is that what you think?'

'I don't know yet,' Swallow answered. 'In all your watching at the Fitzpatrick house, did you ever come across Sarah Hannin?'

O'Donnell shrugged again. 'I saw lots of servants come and go at different times. That name means nothing to me.'

Swallow stood.

'You might be useful to the G Division all right. I suppose you've earned your drinking money.'

He took two 10-shilling notes from his wallet and put them on the table, then he reached into the drawer and drew out a police receipt form. He dipped a pen into the inkwell on the table and handed it to O'Donnell.

'Here, sign on the line to confirm that you've got your pound. It's probably a fair bargain. Remember, you're "Mr Brown" – without an "e".'

O'Donnell hastily scribbled his new signature and thrust the money into his jacket pocket. He stood up and made for the door without a word.

Swallow guessed that precious little of the money would get any distance beyond the public houses in the vicinity of the Castle.

TWENTY-EIGHT

The light was weakening when Swallow left Exchange Court. There was no moon, but the sky was beginning to show the early stars as points of light over the Bedford Tower and the Upper Yard.

He had tried to imagine how the Sarah Hannin investigation might be advancing now that it had been given over to the special detectives working directly from the Under-Secretary's office. He doubted that it would have progressed very far. The effectiveness of the special CID was limited because their accents gave them away. They seemed to have no knowledge of the city's geography. The chances of their making any progress on the case, even if they wanted to, would be slim.

He turned O'Donnell's information over in his head. It was possible that his new informant had simply spotted a way of touching him for an easy pound. Yet he had the feeling that he was telling what he believed to be the truth. If the Chapelizod Gate victims had visited the Fitzpatrick house, then there had to be some connection between their deaths and the murder of Sarah Hannin.

He decided that his homeward progress would be via Merrion Square. It would be a lengthy diversion from his usual route to Thomas Street, but visiting and revisiting crime scenes and locations related to crimes had always been a part of Swallow's investigative approach.

Sometimes he would stand for an hour and watch a house or a street or a stretch of land, mentally rehearsing the movements of those who were players in the drama of the moment. And it had often proven to be profitable. Tonight he felt that he wanted to look at the Fitzpatrick house for a while. If James O'Donnell's information was correct, it was a common location linking the three murder victims of the past week.

He walked to College Green and paused on the pavement opposite Trinity College to allow a tram go by towards Nassau Street. On an impulse he decided to step aboard as it slowed. He would disembark at the corner of Merrion Square.

A man hurried along the pavement behind him, nimbly hauling himself onto the tram as it moved off. He was perhaps 30 years of age, well-built with a trimmed, dark moustache. Oddly, given the warm evening weather, he was wearing a woollen overcoat.

When Swallow stepped from the tram at Merrion Square, the man stayed in his own seat, his face turned to the window and away from Swallow's line of sight.

By now it was close to 10 o'clock, and the lamplighters were making their rounds, moving from post to post, opening the gas-jets and lighting the lemon-white mantles. There was still some brightness in the sky, but the gas light accentuated the darkness descending on the houses on the southern side of the square.

When he reached the end of the railings that abutted the square he had sight of the house. He was not sure what he had expected to see there. Perhaps he had anticipated some of the official traffic that inevitably attends a scene being investigated in connection with a serious crime – uniformed officers on duty, police vehicles, senior officers' transport...

There was none of this at Number 106. If there was anything akin to a crime investigation under way there, no external signs of it were visible. The house was silent with dim lights burning in what Swallow reckoned would be the drawing room, giving out on the square at the first level above the street. Another faint hint of incandescence showed from the windows of the basement.

He moved along the square, easing himself into the shadows where glossy laurel branches overhung the pavement. When he was opposite the house he backed in against one of the garden's entrance gates. He had a perfect view of Fitzpatrick's, but hidden as he was by the branches and the shadows, it would have been impossible for anyone in the house to see him.

He reckoned he was standing more or less in the line of sight described earlier by James O'Donnell. Certainly he would have had a perfect view of any visitors coming to or from the house.

He kept his vigil for perhaps an hour until the light had quite faded and the square was dark save for the pools of yellow under the lamp standards.

The hour yielded little by way of intelligence or information. Merrion Square remained silent. Once or twice a woman's form could be seen fleetingly passing the windows on the first floor of Number 106. Shortly afterwards, somebody closed the drapes on two of the windows on the floor above, presumably a bedroom. Then a faint light glowed behind the drapes.

The light from the basement rooms grew a little stronger. Swallow surmised that the servants had gathered in the kitchen to talk or perhaps play cards at the end of the day. Occasional shadows flickered across the railings outside the house as figures moved about downstairs.

He checked his pocket-watch. It showed 11 o'clock. He had made up his mind to abandon his surveillance and to set out for Thomas Street and Maria Walsh's when he saw a closed brougham carriage draw into the square from the direction of Merrion Street. Two oil lamps flared on the sides, so Swallow could see that the blinds of the vehicle were fully down.

At the same moment he became aware that two men had joined him in the shadows. So silent had been their arrival – one on either side of him – that he felt rather than heard their presence. The carriage drew to a halt directly in front of where he stood, obscuring his view of the Fitzpatrick house. In spite of the warmth of the night, the driver's face was covered with a dark muffler.

His instinctive sense of danger urged Swallow to find his revolver in its shoulder-holster. The more rational part of his brain told him that it would be too slow.

'Our chief wants to have a word with you, Mr Swallow.'

The accent was English. London. The tone was firm, just short of threatening. Swallow could scarcely make out the men's features in the gloom. They might have been twins, wearing similar dark suits and smart Derby hats. He had the impression of men younger than himself, well-built and lithe.

'I'm a detective sergeant of the G Division on duty,' he answered curtly. 'Maybe I don't want to have a word with him.'

'We don't need any unpleasantness, Mr Swallow, now do we?' The second man's accent was identical to the first. 'We know who you are. This is official business. Please step over.'

The door of the carriage opened, and a shaft of light spilled from its interior onto the street. One of the men moved forward and dropped the metal step. In the light, Swallow could see the bulk of a heavy revolver under his jacket. At the same moment, another smaller carriage drew in behind the brougham.

'Please, Mr Swallow, now.' The second man's tone was imperative. Swallow was not being given a choice. He knew that he had made the correct judgment in not attempting to draw his gun. These were not men on a casual errand. He stepped forward to the carriage and climbed in.

The interior was illuminated by two lamps that gleamed across dark leather upholstery and heavy brocade that curtained the windows. The air in the carriage was heavy with oil fumes.

The sole occupant was a man of about Swallow's age, fair-haired with a trimmed moustache and beard, tall and dressed fashionably in a light-coloured suit. He sat well back in the leather upholstery, his hands joined across the top of an ebony cane. His mouth formed a smile, but as he sat opposite Swallow thought that the blue eyes made the moonlight seem warm.

'Detective Sergeant Swallow, it's a pleasure to meet you. I know of your reputation.'

The accent was vestigially Irish but overlaid with an English inflexion. Swallow thought there was a hint of the north, maybe Belfast or County Antrim, in it.

'Then you have the advantage of me. I don't know you, Sir.' Swallow was peremptory.

'Indeed, you do not, Mr Swallow. For the purposes of our conversation you may call me Kelly – Major Kelly. You could say that I am an associate of Mr Smith Berry, whom I think you met recently at Dublin Castle. Now, I believe at this hour of the evening you would normally be on your way towards Thomas Street and to Mrs Walsh's licensed premises. Why don't you allow me to drive you there and we can talk as we travel.'

Without waiting for any response from Swallow, he tapped on the roof of the cab with his cane. The vehicle began to move forward.

Swallow sought to conceal his surprise with as much nonchalance as he could summon. He leaned back into the leather upholstery.

'So, Major Kelly, you obviously know a little about me. What about yourself? What exactly is it that you're a major of?'

'Ah, you don't waste time getting to the point, Mr Swallow. Let me put it this way. Like you, I represent the civil authorities, but at a different level. Should I suggest... a higher level of authority?'

Swallow nodded thoughtfully.

'I know a good bit about the civil authorities, Major Kelly. But I never heard of you.'

'Indeed, that is as it should be, Mr Swallow. My work isn't done in the public eye. My duties are of a, well, more clandestine nature.'

The carriage tilted slightly as it rounded the junction of Merrion Square and Clare Street. The curtain shifted for a moment and Swallow could see that the second vehicle had fallen into line behind the brougham. Kelly waved a hand.

'As you'll have guessed, those are my escort, Mr Swallow. I would ask you to ignore them. They're an unfortunate necessity in my line of work.' He leaned forward in his seat and stared hard into Swallow's eyes.

'Mr Swallow, I want to give you some information and I want to explain certain facts to you. This will be a relatively short journey so it will be very much in your better interests if you listen carefully to me and do as I say.'

Swallow stared back. He had developed his own technique over many years of detective work. Now his eyes bored back into Kelly's.

'Major Kelly, I'm a sworn police officer and a detective sergeant of the G Division. I take orders in regard to what I do from nobody except for my proper superiors.'

Kelly grimaced in what passed for a smile.

'Very right too, Mr Swallow. I like that kind of loyalty. And I like a clear understanding of command and obedience. Nonetheless, you will hear what I have to say.'

'As long as you understand my position in what I have told you,' Swallow said firmly.

'Mr Swallow, initially you were the officer investigating the death of a young woman by the name of Sarah Hannin whose body was taken from the Grand Canal some days ago.'

'You have time to read the newspapers then, Major Kelly? You must have a soft job.'

Kelly ignored the provocation.

'Yesterday you were advised by your superiors that the death of Miss Hannin is to be investigated not by the G Division but by special CID operating directly under the control of the Assistant Under-Secretary for Security, were you not?'

Swallow shrugged. 'I won't discuss my superiors' instructions with you. Detective duties are confidential.'

'Yet you have persisted in these inquiries. Certain evidence, a lady's bag I believe, was recovered by the police at College Street and delivered to you in error at Exchange Court. You did not forward it, as you should have, to the Security Secretary's office. You have challenged your inspector's authority. And I gather that you went so far as to threaten Alderman Fitzpatrick that if you were not given access to his house, you would have a warrant for his arrest too.'

'You must consider yourself very well informed, Sir,' Swallow rejoined coolly.

Kelly laid the ebony cane across his knees. 'I do, Mr Swallow. I do indeed.'

He raised his voice. 'I'm damned well informed. I know that you're trying to maintain what was once perhaps a reasonable reputation as a detective officer. But you won't do it against the orders of your superiors or where you're compromising the safety of the realm. Do you understand me?'

He dropped his voice again.

'The death of this girl is regrettable. It was a brutal and criminal act. Nobody can be other than saddened by it. My colleagues of the special CID at the Assistant Under-Secretary's office have several lines of inquiry. The culprit or culprits will be identified and will be brought to justice. But you, Mr Swallow, will do what you have been ordered. You will have nothing to do with the case. Do I make myself clear?'

Swallow affected a yawn.

'Major Kelly, I don't know who you are. I don't know what authority you claim to have. I'm sure that you think you have very good reasons to interfere in the course of justice. But I am an officer of the Metropolitan Police, bound by oath to preserve the Queen's peace and to prevent and detect crime. I know that Sarah Hannin was murdered, possibly in the Fitzpatrick house, and I know that there's no investigation worth talking about into that murder. I also know that Alderman Fitzpatrick is being shielded by powerful people – probably including yourself – because you need him to perform in some sort of a political pantomime next week.'

He parted the curtain to ascertain where they were. He could see the curtilage wall of Christ Church Cathedral.

'Now, Major Kelly or whatever you are, I can see that I'm almost at my destination. I'll thank you to stop your carriage so I can walk the rest of the way.'

Kelly was silent for a moment.

'Sergeant Swallow, I'd very much prefer you to take my advice,' he said icily. 'Let me put what may be a persuasive line of argument to you. Two vacancies arise within the next 12 months, as I understand it, for promotion within the G Division to the rank of detective inspector. I believe I can tell you that obedience and political discretion will be paramount in the allocation of those promotions. If you can display those qualities, I can tell you now that the rank is yours. Fail to do so and you will be lucky, I promise you, to hold any rank at all in the Metropolitan Police.'

He rapped with the ebony cane on the roof of the carriage, bringing it to an abrupt halt. The door on Swallow's side swung open. Kelly gave a wintry smile.

'I'm sorry that our meeting should have taken place under somewhat tense circumstances, Mr Swallow. As I said earlier, I know of your reputation, notwithstanding that much of it is grounded in successes of quite some time ago. Will you consider what I have said about your promotional prospects?'

Swallow glared at him. 'To hell with you and your promotional prospects. I couldn't give a damn about promotion.'

Kelly nodded with affected sadness.

'I've heard that said too, Mr Swallow. I regret it, although I'm not sure it's as true as you would have people believe. But let me tell you two things further. One, if your plan is to retire and go into the licensed trade here with your close friend, Mrs Walsh,' he pointed in the direction of Thomas Street, 'don't count on it.'

He stroked his trim beard, affecting an air of thoughtfulness.

'You know, Mrs Walsh's licence could be revoked if any irregularities were found in the running of the business. Suppose, for example, it was found that she was employing a member of the police to help her operate the establishment. She could even be prosecuted and end up in jail. Not a pleasant place for a lady, you know, up there in Kilmainham or in Mountjoy.

'Two, your dear sister will shortly qualify as a teacher. Any teaching post has to be approved by the education authorities and, as you doubtless know, the Chief Secretary has control over them. It wouldn't be difficult to find reasons to block any appointment that might go to someone whose connections were considered to be, shall we say, inimical to the Crown.'

Swallow's anger rose. He leaned forward from the leather seat until his face was just inches from Kelly's.

'Now you hear me, so-called Major so-called Kelly. You and I have jobs to do. I have mine and I do it well. You have yours, whatever it may be and however despicable it may be. Sometimes we may have to come into contact and we may have to deal with each other, though I hope it's as infrequently as possible. But if you try to drag my sister Harriet or Maria Walsh into this, or threaten harm to either of them in any way, I swear to God I won't be responsible for what I do to you and your associates. Do I make myself clear?'

Kelly's bland face registered no reaction.

'I don't think you're in a position to make any threats to me, Mr Swallow. Now, good night to you, I hope very sincerely that it won't be necessary for us to meet again.'

He waited until Swallow had stepped down from the carriage. One of the escort party was waiting on the street to close the door after he had dismounted. Swallow stood on the pavement and watched the vehicles as they turned across the street to start back towards the city centre.

The lights were burning in Grant's, and through the half-frosted glass he could see Maria moving purposefully among the customers by the long, mahogany counter. He needed a drink and he needed company. He walked into the bar out of the threatening night.

Thursday June 23rd, 1887

TWENTY-NINE

When Swallow arrived at Exchange Court shortly after 8 o'clock the next morning, the roster sheet showed him detailed as duty sergeant. It was a calculated affront by Duck Boyle; an unspoken charge that since he was not making progress on the murders he could do something useful by manning the desk.

Apart from a couple of men detailed to watch the remnants of the Downes gang in their extended grieving, virtually the full available strength of G Division was once again allocated to security duties.

Swallow found Boyle in the parade room.

'I've got a crime conference on the Chapelizod Gate murders at 9 o'clock.'

'I'm sure ye have,' Boyle retorted. 'An' I'm sure it'll be just as productive as t'others you've been holdin' all week. Take yer conference and get it done with as quickly as ye can. Then yer on desk work here until the afternoon shift comes on.'

'And I'm supposed to be the attending officer at the burial of Sarah Hannin this afternoon. As you know, they have to have a police officer present, and you can be sure that none of the fellows from Smith Berry's squad will demean themselves to it.'

Boyle was momentarily checked. Procedure required that a police officer be made available to ensure compliance with burial requirements. The ordinance went back many years to a scandal involving the burial of paupers' bodies in waste ground so that unscrupulous contractors could pocket the small cemetery fee payable by the Coroner's Office.

'All right,' he acknowledged, 'you can get Mossop to stand in for you when you're doin' that. But remember you're not the investigatin' officer on that case any more. Ye're just there to put a signature on the burial form.'

If the Assistant Under-Secretary's team of detectives was doing any work on the Sarah Hannin inquiry, Swallow picked up no news of it from any of the G-men. Since he was off the case he was unable to inquire officially what the status of the investigation was, or even who was involved.

An hour later, he chaired the fourth crime case conference on the Chapelizod Gate murders.

Pat Mossop and Stephen Doolan arrived at the crime sergeants' office simultaneously. Only four uniformed constables were present. Stephen Doolan's face was healing nicely after his hurling incident. He gestured apologetically to Swallow.

'The superintendent at Kevin Street wasn't willing to let me keep all the boys on this case without any progress. I did well to get these few.'

'So, have we any good news?' Swallow inquired.

There were glum expressions around the room. It seemed as if nobody had the heart to venture anything.

'I'm afraid not,' Doolan said. 'There's nothing come out of questioning the mail-packet crews. We haven't found anything in Hutton's records that might help to identify the carriage. There's nothing coming off the streets about this woman that Vinny Cussen is supposed to have had his boys out looking for. We're not really any further on than we were nearly a week ago.'

Swallow had weighed the advantages and disadvantages of briefing the team on the information he had gleaned from James O'Donnell about the woman and child who had visited the Fitzpatrick house.

On balance he decided against it, at least for the present. He would share the details with Pat Mossop because it would be worth having his experienced opinion on it. But if it became generally known among the G Division that there was a possible link between the Chapelizod Gate murders and Thomas Fitzpatrick's house at Merrion Square it would only be a matter of hours before he would be taken off that case too.

There was a knock on the door of the crime sergeants' room. Pat Mossop opened the door. Swallow saw a constable hand him a large, brown envelope.

'It's from the photographic technician for Detective Sergeant Swallow.'

Mossop handed the envelope to Swallow. He slit the gummed paper seal and took the topmost picture from the bundle of prints. The photographer had softened the exposure so that the artificiality of plaster and paint on the face was minimised. The waxy sheen that glazed the improvised skin had disappeared. The features of an identifiable woman with somewhat prominent eyes were now clear.

He turned the photograph towards Doolan and the others.

'Now, gentlemen, here's something you might have read about in some of the morning newspapers. But you haven't seen it before.'

Suddenly alert, the policemen stared at the picture, a mixture of curiosity and amazement on their faces.

'Jesus, Joe. What is it? How did you do that?' Stephen Doolan exclaimed.

'It's thanks to Dr Lafeyre,' Swallow explained. 'It's a new technique devised in Germany. He's used a system that reconstructs the features on the basis of muscle and bone.'

'How accurate do you think it is, Boss?' Pat Mossop asked.

'Dr Lafeyre thinks it's probably a good likeness. I'm getting a poster with the image printed on it across in Ship Street. It gives us something to start asking questions about, doesn't it?'

Doolan nodded.

'It surely does that. Give us a few copies and we'll start showing them around the city. We'll do the cabmen's shelters, the public houses and so on.'

Mossop distributed the photographs, retaining the master copy. Once he had finished, the conference broke up. The constables moved with a noticeable spring in their step.

The office was quiet. 'Do you want tea, Boss?' Mossop asked. 'I'd say you could do with a cup o' tea.'

When Pat Mossop made a ceremony of brewing tea, Swallow knew he had something he wanted to say. He sat down, accepted the offer and waited while the Book Man poured him a mug of black liquid that looked as if it had been stewing for a week.

'I had an idea about something,' Mossop said, drawing his own chair closer. He added milk to the tea from a pewter jug and dolloped more into Swallow's mug.

He swallowed a mouthful. 'This railway policeman says that the man – or the woman – that he spoke to at Chester gave an address in Dublin at Abbey Street. He said it was 'St Brigid's, Abbey Street.' Now, we know there's no such place, don't we?'

Swallow tasted his own tea. It was bitter and heavy.

'Sure. It doesn't exist.'

'But supposing the policeman got it slightly wrong? Supposing that's just part of the address? Or supposing he mixed up the words…'

'What have you in mind, Pat?'

'Well, Boss, I've been thinking, it could be St Brigid's Abbey. He could have misheard, or maybe he got distracted by the noise of a train or something going on at a busy station. Do you know there's a place called St Brigid's Abbey just beyond Chapelizod, maybe half a mile from where the bodies were found?'

Swallow felt a surge of interest. He had never heard of St Brigid's Abbey.

'Go on, Pat.'

'Well, it's a convent. It's run by an order of nuns. I checked in the Catholic Directory. That's a complete list of all the religious houses in every diocese. These sisters at Chapelizod are what they call "semi-enclosed." They don't have much contact with the outside world, and they don't have many visitors. I've no record of it being checked out in the inquiries.'

'You say this abbey is beyond the village. So it's probably out of the DMP area.'

'Yes, Boss, I checked it on the map. It's in the RIC Dublin County Division. And maybe the RIC would have reckoned that a community of enclosed nuns wouldn't have anything useful to tell them, so why go to the trouble of disturbing the holy sisters?'

Swallow considered Mossop's theory. No trace of the victims had been found in any hotel or boarding house. Door-to-door inquiries had been equally fruitless. Yet they had stayed somewhere in Dublin, probably for two nights. Why not in a convent? A convent just a few minutes' walk from where they had been found…

He forced himself to swallow another sip of Mossop's bitter tea.

'I've followed less promising leads in my time,' he said. 'It's worth a drive out to Chapelizod. But first, I've a bit of information I want to talk through with you. I didn't want to spread it around at the conference because there'd be repercussions. And for the moment I don't want you to put it in the murder book either. It touches on the Sarah Hannin investigation, and that's off limits to us, as you know.'

'Righto, Boss.' Mossop shut the book. 'I understand. Tell me.'

'The business at the Royal Hibernian Academy on Sunday night threw up an unexpected dividend. I questioned this fellow, James O'Donnell, who got caught up in the ruckus there. He's in the Hibernian Brothers, but he's a martyr to drink. So I frightened him, told him we'd pay for good information, and I let him out. But as he left here yesterday evening he saw the picture of the "Chapelizod Gate Woman" in the *Telegraph*. He told me he recognised her. He'd been watching Fitzpatrick's house on the previous Wednesday and he saw her going in, along with the boy.'

Mossop was sceptical. Swallow expected that. It was what made Pat Mossop an excellent colleague on a complex case. He doubted. He challenged. He searched out flaws and infirmities like a ferret.

'Maybe he only wanted to get a few quid, Boss,' Mossop ventured. 'From what you say he has a bad story with the drink. Fellows like that will tell you anything they think you'd like to hear if they can see the price of a few whiskies in it. And even if he wasn't scrounging he might just be mistaken.'

'That's true,' Swallow acknowledged. 'But whether he's right or wrong I think he believes what he told me. He says he saw the woman and child going into Fitzpatrick's. The description of the boy's clothing tallies. It also tallies that the woman had unusually protruding eyes. It's a long way off being conclusive, but it's a possible sighting.'

Swallow stood. 'I'm going over the the Coroner's Court for the Hannin inquest. Then I'm going along to the burial as the attending officer. Will you hold the fort as duty officer for me?'

Mossop grinned. 'Ah sure, I'll use the day to build up my reputation with Detective Inspector Boyle. Don't worry. He'll be very impressed to find me with my nose here in the books all day.'

THIRTY

Sarah Hannin's small funeral cortège made its way in the midday heat through the walkways of Mount Prospect cemetery. Thomas Fitzpatrick's murdered housemaid was to be buried in a newly opened grave of the third class, well away from the grand avenues along which the burial sites of Glasnevin's wealthy deceased are located.

The cortège was not on the scale of Cecilia Downes's obsequies three days earlier, but neither was it the pauper's burial that was accorded to the woman and boy whose bodies had been found at the Chapelizod Gate on the previous Friday morning. The coffin was inexpensive but respectable, made of plain deal with cast-iron handles. It was transported from the Dublin City Morgue by a commercial undertaker in a closed hearse, drawn by a single horse.

There was one mourning car. In addition to a young priest attached to St Andrew's Parish Church on Westland Row, it carried James McDonald and two of the women servants from 106 Merrion Square. The only member of the party who appeared to exhibit any grief was the younger of the women, who sobbed at intervals into a blue cotton handkerchief.

A Dublin Metropolitan Police open car followed the mourners. Swallow sat beside the driver. At the graveside, he dismounted and handed an official form to the foreman gravedigger to sign, then he countersigned it, fulfilling officialdom's requirements in respect of the deceased. The form confirmed the burial of the remains of Sarah Hannin, 'spinster of Merrion Square, in the Parish of St Andrew's, Dublin.' He put the completed form in an inside pocket and joined in with the responses when the priest started the prayers.

At a Coroner's Inquest in Marlborough Street earlier, Swallow had given evidence of seeing the body of Sarah Hannin taken from the Grand Canal. He then read the report of the medical examiner, which stated that the woman had died from injuries to the brain and skull, caused by a heavy, blunt weapon or instrument. The jury had returned a verdict of unlawful killing by a person or persons unknown.

When the prayers had finished, the mourning party started back along the dry, dusty pathway to their car. Swallow saw James McDonald approach the priest and press a white envelope into his hand. The young priest looked duly grateful. He anticipated that the funeral stipend offered by Alderman Fitzpatrick for the obsequies of a member of his household staff would be generous.

Swallow climbed back on board the police trap. His eyes and James McDonald's met as the drivers wheeled their vehicles around to make for the cemetery gate. There was no other sign of recognition. But Swallow thought he saw, perhaps, something akin to distress in the older man's face.

Friday June 24th, 1887

THIRTY-ONE

'I'll be spending a bit of time with Mossop to check out a lead he got last night on the Chapelizod Gate murders,' Swallow told Duck Boyle after the morning parade at Exchange Court. Yet again, every available G-man was on security duty, anticipating the royal visit, now little more than 72 hours away.

'Well I'll be puttin' Detectives Feore and Swift back on general surveillance duties,' Boyle responded. 'They'll be better employed on some proper police work for me instead of runnin' around in circles with you.'

There was no benefit, Swallow reasoned, in publicising Mossop's theory about St Brigid's Abbey. It would probably draw derision from Duck Boyle and it would only serve to distract the team. If it yielded a result, there would be time enough to bring them into the picture.

As the shift of G-men left the office, Swallow remembered his commitment for the theatre in the evening. He thought briefly about cancelling, but it would not be worth the grief, he reckoned. Maria was looking forward to the outing, and Lily and Lafeyre would be disappointed.

The morning newspapers again carried pictures or sketches of Harry Lafeyre's 'Chapelizod Gate Woman' along with reports about the new identification technique. By mid morning, though, no firm leads had come back to the detective office either from Doolan's constables or from members of the public.

Swallow had decided that there would be no point in mounting another crime case conference unless something substantial by way of new information had come in.

Mossop had arranged for a police side-car to be available at Exchange Court for the journey to St Brigid's Abbey. As he exited the detective office, Swallow checked up and down the alley to see if he was still being followed, but he could detect no sign of any surveillance as he and Mossop climbed on board the vehicle.

The police driver was skilful and fast. He took the car along Lord Edward Street and under the Christchurch Arch spanning Winetavern Street. Then he turned west along the Liffey Quays.

The lamp standards on both sides of the river were festooned with red, white and blue rosettes. A forest of Union Jacks fluttered from the pediment of the Four Courts. Most of the decorations had been put in place for the Jubilee itself, but now additional touches were being added for the visit. A group of workmen were draping a huge banner over the arches of the King's Bridge. Swallow could read the words, 'GOD SAVE…' Loyal Dublin was preparing to greet the Queen's grandson.

They crossed the river at King's Bridge and turned west again past Park Gate. Another gang of workers was busy hanging red, white and blue bunting along the park railings in anticipation of the cavalcade to the Viceregal Lodge.

The driver slowed his pace once they reached Conyngham Road. The old coaching route was rutted and uneven. It would bring them directly to the village of Chapelizod and the open countryside beyond the Phoenix Park.

They passed the Chapelizod Gate. Beyond the park's boundary wall Swallow could see the copse of trees where the woman and the boy had been found a week ago. Instinctively he wanted to revisit the scene as was his habit in important crime investigations, but the more urgent task was to see if there was any substance to Mossop's theory.

St Brigid's Abbey was situated north of Chapelizod village on rising ground above the river. Swallow mentally noted the point at which they passed from the DMP's area of jurisdiction into that of the Royal Irish Constabulary.

The driver hauled on the reins, bringing the car to a stop outside a wrought-iron gate, surmounted by a cross and a metal plate embossed with the inscription 'SISTERS OF ST BRIGID'.

Mossop stepped down from the vehicle and pulled on a bell set into the wall. After a minute a grille opened in the gate and an apparently disembodied female voice called out.

'*Laus Deo*… Praise be to God. Who is it please?'

Mossop gave their identities and asked that they be admitted.

'A moment, please,' the voice said crisply, as the metal grille was drawn shut.

One side of the high, metal gate opened noiselessly. A nun in a black and white habit appeared from behind the opened section, bowed slightly and pointed wordlessly along the tree-lined driveway. Swallow wondered at the physical capacity of the slight woman to draw the heavy gate open and shut.

St Brigid's Abbey, Swallow could see, was not a conventional abbey in the architectural sense. It was a Georgian house of middling size, undoubtedly once the residence of some wealthy grandee, with a panoramic view over the Liffey valley below.

Another nun appeared at the main door as Swallow and Mossop climbed the granite steps. She was a tall, angular woman of perhaps 40 years of age, with a fresh complexion and an intelligent face. A plain, silver cross hung on a chain around her neck.

'I am Mother Mary Catherine. I am the Mother Prioress here,' she said, betraying no signal of either welcome or displeasure. Her accent hinted of the west of Ireland. 'Please follow me.'

She led them into a parlour and signalled to them to sit at a polished, oval table topped with a vase of lilies. She seated herself at the opposite side. A brief flexing of her lower facial muscles was an unsuccessful attempt at a smile.

'How may we be of assistance, gentlemen?'

Swallow showed his warrant card, turning it on the table in front of the Prioress.

'I'm Detective Sergeant Swallow,' he told her, 'and this is my colleague, Detective Officer Mossop. We work with the detective branch of the Metropolitan Police at Dublin Castle.'

The nun raised an eyebrow. 'I believe we have not had the attentions of the Metropolitan Police before, Sergeant. On occasion we have contacts with the constabulary, for official purposes to do with the farm or sometimes when animals stray onto our land.'

Swallow was unsure if he and Mossop were being reminded that they were, geographically speaking, out of their jurisdiction. If they were, he chose to ignore it.

'We're investigating the deaths of a woman in her twenties and a young child of perhaps 8 to 9 years, last week at a place not far from here.'

'It's within our area of jurisdiction,' he added to forestall any challenge.

The Mother Prioress nodded, ceding the point, he reckoned.

'We have some reason to believe that they could have visited you here or that they might be known here. May I ask if you or any member of your community would have had any recent contact with persons matching the description I have given?'

Swallow and Mossop could see anxiety in the nun's eyes. Her mouth tightened a fraction.

'I see. Has there been an accident?'

'No, unfortunately we're not dealing with an accident in this case,' Swallow said. 'The woman and the child died very violently. Am I to take it that you have some knowledge of the victims that I have just described?'

She put her hand to her lips. They both saw that her fingers trembled a little.

'I am afraid so, Sergeant,' she said haltingly after a moment. 'I was beginning to be concerned when they did not return to us. And when we heard nothing from them after... what is it... almost 8 days? May I ask what happened?'

Swallow took a deep breath. He could sense Mossop tensing beside him in the chair.

'I'm sorry, Mother Prioress, but what I have to tell you is very distressing.' He paused. 'The woman and the child were shot dead in the Phoenix Park. We believe it happened sometime on the night of Thursday of last week or early on Friday morning – that would be June 16th or 17th.'

The nun bowed her head and blessed herself. 'May the Lord Jesus and his Blessed Mother have mercy on their souls.'

Her expression combined puzzlement and distress.

'She was... very fearful. She was very nervous of leaving the abbey. I felt that she might have believed herself and the child to be in danger.'

'I'm afraid that they were. In mortal danger, it's now clear. Did she say anything about that?'

'She told me that someone was watching her on the tram from the city. I put it down to an over-active imagination.'

'Again, I'm afraid it probably wasn't.'

'But why... who would do such a thing? He was only a little child, a young boy. You will understand that in the abbey we hear very little of what happens in the outside world. I don't understand...'

'These are questions to which we're trying to find answers, Mother Prioress,' Swallow responded. 'I hope that you can help us, as I know you would wish to do.'

She drew herself together, folding her hands on her lap.

'Of course, Mr Swallow. What can I do?'

'At this time we're not sure even of the identities of the victims,' Swallow responded. 'For a start, we need to know with certainty who they were, where they came from, why they were in Dublin and how they came to be staying here at St Brigid's.'

Mossop had drawn his notebook and a pencil from his pocket.

The Mother Prioress had composed herself.

'She... the woman... her name was Louise Thomas – Mrs Thomas. And the little boy – her son – was called Richard. They were referred here by our sister house at Wavertree, near Liverpool. I received a letter from the Mother Abbess there... I can show it to you if you like... asking if we would accommodate them for some days while they came to visit relatives in Dublin. Naturally, I agreed to do so. That would be very much the tradition of our order, you understand.'

'When did they arrive?'

'I believe it was on Wednesday 15th – in the afternoon.'

'Clearly they had left here by the Thursday night or Friday morning. Did they remain here all the time in between?'

'Oh no, they went into the city on Wednesday evening after praying with us at Vespers. I believe they did not return until sometime on Wednesday night because I had to ask a sister to keep watch at the gate to admit them.'

'Do you know how they travelled to the city or where they went?'

'I believe they walked from here to the village at Chapelizod. Mrs Thomas told me they would take the tram that goes from Lucan village into the city. It passes through Chapelizod several times each day. That was before she thought that somebody was watching them, of course. I saw them walk down the avenue. Mrs Thomas was holding her little son by the hand. But I really have no idea where they went in Dublin.'

'Did you notice how she was dressed?' Mossop asked. 'Or was she carrying anything, a parcel perhaps, a bag?'

'There is a very unusual aspect to this case,' Swallow added. 'When the woman was found dead, she was wearing a man's clothing. In fact, we originally believed the victim to be a man.'

The Mother Prioress looked startled.

'How extraordinary. I cannot say I ever saw Mrs Thomas dressed other than would be appropriate to her gender. But yes, perhaps when she left here on the Thursday, I do believe she had a parcel or package with her. I remember seeing her, as I said, holding the boy's hand and with a parcel, yes, a sizeable parcel, under her other arm.'

'You said that the letter from your sister house in England indicated they were coming to visit relatives. Did you – or perhaps any of your community – have any conversation with Mrs Thomas about that, about whom they were to visit or where?'

'We have rules about guests, Sergeant. We offer them shelter and sustenance and we hope they may desire to join with the community here in prayer during their visit. But we try not to pry or inquire too closely about their lives. Often their stories are very unhappy. Of course, if they wish for spiritual guidance, or if they wish to unburden themselves, there will always be a listening ear. Some of our more senior sisters are quite skilled in such matters.'

'And I take it that Mrs Thomas was not one of those guests who wished to avail of such support?'

'If she did, Sergeant, you will understand that I would not be at liberty to discuss it with you. But as it happens, no, she did not wish to engage in any dialogue beyond that required by ordinary politeness.'

Swallow smiled inwardly. Mother Mary Catherine was a woman who would not easily be moved from any position she might strike.

'I understand. May I ask then, whether Mrs Thomas had any visitors or callers during her time spent here with you?'

'Again, Sergeant, if she did, I would have to keep a confidence on the matter. But as it happens, the answer is no, she had no visitors or callers.'

Mossop looked up from his notebook.

'Can you say what time Mrs Thomas and the boy left here on the Thursday?'

'I think it was after the midday meal.'

'Can you say how they were dressed? Could you describe what they were wearing?' Mossop asked.

'I recall that Mrs Thomas wore a navy blue dress and a light coat. I suppose one would call it an outfit. It was very modest and becoming. And she had a rather smart blue-and-white hat. I recall that she did not seem to have any change of dress with her. She wore the same navy blue clothing throughout. As to the boy, I seem to remember some sort of suit. It was a dark brown, I think.'

Mossop turned a new page in his notebook.

'You refer to the child, Mother Prioress, as Mrs Thomas's son,' Swallow said. 'It's not an unreasonable supposition that the child was her son. But did you have any grounds other than supposition to take them for mother and child?'

'Our sisters in Wavertree wrote to me of Mrs Thomas and her son. And I am certain she referred to him as such on a number of occasions here.'

'I don't suppose the Abbey has the equivalent of a register or a guest book where your visitors give details of their address... that kind of thing?' Mossop inquired hopefully.

'I'm afraid not.' The Mother Prioress smiled as if any reasonable person would consider the idea ridiculous.

'How would you describe Mrs Thomas?' Swallow asked.

The Mother Prioress considered silently for a few moments.

'She was somewhat melancholy, I would say. She came across as unhappy and anxious. I had the impression she was a worried, distressed person.

'What might one infer about her background, her class, her general circumstances?'

'She was politely mannered and reasonably well presented but I do not believe she was an educated person. I would think she might have been a servant, perhaps a superior servant. But you understand that I am only speculating in response to your question.'

The nun paused, searching for the rights words.

'Her accent was unusual. I am no expert but it seemed close to what might be the accent of ordinary English people – as distinct from persons of rank. And it had traces of Irish or maybe Scottish in it too. The only other thing I can tell you is that both she and her son had been instructed in the Roman Catholic faith because they were entirely familiar with our prayers and our liturgy in church.'

Not a bad description, thought Swallow. If he could get so much detail in so few words from every detective he worked with he would not be unhappy.

'There is one other thing that I feel I should add about Mrs Thomas,' she said quietly. 'When the Mother Abbess wrote to us from Wavertree, asking that we accommodate Louise and the boy, she told me that the woman was troubled. She said she was not very stable, mentally, and that she could be very difficult to deal with. In fact, she said she was known to be physically aggressive on occasion.'

Swallow nodded.

'You had no… incident of that kind while she was here at the convent, I assume? There was no encounter with anyone that could have led to such a tragic outcome?'

'No, of course not.'

'And you have no idea of anything that might have led to this crime? There is nothing you can tell us that might help to explain why someone would have murdered Mrs Thomas and the child?'

'No, Sergeant. If there were, and if I could tell you, I would. I can only repeat that she seemed to be extremely apprehensive and fearful.'

Swallow decided he did not particularly like Mother Mary Catherine, but he felt that she was probably telling the truth. He reached into his pocket and placed a copy of the photograph of 'Chapelizod Gate Woman' face downward on the table.

'I would like to show you a photograph that you may find upsetting. It is a likeness that has been constructed by scientific methods, and we believe it is a representation of what the dead woman at the Chapelizod Gate would have looked like in life. Would you be willing to look at it for me and tell us if it bears a resemblance to Mrs Thomas?'

The Mother Prioress did not hesitate.

'Certainly I will.'

Swallow turned the photograph over and placed it in front of the nun.

If she found the picture in any way shocking, she displayed no such emotion. She considered it for a moment.

'Yes, Mr Swallow, it is a disturbing image. It is not by any means perfect, but I would recognise Mrs Thomas's features from it. She had rather prominent eyes. I felt they might have indicated some illness or condition.'

Swallow replaced the photograph in his pocket.

'Thank you. You're correct about her eyes. The medical examiner has ascertained that she was afflicted with a number of small cysts. May I ask where their belongings are? I assume they had some luggage or baggage with them when they came?'

The Mother Prioress hesitated. 'Yes… they had one bag, I believe, a sort of portmanteau. But I'm… I'm not sure it's right to interfere with their private things.'

'It may help us to trace their family, if they have any. And it could give us important clues in trying to find out who killed them.'

'I… I don't know.'

'If I have to, I'll get a warrant,' Swallow said sharply. 'I'm entitled by law to secure any evidence that may be material to my investigation. They died violent deaths, and they will not be coming back here for their belongings, I assure you.'

After a moment she stood. 'Very well. If you'll follow me please, I'll take you to the guest-house.'

She led them down a corridor along polished wooden floors under hanging pictures of saints. Two young sisters gliding towards them stood to one side, their eyes cast downward. Exiting through a heavy oak door, they crossed a paved quadrangle to a two-storey building that might once have been a store or a coach-house.

The Mother Prioress unlocked a panelled door and showed them into a sparsely furnished room with bare wooden boards and a narrow gothic window set high in the wall. A small table stood between two iron-framed beds. There was a wardrobe, two straight chairs and a large black crucifix on the wall.

A brown leather portmanteau stood on the floor at the end of one of the beds. Mossop hauled it onto the bed and flicked the two locks to open it.

They emptied it item by item. Women's underclothing, a cheap brush and comb set, two shirts and a woollen jerkin that would have fitted the boy, a bottle of hair lotion, two flannel towels, a box of patent face powder, two bristle toothbrushes and a small tin of chalk paste. Then, at the bottom of the bag, a small leather satchel tied with a frayed blue ribbon.

Swallow untied the ribbon and opened the satchel on the bed.

There was a stylised leaflet with the words of the Lord's Prayer, such as might be hung over a child's bed or in a nursery. There was a photograph of a child of about 4 or 5 years, obviously taken in a professional studio somewhere. Swallow saw a booklet on the attractions of the Blackpool seafront. At the bottom of the satchel he found a post office savings bank book with the name 'Mrs L. Thomas' on the cover.

Swallow flicked the book open. A balance of just over £10 showed on the final page. Not much of a treasure trove, he thought quietly.

A white envelope lay under the post office book. It was stamped at the general post office, Dublin, and addressed to 'Mrs L. Thomas, 37 Clarence Street, Liverpool.' He opened the envelope and withdrew the single sheet of handwritten notepaper. The sender's address and the date were written in a good hand across the top.

143 Francis Street, Dublin
June 10th 1887

It was an address that Swallow recognised instantly. He had been there on Saturday evening at Ces Downes's wake.

He read the letter.

My Dear Daughter Louise,

I am very poorly these days and my time is short and you must come now to claim what is meant for you and for the boy. I very much want to see you and him. You will be safe with the sisters of St Brigid's at Chapelizod, which is not far from Dublin, and I have arranged this with the nuns at Wavertree. You should disguise yourself so nobody will know you when you come here. You would be in great danger if you did not do so. Come to me here as soon as you are safe at St Brigid's.

Your loving mother,

Cecilia Downes

THIRTY-TWO

At the same hour that Swallow and Mossop opened their conversation with Mother Mary Catherine at St Brigid's Abbey, Detective Chief Superintendent John Mallon, head of the G Division, left Dublin Castle's Lower Yard to walk the 100 yards to the office of the Assistant Under-Secretary for Security, Mr Howard Smith Berry.

John Mallon was angry.

Arriving at his office at 8 o'clock, he had scanned the operations and crime reports, starting with the latest developments in security and surveillance.

First he reviewed the allocation of G Division's strength for the coming 48 hours. Since Sunday's incident at the Royal Hibernian Academy he had ordered that the Security Secretary and Alderman Thomas Fitzpatrick should have an armed escort of G-men at any time they moved in public.

The Security Secretary's schedule showed that he would be safely in the Castle for most of the next two days, but Fitzpatrick had a series of engagements where he might be exposed to danger. On Sunday afternoon, for example, he would attend the special Jubilee regatta at Kingstown. The G Division's manpower would be stretched to its limits, he reckoned, but the safety of key public figures had to be paramount in the days running up to the royal visit.

Later in the morning he would speak on the telephone with his counterpart in the Special Irish Branch of the London Metropolitan Police at Scotland Yard. Rumours of a 'Jubilee plot' against the royal family persisted even though the date of the Jubilee proper had come and gone without major incident. There were intelligence reports of powerful explosives being taken down through England to an unknown destination. Senior figures in the Fenian movement were reported to be meeting in Manchester. Every scrap of information coming into the police information network had to be shared and evaluated.

Mallon noted with satisfaction that the two men held in connection with the attack on the Assistant Under-Secretary and Alderman Fitzpatrick at the Royal Hibernian Academy on Sunday evening had been identified, questioned and processed.

With similar satisfaction he read that the obsequies for Pisspot Ces Downes had passed off uneventfully, apart from the demise in the Meath Hospital of a middling-level criminal called Thomas McKnight. Although McKnight had supposedly been the victim of an assault, it appeared from the post mortem conducted by Henry Lafeyre that his injuries were relatively superficial and that his death was due to heart seizure.

He puzzled briefly over a report that Charlie Vanucchi, whom he knew to be one of Ces Downes's senior lieutenants, had been detained at Exchange Court, suspected of some involvement in the death of McKnight. But since Vanucchi had been released without charge, he assumed it had amounted to nothing of consequence.

He read the update on the Chapelizod Gate murders with the sinking sense that the investigation was going nowhere. Dr Lafeyre's application of a new identification technique from Germany had not brought any evident breakthrough. The discovery of the cross-channel tickets, indicating that the dead woman and child had travelled from Holyhead, had not yielded the names of the victims. Without identification, Mallon knew, any investigative trail would go cold, and the chances of solving the crime would rapidly diminish.

It had been a typically mixed bag of good news and bad; the sort that John Mallon could handle with equanimity and a sense of having control of events. But his composure was swiftly dissipated when he opened the green file marked 'Murder of Sarah Hannin at Portobello.'

It contained a single sheet of official G-Division notepaper bearing a grammatically incomplete sentence.

'*File transferred Office of Assistant Under-Secretary for Security on instruction Major Kelly.*'

The single sheet was signed, '*Maurice Boyle, Detective Inspector. June 22nd 1887.*'

Mallon felt his temples begin to throb.

The transfer of a file to Smith Berry's office was not without precedent. It happened sometimes with politically sensitive cases. But where it had occurred in the past it was always on the basis of a direct communication between the Assistant Under-Secretary and Mallon himself. It was unprecedented that it would be done on the say-so of a blow-in like Kelly, and without the express agreement of the head of the G Division.

It was doubly unprecedented that such a file would be referred to him a full two days after the transfer had been effected.

He strode to the door and roared to his clerk to send for Detective Inspector Boyle. When the sweating inspector hurried in 5 minutes later Mallon did not invite him to sit. He slammed his closed fist down on the green file so that everything on the table shook.

Boyle had never seen Mallon in such a fury.

'Why in Hell's name, Boyle, do I read on a Friday morning that a murder file has been diverted from G Division, under your bloody signature, to the Under-Secretary's Office on the previous Wednesday?'

Boyle knew he was trapped. He had broken the one rule that Mallon insisted upon: that he was never to be left exposed with lack of knowledge on a serious case in the hands of the G Division; that any development, no matter how small, must be communicated to him instantly, day or night, whether in his office or in his house. He would generally stand over any decision by a subordinate, even one that turned out to be wrong or ill-judged, as long as he had been kept in the picture as it developed.

'I'm sorry, Sir,' Boyle stammered. 'I… I assumed you'd have been in communication with the Assistant Under-Secretary's office. The paperwork just got delayed a bit, what with the Jubilee, the three murder cases and the men out on duty for the Downes funeral. I'm truly sorry, Sir.'

Boyle was dissembling. Mallon knew that he was trying to play him off against the officials in the Upper Yard who would have the final say in any police promotion or advancement. In all probability, he reckoned, Boyle had been sworn to silence by Kelly or Smith Berry while they reviewed the file quietly themselves over the two days.

'You're a bloody fool, Boyle, and a schemer.' He spat out the words.

'You're unreliable, treacherous, disloyal and worst of all, you're incompetent! I don't know how you got into the bloody job at all, much less into G Division. You're a disgrace to your rank! Get out.'

Having vented his anger on Duck Boyle, Mallon sent a short note to Smith Berry seeking an urgent meeting. A reply came back in 10 minutes, returned by the same constable whom Mallon had sent to deliver the request. The Assistant Under-Secretary for Security would be available to see the head of the G Division at 3 o'clock at his office.

It was a short walk from the Metropolitan Police office in the Lower Yard to the Georgian block that housed the offices of the Under-Secretary and his senior assistants. But the distance that separated the lowly city police from the powerful bureaucrats with their despatch boxes, frock coats and top hats was not to be measured in yards. Mallon was entering a realm where his rank counted for little. It was a place in which he might, in certain circumstances, have a degree of influence, but in reality no independent power.

Smith Berry's office was in the block adjoining the State Apartments. It looked out on to the Upper Yard itself, towards the Justice Gate facing Cork Hill and Castle Street. The Assistant Under-Secretary, in customary morning dress, sat at his desk between two tall windows that reached almost to the ceiling. He rose to shake Mallon's hand and gestured to him to sit opposite.

'I imagine you have something important to report, Detective Chief Superintendent,' he said without preamble.

'Not so much to report, Sir,' Mallon said evenly, 'as to ask your views and, of course, to have your guidance.'

He straightened in the chair. 'Sir, I'm concerned that an investigation – a murder investigation – has been taken from the jurisdiction of my department and transferred elsewhere, without explanation and without the customary procedures being adhered to.'

Smith Berry looked up as if surprised. 'Ah, you mean the woman who was taken from the canal at Portobello on Monday afternoon?'

'Yes, Sir. It's the case of Sarah Hannin. It was being investigated by Detective Sergeant Swallow, whom you will recall you congratulated when you came to my department earlier this week. I'm mystified as to why anybody should feel that he – and I – cannot pursue the matter to a conclusion.'

A smile of what might have appeared as sympathy came across Smith Berry's features.

'I'm sure I understand, Mr Mallon. And I regret that the normal formalities could not have been applied in this case. Yes, the investigation has been taken over by the officers working directly from this office, under the command of Major Kelly.'

He paused as if seeking the right words.

'There was – is – some urgency about the matter, you understand. And it appears that Detective Sergeant Swallow and…' he glanced at some papers on his desk, 'this… Detective Feore… behaved with a good deal less than absolute courtesy and discretion when they visited Alderman Fitzpatrick's home on Monday afternoon.'

Mallon interjected.

'It happens that Alderman Fitzpatrick's home is the place of employment of this murdered woman, Sir. It's where she was last seen alive, at least that we know of. Detective Sergeant Swallow was duty bound to make inquiries there.'

Smith Berry shuffled the papers on the desk.

'Duty has to be defined in different ways in different circumstances, as you know very well, Mr Mallon,' he said reasonably. 'Swallow was planning to search the house, to question the servants, perhaps to question Mr Fitzpatrick himself, on foot of a warrant to be forwarded by you. There are absolutely no grounds for such a course of action. In addition to which, as I said, the detective sergeant and his colleague were belligerent and uncivil to Alderman Fitzpatrick and members of his staff.'

'The application for the warrant hadn't reached me,' Mallon answered evenly. 'Naturally, I would have consulted with your office before advancing it. I recognise that Alderman Fitzpatrick is an important public figure.'

'I'm glad to hear that, Mr Mallon.' Smith Berry seemed to relax a little, sitting back in his chair. 'Nonetheless, I believe we should be thankful that your detective inspector, Mr Boyle, spotted the application in early course and brought it to our attention.'

'The point is, Sir, that nothing would have happened without my signature on the application. We hadn't reached that point. How, may I ask, am I to run the detective division if I am to have serious criminal inquiries simply lifted from my officers without consultation?'

Any relaxation that might have shown on the Assistant Under-Secretary's face vanished. Now his tone was testy.

'Mr Mallon, there are situations in which I am obliged to exercise my authority without feeling myself constrained by what I would describe as polite arrangements. This is one such situation. I am not prepared to risk the possibility of scandal or controversy in or around Alderman Fitzpatrick at this time.'

Mallon chose his words carefully.

'Sir, I don't question your right to take action as you describe. And I share, of course, your concerns that we avoid any public controversy that might embroil a public figure. But this is a murder inquiry and I believe you might have relied on my personal discretion and sense of duty to ensure that any police action would be undertaken with sensitivity.'

Smith Berry swept his papers to one side of the desk with an impatient sigh.

'Dammit, Mallon, that wasn't happening in this case. Swallow and… whatever the detective officer's name is… practically broke into the house. They threatened the servant at the door, and Swallow was completely out of order in the manner in which he addressed the Alderman.'

Mallon knew it was time to cede some ground.

'I'm sorry if that was the case. It shouldn't have happened and I will speak with Detective Sergeant Swallow about it. I should say it's not in character for him, Sir.'

Smith Berry took the cue and shrugged his shoulders as if in resignation. There would be no profit in having a row unnecessarily with the head of G Division. He was Mallon's boss, but he also knew that the Detective Chief Superintendent was highly thought of, not just by the Commissioner of Police, Sir David Harrel, who was influentially connected, but by Chief Secretary Balfour too.

'Look, Mallon, we have the likely future King coming here on Monday. The bloody grocers and tavern-keepers and candlestick-makers that constitute the corporation of Dublin City want to snub him because of what happened back in the damned famine, before I was even born, you realise.'

He paused for breath.

'We can't let that happen. The Queen herself won't even come to Ireland because she feels she's been insulted down the years, along with her late husband, by so-called public representatives here. Mind you, a lot of the same representatives make a damned good living from the government in one form or another.'

He ran a hand through his hair and sighed again.

'Do I have to spell it out? We need Fitzpatrick at this time because he's got the right credentials. He's a nationalist Alderman, the likely incoming Lord Mayor, an authentic Irish businessman who can be seen to run with Parnell and the nationalists but whose greater loyalty is to the Crown – and to us. We need him because he's the acceptable and plausible face of the Irish nation welcoming the representative of the monarch. He'll make the loyal address. He'll be using his Irish charm to persuade the prince that he's as welcome as the flowers in May. We're trying to keep a bloody empire together for God's sake. If we can't keep a small kingdom in order, what chance do we have?'

Mallon permitted himself a short laugh. 'And do we think the future King will fall for this, Sir?'

'It doesn't matter, Mallon.' Smith Berry's impatience was growing. 'That's not the point. From everything I know he's a pleasant dolt. He'll hardly know whether he's in Scotland, Ireland or some damned island off the coast of India. What matters is that the thing is done right. That he comes in to Dublin, gets a good reception, eats a few dinners, gets a degree conferred, unveils a statue or two and then gets back on the bloody ship for home, safely.'

Mallon asked what he knew was the key question.

'And what does Alderman Fitzpatrick expect to get from the government in return for his loyal performance, Sir?'

Smith Berry shrugged again. 'Not a lot that wouldn't have come his way in any event. The Prince hands out a few knighthoods and other baubles. I think he might like to be *Sir* Thomas Fitzpatrick, although as a true nationalist he probably couldn't accept it. And we'll take care to see he gets some contracts for the supply of beef to the army, mainly in Egypt, I believe.'

Mallon nodded, hoping to convey a sense of understanding.

'I see, Sir.' Then, after a moment, 'And where does that leave the inquiry into the death of Sarah Hannin?'

'Why, with Kelly of course. It's not that you can't be trusted, Mallon. But Swallow and his fellows down the line, that's a different story. So it's best to keep them out of the way, at least for the present. Kelly and his men will get to the bottom of it, but in a way that won't cause other problems.'

'Time can be very important in such matters, Sir,' Mallon said. 'It could happen that by the time Major Kelly and his men have completed their inquiries the guilty party – or parties – could have flown.'

Smith Berry waved his hand. 'Oh, I know there's a risk, Mallon. But I think you should talk to Major Kelly. Pool your knowledge, as it were, at this stage. In fact, I believe he's available at this moment if you'd like to have a word.'

Without waiting for a response from Mallon he rang the bell on his desk. Almost immediately a side door into the office was opened and Kelly walked in. He looked as if he was prepared for a day in the country with a walking cane, straw hat and a lightweight flannel suit. He made a little semi-formal bow to Smith Berry and took a seat beside Mallon.

'Gentlemen, I would be glad if you could smooth out any issues that have arisen over this Hannin investigation,' Smith Berry sounded reasonable and cool again.

He inclined towards Kelly. 'Major Kelly, I believe it is accurate to say that Chief Superintendent Mallon now fully understands the sensitivities in this case and the reasons for transferring the investigation to your office. He is, however, concerned lest there be any faltering of the inquiry, and is anxious that you should co-operate with each other as fully as possible in order to bring this to a successful conclusion.'

Kelly extended his hands, palms upward, as if in a gesture of conciliation.

'Of course, Sir, I'd be very glad to have whatever assistance the Detective Chief Superintendent and his men can offer, if they have made any progress on the matter. The file which was forwarded to my office was, well, shall we say, rather thin.'

Mallon felt his anger rising again. He had agreed to co-operate. He had been willing to put the breach of procedure aside. But now his work and the work of his department were being rubbished by this shadowy functionary from God-knows-where.

'It would have been a good deal more substantial by now had my officers been allowed to proceed normally with their investigation,' Mallon said icily.

Kelly grimaced. 'There wasn't much to show after almost 48 hours, Mr Mallon.'

Mallon stiffened. 'Might I ask you, Major Kelly, just what are your credentials that enable you so confidently to offer opinions on the pace at which a particular murder inquiry should proceed?'

'I did my time at Scotland Yard, Mr Mallon,' Kelly said testily. 'You shouldn't misinterpret the fact that I choose to use my military title rather than my police rank. For a start, I wouldn't assume that this is a case of murder. The girl could have slipped into the water by accident.'

'In God's name, have you not read the medical examiner's report?' Mallon shot back. 'It's as plain as daylight that it wasn't an accident. She was bludgeoned to death.'

'That's a matter of opinion.'

'No it is not, Major Kelly. It is a fact. It's there in the clearest English in the hand of the medical examiner himself. What I'm hearing in this conversation is wishful thinking. You don't want to know about any murder here because it's inconvenient.'

Kelly was on his feet. 'That's an outrageous allegation. It's a slander and it's insubordinate. The Assistant Under-Secretary for Security has spelled out very clearly how he wishes this case to be approached.'

Smith Berry raised a calming hand.

'Please, gentlemen. This is inappropriate and unhelpful. Mr Mallon, I'm sure that Major Kelly did not mean to disparage your officers or your department. I would ask you to accept that and to accept the decision I have made. This investigation is to remain with Major Kelly. I assure you, he is an extremely experienced officer and the investigation will be in very good hands.'

Mallon knew his position was lost. He was a relatively powerless police official whose influence weighed little against the authority of Smith Berry and this shadowy creature sent from London, half soldier and half policeman.

'Very well, Sir. I am aware that I am unable to stand against your decision. I have just one question to ask of Major Kelly to which I would like an answer.'

Kelly raised an eyebrow interrogatively. 'Yes, Mr Mallon?'

'I'd be glad to learn the name of your immediate superior at Scotland Yard,' he said conversationally. 'I can say with certainty that I know every one of the senior officers in the crime departments. Was your boss Melville? Jenkinson? Waters? I'd want to be sure that the next time I am in touch there, I will know who to compliment for bringing you on so well in crime detection matters.'

Kelly glared at him in furious silence.

'We have an offence in the DMP disciplinary code known as falsehood or prevarication,' Mallon said after a long, cold interval. 'I don't think, Major Kelly, you'd do very well under it.'

THIRTY-THREE

Swallow instructed the driver to make fast time back to the Castle. 'I'll do that, Sir,' the officer grinned. 'I used to be a Rough Rider before I slowed down to this job. Get a good grip on the rail and sit tight.'

The uneven road was dusty and hot. He sped the car skilfully past the slow-moving traffic, mostly drays and farm-carts as well as a couple of horse-drawn trams. It was coming up on 4 o'clock when they reached the Castle.

The Mother Prioress had protested at first when the detectives said they would need to take the portmanteau suitcase and the personal belongings of the dead woman and child. If it proved necessary, Swallow told her for the second time, he would have a warrant from a magistrate to seize the evidence in an hour.

They might have an advantage for a while, he calculated. The murderer or murderers would not know that the victims had been identified. There might be an interval in which he could gain further information or secure evidence before they knew of the breakthrough.

He briefed Mossop as they travelled.

The portmanteau and personal effects were to be stored under lock and key at Exchange Court. At this time, the officers working on the case would not be informed that they had identified the dead woman and child. Nor would they be told that any link had been established to the late Ces Downes. The news would circulate quickly across the police network. Some constable would drop a careless word or collect a pound for tipping off a newspaper and any advantage would be lost.

Mossop would call in the surveillance reports from the G-men who had watched her house during the closing days of her life. Were there any reports of visits either by a woman and child or a man and child? Simultaneously, a confidential report was to be sought from the City of Liverpool police. What was known of Mrs Louise Thomas with an address at 37 Clarence Street?

Immediately the police side-car drew into the Lower Castle Yard, Swallow leaped down and took the stairs to Mallon's office. The clerk was verging on being obstructive, as usual. The chief was in a foul mood after a visit to the Upper Yard, he said. It might be best to stay out of his way.

'Foul mood or not, he'll need to know what I have to tell him,' Swallow snapped. 'Just go in and say I have news. I need ten minutes.'

When the clerk returned from the inner sanctum and held the door, Swallow realised that there was no exaggeration in what the officer had told him. Mallon was pacing the room in a cloud of tobacco smoke, one hand thrust deep in his trouser pocket, the other running agitatedly through his hair.

'Come in... Swallow... come in.' It was as if, for a moment, he had forgotten his subordinate's name. He made no effort to invite Swallow to sit.

'What it is, Sergeant? I assume your news is important?'

'It's the Chapelizod Gate murders, Chief. I believe we have an identification of the dead woman. And I think it probably means trouble.'

For a moment Mallon looked relieved. Swallow reasoned that he was afraid he would hear that the instruction to stay off the Sarah Hannin case had been disobeyed. He sat down and indicated to Swallow to do likewise.

He rapidly summarised the results of his visit to St Brigid's.

'Detective Mossop reckoned that the address taken by the railway policeman at Chester wasn't quite right. As it turns out, St Brigid was right, but it wasn't St Brigid's on Abbey Street; it was St Brigid's Abbey, out beyond Chapelizod.'

A faint smile of comprehension showed momentarily on Mallon's face.

Swallow recounted the visit to the abbey, the conversation with the Mother Prioress and the search of the guest-room that yielded the letter to Louise Thomas, telling her to come to Dublin.

'I'll let you read it for yourself, Sir.' He passed over the envelope. Mallon studied it for a moment, then he drew out the letter and flattened it on the desk. When he had read it he whistled silently.

'Bloody unbelievable. I'd heard it said that Ces had a son somewhere in England, but I knew nothing about a daughter.'

'I knew her husband, Tommy Byrne, fairly well,' Swallow said. 'I charged him a couple of times for serious assaults. I never heard him talk about having any children.'

'So Ces Downes must have had the child before she met Tommy,' Mallon mused. 'We never found a marriage record for her. And she always used her own name, Downes, rather that her husband's name.'

He picked up the letter and read aloud.

'*I am very poorly these days and my time is short and you must come now to claim what is meant for you and for the boy.*'

'What do you make of that, Swallow?'

'She was dying, of course. I'd read that as a call to the daughter to come to Dublin to get something to her advantage – and the boy's advantage – while Ces was in a position to give it to them.'

'Money, I'd assume,' Mallon said, 'whatever she'd put together.'

'Probably. If you read on, Chief, she says, "*you will be safe with the sisters… disguise yourself so nobody will know you when you come here. You would be in great danger if you did not do so.*" It explains a lot: the man's clothing, and the fact that we couldn't find a trace of them anywhere in the city.'

Mallon glanced again at the letter.

'She tells the daughter to come to the house at Francis Street. "*Come to me here as soon as you are safe at St Brigid's.*" I wonder did our men on surveillance notice anything significant?'

Swallow grimaced. 'I'd be sure that Mossop would have gone through all the intelligence reports. I've told him to do it again, Chief.'

Mallon nodded.

'The Mother Prioress was very clear that Louise Thomas believed herself to be in danger,' Swallow said. 'She told the nun there was a man following her on the tram. I also got a quiet word that Vinny Cussen had his people around the city on the lookout for some woman last week.'

Mallon raised his eyebrows in interest.

'If Ces Downes had money or something valuable to dispose of we'd have a strong motive for murder. And we'd have a few suspects, with Vinny Cussen among them,' he mused.

'Yes, Chief. More suspects than I'd like.'

'Money could just be a partial motive,' Mallon said. 'There might be other factors. There could a revenge angle. Ces Downes made a lot of enemies. We both know a lot of people who would have been quite capable of murdering her daughter and grandson.'

Swallow nodded in agreement. Either Charlie Vanucchi or Vinny Cussen would fit the category. They would both feel that they had served out their apprenticeship loyally and that they were entitled to the fruits of their labours after Ces's death. Or who could guess at the unknown slights or resentments that had built up over many years of collaboration?

Nor would the list of possible suspects be exhausted with Vanucchi and Cussen. Each man was surrounded by a coterie of thugs who would not scruple to kill in order to preserve a cash hoard or to get control of a lucrative criminal business.

'There's a long list of candidates,' he agreed. 'But which of them knew about the daughter's visit?'

'Somebody had inside knowledge,' Mallon said. 'Somebody knew enough about their movements to waylay them inside the Chapelizod Gate.'

'We might have an advantage for the moment, Chief,' Swallow said. 'Whoever killed them probably doesn't know that we've now got an identification. It gives us time to find out a bit more about Mrs Thomas through the Liverpool police. If they have any local knowledge on her, we might be able link her with somebody who knew her plans.'

Mallon nodded. 'You'd need to keep the identification to yourself and Mossop for the moment. If it gets out we could lose the element of surprise. I'm assuming you'll want to take Cussen and his boys in for questioning, probably Vanucchi too.'

'I think that's a bit in the future yet, Sir. We'll keep the information tight and then move in on them when we know more. We could expend a lot of manpower and a lot of time working on the wrong suspects.'

He hesitated. 'There is one other aspect to the case I'd like to put to you at this stage, Chief.'

Mallon's brow furrowed. 'Yes?'

'You know that I've been taken off the investigation into the death of Sarah Hannin, the servant from Alderman Fitzpatrick's house. The investigation has been taken over by the Security Secretary's office.'

'I'm aware of that,' Mallon said icily. 'I discussed it not an hour ago with Mr Smith Berry and his Major Kelly.'

The tone was not lost on Swallow.

'I'm beginning to believe very strongly that there may be some connection between all these deaths, Chief.'

'Tell me more,' Mallon said guardedly.

'The evidence is thin and I'm going partially on instinct. We have two women of similar age and circumstances murdered within 48 hours of each other – maybe less. The killers have attempted conceal-ment in each case. We know that one of the women, Louise Thomas, came in from Liverpool and we know that the other woman was in possession of a new lady's bag from a Liverpool store. And I have a report – unconfirmed but plausible – that a woman and child who seem to match the description of Louise and the boy made a visit to the Merrion Square house on Wednesday evening.'

Mallon looked worried again.

'It's thin. All the same, I wouldn't rule it out. But we're blocked off from the Hannin case. I believe that'll be so at least until after the royal visit is over.'

'Not only are we blocked off,' Swallow said, 'but it seems that I've been put under surveillance – I can only assume it's by Kelly's people. I'm followed around the city, even to the gates of the Castle.'

For a moment Swallow thought that Mallon was about to tell him he was imagining things. Instead, he closed his eyes and leaned back in his chair.

'Tell me, Sergeant Swallow, if you weren't blocked off from the Han-nin inquiry, what would your next steps be? How would you advance your investigation at this stage? I ask this theoretically, of course.'

Swallow knew this was the point, if he were to be honest with his superior, at which he should recount his conversation on Tuesday evening in Naughton's public house with Hetty Connors. This was the time to tell Mallon that he had secured information that Sarah Hannin was probably raised at an orphanage called Greenhills House in Queen's County.

But he could hardly admit that he had used official notepaper to notify the orphanage that an inspector from the Board of Educational Charities was on the way. And he could not tell him that he planned to impersonate that inspector on the following day.

The opportunity for disclosure passed. He could answer Mallon's question without stating anything that was untrue. It had been, after all, a hypothetical question. So his answer would be hypothetical.

'I'd be all over the Fitzpatrick house like manure off a farm-cart. I'd want to examine the dead woman's belongings. I'd want to know all about her: where she came from, how she came to work there, who her friends were. Did she have a boyfriend, or maybe more than one? I'd want to interview the servants and other members of the household individually. And because I think there might be a link to the Chapelizod Gate deaths, I'd be searching for a murder weapon. I'd be searching for a firearm and ammunition of the type that was used to murder Louise Thomas and her son. That's all hypothetically, Sir.'

Mallon appeared to become interested in some papers scattered about his desk. He was no longer looking directly at Swallow.

'Still speaking hypothetically, Sergeant, if you were going to go in and turn over Alderman Fitzpatrick's house, when would you do it? And how would you do it?'

'I think I'd want to question the servants first, Chief,' Swallow answered cautiously. 'I'd search the place from top to bottom. After that, I'd talk to the Alderman if necessary.'

Mallon nodded. He shuffled the papers on the desk to no apparent purpose.

'I think that if Major Kelly and his so-called crack team were going to undertake an operation like that, they'd probably do it on Sunday afternoon.'

Now Swallow was wary.

'I don't follow you, Sir.'

Mallon still pretended to re-order the documents.

'I see that we're providing a security detail on Sunday afternoon for Alderman Fitzpatrick. He's departing his house at noon for the Jubilee regatta at Kingstown. So if Major Kelly wanted to question the servants, for example, or search the house without the risk of being confronted by the Alderman himself, that would be the time to do it.'

He looked up from the desk. For the second time in the conversation, Swallow thought he saw the flicker of a smile.

'But of course,' Mallon said, 'we know that Major Kelly isn't thinking in these terms, even hypothetically.'

THIRTY-FOUR

Swallow did not particularly enjoy *La Fille de Madame Angot*. Although he had looked forward to the outing, he was not in the best mood to appreciate comic opera. He had no time to return to Thomas Street to secure a change of clothes after the sweaty drive in and out to St Brigid's Abbey. He refreshed himself as best he could with soap and cold water at Exchange Court before making his way to the theatre. He would have been glad of a fresh shirt in the warm evening.

Lafeyre's invitation was a gracious gesture, and Swallow felt he should enter into the spirit of the occasion. He had invited them to meet for drinks at the Queen's before the performance. The foyer was crowded and lively, as was usual. Dubliners loved their theatre nights, and the interior was pleasantly cool after the heat of the day. When the final curtain came down, Lafeyre offered them more champagne. Swallow had already decided it was not an occasion for excessive restraint.

It was the first evening in which he could even partially relax since the discovery of the bodies at the Chapelizod Gate. He made the most of it, putting away four or five glasses of Lafeyre's Veuve Clicquot in rapid succession.

They took a late supper at the grill room of Jury's Hotel on Dame Street. Swallow appreciated Jury's with its dark wood and polished mirrors. Even though it was not a place he could afford to frequent very often on a detective sergeant's pay, it remained a good location to watch some of the city's more influential people.

Two silk-hatted, overweight clergymen crossed the lobby. Swallow saw a flash of purple indicating that one was a monsignor or perhaps even a bishop. He surmised that they had dined well.

He saw James Scott, the editor of the pro-establishment *Irish Times* entering the grill room with a corpulent, full-bearded man he recognised as Richard Piggott, a journalist known for his nationalist associations. They made an unlikely twosome, Swallow reckoned. But in Dublin journalism, he supposed, as in many other walks of life, even rivals might sometimes have to engage socially.

Maria and Lily excused themselves to visit the powder-room. Swallow took the opportunity to tell Lafeyre about the visit to the convent and the discovery that the Chapelizod Gate murder victims were the daughter and grandson of Ces Downes.

Lafeyre was astounded. He saw the implications at once.

'Dear God, that's going to make for trouble in one form or another. Isn't it likely that the unfortunate woman and her child were murdered by one of Ces Downes's criminal associates?'

Swallow shrugged. 'That could be so. We still don't have a clear motive. Somebody could have had a grudge perhaps? Or was it for money? We'll probably start by questioning the obvious suspects like Cussen and Vanucchi when we have a bit more information in from Liverpool CID.'

Maria and Lily appeared from the ladies' room. 'I don't want this to go beyond us for the moment,' Swallow said quietly. 'It would upset the ladies. And it just might get out inadvertently.'

Lafeyre led the way to their table. There was some discussion of the operetta, but the talk soon turned to the murders that had shocked the city.

'Is our reconstruction of that poor young woman's face really going to solve this crime for you, Joseph?' Lily Grant asked. She usually addressed him as 'Joseph' in serious matters.

'I hope so,' Swallow answered as he savoured his second glass of Chablis and started on a grilled black sole. 'I've circulated copies of the photograph to every officer on the case. By the time the afternoon shift came on duty there should have been copies at every police station in the city. And, of course, it's been in the morning newspapers as well as in yesterday's *Evening Telegraph*.'

'And if you don't succeed in catching the murderer...?' Maria asked.

Swallow understood the unspoken question she was posing. She knew the pressure he was under. She was asking about their future together. If he failed to solve the case would it mean an end to police work for him?

'Then a very brutal killer is going to remain at liberty,' he said curtly.

'And what's happening about the other dreadful killing?' Lily asked. 'What about the servant girl taken from the canal.'

Swallow did not want to explain that the case had been taken out of his hands.

'I need information on her background. I'm planning a visit tomorrow to the orphanage where I believe she was reared. It's called Greenhills House. It's in Queen's County. So I'm going to take an early train down there to Maryborough and be back by evening.'

'I'm going to go along with Joe,' Lafeyre said. 'I thought you might like to come too, Lily. We could make it a day out in the country? Would we bring a picnic for the fine weather?'

Lily Grant looked far from pleased. 'I thought we were going to take the train to Bray and have lunch there?'

'Yes, I know. But the countryside would be pleasant too. And it's important that Joe gets to make his inquiries at Greenhills.'

'To see the countryside would be nice,' she answered politely but without enthusiasm.

'I know the area well. I grew up not too far away. And in high summer the furze will be magnificent,' Lafeyre said. 'Maria, could you leave the business behind you for the day to come with us?'

Maria seemed no more enthusiastic than her sister, but she nodded acceptance. 'Yes, I think I could do that. I can get Carrie to put together a picnic for us tomorrow morning.'

Swallow caught her doubtful look across the table. He knew that she was worried about him, especially since their conversations of the previous Sunday. A pleasant excursion into the countryside would be harmless, he told himself. It might help to relieve tensions. Apart from a brief visit to the orphanage it would be a day of leisure.

Lafeyre set out a plan. 'I'll depart my house with Scollan at say, 8.30 in the morning to collect Lily at Alexandra College. Then we can pick up Joe and Maria at Thomas Street in time to catch the 10 o'clock train from Kingsbridge to Maryborough.'

There was beef in red wine after the fish course. Lafeyre ordered a Chateauneuf du Pape. Swallow enjoyed the rich Rhone wine and happily assisted Lafeyre in finishing a second bottle. After the meal, Lafeyre's driver, Scollan, took them to Thomas Street.

The bar was silent and dark an hour after closing time. The domestic servants and the barmen had departed or gone to their sleeping quarters. Swallow lit the gas mantle inside the front door.

There was a buff envelope with a crown, addressed to 'Jos. Swallow Esq.' on the floor. Swallow recognised the handwriting as Pat Mossop's. Before he could open the envelope Maria put her hand on his arm.

'I presume that's official business, Joe. You'll want to deal with it, so I'm just going to go straight away to bed. We have an early start in the morning if we're going on this… outing… to Queen's County.'

It was clear that she was no more pleased with the prospect than when it had been proposed in Jury's. Swallow did not want to engage in a conversation that had the potential to become unpleasant.

'Fine, Maria. I'll need to see what's in this, then I'll be on my way upstairs as well.'

The night was humid. Swallow went into the parlour and threw up the sash window to create a current of air. He felt slow and full after the rich meal. He poured himself a brandy from the flask that always stood in the sideboard and opened Mossop's envelope.

He drew out two sheets of police-issue telegram paper. There was also a handwritten note from Mossop.

Sir,

We have two results.

Regarding the gentleman at Fitzpatrick's, Mr McDonald, the Army Paymaster's Office in London came back. Very prompt. There are 12 James McDaniels listed. Two were born between 1827 and 1837, fitting the age group of our man.

One of them is living in Glasgow on a pension.

The other deserted from the King's Own Borderers at York in 1868, aged 38 years at the rank of corporal. He is James Andrew McDaniel, d.o.b. April 17th 1829, in Lanarkshire. So if alive he is now aged 58 years and there is no trace since on the Army records.

This McDaniel was a single man. It seems he was in some serious trouble. The file says he is being sought by the Provost Marshal's Office. I thought it strange that they were still bothered about it now, after 20 years, so I looked into what he had done.

I checked with Dublin Crime Registry this evening. They receive and file all notifications from the Provost Marshal's Office. They came up with it fairly quickly. He is wanted in connection with the murder of a young officer in barracks in York.

It seems that McDaniel was batman to a lieutenant and killed him in the barracks. What the army refers to as an 'unnatural relationship' had developed between them. There was a great stink about it at the time.

The full information from the Paymaster's office is set out in the enclosed sheets.

We also have a telegram from the City of Liverpool Police regarding a Louise Cecilia Thomas, known to reside at 37 Clarence Street, Liverpool.

She has two convictions for assaulting other women. In both cases she escaped imprisonment on payment of fines. Her late husband, Richard Thomas, was killed in an accident while working at Liverpool docks three years ago. He had convictions for assault and theft and served a number of terms of imprisonment.

She and her son, also Richard, aged about 8 or 9 years, have lodged at the above address for about 1 year. She has been employed for about 2 years as a kitchen assistant or assistant cook at one of the Liverpool Hospitals.

City of Liverpool police have no other knowledge. There is no knowledge of further family or relatives.

I thought you would want to have these details as soon as possible.

Yours respectfully,

Patrick Mossop (Detective Officer)

Not for the first time in his detective career, Swallow was grateful for the bureaucracy's insistence on record-keeping in the form of the Dublin Crime Registry, a vast repository of criminal data, housed in a granite-fronted store behind the Castle in Great Ship Street.

The likelihood had to be that McDonald, the butler at Fitzpatrick's, was in reality James McDaniel, wanted in connection with the 1868 murder at York.

He crossed the room to try for a fresher current of air by the window. As his glance fell into Thomas Street he saw a man half hidden in the shadows of a shop door. He crossed the street, and Swallow saw him try the locked door of the public house. Then he went down the side-alley that led to the private entrance.

Swallow put his brandy on the sideboard and sprinted down the corridor. He took the stairs two at a time and dropped quietly though the back window into the small yard. Then he drew the bolt and stepped out into the alley. The man was at the private door, huddled over, as if he were trying to insert something in the lock or peer through the letter-box.

Swallow bounded on him from behind, taking him to the ground. He heard the wind flying from the intruder's lungs. Then he was on him, taking the man's right arm in a sharp lock and twisting it high behind his back. He squealed in pain. With his other hand, Swallow grasped his hair, jerking his head back and around so he could see his face. It was Charlie Vanucchi.

'Jesus, Mister Swalla', will you stop tryin' to break me arm? Let me go,' he hissed, 'I'm only comin' with some information for you.'

Swallow lifted Vanucchi to his feet and pushed him to the wall. Still pushing his arm high behind his back, he ran his free hand along the sides of his coat and trousers. There was no weapon, no jemmy to break a door, no knife to slip a latch. He released Vanucchi's arm and stepped back.

'For Christ's sake, Charlie, what're you doing slithering around the back door here at this hour of the night?'

Vanucchi rubbed his tender wrist where Swallow had grabbed him.

'I came to give you a bit of information Mr Swalla'. I told you Charlie Vanucchi doesn't forget a good deed or the act of a friend. I couldn't come to the bloody Castle, could I? An' I could hardly walk up to you in broad daylight.'

He looked around him. 'I suppose there's a chance you might ask me in and offer me a drink, Mr Swalla? I'm half in shock, you know, after you jumpin' me.'

Swallow led the way through the side door and up the stairs to the sitting-room. He gestured Vanucchi to a chair and reached for the brandy bottle. He poured a shot of the liquor for Vanucchi, who downed it in a single gulp.

'Jesus, that's good stuff, Misther Swalla'. If I could afford that every night I'd be a happy man.' He held the tumbler out.

Swallow dispensed a less liberal tot than before. Vanucchi put the glass under his nose and inhaled deeply. 'Ahhh... that's powerful.'

He squinted at Swallow over the glass. 'Misther Swalla', I'm goin' to give you a bit of information that I think ye should have. It'll suit my purposes for ye to have it. And I'll wager that it'll do you some good if you act on it as you should.'

'Go on,' Swallow said, tipping more brandy into his own glass.

'Well, there's a couple of the younger fellas that did a few jobs for Ces Downes… but they'd be more on the Cussen side of the organisation than they'd be on my side, if you understand.'

'In simple language, Charlie, they're Vinny Cussen's men, so you've no problem giving me a whisper about whatever they're at.' Swallow smiled cynically.

'In a manner of speakin', Misther Swalla, that'd be correct. These young fellas are no help to me. To be honest, they're dangerous and I'd be glad to have them outta my way for a bit.'

'So, what are they at that you think I'd be interested in?'

'Some of these fellas aren't content to make a livin' out of the business. They want to think o' themselves as patriots, idealists, men who'll save Ireland. So they get involved with some of these politicals – the big men that'll drive the English out and give Ireland back to the Irish.'

'So, who are these lads and what are they at?' Swallow asked. He inclined the brandy bottle towards Vanucchi's glass and poured again.

'You'd hardly know them, Misther Swalla'. There's Pat O'Reilly. He's only a lad. About 18, I'd say, but a vicious one. Then there's Eddie Locke. He's a bit older and not too bright. A good man to get over a roof or across a high wall, he is. But he's easily led. The main man doin' the thinking there is O'Reilly.'

'So, what are these young patriots planning?' Swallow asked.

'I'm not 100 percent sure, Misther Swalla'. But I saw O'Reilly the other night with two big, black guns. Like them ones the sailors do have. He was puttin' bullets in one o' them and showin' Locke how the things work. Now, Misther Swalla, as you know very well, there's seldom much use for guns in what we do.'

He took a slug of the brandy. 'So, the next day I meet young Locke when I'm walkin' along on Westland Row, and he tells me he's gettin' to take a train to Kingstown.

'I says to him, "Eddie, what are you goin' to Kingstown for?"… because Eddie Locke wouldn't have any business in Kingstown. He was probably never out o' Dublin in his life. And he says to me, "Oh, we're goin' out to have a look around where the royal prince will be comin' in for a visit." So I says to him, "who's 'we', Eddie?" And he says to me, "Ah, just a few o' the boys I know in the Brothers."

'Then who comes along to meet the two lads at the Westland Row railway station?' He glanced around as if to be sure there was nobody else in the parlour. 'A fella by the name of O'Donnell. He's introduced to me as *Mister* James O'Donnell. And the boys tell me that he's their big contact in the Brothers. He's the main man organisin' whatever mischief they're plannin'. Now, that's good information for ye.'

He drained his glass. 'Misther Swalla', I'm not a man who cares a shit about princes or queens. But I'm puttin' two and two together and I think these fellas are plannin' to do a lot a' damage when that prince comes in to Kingstown next week. They haven't got them two guns for nothin', I'm damned sure.'

Swallow felt a surge of elation at the mention of James O'Donnell's name. He divided the last of the brandy between Vanucchi's glass and his own.

'Yer grinnin' away there, Misther Swalla. Is there a joke that I'm not gettin'?'

'Not really, Charlie. I'm just thinking of the old saying "*the Lord moves in mysterious ways his wonders to perform.*"'

He raised an admonishing finger to Vanucchi.

'What you do now, Charlie, is you tell nobody else about this, do you understand? Don't ask any more questions of either O'Reilly or Locke in case they get suspicious. If you come across the guns, leave them where they are. We'll let this pot boil away for a bit.'

He raised his glass. 'Here's to your health, Charlie. Now, we'll see if we can get you out of here as discreetly as you got in.'

He led Vanucchi to the side door and opened it, allowing a current of warm night air to flow in. Vanucchi slipped into the alleyway and silently vanished.

Swallow climbed the stairs to the bedroom where Maria had drifted into sleep. He arranged his clothes and checked his revolver, laying it carefully, with 12 spare rounds of ammunition, by the bedside for the morning's journey.

He slept. He dreamed that he saw a leering James O'Donnell with his sister, Harriet, somewhere among a crowd of people. He called to warn her that she was in danger, but she was happy and laughing. He called more loudly. In his dream, she could not hear him.

Saturday June 25th, 1887

THIRTY-FIVE

The modest prosperity of the town of Maryborough was founded upon its location at the intersection of the main roads connecting Dublin with the cities of Cork and Limerick.

Lying 50 miles west of Dublin in the flat midland countryside, its central location also made it an important stop for the Great Southern and Western Railway Company. On any given day, thanks to the organisational genius of the company, it was now possible to take any one of up to a dozen trains from the King's Bridge terminus in Dublin to Maryborough and to return before midnight.

Swallow's plan was to take the 10 o'clock morning train from the city, arriving at Maryborough at 11.20. From there they would hire a car and driver to take them to Greenhills House.

Lafeyre was still uncomfortable about having abandoned the planned outing to Bray. Lily's reaction to the change of plan had not been positive. But a picnic lunch in the countryside was compensation of a sort, he reasoned. He knew the area around Maryborough from childhood. If the good weather held up they would picnic on the Heath, a scenic stretch of common land which they would have to cross on their way to the orphanage.

Swallow reckoned they should aim to arrive at Greenhills House at about 1 o'clock, by which time staff and inmates might have had their lunch. Hopefully, whoever would be in charge would be sufficiently impressed by his purported authority to enable him to examine the orphanage records.

They would be back at Maryborough in time to catch the last train to Dublin. He knew the mission to Greenhills was something of a wild shot, but he had a sense that if he could learn about Sarah Hannin's early life it would answer at least some questions. One maxim he had always followed was that when somebody put up obstacles to seemingly harmless information it was invariably worth a policeman's time to get around them.

Swallow and Maria rose before 8 o'clock. In spite of having partaken liberally of Lafeyre's hospitality the night before, along with the brandy he had shared with Charlie Vanucchi, he felt refreshed and alert. His dream of Harriet and James O'Donnell quickly faded.

The clear morning sky indicated another hot day. He washed, shaved and dressed in a light suit whose comfortable fit concealed the Webley Bulldog in its shoulder-holster. Maria went downstairs and helped Carrie the housekeeper to prepare the picnic basket.

Shortly before 9 o'clock, Lafeyre and Lily arrived to collect them in the brougham. The streets were quiet. Shops and offices were not yet busy. By the time the party reached King's Bridge, though, the day was warming.

The railway terminus was quiet too. Swallow bought first-class return tickets to Maryborough while Lafeyre, Lily and Maria waited by the platform. Beyond the ticket-barrier, the engine hissed and rumbled as the driver and engineer went through their checks.

Coming from the ticket office, Swallow's eye caught a shadow moving behind the pillars at the entrance to the terminus. He had an impression of a tall man with a Derby-style hat. Then he was gone from sight.

The train to Maryborough would have stops at Naas, Kildare town and Portarlington. They took the first-class carriage at the front and settled down on the leather banquettes, Lafeyre carefully placing the picnic basket on the seat beside him. On the stroke of 10 o'clock, the train shuddered and started to move out of the sheds into the morning sunlight.

In spite of the serious purpose of their journey, Swallow began to feel a boyish sense of outing. His spirits lifted as the train picked up speed, taking them out beyond the drabness of the city.

The countryside was busy. Farm workers were scything the summer grass or piling it with pitchforks into high-sided carts. Before Kildare, the open plain of the Curragh was a green carpet. They saw a string of racehorses at exercise, loping along in the distance like miniatures from a child's toy-box.

Swallow strained to see how far his eyes could bring him towards Newcroft. His mother would be at her day's work in the business by now. The thought disquieted him. Very soon he would have to square up to the issue of how much longer she could run the place on her own.

'The Hill of Allen,' he told his companions, pointing northward through the window to a low, wooded rise in the flat landscape.

'Not much of a hill, is it?' Maria observed. Her mood had scarcely improved since the previous evening.

'It's the best we can manage around here,' he answered testily. 'Kildare is for flat racing, not mountain climbing.'

'Flat racing and army manoeuvres,' interjected Lafeyre. 'Sometimes they have up to 6,000 men at the Curragh Camp over there.'

Swallow laughed. 'A lot of those fellows helped to fund my medical studies. Some nights the whole camp was drinking their pay in our public house.'

Maria smiled and seemed to relax a little. Lily continued to fasten her artist's eyes to the window, taking in the colours and the detail of the landscape. They might have been any foursome making an excursion to the country.

They left the firm fields of County Kildare and passed into Queen's County. Fenced paddocks and wide meadows began to give way to rushy fields. A little farther, even these semi-arable acres began to yield to bog. Tracts of flat land, yellow with furze, stretched away to left and right. A few substantial farmhouses appeared here and there, but for the most part the dwellings visible from the train were poor cottages.

It required a leap of the imagination, Swallow reflected, to appreciate that these peaceful-looking acres were often a battleground in the cover of night. Police and military faced off against tenants and labourers, organised and encouraged by the Land Leaguers to show their collective strength. Dark deeds were done in fields and country lanes like these between nightfall and sunrise.

Somewhere after Portarlington, the last stop before Maryborough, Lafeyre turned to Swallow.

'You'd better talk us through this. What exactly are we supposed to be doing when we get to Greenhills? I've got a rough idea of what you're doing, but I think the ladies need to know too.'

Swallow saw Maria stiffen slightly. 'It's simple enough,' he said, attempting to sound nonchalant. 'The guardian at Greenhills is expecting a visit from the Board of Educational Charities. So, I'll have to carry myself off as an inspector. I can bluff my way through that role, I think.'

He smiled. 'Harry, you'll have to be my assistant. So, you'll stay quiet and just say "yes" and "no" as seems appropriate when I speak.'

'And what in heaven's name are you trying to find out by impersonating a Board of Education… whatever it's called?' Maria blurted.

'I think the woman we took from the canal on Monday was raised in Greenhills,' he said, 'but nobody is willing to give us any information about her. If we can find out her background it might throw some light on why she was murdered.'

Lily turned away from her landscape-gazing. 'How d'you think you're going to get this information? Are you going to question this guardian?'

'I'm more interested in the records there. Orphanages generally keep good ones,' Swallow said. 'So, if Sarah Hannin was raised there, or if she spent time there, that should be in the registers. And what do inspectors do if they don't inspect the registers?'

'Can I ask what role my sister and I are to play in this charade?' Maria asked pointedly.

'I've been thinking a lot about that,' Swallow said with exaggerated seriousness. 'I've decided that you are to play the role of two ladies of charitable disposition,' he grinned.

'You're travelling around the country with the inspector and his assistant to see some of the more deserving institutions that provide for the needs of orphaned children. You might be considering making an endowment. That way, I'm sure whoever we meet will be more than anxious to accommodate us.'

Lafeyre shook his head in mock disbelief. 'You made the wrong choice of career after medical school, Joe. You could have made it as a great stage actor.'

Maria was not in a mood to make light of things.

'If I had known that I was being brought along to masquerade as a "lady of charitable disposition", as you put it, I wouldn't be here. If I had a day to spare from business I'd be relaxing at home or visiting my friends or taking the air by the sea. I think you've been less than frank, and very unfair with us.'

Swallow winced.

'Look, I'm sorry. I didn't intend it to work out this way. Why can't we just treat it as a bit of a jaunt, like we planned? I'll be in and out of this place in half an hour.'

Maria raised her eyes in despair. 'I don't think you give us much choice, Joe. I'm sure Lily feels the same. We're not in this of our own volition.'

They were at Maryborough on schedule. The station was quiet. Fewer than half a dozen passengers alighted, with perhaps an equal number joining the train as it continued towards its final destination of Cork.

Swallow called a porter who took the picnic basket down from the carriage. In response to Swallow's query he said he could find a car to take them to Greenhills House and back in time to catch an evening train to Dublin.

'It bein' that little bit late in the mornin', Sir, there wouldn't be as much call for the drivers as you'd have with passengers comin' off the early trains,' the man scratched his chin thoughtfully.

'But there's Pat Bracken who's just 100 yards down the road from the station. If yourself and the ladies and gentleman would take a seat in the waiting room, sure I'll have him up here in a few minutes.'

Soon they heard the clip-clop of a horse-drawn car on the cobbles outside the station. Swallow stepped out to the forecourt to see the porter jumping down from a well-maintained trap, drawn by a single pony and driven by a plump man in his fifties, still buttoning his jacket. He had a battered bowler hat perched on the back of his head and a bushy grey beard. He drew the trap to a stop.

The porter took up the lunch box. The others followed him to the car.

'Pat was sittin' at home, Sir, like I said. He'll see you out to Green-hills House now in the best of time. You'll be back then for the up-train later on?'

Swallow tipped him and confirmed that they would return in time to catch the last Dublin train.

'What's your charge to bring us out to Greenhills House and back here for the last train?' he asked Bracken. 'There'll be a couple of hours of waiting in between.'

The driver looked thoughtful for a moment. 'Would you think seven shillings might be reasonable, Sir? There's a good distance between here and Greenhills.'

'That seems fair enough,' Swallow said, even though he thought it a bit on the high side. 'We'll be on our way.'

Bracken settled them into the trap, helping the women first to negotiate the metal step and making sure that they were sitting comfortably.

They clattered out of the station, making for the open countryside past rows of dilapidated cabins and groups of dirty children who stood to watch the car on the rutted road.

Swallow glanced back as they left the station yard. There was the now-familiar shadow with the Derby hat. He seemed to have emerged to watch their departure. Then he stepped back again into the station.

It had to be one of Kelly's agents, Swallow reasoned. On the positive side, if their surveillance was intended to be covert they were not very expert at it. And whatever about the city streets, it would be impossible for anyone to follow them across the countryside without being detected.

Bracken was a considerate driver. He kept the pony at a steady pace, slowing where he knew the road to be particularly uneven or bumpy. Lafeyre and Lily sat to one side of the trap with Swallow and Maria on the other while the driver sat forward. He held the reins lightly in one hand while he filled his pipe with the other.

'Do ye know this countryside at all, Sir? He asked Lafeyre.

Lafeyre smiled but ignored the implicit invitation to give an account of himself.

Swallow answered for him. 'I've a reasonable knowledge of the area. I know more or less the direction we're travelling but I can't say I'd find my way on my own.'

The driver chuckled in his beard. 'Indeed, Sir, it's wild enough out here. There's hardly a signpost to lead ye to any town or village. Have ye heard of the Great Heath, Sir?'

Swallow knew it was notorious in bygone days as a hunting ground for vagabonds, robbers and those on the run from the forces of the law.

'I've heard of it,' he ventured.

'We'll cut alongside the Heath and then turn north,' he gestured with the pipe. 'The stone road ends there and we'll have to take a little boreen – that's what we call a back road here – for about 2 miles up to Greenhills House. It's a tight road, but with the day grand and dry, thank God, there won't be any difficulty.'

'You're the best judge of that,' Swallow responded.

Bracken took a series of puffs from his pipe. 'And what would be the nature of yer business at Greenhills House, gintlemin, if ye don't mind me curiosity?'

'Not at all,' Swallow responded, winking broadly at the others, 'We're calling on behalf of the Board of Educational Charities. Have you heard about the work done by the board?'

'Well, I can't rightly say that I have, Sir,' Bracken answered after a moment's reflection. 'But I wouldn't doubt that it's important.'

'We're in a poor part o' the countryside now, ladies and gintlemin,' he called over his shoulder, deftly changing the subject. 'Ye'll see only a few ruined houses here. These places suffered terrible hard in the famine years.'

Lafeyre knew many such townlands where his grandfather had dispensed medical care among long-vanished communities. Mossy foundation walls were the only lingering traces of the families that starved, succumbed to disease or fled to the emigrant ships 40 years ago.

The ground rose as they came towards Greenhills House. The by-road was little more than a laneway with high ditches, indicating that the land had been drained on both sides. The banks were heavily grown with thorn hedges and occasional single trees; alder and sycamore. Here and there a copse of beech or chestnut stood tall, signifying tenure over time.

'There she is, Ladies and Gintlemin.'

Bracken pointed with the stem of his pipe towards a drab, grey building, now visible through a copse of trees. It was perhaps a quarter of a mile along the laneway.

'Greenhills House,' he announced.

He halted the trap before the main door. A pair of Doric columns flanked granite steps. Green and yellow weeds sprouted from the cracks between the stonework. The paint on the columns was peeled with age. A crescent of what might once have been lawn formed a grassy meadow in front of the building. Greenhills House gave every appearance of decay and neglect.

Lily and Maria, reluctantly acting out their assumed roles as would-be benefactresses, elected to walk in the grounds and to give the impression of examining the gardens.

Lafeyre and Swallow climbed the steps.

'Now,' Swallow said, 'remember, I'm doing the talking. You play along.'

His haul on the doorbell was answered after a minute by a thin young man wearing a shabby, dark suit with a pair of wire-rimmed spectacles sitting on his nose.

'Good afternoon, Sirs. You must be the inspectors. I'm Baxter, the monitor. Please, come in.'

Swallow nudged Lafeyre as they stepped inside. The interior smelled of rotting vegetables. In spite of the warmth of the day there was a pervading sense of dampness.

'So, you're the monitor?' Swallow inquired, endeavouring to assume an expression both grave and knowledgeable that he imagined would be appropriate to an inspector of the Board of Educational Charities.

'Yes, Sir. I'm on duty this afternoon. The children have had their lunch and I'm supervising them in drill. Unfortunately, the Guardian, Mr Pomeroy, is not here at the moment, but he told me to be ready for your visit. Although he didn't say you'd come on a Saturday...'

His voice trailed off.

'We wouldn't usually come on a Saturday, Mr Baxter,' Lafeyre said pleasantly, deciding to play up his adopted role. 'But as it happened we had other business in the area... charitable business, of course. And we have two ladies of a generous disposition with us who might wish to help out... financially, that is, if they are sufficiently impressed. They are now looking at the grounds and the gardens.'

'That is ver... very... edifying,' Baxter stammered. 'Unfortunately, the grounds aren't at their very best at this particular time. We had a gardener who became ill and he... wasn't replaced. Shall I have someone accompany the ladies?'

'I don't believe that will be necessary,' Swallow said reassuringly. 'They would prefer, I am sure, to be allowed to conduct their examination at their own pace and in privacy.'

'Would you like to see the drill class?' Baxter inquired eagerly. 'Because of the good weather we'll be outdoors. Or perhaps you'd like to visit the dining hall and kitchen. There's only an assistant cook there, it being Saturday, but the children...'

'Not at all,' Swallow intervened, 'we won't interrupt what I'm sure is your fine drill-instruction, Mr Baxter. We would, however, like to spend just a little while examining some of the files and records. There are some questions which we have to answer for our colleagues at our next meeting.'

'Then you'll want to go to the office, I assume,' Baxter replied efficiently. 'I have the keys and I can bring you there. Will I have the assistant cook prepare some tea?'

'No, thank you,' Lafeyre smiled, 'that won't be necessary. If you can just show us to the office that will be sufficient, thank you. And you may continue with your work.'

Baxter led them along bare boards, down a sunless corridor into a wing of the house that overlooked the gardens. He opened the door to a high-ceilinged room with grimy bow windows giving out onto a yard. Spreading black patches on the wall and ceiling showed where damp had penetrated. Swallow saw that all of the windows were nailed shut. There was a table with two or three hard chairs.

He reasoned quietly that if these were the conditions in which the officials worked, the lot of the children in Greenhills House could not be a particularly happy one.

Baxter pointed to the shelves that lined three walls of the room.

'All of the files and records are there, gentlemen, as you expect, in chronological order. Is there any particular category you would like me to identify for you?'

'We will want to look at admissions and discharges,' Swallow said. 'That's what the Board is concerned about above all else, as you'll understand. It's a question of making sure that the house is providing value for money in terms of your numbers here.'

'Of course,' Baxter replied. 'The more recent records are on the right and they go back year by year, moving to the left as you face the shelves.'

He made a little bow and backed out the door, closing it behind him. Lafeyre moved across the room and put his ear against the upper panel.

'He's gone,' he grinned at Swallow. 'They were certainly expecting us.'

Swallow nodded. 'It's amazing what can be done with a couple of sheets of paper with a crown on them.'

They set about scouring the shelves, following Baxter's guidance, for the records that they hoped that might yield some information on Sarah Hannin. After just a minute, Lafeyre called out.

'I think this is the section that we want, Joe. "*Records of admissions 1855-1880*".' He drew down a leather-bound journal, date stamped on the spine.

'This covers admissions in the years 1860 to 1863.'

The ruled columns on the left side showed names of children and their dates of admission. Lafeyre leafed through the book, moving through the entries for 1860 and 1861. At 1862, he slammed an open page.

'There she is, Joe.'

He tapped the line. Swallow read the entry.

Family Name: Hannin
Christian Name(s): Sarah Mary

Gender: Female
Date of Birth: June 5th 1862
Date of Admission: October 10th 1862
Date of Discharge: September 1st 1875
General Health: Good

There was a supplementary information panel on the opposite page, but in Sarah Hannin's case, the spaces provided for the place of birth, the names, addresses and occupations of parents were blank.

Swallow reckoned they were fortunate to get even the basic details. Compulsory registration had begun little more than a decade ago. Getting this amount of information on what was almost certainly an illegitimate birth more than 20 years previously was not to be taken for granted.

His eyes ran down the page, scanning the other enrolments at Greenhills House in the year 1862. He gasped at an entry three lines down.

Family Name: Downes
Christian Names (s): Louise Cecilia
Gender: Female
Date of Birth: July 1st 1862
Date of Admission: October 12th 1862
Date of Discharge: September 1st 1875

Unlike Sarah Hannin, the spaces on the supplementary information panel were neatly filled in.

Lafeyre's eyes had also travelled down the page. Swallow was fractionally ahead of him, but their exclamations were simultaneous as they read the entries.

'Christ almighty,' Swallow said.

'As God is my judge,' Lafeyre rejoined.

They read the supplementary panel.

Place of Birth: Rotunda Hospital, Dublin
Family name: Downes
Christian Names: Louise Cecilia
Mother's Christian Names: Cecilia Margaret
Mother Native of: King's County
Putative Father: T. Fitzpatrick
Profession, Rank or Trade of Father: Not stated
Mother's address at time of Admission: 106 Merrion Square, Dublin.

'Ces Downes's daughter, Louise Thomas, was raised here in this place too,' Swallow exclaimed. 'And the father has to be Thomas Fitzpatrick. Look at the address.'

He ran his finger back along the entries.

'I knew it... I knew there was a connection between these damned cases.'

Swallow realised he was almost shouting.

'There had to be a link between the two women,' he told Lafeyre. 'And this is it, here. Or part of it. They were both here in this institution and they're both connected back to Fitzpatrick.'

'But who'd want to murder two women and a child simply because the women were in the same institution?' Lafeyre asked.

Swallow's eyes had been travelling up and down the open record book. Half a dozen entries below, he registered something else.

'Harry, look at this. There's more.'

He ran his finger down the page.

Family Name: Fitzpatrick
Christian Name(s): John Michael
Gender: Male
Date of Birth: July 30th 1863
Date of Admission: November 10th 1863
Date of Discharge: September 1st 1876
General Health: Good
Place of Birth: Rotunda Hospital, Dublin
Mother's family name: Downes
Mother's Christian Names: Cecilia Margaret
Mother Native of: Kings County
Putative Father: T. Fitzpatrick
Profession, Rank or Trade of Father: Not stated
Mother's address at time of Admission: 106 Merrion Square, Dublin

'There was a son too,' Lafeyre almost whispered the words.

'Let's try to get all of this straight,' Swallow tapped his forehead as if to concentrate his powers of reasoning.

'We have two girls – two children – one of whom was the daughter of Ces Downes and Thomas Fitzpatrick, discharged from this orphanage here in 1875.'

'That's it,' Lafeyre agreed. 'There was a relationship between Fitz-patrick and Ces Downes. They have a daughter and a son – Louise and John Michael.'

'So where does Sarah Hannin fit in?'

'I don't know,' Lafeyre answered. 'Louise and Sarah were enrolled here at the same time. Maybe they became friends.'

Swallow nodded. 'Maybe. We know that Louise went to England. Sarah went into service at Fitzpatrick's. I wonder what happened to the boy, John Michael.'

'Did I ever tell you the story of how Pisspot Ces Downes got her name?'

'No, but I suspect you're about to.'

'The received version is that she was a servant in a Dublin house who was accused of stealing by the housekeeper. She took a cast-iron chamber-pot and brained the woman. She never fully recovered. Nor was Ces ever charged.'

'How's that connected to what we see here?'

'I don't know. But my guess is that if the story is true it happened at the Fitzpatrick house and that even then there was some sort of a cover up.'

At that moment the sound of wheels and hooves came through the windows. Swallow peered out to see a side-car coming on the drive to the house.

'Damn. It may be Pomeroy or God knows who else. We'd better get ourselves out of here.'

Swallow slipped the *Record of Enrolments* under his jacket. He saw Lafeyre's look of alarm.

'We need evidence,' he said tersely. 'I'll worry about making it legal when I have to.'

The approaching vehicle swung across the drive past Bracken's wait-ing car. He raised a finger in salute as it swept in behind the house. Swallow and Lafeyre had a momentary sighting of a heavy-set man with a florid, angry face staring quizzically at Lily and Maria who had just walked back from the garden.

'He's gone to the back entrance,' Swallow said. 'Come, we're off.'

They moved smartly along the corridor to the front door. Then they were quickly aboard Bracken's car and moving down the driveway.

As they swung through the gates, Swallow turned to see the man he assumed to be Pomeroy emerge on to the front steps of the house. At that distance he could not judge if the expression on the Guardian's face was fury, alarm or both.

THIRTY-SIX

Lafeyre and Swallow were silent until Bracken's car rounded the bend and Greenhills House with its guardian had disappeared from sight. Lily looked from one of them to the other in alarm.

'Will someone please tell me what's going on? Has there been some sort of trouble?'

Swallow put a finger to his lips indicating silence and pointed to the driver's back. Maria said nothing. She had learned through sharing her recent life with a policeman not to ask questions at certain times. She judged that this was probably one such time.

'Later. I'll explain later. All went well.'

Lafeyre tapped with his foot at the picnic basket on the floor of the car. 'What about lunch?' he grinned, trying to defuse the tension. 'We haven't eaten since breakfast.'

Swallow's instinct told him it would be better to put distance between themselves and Greenhills House. But he knew Lafeyre was anxious to rescue some element of outing from the day's business.

'Not a bad idea,' he said. 'It'd be a pity to waste such a fine day and all of Maria's picnic preparations.'

He tapped Bracken on the shoulder. 'Can you find us a nice spot on the Heath where we might stop to eat our lunch?'

Bracken pulled his ear as if for inspiration. 'I can, Sir. We have a high bank just a bit ahead of us. Nice and shaded and there's a fine view of the countryside. D'ye want me to pull in there for a stop?'

'That would be good,' Swallow replied.

They regained the Heath. Bracken pulled the reins, bringing the trap off the road and calling 'whoa' to the pony. He had chosen a shaded spot with a rising bank of grassy earth, indicating some long-disused ditch or fortification.

'There you are now. That's a fine space for you to put out your refreshments.'

He dismounted from the car, dropped the step and helped his passengers to the ground. He let down a sideboard from the trap and placed the picnic basket on it. Then he led the pony free of the shafts to a grassy spot where it could graze.

'Now Ma'am,' he smiled at Maria. 'I'm sure that you'll want to arrange things yourself.'

The sun was hot. The midland air was heavy and scented with summer. Lily and Maria began to set out the picnic things. The driver stepped away from the car. He struck a match, put it to the bowl of his pipe, drew in deeply and let out two or three puffs. He gestured away to the west.

'Over there now, you'll just see the ridges of the Slieve Bloom Mountains. And over there...' he turned and pointed across the Heath, '...you'll see the remains of the Castle of Dunamase, where the lords of these parts, the O'Moores, had their stronghold.'

Lily had the basket open and Maria had spread out a cloth with napkins, plates and cutlery. Maria's housekeeper had packed a good basket. There was a fresh white loaf, cuts of cold meat and chicken, fruit cake, apples and a bottle of Burgundy.

'Can we offer you something?' Lafeyre inquired of Bracken.

'Not at all, Sir, thanks,' the driver laughed. 'I have me own provisions here.'

He drew a naggin bottle of clear liquid – illicit whiskey Swallow assumed – from his coat pocket. 'I'll stroll a bit and let ye enjoy your party. I won't be far gone. Ye can call me when ye want to move on.'

He ambled away through the yellow furze.

After she had set the picnic things, Lily put up her parasol to create a pool of shade beside the car. Lafeyre started to recount how they had gained access to the records at the orphanage and what they had learned from them.

'So, you're saying that the murdered woman from the Chapelizod Gate was a child of Alderman Thomas Fitzpatrick and this Cecilia Downes and that she was raised there at the orphanage?' Maria furrowed her brow in concentration. 'And Alderman Fitzpatrick's servant, the girl taken from the canal, was raised there too, at the same time?'

Lafeyre nodded.

'And they had another child also – a boy – John Michael?'

Lafeyre nodded again. 'The records show that Cecilia or Ces Downes had children by Fitzpatrick, at least two. On both occasions the children were lodged at Greenhills House under their mother's name.'

'And at some point Ces Downes abandoned her life as a servant and became a professional criminal,' Swallow added. 'Or, more accurately, she went back to being a criminal.

'The police picked up rumours that she had children. But there weren't any available records to confirm that. Louise must have gone to live in England after leaving the orphanage. At some point she took the family name, "Thomas." She may have married a man called Thomas. Or Thomas may have been an alias, perhaps taken from her father's name. We don't know yet.'

'We also know that Louise, Ces's daughter, then became mother to at least one child,' Lafeyre said grimly. 'And that child was murdered with her.'

Swallow could see comprehension and distress in Maria's eyes.

'It's a dreadful story,' she said quietly. 'I hope you've learned what you came here to find out. And I hope you can solve these terrible crimes. But I wish you could have found some other way of getting this information. I don't want to be involved in this sort of thing any more. Nor, I'm sure, does Lily.'

She shot an angry look at Lafeyre and Swallow. 'I hope you both understand that.'

The women had completed laying out the food when Bracken's pony looked up sharply from its grazing and cocked its ears. At that moment an open car with four men clattered in from the pathway across the grass. The car slewed to a halt beside them, the horse snorting from its gallop.

Swallow recognised Richard Pomeroy, the guardian from Greenhills. The man sitting beside him was the shadow with the Derby hat that he had seen twice earlier in the day. The other two looked like labourers or farm-hands. Swallow saw the driver take up a long, black cudgel from the seat beside him. His companion held a double-barrelled shotgun.

Pomeroy dismounted. The man with the shotgun raised the weapon to shoulder height and levelled it. Pomeroy's driver climbed down and ran to take the bridle of Bracken's horse where it had resumed its grazing.

'I don't know who you damned people are,' he hissed, 'but by God you've made a serious mistake here today. Wherever you're from, you're not from the Board of Educational Guardians.'

He stepped forward. 'You've got property belonging to Greenhills House that you've stolen. I'll give you one chance now to return it to me.' He extended his hand.

Bracken suddenly emerged from the side of the clearing. He saw the man holding his pony's bridle and shouted.

'You there, leave go of my horse...'

At the sound of Bracken's voice the man with the shotgun swivelled and fired. Orange flame spurted from the twin barrels. Bracken's hat flew into the air, carried off by the blasts. He stood, frozen in shock but apparently uninjured with the shots gone high.

Lafeyre's reflexes were instantaneous.

He caught Lily's waist and pushed her down behind Bracken's car. Swallow saw a revolver appear in Pomeroy's hand. The man with the Derby hat leaped from the car, lost his balance and landed, cursing, on the grass. The man with the shotgun was fumbling to reload his weapon.

Swallow drew his Webley Bulldog from its shoulder holster. He levelled the revolver at Pomeroy.

'I'm armed. Drop your weapon. Drop your weapon! And tell that man to drop the bloody shotgun!'

From the corner of his eye, Swallow saw Maria's arm rise in an arc to hurl the Burgundy bottle at Pomeroy. It hit him full across the forehead. There was a yell of pain. He splayed his fingers, dropping the gun to the ground. Then his hands went up to the bleeding gash over his eyes as he sank to his knees.

The man with the shotgun had reloaded both barrels. He snapped the weapon shut. Swallow swung the Bulldog to point to his chest.

'Put down the bloody gun. Put it down or I'll shoot, I bloody well swear it.'

The man raised the shotgun to his shoulder. Swallow lowered the angle of the Bulldog and fired a warning shot into the ground.

The man with the shotgun started to take aim.

Swallow swung the revolver up and fired instantly. The massive .44 calibre bullet hit the man's left leg above the knee. Swallow saw a spout of bright red blood as he cartwheeled from the car down to the grass.

The shotgun flew from his hands and clattered against the side of Bracken's car. Lafeyre stepped forward and seized the weapon as it came to earth.

Suddenly, Bracken swung a heavy fist at the man who had been holding his horse's reins. He shouted something that Swallow could not catch. The horse and car lurched forward, knocking against the man. He grabbed at the animal's harness for support, but Bracken wrestled him forward to the open ground.

'Ye blackguard,' Bracken spat. 'Would ye try to take me horse?' He kicked the man twice, hard, in the back and ribs. Then he kicked him again and hauled him to his feet. The man staggered to Pomeroy's side and raised his hands over his head, moaning in pain.

Lafeyre had broken the shotgun at the breach. He hurled the cartridges far away into the furze, then he threw the weapon to the ground and went to where the wounded gunman was lying on the grass. The blood was coming in spurts from his leg. From the corner of his eye Swallow saw the shadow – now bareheaded – pick himself up and sprint to the bank of high ground to disappear from sight.

Lafeyre ran an expert hand along the wounded gunman's leg.

'Take the coat off one those fellows,' he told Lily, gesturing to Pomeroy and his driver. 'Tear out the lining. I need two or three long strips to make a tourniquet, hurry.'

He drew a penknife and sawed at the wounded man's trousers. Lily slashed the lining on the driver's jacket, using one of the picnic knives. She handed two strips of the material to Lafeyre. He lashed them around the wounded man's upper leg, hauling on the ends before tying two firm knots into place.

Lafeyre snapped at Pomeroy who had clamped a handkerchief to his bleeding forehead.

'Delay for even a little while and your man will die from blood loss. Put him into your car and get him to the infirmary at Maryborough as quickly as you can.'

Swallow jerked his Webley Bulldog towards the attackers' car. He shouted at the other two.

'You heard that. Get him into the car and get to hell out of here before I change my mind and shoot all three of you.'

Pomeroy's gun lay on the grass where he had fallen. Swallow opened the magazine, ejected the ammunition and threw it as far as he could across the high bank. Then he flung the weapon itself into the furze in the opposite direction.

Pomeroy's forehead was still bleeding from where the Burgundy bottle had hit him. But he took the injured gunman's legs while his companion lifted him under the arms.

By now the pain from the man's shattered leg was coming through. He screamed as they put him on the floor of the open car. The driver cracked the horse's reins to start the vehicle moving across the grass and back on to the roadway.

Swallow emptied the spent shells from his own revolver and reloaded the chambers.

Bracken was nursing a bruised hand.

'Jesus Christ, I didn't bargain on this. We could have all been killed, murdered. Let me get home out of here… come on. I have a safe way back to the town that'll keep us off the roadway. We have to move fast.'

'There isn't time to take care of this stuff.' He gestured to the picnic things on the sideboard that he had earlier let down from the car. With a sweep of his arm he tumbled the food, crockery, glasses and cutlery into the grass.

He let down the step and quickly helped Lily and Maria to board the car. Swallow and Lafeyre followed. He touched the pony's flank with his whip and picked up speed as soon as they reached the track he had chosen across the back of the heath.

'In the name of God and his Holy Mother,' he shouted to Swallow as the car bucked and rattled beneath them. 'What's goin' on here? I thought ye told me ye were from the Board of Education. There's nothin' much to do with education about that business back there, is there?'

'Police business,' Swallow shouted back, 'I can't tell you any more than that. I'm sorry for getting you involved, Mr Bracken.'

Bracken spat over his shoulder into the ditches flying by. 'Ah dammit, you should 'a told me what you were at before we set out. I'd have brought me own shotgun along. And who are them bastards back there?'

'To tell you the truth, I'm not sure myself,' Swallow said. 'And even if I knew, you might be better off not hearing it.'

'Well, you're a fair shot with that big revolver, anyway,' Bracken retorted.

'You're well able to take care of yourself as well, Mr Bracken, from what I saw,' Swallow said.

Bracken nodded grimly. 'Ah, sure I did a bit o' boxin' in the army. I was in the Leinsters over at the Crinkill barracks near Parsonstown. And I'm not past it yet, if I have to deal with a couple of blackguards.'

Half an hour of fast driving later they drew into the railway station at Maryborough. Swallow had half expected to encounter some of Major Kelly's agents waiting for them, but the platform was empty. There was nobody in the waiting rooms apart from two women with a small child.

Swallow paid Bracken his fare and added a further shilling as a tip.

'Ah, sure it'll cover the cost of me hat,' Bracken grinned, pocketing the money.

The four travellers stepped down from the car. In the distance Swallow heard the whistle of the approaching Dublin train.

THIRTY-SEVEN

'We did well to make it back without any further encounters with your persecutors from the Upper Yard,' Lafeyre said, sipping at a stiff whiskey. They were seated in the drawing room of his house on Harcourt Street.

'I'd guess that Major Kelly and his gang mightn't be so keen to get in your way again after what happened out on the heath,' he said with unconvincing jocularity.

'If that fellow with the shotgun ever walks again I suspect it'll be with a bad limp. And as for your shadow with the Derby hat, I doubt if he's stopped running yet.'

Scollan had met them at King's Bridge with the brougham. Once the train came to a halt, Swallow had scanned the platforms and the station concourse to see if he could spot anyone who might be waiting, whether to shadow them or to confront them, but there was no surveillance that he could detect.

'It wouldn't take Kelly's people long to work out what we've learned at Greenhills House,' Lafeyre said. 'They know that we've had access to the records. That's what sent Pomeroy and his gang after us.'

'I'm surprised the registry books weren't already destroyed,' Swallow mused. 'Pomeroy and his people would have understood the significance of records linking a public man like Fitzpatrick with two young children committed to their care.'

Lafeyre grimaced. 'I suspect it's precisely because they did understand it that they held on to the records. And it's why they came after us. That sort of information is valuable. You can be sure that Mr Pomeroy and his associates were able to get their money's worth out of Fitzpatrick over the years, knowing that they had the goods on a wealthy businessman.'

Swallow had a mental image of two young children in Greenhills House, an inconvenience to the parents who had brought them into the world and a source of profitable extortion for Pomeroy. His exhilaration at the breakthrough in the investigation gave way to a sense of anger.

He raised his glass to his lips. The spirit showed amber against the evening light from the windows giving onto Harcourt Street.

He was tired. The strain of the day's events and the knowledge that he had brought them unwittingly into danger bore in on him.

'I'm truly sorry for putting Lily and Maria in harm's way,' he said. 'I'll acknowledge that the idea of impersonating an education inspector was taking a chance. But I never imagined that there'd be an attempt to injure or kill anyone.'

Lafeyre shrugged. 'I went along with the impersonation idea. I can't say I approved of it, but it was relatively harmless. I wouldn't have anticipated what we encountered either.'

'It's a detective's job, or part of it, to anticipate the unanticipated,' Swallow said quietly.

'There isn't any point in flagellating yourself,' Lafeyre said. 'The issue is what happens next.'

'I want to isolate McDaniel the butler and question him,' Swallow replied after a pause.

'All the threads of this business lead back to Merrion Square. Mallon has marked my cards that Fitzpatrick will be away from the house tomorrow afternoon. That would be the time to go in. Mind you, he didn't offer to give me a warrant. He won't take that risk.'

'You see this butler fellow as the key to this?'

'He's an army deserter who's wanted for a murder more than 20 years ago. He's vulnerable. And I think he knows a lot.'

Lafeyre smiled. 'It sounds as if Mallon wants it both ways. But there's a route around the warrant problem, if you really wanted it. It mightn't be wise but it would be legal.'

'What have you in mind?'

'I'm a Justice of the Peace, remember,' Lafeyre said. 'I have most of the powers of a magistrate. What's relevant in this case is that I can issue a search warrant on information sworn before me by a police officer.'

Swallow realised that Lafeyre was technically right. The medical examiner had been appointed as a Justice of the Peace to facilitate searches for evidence when he was working on criminal cases with the police. The authority was rarely invoked, but Swallow knew there had been instances where it had.

He shrugged.

'Well, my career prospects wouldn't be described as great at the moment anyway. So it probably doesn't make much difference whether I'm wise or foolish at this point.'

'How would Mallon react, do you think? He's the only one you need to worry about,' Lafeyre said. 'From what you say he'd have to express disapproval officially, whatever his real sentiments.'

Swallow smiled. 'I think he'd be happy to pull a fast one over the crowd in the Upper Yard. If you're prepared to sign the warrant, Harry, I'm willing to go into the firing line.'

Lafeyre nodded. 'Then it's best done sooner rather than later.'

'I agree.'

'So what's the sequence from here?'

'I'll start with questioning McDaniel. Then I'll want to search for possible murder weapons and seize any personal effects belonging to Sarah Hannin that might give us some clues or evidence.'

'What you want from me is a warrant to enter and search in the belief that you may secure evidence concerning a felony, specifically murder?'

Swallow knew that Lafeyre would be punctilious in the drafting of the warrant.

'Yes,' Swallow nodded. 'Fitzpatrick is to depart from Merrion Square at 12 noon.'

'I'll draw up the warrant in the morning,' Lafeyre said. 'It'll be dated for June 26th if you're sure you want to do this tomorrow.'

'I'm sure,' Swallow said. 'If anyone raises the alarm it will take the crowd in the Upper Yard that bit longer to respond and pull me out. Because that's exactly what they'll do, at gunpoint if necessary.'

'How will you get your manpower together without raising suspicions in Exchange Court?' Lafeyre asked. 'You won't want word of your plans to get to Boyle or Mallon.'

'I'll be able to muster a few men,' Swallow replied. 'I'll get Pat Mossop and Mick Feore, maybe young Shanahan and Collins. I think I can probably get Swift too. And Stephen Doolan should be able to round up a few uniformed lads for me.'

Lafeyre looked doubtful. 'Not an overwhelming show of force, I'd say.'

'It'll have to do. All of those G-men are good even if some of them are a bit inexperienced. And I'd always count on Stephen Doolan where there's work to be done. I'll assemble them at the morgue at 11 o'clock tomorrow morning. I'll formally apply to you for the warrant and we'll aim to be at the Fitzpatrick house for 12.30.'

Lafeyre refilled the whiskey glasses. He added water to his Tullamore and pushed the jug to Swallow.

'What are the priorities once you get into the house?'

'We'll have Doolan's men do the searches. The G-men will secure the house and the staff. I'll take Pat Mossop with me and we'll question McDaniel. He's the first target as I see it.'

Lafeyre sipped at his Tullamore, turning the plan over in his head.

'After that, we'll just have to see who else will come into the net,' Swallow said.

He drained his whiskey.

'That was welcome,' he nodded at Lafeyre. 'Now I've to go and visit my squad members to tell them they won't be paying their usual Sunday morning respects to the Lord. I don't expect I'll be very popular in some houses tonight.'

Detective Pat Mossop rented rooms over a poulterer's shop on Aungier Street. He answered Swallow's knock on the side door in his shirt sleeves, holding a handful of playing cards. A small, brown dog came up behind him, wagging its tail. In the background Swallow could hear the squeals and calls of the young Mossops.

Mossop invited him to come through for a cup of tea or a glass of lemonade. There was a card game underway in the cooler outdoors of the poulterer's yard behind the shop. He would be welcome, Mossop insisted, but he declined. There would be a poor reception from Mrs Mossop, he reckoned, when it emerged that he wanted her husband on duty at 11 o'clock on his supposed rest day.

'Were there any new developments, Boss?' Mossop asked. 'Did anything come in during the day?'

'Nothing you weren't aware of, Pat,' Swallow told him. The less the Book Man knew about events at Greenhills and on the Heath the better. 'Go on with your game now.' He laughed. 'Just don't let yourself be beggared by those young card-sharps out there.'

Mick Feore, a single man, lived in a half-board lodging house not far away in Digges Lane. Swallow knew that his landlady was a constable's widow who was accustomed to police messengers calling at unexpected hours. She had no idea where her lodger might be, she told him. But she would deliver the message. He would be at the City Morgue in the morning.

He retraced his steps to Kevin Street where he could send a telegraph message to Kilmainham, instructing a beat man to deliver a duty order to Stephen Doolan's house at Mount Brown.

His last call for the evening was at Exchange Court.

Eddie Shanahan and Martin Collins were 'live-in' men. Newly appointed G-men were required to billet in the detective building for at least a year, sleeping in the dormitory on the top floor. 'Live-in' men could not be off the premises any later than 11 p.m. without special permission or unless they were on outdoor duty.

What some might consider a restrictive regime was, in fact, usually welcomed by young officers. The accommodation and messing was good value at seven shillings a week deducted from pay at source.

Shanahan was out with permission, but Collins was already lying in his cubicle in the top-floor dormitory, smoking a cheroot and reading a newspaper. He jumped from the bed when Swallow appeared.

'Eleven o'clock in the morning at the City Morgue? I'll be there, Sergeant. And I'll have Eddie Shanahan with me.' Swallow surmised that Collins was still smarting from the fiasco of 'Tiger' McKnight's supposed dying declaration. He seemed anxious to please.

Grant's was in darkness by the time Swallow reached Thomas Street, but a light on the first floor told him that Maria was not in bed. He climbed the stairs and found her seated in the parlour. She had just finished counting the day's takings.

She looked drained. Her forehead was furrowed. Worry lines had formed along her cheeks. He saw something between anger and hurt in her eyes.

'You must be very tired,' he said. 'It's been a long day.'

She nodded and raised her hand to her forehead, kneading her brow between thumb and forefinger.

'I'm sorry I couldn't get in earlier,' he said awkwardly. 'I had to make arrangements for tomorrow.'

She shook her said. 'Don't apologise. It's your work, I know. I'm sure that after what happened today you have to take action quickly. Did you…'

She gave a little sigh, as if reluctantly releasing her emotions. He moved forward to where she sat, extending his arms. She raised a hand to stop him where he was.

'I'll be fine in a moment. I'm probably a bit in shock after today. I can't get out of my mind what happened... what nearly happened. My sister might have been killed or injured, or it could have been you, or Harry.'

She took her hand from her face.

'I don't think I can be involved any more in all of this.'

'It's not going to happen again,' he said gently. 'It shouldn't have happened. I know I'm to blame. But I'll never again allow any situation like that to come about. I'd ask that you consider what I'm trying to deal with here. There are two women and an innocent child murdered.'

She sighed again.

'It isn't just about what happened today.' Her tone had hardened. 'It's the uncertainty of everything. I don't know what's to happen with our lives. I don't know why or how we got ourselves into this situation. But it's too difficult for me, just drifting along like this. I won't endure it and you can't expect me to. What happened today just... brought things to a head for me.'

He felt unable to respond. 'I don't know... Maria... I have no idea what to say.'

Her eyes lit.

'Well that's a great part of the problem, Joe. You don't know what to say. You don't know what to do. So if you can't make up your mind, I'll have to make up mine. I think perhaps it's time you considered making some new arrangements for your accommodation... and for your life.'

Sunday June 26th, 1887

THIRTY-EIGHT

S unday was to see the peak of the heatwave. By the time Swallow's squad assembled at the Marlborough Street morgue the sun was already starting to bake the city pavements. All of Ireland was sweltering. Later in the day a record temperature of more than 33 degrees would be noted 50 miles inland at Kilkenny Castle.

Swallow absolved himself from any religious duties. Shortly after 10 o'clock he left Thomas Street and walked to the Castle. John Mallon's house was in the Lower Yard, facing the Chapel Royal and the Record Tower. When he rang the bell, Mallon himself opened the door.

The Chief Superintendent of the G Division was, as usual, impeccably dressed. Swallow reasoned that he had attended an early Mass in one of the churches close by the Castle. The aroma of a cooked breakfast wafted from the back of the house. Somewhere in the background Swallow heard the sounds of crockery being laid out and a woman's voice calling to a child. Mallon was in domestic mode. But it was not uncommon for his domestic tranquillity to be interrupted when important intelligence had come to hand.

'I'm sorry to disturb you, Chief,' Swallow said. 'Would it be convenient to brief you on something significant that has come up? It won't take long.'

Mallon led him into the parlour.

'It's concerning the royal visit next week,' Swallow said when Mallon had gestured to him to take a chintz-covered chair by the empty fireplace.

'I've received confidential information that there's to be some sort of incident or attack on the prince at Kingstown very shortly after he arrives on Monday.'

Mallon's brow creased. 'Have you got details, Swallow, and a reliable source?'

'I have some details. There's at least three involved, possibly more. Two are O'Reilly and Locke, members of Ces Downes's gang and involved in the Hibernian Brothers. They're young fellows, not yet 20 in either case. A third is James O'Donnell, the individual I arrested last Sunday at the Royal Hibernian Academy in connection with the attack on Alderman Fitzpatrick and Mr Smith Berry.'

Mallon drew a small notebook and pencil from his pocket. He was silent for a moment as he jotted down the details.

'I don't think these two... Locke and O'Reilly... have come to prominent notice,' he tapped the notebook. 'I know about O'Donnell of course. But how does it happen that he's out? Shouldn't he be in a cell at Kilmainham?'

'He didn't actually have a gun at the Hibernian Academy. It was the other fellow, Horan. O'Donnell agreed to co-operate and act as an information source for us, so I let him out.'

Mallon grunted. 'Well, if he's your informant on this business, it sounds as if you took the right decision. What else do we know?'

'Thanks, Sir,' Swallow replied, choosing not to correct Mallon's assumption that O'Donnell was the source of his information.

'I believe Locke and O'Reilly are in possession of two revolvers with ammunition. From what I know the weapons are probably Navy Colts. I understand they plan to travel to Kingstown on Monday and to be in the crowd when the prince steps ashore.'

Mallon whistled silently. 'Navy Colts – a good handgun for an assassination. They've got accuracy over distance and a heavy punch. The Americans designed them for close-quarter use. They claimed a lot of lives in the Civil War.'

Swallow nodded. 'Yes, Sir. They're hard to come by. But from what I know the suspects have got them and they've had instruction in how to use them.'

Mallon's face was creased in strain. 'What's the best thing to do? It might be safest just to take them in now and decide what to do with them when the royal visit is over?'

'The problem with that, Chief, is that we don't know how many others there may be in the gang. I'd suggest it would be better to put a full-scale surveillance on them and try to catch them red-handed, along with whoever else might be involved.'

'There are risks in that,' Mallon mused. 'But you're probably right. If we lift these three now we could simply alert any others and give them the time to put together another plan.'

Mallon stood. 'Leave it with me. I'll be across in my office directly after I've had my breakfast and I'll arrange to have the three of them shadowed. We'll keep on their tails and pounce when the moment is right. Tell me, is O'Donnell sufficiently valuable to us to have him… shall we say… make good his escape? Or would that simply raise suspicions that he's been working for us?'

Swallow thought for a moment. 'I'd say it's best to bring him in with the other two when the arrests are made. I'll find a way of springing him that won't arouse any suspicions among his own crowd.'

He was conscious that he was delivering a full-blown lie about his intentions for James O'Donnell.

'That's how it'll be then,' Mallon said, moving towards the door. 'This is work well done, Swallow, damned well done.'

Swallow reflected how little either the Chapelizod Gate murders or the Sarah Hannin case obtruded into John Mallon's priorities when a security issue presented itself. And if either man's mind had run to Thomas Fitzpatrick's scheduled absence from his house at Merrion Square in the afternoon, neither one of them mentioned it.

* * *

At noon, Swallow and his squad set off from Marlborough Street in two open cars. The four constables that Stephen Doolan had recruited were perspiring in their buttoned-up tunics. The G-men would have shed their own jackets were it not for the bulky revolvers in their shoulder-holsters underneath.

Cab men had gathered into the shade of a sycamore that overhung the railings at the corner of Merrion Square.

One driver was dousing his animal with cool water from the stone trough at the head of the cab stand. Swallow could see through the trees that some of the nurses from the houses around the square had already taken their young charges out of the sun's glare into the shadows of the beech and oak that sheltered the lawns.

Doolan sent two of his constables to the mews laneway behind the Fitzpatrick house. He posted another to the tradesman's entrance where a flight of steps went from street level to the basement.

Swallow and Mossop climbed the steps to the hall door for the second time in six days. Stephen Doolan came behind in uniform. Swallow pulled on the bell cord. Children's laughter floated across from the gardens, but he could hear the bell ringing faintly somewhere inside the house.

McDonald opened the door almost immediately. Swallow stepped past him into the hallway and brandished Lafeyre's warrant under his nose.

'Detective Sergeant Swallow, G Division,' he said unnecessarily.

'I have a warrant to search these premises for evidence in relation to the murders of Sarah Hannin, Louise Thomas and Richard Thomas, a child. This warrant also states that I may detain and question any or all persons found within these premises in relation to the deaths of Sarah Hannin, Louise Thomas and Richard Thomas. Do you understand?'

McDonald moved as if to block the G-men. 'Mr Fitzpatrick… won't permit this. You can't come in here like this.'

Swallow folded the warrant into his pocket. 'I'm afraid you're mistaken. And I'll discuss that with Mr Fitzpatrick in due course, if he wishes. In the meantime, the officers with me will start their search of the house. Please tell me who else is here now.'

For a moment it seemed as if McDonald would refuse to answer.

Then he stepped back. 'I am in cha… charge of the house. There's… ju… just some other servants here now.'

Swallow snapped. 'Who are they?'

'There's the cook… downstairs, the groom in the coach-house and there's Joan the housemaid. The coachman is gone wi' Mr Fitzpatrick.'

Pat Mossop scribbled the details in his notebook.

'Please assemble them immediately,' Swallow instructed. He turned to Mossop.

'Get their full names and the usual details including their home places. And you can call in the others now.'

Mossop waved from the open hall door. Feore, Collins and Shanahan, who had been waiting in the open car across the street, sprinted up the steps and into the house.

Swallow posted Shanahan inside the front door.

'Nobody leaves and nobody enters without my permission. If necessary draw your revolver to prevent anyone entering the house or interrupting our search,' he said.

'You cover the back along with Collins,' he told Mick Feore. 'Nobody moves in or out through the mews.'

He took the granite back stairs with Mossop to the basement where McDonald had assembled the servants.

They were young. The groom and the housemaid looked scarcely 20. The cook was perhaps 25 or 26. McDonald, standing beside the little group, could have passed for their father.

A cloying odour of cooking pervaded the basement air. Swallow crossed the stone-flagged kitchen to stand by an open window where he hoped the smell might be diluted.

'I apologise for having to disturb you from whatever you may have been doing. I'm Detective Sergeant Swallow of the G Division and I'm investigating the death of Sarah Hannin, as well as the deaths of Louise Thomas and her son, Richard, who were murdered at the Chapelizod Gate of the Phoenix Park 10 days ago.

'I'm going to require each of you to answer some questions from the officers I've brought with me. I have a warrant that gives me authority to search this house and to question any persons here in connection with these deaths.'

He tried to read the servants' faces. He saw nervousness, which was to be expected, but nothing more. The cook glanced sideways at McDonald as if seeking his opinion.

'You have to answer all of the officers' questions truthfully and fully,' Swallow said sternly. 'If you do that you'll have nothing to fear. If you don't do so, I will arrest you and bring you before the courts for obstructing the course of justice. Is this clear?'

There was a murmur of acknowledgment.

'You will have to remain in the house until we've finished. There's a policeman at the front door and at the back door to make sure of that. Now, the first thing I need is for someone to show Sergeant Doolan here the accommodation occupied by Sarah Hannin and any belongings of hers that there may be here. Which of you can do that?'

'I can do that, Sir, if you please,' the young housemaid offered with an alacrity that brought a reproving glance from McDonald. 'She and me shared a room up at the top of the house.'

'Good,' Swallow said supportively. He recognised her as the young woman who had wept at Sarah Hannin's burial. 'What's your name?'

'I'm Joan, Sir.'

Doolan and a constable started for the stairs with the housemaid. The other constables and G-men began their search of the house and the outbuildings.

'Now, Mr McDonald,' Swallow turned to the butler. 'Could you find us some quiet place where you can talk to Detective Mossop and myself without being disturbed or overheard?'

THIRTY-NINE

McDonald led them to a dim, rectangular room off the kitchen. He drew three straight-backed chairs around a long, pine table.

There was a patina of oily green on the walls. The floorboards were scrubbed bare, but the room was suffused with the same smells of grease and food as the outer kitchen. Swallow surmised it was the servants' dining space.

McDonald sat, placing himself at the head of the table. He looked angrily at Swallow.

'Ye may have some sort of warrant, Sergeant. But by the time this is over you'll be a sorry man, believe ye me.'

The tone was threatening, with the Lowlands accent coming through.

Swallow took the opposite chair. If it was McDonald's tactic to try to provoke him he would not respond. Mossop sat, opened his book and placed it on the table.

'McDonald, I want to ask you some questions about what happened in this house on Wednesday June 15th when Mrs Louise Thomas came here with her young son, Richard,' Swallow said.

McDonald looked stonily ahead.

'I don't think I can be o' any help to you there, Sergeant.'

Swallow rephrased the question.

'A woman and a young boy came to this house on that evening. They matched the descriptions of the woman and boy subsequently found murdered at the Chapelizod Gate of the Phoenix Park. No doubt you read about those crimes in the newspapers or heard about them. Now, I want you to tell me about the woman and the boy who came here.'

'If they came here, I didna' see them.'

'So you're saying they might have been here?' Mossop said testily.

McDonald scowled at Mossop as if irritated by the Book Man's intervention.

'I don't know if you realise the situation that you're in,' Swallow snapped.

'I warned the others. If I don't get full answers to my questions I'll have them charged with failing to co-operate with the police. The same applies to you.'

McDonald shrugged. Swallow decided to play what he hoped would be his shock card.

'I'm warning you for the last time that I won't be put off by any word games and I won't accept a refusal to answer my questions. I expect your fullest co-operation, Mr McDonald – or should I say, Corporal McDaniel.'

Swallow had never known a sentence to elicit anything as dramatic as the reaction of the elderly man sitting opposite him. His fists crashed on the pine boards so forcefully that Swallow felt the table legs quiver. The colour drained from his face. His lower lip began to tremble.

'You should understand, McDaniel,' Swallow said coldly, 'that we have your records. I know your history.'

He paused to let it sink in.

'All I have to do is send a telegram and you'll be back at York Barracks the day after tomorrow facing a charge of murdering the officer you served as orderly.'

The butler's face was grey. He raised a hand.

'Wait... wait a moment... stop please. You're... on the wrong track, Swallow. If you think that anyone here at this house had anything to do wi' the death of Sarah Hannin or anyone else... you're mistaken.'

The tone of defiance had gone. Swallow felt a surge of retributive pleasure.

'You'll find it hard to convince me of that, McDaniel. And you'll find it hard to convince me that you haven't anything to do with the deaths of Louise Thomas and her son. We know that she was the daughter of your employer, Thomas Fitzpatrick.'

He paused again to let McDaniel consider the implications.

'We also know that you're a man who has killed in the past. If you could kill that young officer in York you could kill two women and a child here in Dublin.'

This was the point, he knew, at which a denial, if there was to be one, would come.

Beads of perspiration broke out on the butler's forehead. He drew a handkerchief from his suit pocket. Pat Mossop put down his pencil and got to his feet.

'I'll see if I can get you some water from the kitchen.'

'Stay where you are, Pat,' Swallow commanded. 'Corporal McDaniel won't die of thirst before he tells us what he knows.'

Mossop silently resumed his seat and took up his pencil again.

The butler mopped his perspiration. Then he twisted the handkerchief between his fingers.

'Ye know who I am. I won' deny that my name is McDaniel,' he said finally. 'But I'm tellin' you again, nobody here had anything to do with the deaths of any woman or the wee child.'

His throat dried.

Swallow nodded to Mossop. 'You can get that water now, Pat. Corporal McDaniel has stopped pretending that he's somebody else.'

Mossop returned from the kitchen a few moments later with a jug and three tumblers. He poured a full glass for McDaniel, who drank half of it down in one gulp.

The Vartry water was cool. Swallow drained the glass that Mossop had put before him and poured himself another.

The sound of heavy boots on the stairs above signalled the progress of Stephen Doolan and the others as they continued their search of the house.

McDaniel drank again. In spite of himself, Swallow felt a twinge of sympathy for him. The butler spread his hands, palms upward, as if pleading. After a few moments he found his voice again.

'There isn't any way you'd understand wha' happened in York. It wasn't like they said at the time... but I knew I wouldn't be believed,' he said hoarsely.

'I expect you know what they do in the army to people like me. They'd have made me out to be a... a monster, and then they'd hang me.'

Swallow remained silent.

'There was a... misunderstanding,' McDaniel resumed. 'He said I was insubordinate. He struck me on the face. I hit him back and he fell down. I think he struck his head on the floor. When I saw he wasn't movin' I took my chance before they could put me in the Glasshouse. I made a run for it. Anyone would do the same in that position...'

333

'If he struck you first it was provocation,' Mossop said. 'You'd very likely have got off with manslaughter.'

McDaniel laughed bitterly.

'You haven't had any experience of army justice. I'd have been condemned just for crossin' the line between ranks, steppin' out of my class. A… friendship between two officers would be a problem. But between an officer and an enlisted man, that'd be worse than treason.'

His mopped his forehead again.

'I got away on a packet crossing from Liverpool. For a long time after I came here, I used to fear that I'd be caught. But I kept my head down. I'd been trained to look after officers… gentlemen. So, I answered some of the advertisements in the newspapers and I was able to go into service with old Mr Fitzpatrick and Mrs Fitzpatrick. That was the father and mother of Alderman Fitzpatrick.'

'Did the Fitzpatricks – old Mr Fitzpatrick, as you call him – know about your past? Did they know about York?' Mossop asked.

'Not at first. There were some reports in the newspapers. I think old Mr Fitzpatrick came across them and he worked it out himself. But they weren't the kind of people who'd be out to judge you. You know wha' I mean? If I did me work and did it well, that was all they worried about.'

'And you continued in service for their son after the older Fitzpatricks died?' Swallow asked.

McDaniel nodded.

'Yes, I've been here… since I… since I left the army behind me. I was taken on as a groom. About a year after I started, there was an old butler here whose health failed. He had to be paid off and I was offered the job.'

He looked from Swallow to Mossop and back again. 'I was never in any more trouble. You won't find anything against me.'

A clock struck somewhere in the house.

'How did you know about… wha' happened back in York?' McDaniel asked when the chiming had stopped.

'Murder doesn't just fade away,' Swallow said. 'There are records. And there are witnesses. You can be sure that there'll be enough people at your trial who'll remember what happened.'

McDaniel ran his fingers through his thin, grey hair. Then he covered his eyes. The backs of his hands were veined and mottled.

'It was all a long time ago. I'm not young. I don't think they're going to hang me a' this time o' my life, will they?'

'I wouldn't count on that,' Swallow said coldly. 'They executed a man of 82 a while back in Bristol. But if you can help us in regard to the deaths that we're investigating here we might be able to leave the Provost Marshal's office out of this.'

He paused. 'I don't see any great profit in hauling in an army deserter after all those years. We've got bigger fish to fry. But, by God, you'd better give us the whole story or you'll be in handcuffs and on your way to the Glasshouse by nightfall.'

McDaniel's face contorted in stress. He extended the thin, bony fingers again to cover his eyes as if to block out the reality around him.

Swallow slammed the table.

'I'm damned sure you know who killed the woman and the child. They visited this house 24 hours before they were murdered. Now stop playing games and tell me the fucking truth. Because if you don't you'll be swinging on a rope in York barracks within the month.'

McDaniel took his hands from eyes. 'Do you know what you're askin' o' me?' His tone was pleading.

'We're not fools, McDaniel,' Swallow said, injecting a momentary softening into his tone. 'But I don't think you're a fool either. You'd better co-operate with us now.'

There was no sound in the humid dining hall other than a wasp buzzing noisily around the window.

'If I talk, I'll tell you everything you need to know,' McDaniel said after an interval. 'But will you swear I can walk away from this business and that I won't have you comin' after me?'

'I think that would be a fair bargain,' Swallow said. 'I don't give a toss what you did back in York. But I've got three murders to solve here in Dublin, and if you don't give me every scrap of information you have about them, I'll shorten whatever is left of your unhappy life.'

He turned to Mossop. 'What do you say, Pat?'

'I'm with you, Boss,' Mossop replied. 'Go on,' he gestured to McDaniel.

'But like Sergeant Swallow says, it'd better be the real thing. Half a story isn't any use to us at this stage.'

FORTY

McDaniel seemed to have regained a degree of composure. Swallow wondered if he had found some relief in the realisation that he had no choice now in what he had to do.

The butler had joined his hands, locking the fingers. He might have been about to say grace or set out the day's duties to the servants.

'I'm beyond makin' a start at something else,' he said. 'I have a few pounds saved from my wages and that'll have to keep me going. It's no'a lot, but I'll take my chances as long as I don't have to face back to the army.'

'I've given you my word.' Swallow said. 'What happened in York won't be opened up if you're completely straight with me. But there's to be no holding back, is that clear?'

McDaniel nodded.

'When I came here first, young Master Thomas, as I called him then, was sowin' his wild oats. He was always after the female servants. Old Mr and Mrs Fitzpatrick knew he was liable to be foolish. It became part of my job to keep an eye on that sort of thing and to let them know if… if there were any issues to be dealt with.'

He looked past Swallow towards the window as if reaching for details buried in memory.

'It was different when this new housemaid, Cecilia, came along. Not greatly beautiful but she had a very strong personality. Young Master Thomas fell for her. The mother and father – old Mr and Mrs Fitzpatrick – didn't especially take any notice of it. Until one day he told the old pair that Cecilia was pregnant and he was goin' to set up house wi' her.'

So far, what McDaniel had told them tallied with what Swallow had learned from the records at Greenhills House.

Pat Mossop interjected. 'You're saying that Ces Downes and Thomas Fitzpatrick set up house together?'

'That's it,' McDaniel said. 'He leased a house over near Charlemont Street. The pretence first was that Cecilia was a housekeeper. Then she started callin' herself 'Mrs Fitzpatrick.' Could you believe that? The child was born, a wee girl. That would have been Louise. A year later there was a little boy born too.'

'What happened to the children?' Mossop asked.

'They were sent away. Then young Master Thomas wanted to come back here. He said the house at Charlemont Street wasn't suitable.'

He drank more water. Swallow watched his hands holding the glass. They were steady.

'Cecilia saw herself as bein' in a special position. She fought wi' everyone. She started to steal, or maybe I should say she started stealin' again. Finally, old Mr and Mrs Fitzpatrick convinced Master Thomas that the relationship had been a mistake. The passion had cooled. She was paid off and then she was gone.'

'And that was that,' Mossop said. 'It was all neatly tied up. Did the other servants at the house know anything about this?'

'It was kept from them as much as possible,' McDaniel said. 'It wasn't easy. There was another child before all this, born to Cecilia Downes here in the servants' quarters.'

Swallow started. His examination of the registers at Greenhills had disclosed the births of just two children.

'A third child? Thomas Fitzpatrick – Master Thomas – was he the father of this third child too?'

'I'm sure that was so,' McDaniel said. 'Cecilia managed to hide the fact that she was expectin' until close to the very end. Nobody spoke about it afterwards. I remember that she was back at work around the house the next day.'

Swallow paused. Mossop's notes in the murder book were running behind McDaniel's narrative.

'I know about two children. They were Louise, later known as Louise Thomas, and John Michael,' Swallow said. 'What happened to the third?'

McDaniel let his gaze go to the window again. 'She said it died, that it was stillborn. But I know it wasn't. To this day I don't know if it was a boy or a girl. I heard it cryin' for a while. But we never saw it.'

He turned back to Mossop. 'I know that Master Thomas put the baby out there… in the garden.' He pointed towards the window.

The air in the room was stifling. Mossop crossed to the window and hauled the sash down as far as he could in an attempt to increase the circulation. It made no difference other than causing the G-man to perspire further with the effort.

Then McDaniel began to sob, gently at first, but within a few moments breaking into open tears.

'Did Sarah Hannin know when she came to work here that Thomas Fitzpatrick was the father of her friend Louise at the orphanage?' Swallow asked.

McDaniel blew into his handkerchief and wiped his eyes.

'I don't know. It's a good question, Sergeant Swallow. I suppose you're thinkin' that if she did know, it might in some way explain what happened to her.'

Swallow smiled icily. 'And yours is a good answer, McDaniel. If you knew that she was aware of all this, it could give you a motive for wanting to silence her.'

McDaniel shook his head. 'I never asked her. And I'm telling you again, I never harmed her in any way.'

'But you knew that she came from Greenhills orphanage and that she'd been there at the same time as Louise,' Swallow persisted.

'Yes. But it wasn't somethin' ever spoken of.'

'So, when were these two children sent down to the orphanage?' Mossop asked.

'I don't ever remember them being here in the house. They sent Cecilia out to some place in Wicklow for the births. It's my belief they went from there to the orphanage.'

'So, go on,' Mossop prompted McDaniel, 'what happened to Louise after she left the orphanage?'

'I think Master Thomas always kept a bit of a flame goin' for Cecilia. After she go' her settlement she went back to her own people and her own class. But Master Thomas would send her money and often she'd write looking for help on various things.'

McDaniel paused.

'I've… I've… seen some of the letters on his desk. She wrote well. She even came back to the house here once in a while. And he always had an eye out for the children while they were in the orphanage.'

'And the little boy, what happened to him?' Swallow asked.

'It's my understandin' that he died. That's what Master Thomas told me once. I don't know when or where or how it happened.'

'How much did Louise know about all of this as she grew up in the orphanage?' Mossop queried.

'I don't think she knew much. I went wi' Master Thomas down there two or three times. He didn't abandon the children completely, you know. He'd go down to see them, maybe once a year. I know he paid the Guardian there, a fellow called Pomeroy, to make sure the children got good medical care, extra food, that kind of thing. He isn't a hard-hearted man.'

Lafeyre was on the mark, Swallow reflected silently, in his speculation that the guardian of Greenhills had known how to exploit Thomas Fitzpatrick's responsibilities.

'So she didn't know he was her father?' Mossop asked.

'I don't think so in the early years. But I'm sure as time went on she began to work things out. I think the children believed he was a kind visitor. That's how Sarah Hannin ended up workin' here.'

'I don't understand,' Swallow said.

'She was Louise's wee friend at the orphanage. When Master Thomas would visit, they'd always be together. And when the time came for them to leave, Louise went across to England and Master Thomas offered to take Sarah into service here.'

'What do you think Louise and her child were doing in Dublin last week?' Swallow asked.

McDaniel shook his head.

'I've told you already, I can only guess. Her mother was dyin' after a life o' crime, as I heard it. The Fitzpatricks were right about her. She had a bad streak. She just reverted to type.'

'So, I ask you again, do you know what Louise and the boy were doing back in Dublin?'

'How would I know? Maybe she came to see her dyin' mother.'

'Maybe she wanted to see her father too. We know she was at this house on the Wednesday evening before she was murdered.'

'I wasn't here. So if she came here, I didn't see her, like I told you.'

'But Sarah Hannin saw her.'

'I don't know that. Sarah told me she wanted the evenin' off to meet someone. I couldn't spare her. But if one of the staff wants to have a visitor call in during their meal break, I'm generally willin' to allow it.'

There was a sharp rap on the door. Stephen Doolan put his head in to say that the search of the house had been completed.

It afforded a natural break in the questioning. Swallow and Mossop needed time to consider what they had learned.

'We're going to stop there for a while, McDaniel,' Swallow told the butler. 'Rest yourself for a bit. But you're not to leave the room. Detective Mossop and I have to consult for a while with the other officers.'

They left him staring at the green walls.

FORTY-ONE

An hour later they resumed the questioning of James McDaniel in the small, claustrophobic room that was the servants' dining space at 106 Merrion Square.

Stephen Doolan's men had searched the bedroom on the top storey of the house that Sarah Hannin had shared with the other maid. They located some personal belongings including some letters from other former residents at Greenhills, but there was nothing that offered any information about the dead girl's family or background.

They had found nothing that might have been a murder weapon. There were no bloodstains or signs of recent or unusual cleaning or scrubbing. If Sarah Hannin had died in the house, any clues to what might have happened had been thoroughly eradicated.

With the house secure, Detectives Feore and Swift questioned the housemaid. Collins and Shanahan interrogated the cook and the groom.

Swallow conferred in the kitchen with the G-men.

'The housemaid is only a kid,' Mick Feore said. 'She's intelligent. She liked poor Sarah and she's very upset. She wants to be helpful but she knows nothing.'

'It's the same with the other two,' Shanahan nodded. 'I wouldn't describe them as friendly, but I don't think they have anything useful to tell us.'

Swallow and Mossop sought the fresher air in the garden at the back of the house. It was still warm but it felt healthier after the greasy odours of the basement.

Mossop nodded towards the narrow strip of ground that ran to the coach house. 'If McDaniel is telling the truth about the dead baby it's over there somewhere. And God knows what else there might be. There'll be a fair bit of digging by the time we're finished.'

They resumed their seats at the pine table with McDaniel.

'What you've given us so far is background,' Swallow said. 'We still need to know what transpired here between Louise Thomas and Sarah Hannin. Did anything happen that could explain Sarah's murder?'

'I've told you. Nobody here harmed Sarah. And nobody here harmed Louise and the boy. I swear it.'

Mossop was exasperated

'How can you be sure one of the servants didn't kill Sarah Hannin for some reason? Or Mr Fitzpatrick himself might have done it for all you know. Or was there a man keeping company with her, for example?'

McDaniel looked beseechingly at Swallow.

'I told you there wasn't to be any holding back on me,' Swallow said sharply. 'If you want me to keep my side of the bargain you'll need to do better than just repeating yourself and telling us you know nothing.'

Perspiration broke out again on McDaniel's forehead.

'I can't tell you wha' I don't know. But I know that nobody from this house had anythin' to do with wha' happened at the Chapelizod Gate.'

He paused to wipe the rivulets from his forehead.

'I know that because I saw… Louise Thomas… and the boy dead in the park before they were found.'

Swallow felt as if something hard had hit him in the chest. Mossop's mouth opened in shock. The only sound in the airless room was McDaniel's breathing.

'Would you repeat that please?' Swallow said eventually.

'I've told you, I was at the Chapelizod Gate on Thursday night and I saw them dead.'

'Why were you at the Chapelizod Gate on Thursday night?' Swallow asked quietly.

'Mr Fitzpatrick told me Louise and the boy were in Dublin and he wanted me to take the clarence to the Chapelizod Gate to collect them.'

McDaniel licked at dry lips. Mossop poured more water into his tumbler. He drank quickly.

'I can still handle a carriage. I was to bring them to a hotel on Rutland Square. He was goin' to see them there. I was told they'd be at the Chapelizod Gate at 9 o'clock. When the clarence was ready, I drove up there and I waited on the grass just inside the gate.

'When they hadn't appeared by around 10 o'clock or so, I had to go to answer a call of nature in the trees. Then I saw the two bodies... lyin' there. I thought they were sleepin' or somethin' and then I went over and saw the blood. I didn't realise who they were because... you know... she was wearin' men's clothes. But then I knew it had to be Louise and the boy.'

'So, what did you do?' Mossop asked. 'Why did you not call the police?'

McDaniel jerked his head.

'For God's sake, how could I? I'd be done for. I drove as fast as I could to the hotel at Rutland Square and I saw Mr Fitzpatrick. He didn't believe me. He was in shock himself. I didn't blame him because I was in a terrible state. When I told him what had happened and when he realised I hadn't gone mad or somethin' we came straight back to the house here.'

'So why didn't Mr Fitzpatrick notify the police at that stage?' Swallow asked.

'He was out of his mind wi' upset. It was his daughter, even though he had kept his distance from her. And the boy was his grandson. But if he got involved, if he'd admitted to knowin' anything, it would all have come out into the open, about Cecilia, the children, the dead child in the house here, all of that. He said we'd have to let things take their course.'

'A bloody cold decision in all the circumstances,' Mossop said. 'For Jesus's sake, this was his own flesh and blood. Didn't he want to know who had done this, or why?'

McDaniel shrugged. 'That's not for me to say.'

'What happened? Who killed them?' Swallow interjected. 'Who does Mr Fitzpatrick think killed them? Surely to God there'd be no other question in his mind, or in yours.'

McDaniel stammered. 'I... think you'd n... need to ask him what he believes.'

'Unfortunately he's not here,' Swallow said angrily. 'At least he's not here yet. But you are. And you're supposed to be answering my questions. Now if you don't do that our deal is off and you're going back to York.'

'I'm tellin' you what I know,' McDaniel pleaded. 'Mr Fitzpatrick knows more. I don't want to say anythin' to you that I can't stand over. There isn't any point in my tellin' you what I don't know, is there? I'm no' goin' back on what I promised.'

Swallow decided to change tack. 'Now that you've told us about Louise and the boy, don't you think you should tell us what you know about the death of Sarah Hannin?'

'I know nothin' about what happened to her. I saw her here on Sunday evening and that was all. She went out just the same as she often did.'

'For the love of God, come on McDaniel,' Mossop raised his voice. 'Louise and her son are murdered at the Chapelizod Gate and 48 hours later her friend Sarah is found dead in the canal. Are you seriously saying these are unconnected, random events?'

'I don't know, I tell you.' McDaniel's voice was pleading again. 'I've asked Mr Fitzpatrick about it and he doesn't understand it either. I swear I don't know anythin' beyond what I've told you.'

'So you talked about it with Mr Fitzpatrick?' Mossop shot back.

'Of course I talked abou' it. Every one of the servants here is upset and terrified. But Mr Fitzpatrick doesn't want to hear about it. He has public duties to perform and he doesn't want anythin' to cut across those duties. He told me that he'd given all the help he could to the people at Dublin Castle and that they were doin' what they could to get to the bottom of it.'

'I need to talk privately to Detective Mossop again,' Swallow said.

They withdrew to the outer kitchen.

'What do you think?' Swallow asked once they were out of earshot. 'Did he just come on the scene as he says, or was he involved in the killings?'

'I'm not sure, Boss,' Mossop answered. 'But he's in terror that we'll send him back to the army. He knows we can do that. In a way I'm inclined to believe him.'

'I think so too, but at very least he's a significant witness and he's keeping information back. He's pointing us to Fitzpatrick, but he won't tell us what Fitzpatrick knows. The next step has to be to hold Fitzpatrick for questioning when he arrives home.'

Mossop shrugged. 'Jesus, that'd be putting our heads into the tiger's jaws, wouldn't it? If we grab Fitzpatrick, the Upper Yard will see it as a declaration of war.'

He forced a grin. 'But you're the boss. Give the order and I'll follow where you go, within reason of course.'

'Then let's get McDaniel across to Exchange Court and we'll wait for Fitzpatrick. The regatta ends at 6 o'clock.'

'I'll have a couple of Doolan's men take McDaniel to the Castle,' Mossop said. 'But if we're not handing him over to the military do we have a charge to hold him on?'

'We said we'd keep the Provost Marshal out of it if he was fully honest with us,' Swallow said coldly. 'He hasn't done that. So I don't feel any obligation.'

Mossop looked taken aback.

'He's given us a lot, Boss. You can understand if he doesn't want to drop his employer in the manure heap, betray him, as he'd see it?'

Swallow shook his head sadly.

'Jesus, but you're very soft, Pat. Lock him up on a charge of obstruction then. And when we're done with this business you can let the old bastard go.'

FORTY-TWO

The draining heat of the warmest day in Dublin's records was start-ing to abate when Alderman Thomas Fitzpatrick returned home.

Swallow and Mossop had waited for more than three hours after they finished questioning McDaniel. Swallow had spent some of the time admiring the paintings, fine furniture and *objects d'art* that filled the reception rooms of the house.

In the library he found a variety of fine paintings: two Osbornes; a small Vermeer; an early Constable landscape and any number of lesser products of the English, French and Irish schools.

The drawing room was dominated by portraits in baroque, gilt frames. An engraved plate at the foot of one told Swallow that it depicted Thomas Fitzpatrick Senior and his wife. In the sharp eyes, strong jawline and heavy build, Swallow recognised the resemblances between father and son.

Rich carpets ran from wall to wall. Four classical busts, emperors or gods that he could not identify, stood one in each corner. In the dining room, a pair of Jacobean sideboards displayed an array of fine English and French china. The house bespoke the wealth that the Fitzpatrick family had accumulated over generations.

Hunger drove Mossop downstairs to the kitchen. He procured two plates of bread and cold beef along with two mugs of milk. They were glad of their sustenance as the hours ticked by.

Later, they positioned themselves in the morning room so that although they were in shadow they had a clear view of the street below.

Shortly after 7 o'clock Fitzpatrick's clarence came up the square, a police side-car with his plain-clothes escort perhaps 20 yards behind.

Fitzpatrick dismounted and started up the steps. The escort driver momentarily reined in his horses to see his charge reach the safety of his house.

Swallow and Mossop heard the heavy door swing open and then bang shut. The escort car moved off and disappeared out of view.

They heard Fitzpatrick's voice from the hallway. 'McDonald, where are you, man?'

Swallow opened the morning room door and stepped into the hall. Mossop was a pace behind.

Fitzpatrick's face was flushed from a combination of alcohol, the sea air and the strong sun of the day. His eyes registered puzzlement and then anger at the sight of the two G-men emerging from his morning room.

'What the hell are you doing here? How dare you... how dare you enter my house... Sergeant...?' He sought to recall Swallow's name and failed.

Swallow took Lafeyre's warrant from his pocket and held it out.

'It's Detective Sergeant Swallow, Sir. I have a warrant signed by a Justice of the Peace giving me authority to search this house and to detain and question any persons I find here in connection with my investigations into the deaths of Sarah Hannin, Louise Thomas and her son, Richard.'

Fitzpatrick sobered instantly. He scrutinised the warrant in Swallow's hand.

'I don't recognise the signature on this... thing. I don't know who signed it. You might have signed it yourself for all I know. I don't have to talk to you... That damned paper isn't even legal. Now... get out of my house this instant!'

He shouted towards the stairway. 'McDonald! Wherever the hell you are, get out here at once!'

'I'm sorry to tell you that you're wrong, Sir,' Swallow said with exaggerated formality. 'The warrant is legal and I'm authorised to enforce it. And Mr McDonald – or should I say Corporal McDaniel – is not here. He has been helping us with our inquiries and is now lodged in Dublin Castle.'

Swallow's articulation of McDaniel's name did not appear at first to register with Fitzpatrick.

'I won't waste my time talking further with you here, Sergeant. I'm calling my coachman and I'm driving to the residence of the Assistant

Under-Secretary. I was with him not half an hour ago. I'll have you dismissed from the police – and your colleague too.' He snorted angrily towards Mossop.

'Your coachman will have been held as a possible witness by police officers at the back of the house, Mr Fitzpatrick,' Swallow said evenly. 'I think it might be wiser if you were to agree to talk to me willingly.'

He gestured to the room. 'Maybe if we can take a seat somewhere it would be best. There are a great many questions arising from our interview with Corporal McDaniel… questions concerning the deaths of your daughter and your grandson.'

This time Swallow's words penetrated. Apprehension flickered in Fitzpatrick's eyes. Then, without a word, he led the way into the morning room.

He took an armchair by the mantlepiece. Swallow took the facing chair. The room was warm with the retained heat of the day.

'Mr Fitzpatrick, I know that the woman murdered at Chapelizod Gate in the Phoenix Park on Thursday evening or Friday morning of last week was Louise Thomas. I know that she was your daughter and that the boy found with her was your grandson.'

He paused. 'I imagine that you're suffering the grief that any father or grandfather would suffer at a time like this. I'm sorry for your loss.'

Fitzpatrick shifted in the chair. Swallow saw perspiration glistening along his collar and on the backs of his hands.

'I'm thankful… to you… for your sympathy,' he said flatly.

'Will you tell us what you know about the circumstances of their deaths, please?' Swallow said.

After a few moments, Fitzpatrick placed his hands palms downward on his knees as if to steady himself.

'I don't know if you or anybody else could understand… the grief that I have had to deal with for a very long time. There is a lot that you don't know.'

Swallow shook his head.

'That's not altogether true. I know why and how Sarah Hannin came to work in this house, I know about your relationship with the late Cecilia Downes, about your children and about the infant that's buried just a few yards away from where we're sitting now.'

He paused. 'And I also believe that I know – as you know – the identity of the person who killed your daughter and your grandson.'

Fitzpatrick sighed. Swallow could not estimate if it indicated relief, sorrow or both.

'If you know about Cecilia and about the children, then you do know a lot, Sergeant Swallow. Is it wise for me to let this conversation go any further?'

'Whether the conversation is to be taken further is a judgment you have to make for yourself,' Swallow said. 'But I have my duty. And I must warn you that anything you say after this will be taken down by Detective Mossop and it may be used in evidence. Do you understand?'

Fitzpatrick gave a thin laugh. 'You don't need to go on with that, Sergeant. I had hoped maybe…'

His voice trailed off. He drew a handkerchief from his pocket and wiped first his hands and then his face.

'There's a bigger picture here that I don't think you'd understand, Sergeant. There are considerations that go beyond my personal affairs and beyond the concerns of the police.'

'Please don't assume I'm incapable of grasping an issue outside of what you call the concerns of the police,' Swallow said sharply. 'Tell me what you mean by a bigger picture. I'll do my best to get my mind around it.'

'Let me make it clear, Sergeant, that I have had no part in the terrible events of the past week,' Fitzpatrick said emphatically. 'I would never – could never – have allowed any harm to come to my own flesh and blood. And as for the unfortunate housemaid here, Sarah, why would I harm someone who I had treated with nothing but kindness since childhood?'

'Then you might explain to us what Louise and the boy were doing in Dublin and why you ordered McDaniel to pick them up in your carriage at Chapelizod Gate,' Swallow said.

'I gather from what you say that McDonald – or McDaniel as you have identified him – has told you what he knows,' Fitzpatrick said.

'I'm sorry, Sir, but I won't reveal the sources of the information I have.'

Fitzpatrick looked slowly around the room as if seeking some reassurance in familiar surroundings.

'I became… attached… to Cecilia Downes. It was a foolish, youthful mistake on my part. The differences of class and position could never be bridged. It was unjust to everyone, including Cecilia. So I ended it, under pressure from my late parents, and I… made all the necessary arrangements for the children. It had to be in secret. If it came out I would be denounced by the church and shunned in business. And I'd have been destroyed politically.'

He paused.

'Cecilia was utterly wayward. I suppose that was part of the attraction for me. She didn't accept authority. She didn't accept her position as a servant. She didn't respect the laws of property or anything else. She was a born troublemaker and unfortunately a born criminal, as I'm sure a policeman knows better than anyone.'

He hesitated. Swallow wondered if he saw a glistening in Fitzpatrick's eye.

'I never married. It wasn't because there weren't plenty of suitable young women around Dublin. I think it was because I had made such a terrible mistake. I made a whole series of mistakes. And I was afraid of making more.'

'With respect, Mr Fitzpatrick, I don't need to hear about that aspect of your life,' Swallow interjected. 'Could you confine yourself to recent events?'

'No, of course you don't,' Fitzpatrick said sadly.

'Cecilia and I made arrangements for the children. But we came from different social situations, different values. She was content to see Louise go to Liverpool and learn to work in service, first with the nuns at Wavertree and then with some of the city hospitals. Those were the horizons of her ambitions, I suppose.'

'Did you know anything about your daughter's recent life in England, Mr Fitzpatrick?' Swallow asked. 'Did you know that she was living in poor circumstances, that she had health problems, that her husband was dead?'

Fitzpatrick nodded. 'I didn't have a lot of detail. But I was aware that her circumstances were... problematic.'

He raised a hand as if to ward off Swallow's disapproval.

'Naturally, I wanted something better for my children. But my son was the only one within my influence. I arranged for him to be given a new identity. I had him enrolled in a good boarding school. Then he went on to Trinity College. At first, he thought I was just a benefactor. A few years ago, I thought it better to tell him who he was. But he decided that he wanted to continue with his new identity and to live his own life. I think that was probably for the best. It was his decision.'

'So, you abandoned your daughter?' Mossop interjected. 'You left her in the care of a woman you knew to be emotionally unstable... and a violent criminal.'

Fitzpatrick nodded slowly.

'I'm not proud of it now. But it seemed an easier solution to have the girl taken care of by her mother and the boy by his father. It happens, you know.'

'I'm not judging your actions, Mr Fitzpatrick,' Swallow said, throwing a silencing glance at Mossop. 'I'd prefer if you resumed your narrative of what happened last week.'

Fitzpatrick nodded again.

'Cecilia knew that she was dying. She wanted to ensure that Louise got whatever she could leave her. And we had agreed that I'd make a settlement on the girl as well.'

'So Ces – Cecilia – wrote to her daughter – your daughter – Louise Thomas, asking her to come to Dublin?' Swallow asked.

'I don't have any direct knowledge of that. But I imagine so, yes.'

Mossop looked up from his murder book. 'Why was all the secrecy required? Why did she have to disguise herself as a man?'

Fitzpatrick looked at Mossop as if he was addressing a child.

'You're a policeman. Are you saying that you couldn't see the dangers she faced coming back to Dublin? Any of the gangsters around Cecilia would kill her daughter without a moment's hesitation.'

'I suppose so,' Mossop acknowledged. 'But in the end, the disguise didn't protect her or the child.'

'Did Louise get her inheritance, if I can call it that, from her mother before she died?' Swallow asked.

'Cecilia sent me a message to say that she was going to give Louise the money she had put away,' Fitzpatrick said. 'I don't know how much there was. She said she wanted me to give Louise whatever I had provided for them as well. She said that they were going to go to make new lives in America or Canada as soon as they could.'

Fitzpatrick hesitated. 'If they were planning to make a fresh start in the new world I felt it would be a final discharge of my duty to provide them with something to establish themselves.

'Cecilia said that Louise was afraid to travel on the tram back into the city. She believed someone was following her. She said I should have them collected at the Chapelizod Gate of the Phoenix Park at 9 o'clock on Thursday evening. I was puzzled at the location, but I realise now they must have been staying somewhere nearby.'

He hesitated. 'I didn't want to meet them here at the house, you understand. I had a bank draft as well – a thousand pounds – ready for them. So I sent McDonald – McDaniel – in the clarence. When he got there, he found them shot, just inside the gate, among the trees.'

There was a long silence, broken only by the sound of Mossop's pencil filling the pages of the murder book.

'We know that Louise and the boy had come to this house on the previous evening, the Wednesday, to meet Sarah Hannin.' Swallow said. 'Can you tell us why?'

'I don't know why you persist in trying to link all these matters,' Fitzpatrick snapped. 'Louise and Sarah were in the orphanage. I arranged for Sarah to have a position here in this house. But whatever happened to Sarah Hannin has nothing to do with the deaths of my daughter and grandson.'

Swallow grimaced. 'It seems a very extraordinary coincidence to have three murders linked back to this house, Mr Fitzpatrick. When did you last see Sarah Hannin?'

'I believe it was on Sunday afternoon. I came out of my study and saw her going down the hall to the basement. It was perhaps about 6 o'clock.'

'Do you have any idea who might have wished to do her harm? You can't really believe there's no connection between her death and what happened to your daughter and grandson.'

Fitzpatrick's expression became agitated. He sighed again.

'I would hope that you recognise I'm being very frank with you, Sergeant. I've told you things here this evening that I never believed I would discuss with a living soul. But I tell you, as God is my judge, I know nothing of what befell Sarah Hannin. I'm as much at a loss about what happened to her as you seem to be.'

Swallow stood. He walked to one of the windows overlooking the square. Then he turned to face Fitzpatrick.

'I have to tell you that I'm going to charge you with misprision or concealment of felony. That relates to withholding information concerning the deaths of Louise and Richard Thomas. And I may additionally put charges to you relating to concealment of the birth of Cecilia Downes's child and the death of that child in this house. Do you understand?'

Fitzpatrick was silent for a moment.

'I know what the offences mean,' he said eventually. 'But this doesn't have to come out immediately, does it?'

Swallow shook his head.

'I don't think concealing information on a double murder is something that can be kept under wraps. You'll be charged and remanded in custody. You'll probably want to convey a message to the authorities, Mr Fitzpatrick, in order to explain that you can't be available for public events next week. If you would like a little while to compose a letter to whomever you think appropriate along those lines I'll ensure its early delivery.'

Fitzpatrick shrugged in resignation.

'It's a great pity. It would be good for Dublin to be seen to be warm in its welcome for the Queen's grandson. This city needs all the trade and business it can attract. They mean employment for a lot of people. When I said that there were issues here that were broader than the concerns of the police, that's what I meant.'

Swallow nodded. 'Mr Fitzpatrick, I don't deal in such matters. I understand what you're saying. But as a police officer I can't be influenced by it.'

Fitzpatrick smiled. 'There's one other thing, Sergeant. It concerns the child that's out there in the garden. Ces wasn't in her right mind. When the child died, when she… ended its life… she wasn't well. I would never have allowed any harm to come to it. But when it was done, it seemed the most sensible thing to just… dispose of it.'

'In due course you'll need to show us where you put the child, Mr Fitzpatrick,' Swallow said. 'And you understand that we'll have to do whatever is possible to recover any remains – however slight.'

Swallow felt tired. He resumed his seat opposite Fitzpatrick.

'Mr Fitzpatrick. To be frank, you haven't told me a great deal that we hadn't already pieced together. But you've yet to tell us about the one subject we need to hear you on. You need to tell us about your son.'

'You want to hear about my son?'

'Yes, Mr Fitzpatrick, your son, John Michael.'

Fitzpatrick closed his eyes as in physical pain.

'Perhaps having listened to me, you can understand why I went to such lengths to protect him. And you'll understand that I never could have expected that he would go to such extremes of violence to eliminate a threat to himself, as he saw it. Or maybe it was to have his revenge on his mother and his sister or on me, I'm not sure.'

'Please go on,' Swallow said.

Fitzpatrick opened his eyes. He smiled sadly.

'John Michael didn't die. When I separated from Cecilia and the children were sent away I immersed myself in public life and in commerce. I tried to write Cecilia and the children out of my life as if they never existed.'

He paused for a moment.

'Later, I realised that I couldn't turn my back on my own flesh and blood. I wanted to take them out of Greenhills and to bring them up here. But Cecilia was so bitter that she insisted on denying me that happiness, even if it meant that they would stay in the institution. Finally, we agreed that when the children reached the age at which they would be discharged I would take charge of the boy and arrange for him as I wanted.

'I saw him set up in life as best I could with a new name. When he had advanced a bit in his schooling I told him who I was... that I was his father. He was very angry at first. But in time I think he realised that it was in his own best interests to accept his new circumstances and to go along with the arrangements.'

Mossop was incredulous.

'You're saying he knew you had thrown him into an orphanage as an infant but he was willing, in spite of all that, to have cordial relations with you as father and son?'

'At first he accepted the situation as it was explained to him. But it wasn't easy. He was often very angry and bitter in conversation with me. Who could blame him? But increasingly that anger and resentment came to dominate his personality. It seems that there is much of his mother's violent instinct in him. And it seems that those instincts have led to tragedy.'

'What are you telling us, Mr Fitzpatrick?' Swallow asked. 'You'd be best to speak plainly because I believe I know the answer to my question already, if that makes it easier for you.'

Fitzpatrick shook his head sadly.

'I think I underestimated you, Mr Swallow. My son was the only other person I told that McDaniel was to meet Louise at the Chapelizod Gate. The implication is obvious, is it not?'

'I'm afraid so, Sir,' Swallow said.

'Where can we find your son, Mr Fitzpatrick?' Mossop asked gently.

'He's a fine young man in many ways, and I'm proud of his accomplishments as any father would be. He works as a journalist, quite a successful one too. Now he writes and works under a *nom de plume.*'

'Can you give us that name please?' Swallow asked.

'My son is known as Simon Sweeney.'

FORTY-THREE

Just before midnight, Swallow and Mossop, with a party of uniformed constables, knocked on the door of the four-storey house on Lower Ormond Quay where Simon Sweeney of the *Evening Telegraph* had his rooms.

There was no traffic on the street, and they could hear the flow of the river lapping against the granite of the Liffey embankment. A quarter Moon hung over the square-towered spire of Christ Church Cathedral. It was a midsummer night in which there would be no real darkness. Away to the west, where the river flowed in from the flat countryside, there were still traces of red in the sky.

A constable covered the door that led to the servants' quarters below street level. Swallow posted two others, with Mick Feore as armed backup, behind the house, where the coaching entrance gave out onto Strand Street.

An hour earlier the G-men had left the Fitzpatrick house at Merrion Square, exiting through the mews. A DMP closed carriage stood by the gate with doused lamps and the horse's harnesses muffled.

They placed Thomas Fitzpatrick in the carriage, handcuffed between Pat Mossop and a uniformed officer. Swallow took position up front with the driver. Detectives Eddie Shanahan and Mick Feore flanked the vehicle on foot until they reached the end of the mews laneway.

At the end of the lane another closed carriage waited under a pool of gas light. Two men stood on the pavement on either side. As the carriages drew level, Swallow ostentatiously turned back his jacket, drew his Webley Bulldog and laid it across his knees. Shanahan and Feore already had their guns drawn.

Major Kelly stood in front of his men under the street light. He too had drawn back his coat to reveal his weapon in its holster. Swallow saw that the man beside Kelly was holding a shotgun, barrels pointing downward, half concealed by his side.

Kelly tipped his hat. 'Good evening, Sergeant Swallow. I trust that you've had a successful day.'

'Yes, Major Kelly. I've had a very good day, thank you. I'm on my way to Exchange Court with a prisoner and a signed statement taken under a warrant issued by a Justice of the Peace.'

Kelly appeared to consider this information for a moment. Then he raised his hands, palms upward, suggesting a sense of helplessness.

'A signed statement, secured under a warrant issued by a Justice of the Peace? Then it would appear that I can be of little assistance to you.'

'I believe so, Major Kelly. Matters have moved on.' Swallow saw the man with the shotgun shift the weapon uneasily. One of his colleagues moved closer beside Kelly, his right hand resting on the butt of his revolver.

Kelly stepped forward onto the roadway.

'As you can see, my fellows have come prepared for any difficulties that might arise. And I can see that your men are similarly equipped. So, rather than cause an incident that could be very nasty, it seems that I shall have to accept that matters, as you say, have moved on.'

He gave the cold smile that Swallow had seen on the night they had talked in the carriage.

'In that case, Sergeant Swallow, I can do no more than give you my assurances that I won't forget you. And your failure to take good advice will be remembered.'

Swallow did not reply.

'Go ahead,' he ordered the driver.

* * *

It took four or five hard bangs before a woman's voice called out from inside the front door of Simon Sweeney's lodgings at Ormond Quay.

'What do ye want?'

Mossop put his mouth to the letterbox.

'It's the police, G-Division detectives. Would you open the door please, Ma'am?'

A beam of candlelight showed at the crack between the door and the jamb. Then the elderly woman drew it open, reassured by the sight of uniforms.

'In the name o' God almighty, what do ye want at this hour o' the night?'

'I'm Detective Sergeant Swallow, Ma'am. Can you tell us where we'll find Mr Sweeney who lives here?'

The woman pointed up the stairs in the darkness. 'His rooms are up on the second landing there. It's the big oak door facin' down the staircase. But I don't know if he's in. He can often be late, you know, what with his workin' at the newspaper.'

Mossop struck a match to a police lantern. They climbed the stairs following the thin, yellow light. Taking up positions on either side of the door, they drew their revolvers. The constables waited on the stairway. Swallow knocked sharply on the pedimented door.

'Yes? What is it?' The reply from inside was immediate.

'It's Detective Sergeant Swallow here. Can I have a word please, Mr Sweeney?'

A shuffling sound was faintly audible through the door.

'It isn't convenient just now. Can't it wait until the morning?'

'Not really, I'm afraid.'

'What's it about?'

'We've made some progress in the investigation and I need to talk about the material you carried in the *Evening Telegraph*.'

The ruse wasn't entirely untrue, Swallow reflected.

There was more shuffling. A flicker of light passed over their feet from the crack underneath the door. A bolt was drawn and Simon Sweeney, fully dressed, opened the door with one hand, a lighted candle in a holder in the other.

Swallow stepped forward, pushing the barrel of his revolver hard into Sweeney's chest. Mossop put his weight to the door to swing it fully open. It connected hard with Sweeney's shoulder, sending him staggering back into the room. The candle in its holder flew from his hand.

The two G-men stepped into the room, followed by the constables.

'Raise your hands over your head and don't move,' Swallow barked. Mossop deposited his lantern on a table and covered Sweeney with his own revolver.

'What in the name of God is going on?' Sweeney shouted angrily. 'Are you out of your mind, Swallow?'

'Where's the gun, Mr Sweeney? We know you have a revolver. Tell me where it is please.'

'I don't know what you're talking about, Swallow. What do you think you're at?'

'I think you know very well what I'm at,' Swallow snapped.

'Simon Sweeney, also known as John Michael Downes or John Michael Fitzpatrick, I am arresting you on suspicion of murder,' Swallow said. 'I have reason to believe that on or around June 16th or 17th last you murdered Louise Thomas and Richard Thomas, at a place within the Dublin Metropolitan Police District, contrary to common law.'

Even in the weak light of Mossop's lantern Swallow could see shock on Sweeney's face.

'You're wrong. You're completely wrong, Swallow,' he said. 'I never…'

'You're not obliged to say anything, Mr Sweeney, unless you wish to do so,' Swallow added. 'But if you do say anything, it will be taken down and it may be used in evidence.'

'Now,' he gestured with his revolver towards an armchair, 'please sit… you can bring your hands down but keep them on your knees where I can see them. I'm asking you again, where is the gun?'

'What bloody gun? I don't know what you are talking about, Swallow.'

'Do you have gas light here Mr Sweeney?' Mossop asked patiently.

Sweeney nodded, pointing to the wall behind the detective. Mossop opened the jet and put a match to the mantle. After a few seconds the glow strengthened and the room brightened.

Swallow nodded to the constables. 'Start your search. Mr Sweeney will be having a conversation with Detective Mossop and myself.'

He turned back to Sweeney.

'Mr Sweeney, I know that you're the natural son of Alderman Thomas Fitzpatrick and Cecilia Downes. I have to tell you that Detective Mossop and I have spent some hours earlier today with Alderman Fitzpatrick. Based on the information that he furnished to us, as well as other evidence that has emerged, I know that you are responsible for the deaths of Louise Thomas, your sister, and of her son, Richard, who was your nephew.'

Sweeney stared silently into the half-light of the room.

'Have you heard what I said and do you understand it?'

'It doesn't matter what Alderman Fitzpatrick told you,' Sweeney said. 'To hell with that man and whatever he says. It's just hearsay and that isn't evidence.'

'It would be best if you told us the truth at this stage, Mr Sweeney,' Mossop said.

'Tell you the truth about what?'

'I believe you know very well what we mean. We want to hear why you took the lives of your sister and her son.'

'I've told you, I don't know anything about that. You came to me for help, remember, Swallow? You wanted me to help you to get Dr Lafeyre's reconstruction of the woman's face into the newspaper.'

'Yes, of course, Mr Sweeney, and that was very helpful. But you've known a great deal more about this case that you have pretended from the beginning.'

'That's nonsense,' Sweeney retorted. 'I facilitated you, Swallow, for all the good it seems to have done. This is fine thanks for my co-operation and the newspaper's assistance.'

'It isn't really nonsense,' Swallow said. 'You gave yourself away on the first morning when you came out to the crime scene with your colleagues.'

He saw a look of anxiety flash in Sweeney's eyes.

'What do you mean?'

'You were the only one of the reporters who knew that the victims had been shot. You asked me 'who would shoot a man and child?' You were clever enough to pretend you thought it was a man and a boy, even though you knew that the adult was a woman, your sister. But at that point nobody had said anything to indicate how they had died.'

'It was a guess, for God's sake. It was a slip of the tongue along with a good guess.'

'It could have been. That's why I wasn't sure all week what I was dealing with. But as it turns out, it wasn't a guess. You knew what none of the other pressmen knew. And you let it out.'

One of the constables re-entered the room, carrying a wooden box.

'You'll want to see this, Sir,' he told Swallow, setting the box down on the table. He opened the hinged lid. 'It was under a loose floorboard in the gentleman's bedroom.'

Swallow withdrew a Smith and Wesson .38 revolver and a cardboard carton of ammunition. He placed them on the table. Then he lifted the carton and held it before the light to read the label.

'Jupiter .38, low-charge cartridges. They're very suitable for short-range or target firing, are they not?'

'The gun is mine, of course,' Sweeney snorted. 'If that's what you were looking for you should have said so. It's perfectly legal. I was issued with it in the Officer Training Corps at Trinity. I was on the shooting team there. Every cadet has to buy one. You should know that.'

'So what's the necessity to conceal it under the floorboards?' Mossop asked.

'It's for safety, of course. I'd have thought the last thing a policeman would want to hear is that a gun was left lying around where someone could find it. I didn't want the chambermaid or the landlady to find it. For all I know any of them could be involved with the Fenians or the Land Leaguers.'

'It's useful for the purposes of my investigation that you've confirmed that the gun is yours, Mr Sweeney,' Swallow said. 'But not every cadet would have these low-charge cartridges. These would be issued to members of the OTC shooting team. Low-charge is used for target practice and in shooting ranges. That narrows the field a bit.'

He replaced the carton and the revolver in the box. Sweeney shook his head as if in disbelief.

'That's all a bit thin, Sergeant. For God's sake, give over on this nonsense and let me go to my bed.'

'Your sister and her child were shot with low-charge ammunition, Mr Sweeney.' Swallow picked one of the cartridges from the cardboard box.

'Just like these Jupiter .38s. A man would use those if he was engaged in target practice or if he was in competition on a shooting team. Let's say the college shooting team at Trinity?'

Sweeney waved his hand. 'Yes, I was on the college shooting team. So were ten others. And you could buy those cartridges in any one of a dozen gun shops around the city.'

Swallow replaced the cartridge. 'That's true. But it's not all, Mr Sweeney.'

He dug his hand into his jacket pocket and produced two twisted lead slugs. He placed them side by side on the tabletop.

'It's unlikely that you know much about the science of ballistics, as it's generally called, Mr Sweeney. It's the matching of bullets to the guns they've been fired from. Professor Alexander Lacassagne is the authority in the area. He's a French scientist. He discovered how to match the scratches and grooves on an expended bullet to the barrel-markings of a particular gun. With the short-barrelled revolver, firing a low-velocity bullet, it's absolutely accurate.'

He gestured to the tabletop.

'I can promise you, Mr Sweeney, that it will be no challenge – no challenge at all – to prove to a criminal court that the .38 bullets that we recovered from the bodies of Louise Thomas and her son were fired from your revolver.'

'Now,' he prodded with his finger at the two twisted slugs, 'it would make it all a lot easier for everyone, yourself included, if you would start at the beginning and tell us what happened last week at Chapelizod Gate.'

Sweeney clasped and unclasped his hands. Swallow and Mossop waited. The only sound breaking the silence of the warm night was the hissing gas jet on the wall.

'It wasn't meant to happen. I only wanted to frighten her,' he said finally.

'I wanted her to leave Fitzpatrick... my father... alone. She was intent on bleeding him for all she could get... and then destroying him as well. He was going to hand money over to her and hope that she'd go to America. But I know that wouldn't have been the end of it. I knew that even if he paid her off she'd still try to destroy him.'

'So what happened, Mr Sweeney?' Mossop asked, his pencil poised over his notebook.

'It hasn't been easy for me, living in denial. Can you imagine if you had to live an artificial life? My father provided for me eventually, when his conscience eventually caught up with him. He saw that I was educated. His influence got me a job in the *Telegraph*. Because of who he is I was able to get introductions to important people. That helped me to be a successful journalist.'

He paused. 'Some people would say I was lucky. But it's hard when you can't be who you are. And it's hard when you realise that you're a bastard – the unwanted offspring of a relationship that shouldn't ever have happened between a weak man and a bad woman.'

'Go on,' Swallow said impatiently, 'we know enough of the family history. I want to know what happened last Thursday when you went to Chapelizod Gate.'

'You think you know the family history, Sergeant? Well, maybe you know the facts. But you don't know what I had to endure. I spent 12 years along with my sister in a damned hole called Greenhills House. Can you imagine the misery and the loneliness and the cold and the hunger?'

He brought a fist down angrily on the arm of his chair.

'I don't just mean hunger in your stomach. I mean the hunger of isolation and the lack of any love or affection, under the charge of a so-called guardian. And then, at the end of it all, I had to accept that I had been flung in there, locked away for the years of childhood, because it didn't suit my mother and father to raise the children they had brought into the world.'

Swallow had a momentary recollection of the smells of damp and stale vegetables at Greenhills House. He saw the angry, florid face of the guardian, Richard Pomeroy. Then his mind switched to the image of the dead child inside the Chapelizod Gate, its hands clasped in death, side by side with its murdered mother. Any incipient pity for Simon Sweeney quickly died.

'It's not a justification for murder,' Mossop said. 'Your sister wasn't to blame for what your parents did, much less her innocent child.'

'My sister was like her mother – my mother. She inherited her low ways and her low standards. I won't defend my father but at least he tried to see his son well provided for. My mother was content to see her daughter work as a skivvy in England. And her daughter didn't seem to want any better for herself.'

'I've told you I don't want to hear any more family history,' Swallow said impatiently. 'I've asked you to tell us what happened at Chapelizod Gate.'

'It… it wasn't what I intended. I had lunch with my father that day at his club. We do that maybe once every couple of weeks. He gives me an insight into what is happening among the nationalist politicians, and I can make arrangements to secure column space in the newspaper for his speeches.'

He laughed bitterly. 'Anybody looking at us together would have seen a prominent public figure dining with a journalist from an influential newspaper. It was very strange, very bizarre. When we would meet it was as if I was dining with two different people at once. At one moment I was talking to a man who had revealed himself as my father. And in the next snatch of conversation he was a politician.

'On that day he told me that my sister, Louise, was in Dublin. He said she wanted money and that if she didn't get it she would reveal everything about him and about the Fitzpatrick family. She would find some newspaper or gossip sheet to write it all. Louise knew that would destroy him and that he'd be shamed out of public life.'

'He told me that McDonald was to meet her at the Chapelizod Gate and bring her to a hotel on Thursday evening. He asked me if I would come to meet her. I think he saw brother and sister embracing and reconciling, that kind of thing. I didn't want to argue with him so I said I would be there.'

'What was the necessity to meet her at the Chapelizod Gate?' Mossop asked.

'She didn't want anyone to know where she was staying. My mother was close to death but she sent the message to have Louise met at a safe place. It seems that she was in fear of her life because she thought my mother's criminal gang would kill her. So, I went up there. I took the tram to Islandbridge and then walked to the Phoenix Park. All I wanted to do was frighten her, to silence her and to tell her to get to hell out of Dublin and Ireland. That's why I took the gun.'

'So, what happened to make you do what you did?' Swallow asked.

'I was puzzled because I saw a man and a child. Then I recognised her in spite of the man's clothing. But I hadn't expected to see the child with her. Fitzpatrick never told me that she had brought the boy across from England. At first she didn't know me. We hadn't met since we left the orphanage. But when she realised it was me she flew into a rage and started to abuse me.'

Sweeney swallowed nervously. Swallow could see stress building.

'She swore at me. She said I had got all the privileges and that she had got nothing. Then suddenly she took a knife from somewhere and went for me. So I stepped back and I took out the gun. The boy began to scream. She went to stab me with the knife and I moved away but she kept on coming at me. So fired one shot at her. Then the child screamed again and ran over to her. I fired a second shot and it hit him. I didn't mean to.'

'When they didn't move I realised they were both dead. I knew that if they weren't identified I'd have a better chance of escape. So I took anything that might identify her. She had a ring so I took it off. There was a bundle of clothes and a bag with some women's things wrapped up in a parcel. And... I... I... used her own knife on their faces so it would be a bit more difficult for anyone to recognise them.'

'I was only there about 10 minutes or so. It was starting to get dark and I saw the clarence coming across from Chesterfield Avenue. So, I slipped in behind the copse and then out of the park through the Chapelizod Gate. I walked to Islandbridge and dropped the knife in the river along with the parcel and her things.'

He looked at Swallow. 'Now, I've told you all you need to know, Mr Swallow. But I didn't set out to murder anyone. Louise attacked me without provocation.'

He laughed bitterly. 'My only regret is that I won't be able to write the report on this for the newspaper.'

'No,' Swallow said. 'You won't. And if you were to write what you have just told me it would be a tissue of lies. Louise and Richard were shot at point-blank range, executed deliberately. The powder burns on their skin show that the gun was practically touching them when you fired the shots. You think you can put up a story of self-defence or provocation to a court? It won't work. You'll be convicted of wilful murder – twice.'

Sweeney's face had frozen as in shock.

'I'm telling you the truth. But if... if that's the evidence that you're going to give, they won't believe me. They'll hang me.'

'You can tell your story in court, Mr Sweeney,' Swallow said reasonably. 'And I imagine that your father won't see you left without the best legal representation he can afford. Although I think he'll need a few pounds for his own defence as well.'

He stood. 'Would you please stand and put your hands together to enable Detective Mossop to handcuff you. I'm taking you now the detective office at Exchange Court where I will formally charge you with the murders of Louise Thomas and Richard Thomas.'

'The handcuffs won't be necessary, Sergeant,' Sweeney said. 'I'll go along voluntarily.'

'It's actually a bit late for that. You're under arrest and that doesn't give you any choice. Put your hands together, please.'

Sweeney stood and put his hands out. Mossop snapped the handcuffs on his wrists.

They went down the two flights of stairs to the street. A police side-car with flickering oil lanterns stood waiting by the kerb.

Mossop stood to one side of the car door. 'I'll help you up there, Mr Sweeney.'

Sweeney stepped forward. Then his handcuffed fists swept up and took the G-man full in the throat. Mossop gagged as he went down on the pavement beside the car. Sweeney's hands grabbed under the detective's jacket, finding the butt of his revolver. He swung around, the gun gripped between his manacled hands.

'Tell your men to stay back, Swallow. I'll shoot them. Don't doubt me.' Swallow heard the click as he cocked the hammer.

'Don't be mad, Sweeney!' Swallow called. 'Where do you think you're going to get to?'

Sweeney glanced along the street. As he did so, Mossop's right hand shot out, grasping his lower leg.

Sweeney screamed. 'Let go, back off!'

The manacled hands came down, lashing the gun barrel across Mossop's face. Swallow heard it connecting. But Mossop held on, squirming sideways to get a better grip on his quarry.

'I warned you!' Sweeney shouted again. He pointed the gun at Mossop's chest and fired. The shot boomed across the street, echoing off the darkened house-fronts. The impact of the bullet propelled Mossop backward to the pavement again, his grip broken, blood spurting from his upper chest.

Sweeney moved back, half running, half stumbling, past the car. Swallow and a constable knelt simultaneously and leaned over Mossop. His eyes were wide in shock.

'The bastard… with my own fucking gun… I had him…'

'Get him into that car and around to the Jervis Street infirmary,' Swallow ordered the constable. 'Move now. Get them to stop that bleeding.'

Sweeney had crossed the quay. He ran towards the Ha'penny Bridge, the pedestrian walkway connecting across the river. Once on the other side, Swallow knew, he would easily lose himself in the alleys and courts of Temple Bar.

At the sound of the shot, Mick Feore had sprinted from his post in Strand Street. Rounding the corner to Ormond Quay he saw the handcuffed Sweeney running to the bridge. He pounded across the street and threw himself forward, taking one of the fugitive's legs in a half-tackle.

Swallow saw Sweeney stumble. The gun flew from his hands and clattered to the street. Sweeney kicked out with his free leg. His shoe connected with Feore's jaw, sending him backward against the quay wall. Now he had a clear path. Swallow started to run, but he was still 50 yards from the northern end of the bridge when Sweeney was halfway across.

Sweeney halted. He looked back and then forward again. Two patrolling constables in night-capes had appeared at the other end of the bridge, blocking off his line of escape. If they were anything less than alert he might surprise them and barge his way past. But the likelihood, he knew, was that they would see him running in handcuffs and seize him.

As Swallow ran he saw Simon Sweeney hoist himself onto a cast-iron lamp standard and step out over the guard rail. The two constables broke into a run. They were seconds from him, night capes flying behind them, as he plunged feet first into the dark, fast-flowing Liffey.

Swallow, Feore and the uniformed officers scanned the water until their eyes were aching. The others strained out across the granite parapets on both sides of the river, eyes sweeping over and back across the currents, but Sweeney did not come to the surface.

FORTY-FOUR

The heatwave broke on the 10th day. The skies over the city started to show trails of grey cloud that darkened during the morning. At noon, a breeze stirred from the west and the temperatures dropped. It stayed dry but the air was softer, indicating that the rain was not far away.

At 4 p.m., His Royal Highness, Prince Albert Victor, the eldest grandson of Queen Victoria, stepped ashore at Kingstown Harbour, accompanied by his younger brother, Prince George.

Two military bands took turns to play on the pier. People lined the promenade in sufficient numbers to please the official welcoming committee. The chairman of the Harbour Commissioners made a speech. The royal visitor smiled and nodded and waved before moving towards the special train that would convey him and his party to the centre of Dublin.

Among the crowd on the promenade, detectives from the G Division watched Patrick O'Reilly and Edward Locke, two young men known to them as members of Dublin's criminal underworld and associates of the organisation calling itself the Hibernian Brothers. Other G-men watched a somewhat older man known to them as James O'Donnell, also a member of the Hibernian Brothers, and listed in police files as unpredictable and dangerous.

Earlier in the day, the officers had noted O'Reilly, Locke and O'Donnell drinking together at a public house on Westland Row in the city centre. Later they travelled out of the city by tram, dismounting for further 'refreshments,' as the G-men recorded it, at another public house near Booterstown. From there, two hours later, they took a second tram to Kingstown and visited a bar on Marine Road, close to the harbour.

When they emerged, shortly after 3.30 p.m., it was noted that O'Donnell was unsteady on his feet. The three walked to the promenade, joining the crowds of onlookers above the railway platform where the prince would take the train for the city.

At this point, the subjects separated. Two officers watched O'Donnell as he started to move through the crowd, apparently leaving his companions.

The heavier of the two G-men closed with him, seized his left arm and drove it hard up his back as he clicked the handcuffs around the wrist. For good measure, he drove a hard right fist into the prisoner's solar plexus, causing him to gag as his knees went from under him.

When the prince turned to wave before stepping into the train, the other G-men saw O'Reilly and Locke move forward in the crowd. Within seconds they were on them, the first officers pinioning their arms while others plunged their hands into the men's pockets to fasten on the Colt Navy revolvers that they were carrying.

A woman cried out at the commotion. A top-hatted gentleman looked cross and called out, 'what the devil...?'

One of the G-men showed his warrant card.

'We're detective division... police business here.'

The gentleman looked momentarily bemused. Then he turned his back to resume his cheers for the royal visitors.

The G-men hustled their captives to a closed car that had been waiting at Marine Road. Before the royal train had cleared Kingstown Station, the police vehicle had started towards the city.

The three prisoners were lodged in separate but adjacent cells at Exchange Court. O'Reilly and Locke screamed curses at the G-men. James O'Donnell defiantly sang a couple of verses from a patriotic ballad before falling silent.

Half an hour later, Detective Sergeant Joe Swallow entered the holding area. He registered his presence with a brief visit to O'Reilly and Locke in their cells. Were they ready to make formal statements about what they had been doing in Kingstown, armed with Navy Colts, as Prince Albert Victor stepped ashore?

After predictable torrents of abuse from the two prisoners, he went to James O'Donnell's cell and flung the heavy door open.

'Come on out, O'Donnell. I'm sorry about the misunderstanding. You did great work there for us,' he called in a voice sufficiently loud to be heard in the adjoining cells occupied by O'Reilly and Locke.

A bewildered James O'Donnell, afflicted with the pains of alcohol withdrawal and approaching sobriety, staggered out of the cell to freedom.

Patrick O'Reilly was surprised an hour later when the duty officer admitted his mother and brother for a brief visit. Shortly afterwards, both men were further surprised to be allowed to consult with a solicitor known to G Division as an active supporter of the Hibernian Brothers.

By nightfall the word was around the city that O'Donnell was an informer, a G-Division spy, a traitor. By the next morning, the Hibernian Brothers let it be known that there was a price of £100 on his head, payable in cash to anyone who would discharge the patriotic duty of ending his life.

Some time over the next 72 hours, G-Division detectives learned, James O'Donnell made his way to Queenstown and purchased a one-way, third-class ticket to New York. A police agent on the voyage reported that he was seldom sober on the crossing to the New World.

* * *

At mid-morning, a nervous young woman had presented National Bank of Ireland bonds with a total value of more than £1,200 to a teller at the bank's head office at Dame Street.

Two lines of green ink had been struck through the name of the original bond-holder, which could still be clearly read as 'Cecilia Downes.' A new name, 'Mrs Louise Thomas,' now appeared on each bond. The alterations had been witnessed and initialled by Horace (widely known as 'Fish') McGloin, the principal and sole member of a law firm located at Essex Street. The young woman said she wanted to exchange the bonds for cash.

Although the teller had 10 years of experience in the cashiers' department he had never before been asked to provide such a large sum across the counter to a single customer. Nor was it usual for individuals of the woman's social class, as indicated by her speech and dress, to have business with the bank.

When the teller had examined the bonds he asked the woman for proof of her identity. She became evasive and then upset. The teller noted that although she claimed to be Mrs Louise Thomas, she wore no marriage ring. He asked her to take a seat and to wait. He beckoned to the branch porter and whispered to him. The porter stepped into the street and signalled to a constable.

When the constable questioned the woman she became aggressive at first, then she admitted that she was not Mrs Louise Thomas. She claimed she was a friend of Mrs Thomas and that she was acting on her behalf. When the constable asked her give her own name, she declined. He then told her he would have to take her to the police station at College Street.

An hour later, after questioning in the station, she said she was Henrietta Connors, known as 'Hetty.' She told the officers she was 18 years of age and that she was employed as a domestic at Sir Patrick Dunn's Hospital.

She insisted that she was a friend of the woman whose name appeared as the new beneficiary on the bonds, Mrs Louise Thomas. But she was unable to say where or how Mrs Thomas might be contacted in order to verify this.

After another hour she changed her story, claiming that she had found the bonds on the street. When it was clear that the police officers did not believe her she gave yet a different version. The bonds had been given to a friend of hers for safe keeping. And the friend, in turn, had given them to her.

The officers wanted the name of this friend. They told Hetty Connors that she had to realise that she was now in mortal danger as far as the law was concerned. Then she gave her friend's name: Sarah Hannin.

Was this the same Sarah Hannin whose body had been taken from the canal a week previously? It was, she agreed. The station sergeant sent for a side-car and told the station orderly to notify Detective Sergeant Swallow that he was bringing a prisoner to Exchange Court.

Later, after questioning by Joe Swallow and Mick Feore, Hetty Connors finally broke down and abandoned her story about being given the bonds for safe keeping by Sarah Hannin.

Swallow told her that she would be charged with the murder of Sarah Hannin and unlawfully receiving the bond. He added that he had seen a woman hang at Tullamore jail for murder a year ago. Hetty Connors reflected for a short while, then she inquired if she might avoid such a fate by telling Swallow the truth.

He said he could not give any assurances until he heard what she had to say. But if it was the case that she was not directly involved in violence, and if she were willing to give evidence against Sarah Hannin's murderer, then it might be possible for her to be dealt with more leniently.

She considered this for a few moments, then she gave her final version of what had happened.

On Wednesday evening of the previous week, Louise Thomas, with her young son, had come to visit Sarah Hannin at 106 Merrion Square.

As Hetty Connors understood it, Louise wanted Sarah to mind some important papers she had been given by her dying mother. She was in fear of the criminals who were her mother's associates.

When Louise and her son had left, Sarah went to her room and looked through the papers. She knew enough to recognise that the bonds were valuable. She kept them in a small bag that Louise had brought to her as a gift from Liverpool.

The next day, when Sarah met Hetty by the canal, she was carrying the bag. She showed Hetty the papers. She was nervous about being given such a responsibility. She said she did not dare leave the papers in her room but that she was equally frightened at having to carry them with her.

Hetty might have been illiterate, but she knew that the bonds represented a lot of money. She arranged to meet Sarah again the following evening. Then she told Tony Hopkins, her criminal mentor and her lover, about the bonds.

Hopkins had concealed himself on the towpath near Baggot Street Bridge. When Hetty and Sarah walked by, Hopkins leaped from his hiding place to grab Sarah's bag. When she struggled he hit her in the face with his fist. Then he hit her again with an iron bar. When she started to scream he hit her a third time, very hard.

Sarah collapsed to the ground. Hopkins opened her bag and took the bonds along with a few coins. Then he pitched the bag into the reeds along the canal bank.

After Hopkins's second blow there was no stir from the injured girl. Hetty said she tried to revive her but realised that she was dead. Hopkins then lifted the body and pushed it over the bank, into the water.

Could she not have prevented Hopkins from using lethal force on Sarah Hannin, Swallow asked. 'No,' she said. And at any rate, she added, Sarah Hannin had been 'having relations' with Hopkins. In the circumstances, Hetty was not particularly distressed by Sarah's fate.

An hour after Hetty Connors had made her 'X' on her statement, two G-men arrested Tony Hopkins at a public house in Hawkins Street.

He was brought to Exchange Court and confronted with the signed statement. He said that he had been in Naughton's public house in

Crow Street, drinking with friends who would vouch for him, on the Sunday evening that Sarah Hannin was murdered. When Swallow charged him with her murder he replied, 'I am not guilty.'

* * *

Prince Albert Victor and his entourage had time to spare in the afternoon.

The reception at the City Hall at which a prominent figure was to present him with a loyal address was cancelled without explanation. Dublin City had no official welcome for the grandson of the Monarch on her Jubilee.

Instead, he was escorted directly by a detachment of hussars from the Westland Row railway terminus to the Viceregal Lodge in the Phoenix Park. The streets were gaily decorated but the crowds were thin. In the evening the prince dined at King's Inns with the Honourable Benchers. After that he presided at a grand banquet and ball at Dublin Castle.

* * *

At about the time that Prince Albert Victor was finishing dinner in St Patrick's Hall in Dublin Castle, Detective Sergeant Joe Swallow and Harry Lafeyre, the City Medical Examiner, were emerging from the Dublin City Infirmary at Jervis Street.

The infirmary's surgical team had successfully removed the bullet from Pat Mossop's upper chest. It had not struck the heart or any of the larger arteries. After they had extracted the slug, the surgeons had packed and stitched the wound, successfully staunching the loss of blood.

'He'll be damned sore for a couple of weeks and he'll need a regime of laudanum to keep the pain at bay,' Lafeyre told Swallow as they emerged out onto Jervis Street. 'But he should be well as long as he's given plenty of time to recover and kept in a place where the wound won't be infected. That means here in hospital.'

Mossop had lapsed in and out of consciousness during the day. But with the bleeding stopped he began to settle and gain strength. Around noon, he had come to wakefulness. His eyes focused on Swallow at the bedside.

'Did the bastard get away, Boss?' he asked.

'No, Pat. He didn't get away at all,' Swallow said, 'don't worry about that now. Just get plenty of rest and you'll be well.'

'Sorry about the bloody gun, Boss,' Mossop muttered. 'From now on, I'll put the handcuffs on from behind.'

* * *

Swallow and Lafeyre went to Lavery's, the public house frequented by the medical staff from the Jervis Street Infirmary.

The awaited rain had not come and the night was muggy. Swallow ordered two cooling pints of MacArdle's Dundalk ale at the counter.

Lafeyre had just returned from Merrion Square, where he had conducted a preliminary examination of what appeared to be infant remains, exhumed by searching constables from the garden at the rear of the Fitzpatrick house.

The tiny, skeletal fragments offered the City Medical Examiner no clues as to the gender of the infant or the cause of death. He could only estimate that it had been in the ground for years rather than months or weeks.

Swallow took Lafeyre through the interviews with McDaniel and Thomas Fitzpatrick.

The morning and the evening newspapers had variously detailed accounts of the late-night arrest of a man at a house at Lower Ormond Quay, the shooting of Detective Officer Mossop of G Division and the final, desperate jump by the suspect into the river.

Lafeyre took a sizeable draught of his MacArdles. The ale was energising and refreshing.

'I suppose there's a possibility he swam out of it,' he said. 'From what you tell me, he could have made it to the quay wall in the darkness and hauled himself up at one of the mooring steps.'

'It's possible but I'd say it's unlikely,' Swallow answered. 'Not with the handcuffs and a full tide flowing down to the bay. I saw his face as he went off the bridge. It was the look of a man in despair. You'd probably do the same yourself. The alternative was the rope.'

'What will happen to Fitzpatrick?' Lafeyre asked.

'Do you mean in terms of what the law will do?'

'Of course. His political career is over.'

'He'll be a while in Kilmainham Jail, but he mightn't even go to trial. There isn't a case you could build from the few scraps of bones you saw out there today. Even if you could show that the infant died violently, Fitzpatrick would very likely say that it was Ces that did the deed. And she probably did.'

'But he concealed his suspicions – his knowledge – that Sweeney had murdered his own sister and her child at the Chapelizod Gate.'

'I threatened him with misprision of felony – essentially withholding knowledge of a crime on that. But it's damned hard to prove.'

'So what about Hetty Connors and her fellow – Hopkins?'

'She's no fool. She knows her only way out is to swear informations against him. I expect he'll hang on her evidence. He saw a big prize and he was willing to use whatever violence might be necessary to secure it. Personally, I think she's as bad as he is. She mightn't have expected that Hopkins would kill Sarah Hannin. But I suspect she didn't try very hard to stop him.'

Lafeyre called for two more pints. Swallow drained his own glass. He eyed Lafeyre carefully.

'Will you be all right with the fellows in the Upper Yard over the fact that you issued that warrant to search the Fitzpatrick house? They know that you went against them. They're not likely to forgive and forget. They could try to challenge your contract as medical examiner.'

Lafeyre smiled. 'Ah, we'll see. But, you know, nothing succeeds like success. The Chapelizod Gate murders are more or less cleared up because of that warrant. And Thomas Fitzpatrick is a busted flush now. They won't have any interest in protecting him any further. Why would they want to pick a fight with me? I've got a few connections in high places myself and I wouldn't be slow to use them, I promise you.'

He paid the barman for the drinks and scanned Swallow's face.

'And what about yourself? How will things work out now between yourself and Mallon? And how will it go with Smith Berry?'

Swallow downed a third of his pint.

'I don't much care at this stage. I always thought that the law came before politics and that good police-work would be backed up by the people at the top. I'm not sure that anyone in authority shares that view. There's big stakes being played for in this country. And there won't be much tolerance extended to an awkward policeman who won't do what he's told.'

Lafeyre shook his head in disagreement.

'I'd hate to see you throw it in now. I think when all this washes through you'll come out of it well. Go and sleep on it and see what tomorrow will bring.'

They finished their ale and walked towards the river. Lafeyre hailed a cab at the quay and Swallow started for Grattan Bridge.

EPILOGUE

Swallow crossed the river and made his way up Parliament Street towards the Castle.

The lines of carriages that had brought the guests to the state dinner jostled in uneasy order on Cork Hill. Drivers stood about, smoking and talking in the night air. The city gaslights reflected off the bevelled windows of the larger carriages. Some of the drivers kept their car lamps burning too.

When the tableau started to remind him of a Venetian *carnival* that hung in the National Gallery, he checked himself. Life was life. Art was art. He had to stop trying to define one within the other.

The strains of the orchestra playing in St Patrick's Hall drifted down Cork Hill into Parliament Street.

Gaggles of children from the tenements had congregated at vantage points on steps and window-ledges, hoping to wheedle a few coppers from the guests as they would make their way back to their carriages.

Some of the more daring urchins whistled at the sentries in their ceremonial uniforms at Cork Hill Gate. Others jeered at the policemen placed at intervals along the pavement, safe in the knowledge that none of them dared to leave their assigned place of duty.

Swallow wanted to avoid the crowds. He turned down to Dame Street and went into the Castle by the Palace Street Gate.

In the Lower Yard he saw that the lights were burning in John Mallon's office. That was unsurprising. With the security of a royal visitor at issue, the head of the G Division would not turn in until he could be sure that Prince Albert Victor was safe in his bed, or at least within the sanctuary of the Viceregal Lodge in the Phoenix Park.

376

Swallow wanted to check at the police telegraph room to see if any additional information had come through from Liverpool concerning Louise Thomas. As he started towards the police office he saw John Mallon step out of the shadows where the high archway connected the Upper and Lower Yards.

Swallow guessed that Mallon had taken a vantage point from which he could survey the full sweep of the Upper Yard.

At one end of the spacious quadrangle were the entrances to the State Apartments and St Patrick's Hall. At the other were the gates leading out to Cork Hill. This was where the royal party would enter and exit the Castle and it was where the prince would be most at risk, moving through a large crowd in a confined space.

'Bloody nerve-wracking,' Mallon said quietly. 'We've got three more days of this. You've been over at Jervis Street to see Mossop?'

'Yes, Chief, he's doing well. Dr Lafeyre was with me. He says he could be a couple of weeks in there.'

'Mossop's a good man,' Mallon said, 'I'd give him as much time as he needs so that when we can get him back he'll be in good order.'

He gestured to the upper window. 'Come on upstairs. We could both do with a drink.'

In Mallon's room, the head of G Division opened a bottle of Bushmills whiskey and poured two heavy measures. He handed one to Swallow.

'I know you like your Tullamore, but that's good Ulster stuff. It's from Antrim.'

They sipped the whiskey neat.

'That was a damned good whisper you got on that fellow O'Donnell and his two pals, Locke and O'Reilly,' Mallon said. 'I don't know that they'd have been able to get an accurate shot from where they were, even with those Navy Colts. But the very fact of an attempt being made on the prince's life would have been a disaster for us.'

Swallow was silent. He wondered what his sister would have to say about the object of her romantic interests when next he met her. But she was safely out of the frame. And James O'Donnell, with a death sentence hanging over him from the Hibernian Brothers, would not be back from America for a long time – certainly long enough for Harriet to lose interest.

He made a mental note to check how her examinations had gone. It would be a poor bargain to have extricated her from the mischief-making of the Hibernian Brothers only to have her fail in her teacher training studies.

'Thanks, Chief. It comes down to a lot of donkey work – and using your informants well, as you say.'

'And you got a result earlier on the Sarah Hannin case,' Mallon said conversationally.

'It fell into our lap. If the girl – Hetty Connors – hadn't tried to pass off the bank draft, we'd still be nowhere.'

'A lucky break is a lucky break, Swallow. But you make your own lucky breaks sometimes. You followed her into Naughton's in Crow Street when you might have just walked on.'

'I was on the wrong track though. I was fairly sure that someone in the Fitzpatrick house was responsible for Sarah Hannin's murder. It turns out to have been a simple case of robbery with extreme violence.'

Mallon smiled. 'You were off the case, Swallow. It was up to the clever fellows in the Upper Yard to solve it. They weren't exactly making great progress, were they? And it wasn't just a simple case of robbery. You felt there was a link between Chapelizod Gate and the Hannin death. And you were right.'

A flicker of a smile crossed Mallon's face.

'Wasn't it fortunate that Fitzpatrick was at the Jubilee regatta when you went in at Merrion Square?'

'Yes, Sir,' Swallow said impassively, 'very fortunate indeed.'

'Mind you, organising a search and arrest on the basis of Harry Lafeyre's warrant isn't something I'd want to encourage as an everyday method of doing police business.'

'It was all perfectly legal, Chief.'

'Legal, yes, but… well, you took the risks. Nobody forced you.'

'I suppose so,' Swallow acknowledged. 'Will there be… consequences… do you think?'

Mallon was silent for a moment.

'I hope not. The game's gone against our political masters now and they know it. They're very pragmatic people, in my experience. Fitzpatrick is a lost cause, a beaten dockct, as the bookies would say. They can't rehabilitate his reputation.'

He sipped at his Bushmills. 'Fitzpatrick is politically dead. And there's nobody will run faster from the stench of a rotting political corpse than the civil servants. So will there be consequences? No, not of the kind that should worry either you or me, I think. Be sure, they won't forgive or forget the fact that a couple of G-men thwarted their grand design. But they wouldn't dare to take any action – at least not at this stage.'

'But in the longer term?'

'Let me put it this way. I wouldn't hold out fervent hopes of seeing your name on the G-Division promotion list in the very near future. You know I don't have the final say in that.'

Mallon poured another two good measures of Bushmills.

'I'd like to be able to tell you something different. But there are realities we have to live with. I got to where I am in spite of my religion and my background and because I knew how to play the system. You're not that kind of man. You're a first-class policeman and detective, but you buck the system. They don't trust you. They never will. You can walk on water and it won't be acknowledged. I'm sorry, but that's the reality of it.'

He chuckled as he drank from his whiskey glass.

The chuckle died. There was an earnest look in Mallon's eyes.

'Do you not think it might be time for you to look for that transfer to uniform? You'd move to inspector and maybe up to superintendent in a few years. Would you not send in the application? I can probably make sure that it goes the right way. And when you're at it, you could make a decent woman out of Mrs Walsh and take her on a nice honeymoon to Killarney or some place. Great scenery for painting there, you know?'

Swallow felt himself flush.

'I'll think about that, Sir. It would be a big decision for me to take. There are… personal considerations,' he said flatly.

Mallon caught his tone. He changed the subject.

'I've read the two statements that you and Mossop took from McDaniel and Fitzpatrick. It's hard to credit that people could put up pretences and bury the truth over, what, more than 20 years.'

'I think it took its toll on Fitzpatrick,' Swallow said. 'In a way I think he was relieved to have it all come out.'

Mallon looked doubtful. 'He paid a high price to protect his wealth and his family's place in society, as he saw it. He lost the woman he probably loved. He lost his children. And now his reputation is gone as well.'

'And it's hard to think that a woman like Ces Downes could keep her secrets over the same long time,' Swallow mused. 'I guess both of them felt they were doing the right thing for their children. Different people have different natures. They want different things out of life.'

'Human nature,' Mallon snorted. 'It's a brute nature that allows your own daughter to be raised in an orphanage and your son to be raised as a stranger – even if he's well looked after in the material sense.'

He drank from his Bushmills again. 'We're talking about old-fashioned greed and avarice, Swallow. Fitzpatrick was going to get rich – richer than he is – with government contracts. And Ces Downes knew that as long as she stayed quiet about her past she could count on Fitzpatrick's protection in all the years that she was engaged in crime.'

Swallow could see the summer night darkening through the window.

'Yet you'll hear that she could be good to those she had a soft spot for.' he said. 'You'll find those who speak well of her.'

Mallon nodded.

'We've both seen that in police work, Swallow. You learn that the worst blackguards can perform acts of what seems like kindness. Do you know *The Pirates of Penzance*?'

'I haven't seen it performed, Chief. But I know of it.'

Mallon grinned and broke into a low baritone.

When a felon's not engaged in his employment
or maturing his felonious little plan
his capacity for innocent enjoyment
is just as great as any honest man.'

Swallow wondered if the head of G Division might not have had enough Bushmills for the evening.

* * *

He walked through the Lower Yard and the Palace Street Gate, making for Thomas Street and Maria Walsh's.

The ale he had drunk with Lafeyre and the stiff Bushmills poured by Mallon had combined to blur his senses. He felt tired with a deep sense of anti-climax.

He thought about John Mallon's advice. It was wrong that his choices should be between retirement, going into uniform or remaining in the rank he held until the end of his service. It was hard to think of carrying on, watching time-servers like Boyle move ahead of him. But if he left, he was certain, he would have to make up his mind finally about his relationship with Maria. He was not ready to do that, just yet.

At the corner of Fishamble Street and Christchurch Place he saw Duck Boyle. The inspector was carrying a heavy book under his arm. They greeted each other without much warmth.

'Do want a drink?' Swallow asked reluctantly, feeling that he should not be ungenerous close to his own turf.

'Nah, thanks Swalla', I'll pass this time. I have to get home to do a bit of work, studyin' for the superintendents' exam.'

He waved the book.

'Do you know what... I'm readin' here? There's a fella out in India... He has a theory that in a few years we'll be able to identify every single human bein' be the ridges on their fingertips. He's writin' about what he calls 'the science of fingerprints.' Did ye ever hear the like... he must be a right eejit.'

Swallow thought he could already see the gold braid glinting off Boyle's new uniform.

* * *

In the morning, after 13 days of drought, the rain started to fall on the city. It came in from the west as a light drizzle and gradually built to a steady, slanting downpour.

Soon it obscured the mountains and the harbour and the high facades of the public buildings. Then it began to veil the features of the houses and the churches from the people hurrying along the city streets. At noon, with visibility at the water's edge down to a few yards, the men combing the shoreline along Dublin Bay gave up and stopped searching for Simon Sweeney.

The End